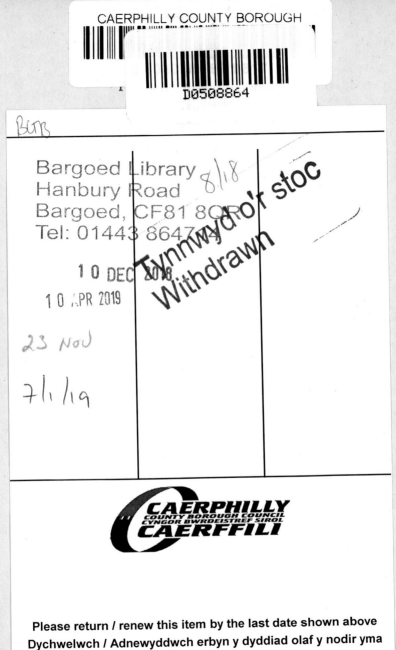

Hester Browne lives in Herefordshire with her dog, her 1962 Mini and her vast collection of red lipsticks. She is the author of numerous bestselling novels including *The Vintage Girl*, *The Little Lady Agency* and *The Runaway Princess*.

ALSO BY HESTER BROWNE:

Little Lady, Big Apple

What the Lady Wants

The Finishing Touches

Swept off Her Feet

The Runaway Princess

The Vintage Girl

The Honeymoon Hotel

The Little Lady Agency

hester browne

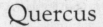

Quercus

First published in Great Britain in 2005 by Hodder & Stoughton
An Hachette UK company

This edition published in 2018 by

Quercus Editions Ltd
Carmelite House
50 Victoria Embankment
London EC4Y 0DZ

An Hachette UK company

A CIP catalogue record for this book is available
from the British Library

PB ISBN 978 1 78648 718 6
EBOOK ISBN 978 1 78648 717 9

10 9 8 7 6 5 4 3 2 1

Printed and bound in Great Britain by Clays Ltd, Elcograf S.p.A.

For PAR, a good lass, a wise woman, and a true lady

I

My name is Melissa Romney-Jones, but you can call me Honey. In the past, when people asked me to describe myself, I used to say I was one of Nature's organisers. Reliable. Sensible. A bit, you know, *shy*. My friend Gabi would have said I was a domestic goddess in practical shoes, but then she always took a positive view of my hips. My flatmate Nelson would have said I was too bloody nice for my own good, and then would have been unable to resist making some crack about my clueless taste in lounge lizard men.

Ask about Honey, though, and you get a much more interesting description.

Honey is a supercharged whirlwind, Mary Poppins in silk stockings. I've dated over fifty men this year alone, seven of whom were gay; I've been married temporarily to another fifteen; I've sent seventy Mother's Day cards, all to different mothers, and dispatched armfuls of flowers to sisters, secretaries and secret amours; I've been a live-in girlfriend to twenty-one bachelors and a vengeful ex-girlfriend to another three men keen to return to bachelorhood; I've transformed forty-three frogs into princes by dragging them round the shops and into barbers' chairs; I've cured nine men of nail-biting, found gifts for fifteen godchildren, and arranged no fewer than thirty-one very successful parties.

I've also attended five weddings. Three as Honey, one as Melissa and one, very confusingly, as both Honey and Melissa at the same time.

How I got myself out of that particular tangle is a tribute to the magical powers of feminine charm and good manners. How I got myself *into* it is rather more complicated . . .

My golden rule has always been to look on the bright side, no matter what. With all the complications in my life, I've had to. Notorious father, unsupportive sisters, constant cash-flow dramas, multiple schools . . . But if you can find three good things about any given situation, no matter how dire, I guarantee you'll forget the rotten stuff.

The three best things about my job with the Dean & Daniels estate agency were as follows: first, it was highly satisfying to know I was helping people to find somewhere perfect to live. Second, the hours weren't too long. And third, the office was terribly convenient for the shops, on the rare occasions that I ever had any money to spend.

I won't go into the rotten stuff. You can probably guess it for yourself.

According to my job description, which I wrote myself since no one else had ever bothered to sort it out, I was Personal Assistant to Hughy, who sold two-bed and three-bed houses, and Charles, who specialised in mews. It was my job to calm them both down and smooth everything over, and, although I say it myself, they only believed they were efficient because I left no trace.

'No shopping bags, Melissa?' simpered Carolyn, the office manager, when I bowled in after lunch – on time, I might add. 'Your credit card lives to fight another day?'

'My credit card is just fine right now,' I said with as much dignity as I could muster. And then, because I'm pretty hopeless at lying, even when I'm trying to be dignified, I added, 'Anyway, nothing fitted. I'm just not the right shape for modern clothes.'

'Fashion is a cruel mistress.' Carolyn folded her arms over her flat chest, and gave me one of her smug looks. She wore a lot of sleeveless Joseph tops, just to prove she had money to chuck around and didn't need a bra.

'Mel's an hourglass,' said Gabi, adding, 'whereas you're just ghaaaastly,' under her breath in a grating Sloane accent.

I mouthed a 'thank you' at her over my monitor. I wished I had Gabi's confidence. Particularly in my figure; she thought I should embrace my billowing curves and wiggle around in skin-tight Capri pants and straining blouses, like Gina Lollobrigida or Jayne Mansfield. In my head, I did entertain the idea, honestly. But out in the real world, I didn't have the nerve.

Gabi was my best friend at Dean & Daniels. We were united in our loathing of Carolyn and our mutual desire for a real Kelly bag. That's about all we had in common, but we got on like a house on fire, despite the fact that she claimed to hate posh girls (the office is packed with them) and stupid Hooray men (who made up the other half of the staff). I often wondered what she was doing working somewhere like Dean & Daniels, but I think it was because she got a malign pleasure out of running rings round everyone: Gabi's filing was so baroque that you'd need to have worked in code-busting at Bletchley to find anything unaided.

'It's nice of you to see it like that,' I said, and automatically checked my emails in case there was any communication yet from Orlando, the on-off love of my life. We had been off for a few months now, but I lived in hope that he might change his mind. Still nothing. My heart broke a little, yet again, but I rallied myself before Gabi's eagle eyes could register any signs of weakness. A big sigh slipped out.

'Oh, come on,' she said. 'Ignore the numbers on the labels – they don't mean anything.'

'Don't they? Good job I'm handy with a needle and thread or I'd never have a thing to wear.'

'Mel, I would kill for your figure,' said Gabi sternly. 'Your tiny waist.' She grimaced. 'Your proper lady's bosom.'

I smiled because it's rude to refuse a compliment, even if you don't quite believe it. 'Oh no, you wouldn't. Bones are so much more elegant.'

'I don't know,' said Gabi, shooting a sideways glance in the direction of the photocopier. 'Nothing worse than those posh Fionas who trail up and down outside, all skinny and blonde like malnourished Afghan hounds,' she went on, making sure Carolyn could hear her. 'What a fecking waste of space they are. Chalet girls surfing the King's Road on Daddy's magic credit card, in between ironing their hair and planning their next ski trip.'

Gabi said this at least once a day, and yet it never apparently registered with her that I'd spent *my* year out running a chalet complex in Val d'Isère. I spent more time tidying up the various love affairs and broken friendships than I had done tidying chalets.

'Gabi, *I* was a chalet girl,' I protested gently.

'Oh, yeah.' She stared at me, then shook her head. 'Jeez, I always forget you're one of them.'

'Why?' I ignored the 'one of them'.

Gabi shrugged. 'Well, you're working, for a start. And you just get on and *do* things. You don't keep banging on about where you buy your puffa jackets and who your daddy is.'

I was about to remind her why my father was the last person I'd want to be discussing when the office door opened and the boys steamed in, fresh from one of their long lunches.

Only it occurred to me that this hadn't been a very long lunch and they weren't looking their normal jolly selves. In fact there was no steaming at all.

'Early?' mouthed Gabi to me, looking at her watch.

'Yes, we are back early,' snapped Quentin. 'Because there's a lot to do.'

Quentin was the company director and the main man for serious three-million-plus houses. He did nothing all year, until the City bonuses rolled in, then he was rushed off his feet. Carolyn was meant to be his PA, but all she seemed to do was book mysterious lunches with clients I knew he didn't have and order flowers for his very sweet and undeserving wife, Letitia.

The other boys slunk into their seats and started making subdued phone calls, which wasn't like them at all.

'Melissa, would you come into my office?' said Quentin. 'And bring a pot of coffee and some cups with you.'

'Oooh, Melissa,' smirked Carolyn who had reappeared out of nowhere, much in the manner of Mr Benn's shop-keeper. Her coral lipstick looked very fresh and brought out the nicotine stains on her teeth beautifully. Gabi swore blind Carolyn couldn't be a day under thirty-five, despite the desperate palaver of her 'thirtieth' birthday party the previous year. 'It'll be about that skirt, I'd bet.'

I tugged the hem down. It was my favourite skirt because I had spent ages microscopically adjusting the seams so it fitted at both the waist and hips, but I must admit that it did have a habit of riding up. 'What's wrong with it?' I asked.

'Nothing wrong with that skirt,' said Hughy and, as he walked past, the cheeky article gave my bottom a firm slap. 'Miss Monroe.'

Gabi giggled and I blushed bright red.

Hughy hadn't joined the others for lunch, hence his cheerfulness; a while ago, I'd arranged for him to have private lunchtime Pilates lessons to cure his terrible back problems – now all too cured, it seemed.

Carolyn's eyebrows dropped immediately and she looked as if her lunch was repeating on her.

'It's too short,' she snapped. 'You're in an office, not a cabaret.'

Then she disappeared into her office with a handful of brochures for Chelsea loft conversions.

'Ignore the scrawny witch,' said Gabi loudly. 'Her nicotine patches aren't sticking. I saw her in the loo trying to fasten two on at once with sellotape.' She paused. 'If she carries on like this, I'm going to offer to staple them on for her.'

I sniggered, and whinnied, 'Oh, Gabi!' in my best Carolyn impression. It wasn't as good as Gabi's impression, which came complete with a jerky array of hairflicking gestures and poker-faced scowls.

'Well, she deserves it . . .' Gabi wagged her stapler at me. 'Now get in there and do some of that upside-down reading you're so good at, eh?'

'Will do.' I pulled my hem down as far as it would go and checked that my white blouse was safely buttoned up. Then I made the coffee, got my notebook and walked over to Quentin's office, wondering what it was I'd done that he wanted to discuss so privately.

Quentin was sitting at his desk with his fingers steepled and a serious expression on his face. I'd seen this expression before, on my father; it was the first stage of the school-report reading process, which would begin with an unconvincing display of sympathetic calm and end with Daddy bright red up to his ears, roaring, '"Melissa must try harder"? Too bloody right she should at seven thousand pounds a term!'

I steeled myself not to cry whatever Quentin said, because I made it a rule never to cry in public: it doesn't help, except as a very, very last resort.

Quentin waited for me to sit down and I perched on the edge of the leather chair, with my knees clamped together, as drilled into us in Home Economics classes at school. I noticed that Carolyn hadn't been watering Quentin's weeping fig and made a mental note to give it a good soak later.

'Now then, the lovely Melissa,' said Quentin, unctuously. 'Thanks for the coffee. How long is it you've been with us now?'

It was a stupid question, because my file was open on the desk in front of him. One of the files that I'd dragged out of the paper-y jungle when I arrived at Dean & Daniels, the jungle I'd reorganised and updated on the computer system. But I didn't point that out, I just said, 'Eight months next week.'

'Indeed. And you've certainly made your mark on the office.'

I gave him a really big smile because it wasn't often

that Quentin said nice things like that to people. It was true though. When I'd arrived, the office had been in a dreadful state. It had taken me ages to sort it out, but now everything ran like clockwork. Gabi said I should have made a bigger deal about what I'd done, but for an easy life, I let Carolyn imagine it was still all her own work. I'm terrible at blowing my own trumpet. It's much easier to blow other people's – then everyone's happy.

'Thank you,' I said. 'It's nice when everything's running smoothly.'

I hoped that didn't make me sound like a dreadful prig. I had this morbid fear that everyone in the office thought I was deadly boring because I knew how to do double-sided photocopying.

'Yeees.' Quentin shifted about a bit in his chair. 'Yeees, you do a really sterling job, and that rather makes what I have to say next somewhat difficult.'

'Spit it out,' I said cheerfully, pouring the coffee. How bad could it be? Clearly my skirt was fine, or else he wouldn't have suggested I sat on this particular chair. Maybe he wanted to promote me, I thought. Stranger things had happened.

'Melissa, it's—'

'One sugar, isn't it?' I said, leaning over the desk to hand him his cup.

Quentin looked up, straight into my cleavage, looked down at the desk, and swallowed rather hurriedly. 'Oh er, yes, thank you.'

At this point the door opened and Carolyn's head popped round. When she saw me she looked furious; presumably she was dying for Quentin to rollock me about my skirt, so I sat down again quickly.

Quentin made a faint gesture to me around his tie area

and I looked down to see my blasted middle button had burst open again. I try to reinforce the buttonholes, but the power of gravity can't always be checked.

'I'll leave you to it, Quentin,' said Carolyn frostily. No word of apology, mind. I often wondered exactly who the boss was.

Hatches safely battened, I stirred some cream into my coffee and resumed my perch on the edge of the chair.

Quentin smoothed down his quiff and re-steepled his fingers. This time he stared fixedly at my file while he spoke. 'Now, Melissa, I'm afraid I have some bad news for you. It's bad news for the whole company, really. Well, bad news and good news.'

I widened my eyes.

Quentin looked up, coughed and took a big gulp of coffee. 'The good news is that Dean & Daniels is being incorporated into Kyrle & Pope, a very prestigious New York estate agency.'

'How marvellous!' I said, warmly.

'Yes, well, head office have decided that it would make more sense to merge the Chelsea and the Knightsbridge offices of Dean & Daniels into one large flagship branch, with state-of-the-art computer facilities, architectural simulations, and recreational areas for our clients.' Quentin was really warming to his theme. 'Kyrle & Pope want to provide the most complete house-buying experience possible for their international clientele, from arranging the mortgage to finding the best vase for displaying architectural flower arrangements in the hall.'

'What a fabulous idea!' I said, impressed. 'I've always thought we should organise a sort of collaboration service with Peter Jones, you know, a helping hand for those male clients who might not have a woman's touch when it comes to decorating their lovely new home.'

It occurred to me that this was exactly the kind of thing I would be excellent at, and I was about to demonstrate my initiative by suggesting it, when an ominous 'sympathetic' expression swam over Quentin's red face.

As I recall, this was the expression that accompanied Daddy's enquiries as to whether I'd been ill for significant portions of the term to have missed so much information. Even when he knew very well that I hadn't.

I gripped my saucer tighter.

'Now, the bad news is,' intoned Quentin, 'that for every advance in business there are usually some casualties, and since we're merging our staff with Knightsbridge and taking on some American agents too, we're forced to let some personnel go.'

'Oh dear!' I gasped, thinking of poor Hughy and Charles, and I crossed my fingers under my coffee cup. I knew for a fact that Hughy had a big holiday planned for three months' time, and Charles had the most horrendous mortgage. I helped him fib on the application form.

'So you're not the only redundancy to be made from this office, but believe me, you're the one everyone will miss most, and I include myself in that.'

'Thank you very much, that's so sweet of you,' I replied, with another big smile. Really, I thought, Quentin could be quite charming when he tried.

Then it dawned on me that I'd just been sacked.

An ominous lead weight settled at the pit of my stomach. Not *again*. Oh God.

The door opened and Carolyn's haystack of blonde hair appeared a good two seconds before the rest of her.

'Not *now*, Carolyn!' snapped Quentin and she scuttled out.

I bit my lip and replaced my coffee cup on Quentin's desk so I could think better.

Part of me wanted to burst into tears, hammer my fists on the desk and demand my job back, if necessary on the grounds that, unlike Carolyn, I didn't fake my typing certificate, but I knew this wouldn't work, and more to the point, it would be spectacularly undignified. So I pulled myself together, as I'd been brought up to do, and glued a big smile on my face, despite the cracking sensation I felt inside.

'Oh dear,' I croaked. 'Oh . . . dear.'

Quentin looked genuinely cut up, which is where he started to deviate from the Daddy Plan. 'It's only because you're the newest PA,' he apologised. 'Really, you've worked much harder than most of the other brainless— er, young girls we *normally* seem to have working here. And you certainly brighten the place up no end. I'd be happy to give you a glowing reference. And of course, there'll be severance pay to see you through.'

God! The rent!

The overdue rent. And the small matter of the phone bill. My salary barely covered bills at the best of times.

I tried to smile bravely. 'Well, that will help. I know it's none of my business but does this mean . . .' I cast about for a tactful way to put it. 'Um, are Charles and Hughy . . . ?'

'Charles and Hughy?' Quentin looked surprised, but shook his head. 'No, they'll be heading up the flagship with me.'

Good. Well, I was pleased about that, at least.

'Is there anything else?' I asked.

'No,' said Quentin, 'that's it.' And he looked a bit sad.

Gabi took the news very badly. If I didn't know she was a tough nut, I'd have sworn she was crying for real.

'Don't leave me here with Carolyn!' she pleaded. 'It'll be like working the night shift with Dracula. In a blood donor unit.'

'I won't be leaving you here, you idiot,' I said. 'You'll all be shipping out to Knightsbridge.'

'Oh God,' moaned Gabi and sank her head onto her folded arms.

'Think of the shopping, Gabi!'

'I am,' she groaned from underneath her sleeves.

Quentin's office door opened and everyone froze until he barked, 'Jeremy? A word? ASAP?'

The door closed. Jeremy walked over in a silence so extreme I could hear his Gucci loafers squeaking.

'Sooo, skirt too tight then?' simpered Carolyn in passing. Her face looked so innocent that I couldn't help wondering if she'd been listening in.

'Nothing wrong with my skirt,' I said, lifting up my chin so I could look her in the eye that didn't squint. 'In fact Quentin thinks I brighten up the place no end.'

'Brightened,' Carolyn corrected me smugly, then looked cross with herself.

'I don't know what we'll *do* without Melissa,' wailed Gabi. 'Apart from the small matter of the office grinding to a halt, she's the only one who knows how to work the coffee machine without getting it full of grit. Quentin must have gone insane. Why has he sacked *you*?'

You can't tell Gabi anything and expect it to stay secret.

Hughy had got into loads of trouble that way, with Gabi answering my phone and telling clients what other people were offering. I, on the other hand, prided myself on being the very soul of discretion.

'I've been *made redundant*,' I reminded her, putting on a brave face. 'These things happen, don't they? No sense in getting bitter about it. New challenges and all that.'

As Gabi sank her head back into her hands, I struggled to think up three positives about the situation.

More time for dress-making at home – the pocket money sideline that had saved my bacon with the rent more than once already.

No more fighting Carolyn's inept filing.

Um, sometimes things go wrong for a reason?

For once, none of them made me feel much better.

There really aren't that many rewards for being nice, not in real life. I suddenly wished I could throw an all-out hysterical bitch fit – God knows I'd seen enough at home – but I just couldn't. For a start, I didn't know what you were meant to do once you ran out of bitchy hysteria. Rush away? Vanish in a puff of smoke?

'Well, I'm sure Daddy will bail you out,' said Carolyn nastily. 'Slip you a couple of thousand for a skiing holiday to get over it.'

'No, he will not,' I retorted.

I didn't need to pretend to be dignified here, because it was true. My father had always made a huge deal about how my sisters and I wouldn't get a penny until we're fifty. He reckoned that if anyone wanted to marry us for our money, they'd have to stick around for at least twenty-five years to get it.

His actual words were, 'If they want to get into my daughters' pants, they can bloody well pay for it up front.'

Not nice, is he? I think thirty years in Parliament does that to you.

I used to think it was because he wanted us to earn our own money and be independent, or at least marry for love, but the older I got, the more I realised that Daddy liked to make sure his was the only name on the cheque-book. Maybe there was a tax break in it too somewhere. Maybe there wasn't actually any money. Cash flow was ever a mysterious force in our family. There was never enough for Mummy to buy new clothes, for instance, but always enough to restock the wine cellar.

Anyway, unlike my confetti-happy sisters and my poor subjugated mother, I vowed at an early age that I'd never be a household slave to any man, especially my father, so I made a point of always earning my own money, what little there was of it. Apart from which, Daddy and I didn't see eye-to-eye about, well, previous loans.

'I don't get a penny from my parents,' I insisted.

'Daddy not paying your bills?' said Carolyn with great surprise. 'Do me a favour.'

Gabi looked shocked too. Her boyfriend, Aaron, was a maths whizz who did something complicated with spread-betting in the City; he earned a small fortune, but had no time to spend it, so Gabi's main purpose in life was getting her hands on his cash and redistributing it amongst deserving shops, salons and spas. She was the Robin Hood of Bluewater, basically. 'How else can you afford to work here on this salary?' she demanded. 'It doesn't even cover my credit cards!'

I looked from Gabi's sagging jaw to Carolyn's spiteful moon-face and the red-faced agents in the background, all making panicky calls to their girlfriends, and felt rather affronted. I was no blonde Daddy's girl. I wasn't even a blonde, for heaven's sake.

'I pay my own way,' I said. 'I have done since I left college. This and my, um, side projects cover the bills, thank you very much.'

Carolyn hooked up her eyebrows in a very inelegant enquiry. 'Side projects?'

I wasn't going to mention my dress-making to Carolyn. It was the big office joke that I was a 1950s throwback already, what with my girls' school education and my pearl earrings. In *fact*, I made gorgeous T-shirts, embellishing baby-soft cotton shirts with tiny beads and sequins. I only did them for friends, but even so it was quite a lucrative hobby, given that I mainly did it to keep my hands busy and out of the biscuit tin while watching television.

But Carolyn wasn't interested in that, and I wasn't going to tell her.

'Yes, side projects,' I said and shut my lips tight. My head was beginning to throb with tension and hurt.

'How fascinating,' she said, sounding bored. 'Now, come into my office so we can talk about your P45. Why don't you take your outstanding holiday now, and have the rest of the week off?'

There are many marks of a true lady, but I believe that one of them is to walk with her head held high into the office of redundancy, while her world falls apart around her. Which I did. For the third time in eighteen months.

2

Thank God for Nelson Barber, the flatmate from heaven.

And I did thank God for him, every time I passed a delicatessen and saw how much stuffed olives would cost if I had to buy them ready-made instead of enjoying their hand-wrought brothers in the comfort of my own house.

Nelson and I have known each other for years and years. His father was at school with mine, only his dad's a perfect gentleman with a passion for British naval history – hence Nelson and his brother, Woolfe. Nelson's three best points are: he's a fantastic cook; he makes me laugh when I'm feeling sorry for myself; he has a very kind heart beneath his grumpy exterior, and he appreciates good manners. OK, four good points. To be honest, I can't stop at four – he has loads.

In fact, it's easier to do Nelson's only three bad points: he frequently acts like an off-duty High Court judge; he has very thick brown hair which clogs up the shower; and he derives disproportionate pleasure from taking the mickey out of my occasional faux pas.

But I can forgive all that because he understands me perfectly and knows when to keep quiet and offer comfort food.

Hence the first thing Nelson said when I walked through the door, looking and feeling completely shattered, was,

'I've just tried this new recipe for chocolate orange cake – can I twist your arm and make you taste it?'

I was forced to admit to myself that that was what you want at the end of a day like today; not rampant sex, or stacks of red roses leaning up against your front door. Not that either had ever been on offer to me.

'Just a tiny, tiny slice,' I said. Then, when I saw the somewhat literal angle his knife was making, 'Er, maybe not that tiny, darling.'

Nelson handed me the wedge of cake and a fork to shovel it in with, and didn't even ask me what had made my hair so flat and my eye make-up so smeary. But I knew he knew something was badly wrong because he didn't mention the rent, even though it was now over a fortnight late.

When I'd devoured the first slice of cake (divine), and Nelson had cut me another giant wedge without me even having to ask, I bit the bullet and filled him in.

'I've been made redundant,' I mumbled through a mouthful of ganache. Sharing the news with Nelson took a tiny sting out of it, but not very much.

'Why? And from when? And,' he added, ever the pragmatist, 'with how much severance pay?'

'Oh, I don't care about that,' I said, sinking onto the sofa and surreptitiously easing the strain on my skirt zip at the same time. 'I mean, it wasn't ideal, but I *liked* working there, and I *hate* interviews. I'm just not very good at selling myself. I know how good I am at my job – I just can't sit there boasting about my typing speeds.'

Nelson climbed over the back of the sofa and settled himself at the end opposite me. His best jeans were covered in flour and he was wearing socks, but I let it go. 'Do you want me to talk about the legality of them firing you like this?'

'No, not really.'

'Well, how are you for cash?'

'I have a little,' I said.

'Enough for half a phone bill?'

The mere thought made me flinch. 'Is that bigger than half an electricity bill?'

'Try a quarter of the electricity bill.'

I bit my lip. 'Oh God, I hate owing money. It's just so . . . humiliating.'

'Don't bite my head off, but why not call your dad?' suggested Nelson. 'Ask his advice. He owes you that much. And if he can't find you a job, he should at least lend you some money until you sort yourself out.'

I noticed Nelson said 'lend', not 'send'. He knew my father too well.

'No. That's not going to happen,' I said, slightly evasively. I still hadn't exactly come clean with Nelson about why Daddy was even less likely than normal to bail me out this time. Nelson had a very low opinion of my boyfriends in general and confessing all about the Perry Hamilton incident – and its financial ramifications – would just have put the tin lid on it.

'Oh, don't be so proud, Melissa.'

'It's not pride. It's . . .' I wasn't sure it wasn't pride, actually. 'It's dignity,' I said instead.

'It's stupidity, that's what it is.' Nelson looked unusually ticked off. 'He should support you, and he doesn't. *No one* in that family supports you. He's throwing money at Emery, the most *foolish* girl I've ever met, just because she's getting married to a serial womaniser, and if anyone needs a bit of help it's you, since you're all on your own and that creep Orlando's never going to—'

'Nelson!' I exclaimed, before I had to hear him say what was inevitably coming next. 'No!'

'Sorry, sorry . . .' He held his hands up in front of his face. 'I didn't mean it to come out like that, honestly.'

But all the tears that I'd managed to bottle up while I was at work were rushing up my throat now, hot and choking. I felt so miserable. And to my surprise, I realised I was rather angry too. I could feel my face burning red. It was too mean of Nelson to bring up the marriage thing. Emery, my sister, was two years younger than me, and getting married at the end of the year, albeit to a man whom I'd never actually met, while I remained an on-off spinster who couldn't even afford a cat to grow wrinkled with. It wasn't that I lacked a romantic soul, either. Maybe I was *too* romantic.

Nelson looked guilty and stretched out a comforting hand towards my knee. He patted it awkwardly. 'Oh God, listen, what do I know? Maybe he'll come back from this . . . "break", or whatever you've called it, and decide that you're meant to be together after all, and . . . Oh, sorry. I'll just shut up, shall I?'

The well-meaning kindness in his voice set me off afresh. I had thought Orlando was The One. I honestly still thought he might be. But then I'd thought Perry was The One too. And Toby and Jacques before him. But I hadn't loved any of them the way I loved Orlando. I truly believed that he was the one I'd been saving myself for. And that made his desertion even harder to bear, since he'd galloped off into the sunset 'to think about what he wanted from life' with my dignity, my heart and, well, other prized gifts. Nelson, needless to say, claimed he knew Orlando was a reptile straight away.

But I *didn't*. That's what comes of getting most of your romantic education from paperback books, and a mother who insists that True Love Conquers All despite being married to an out-and-out cad.

That was why I was still secretly hoping he might come back and prove me right, and Nelson wrong.

'Oh, bloody, bloody hell!' I screeched, and marched into my bedroom. There was only one thing that could calm me down now. I needed to wreck something, really break something up, so it could be me inflicting the damage instead of it happening to me.

I yanked open my sewing basket and pulled out a T-shirt I'd been stitching for a friend of Emery's: rainbow rows of tiny sequins and pearls.

I barely even registered how long it had taken me to get that far, or how much she was willing to pay for it, or how many beads there were, nestling on the peachy-soft cotton.

'Oh, Mel, don't!' Nelson's voice drifted through from the sitting room. But I had what Mummy calls the red mist on me, and the T-shirt got it, with both blades of my embroidery scissors.

Nelson came in, in time to see me slashing away in a fury, beads and sequins and threads and tears flying around and sticking to my face.

'Sweetheart, calm down,' he muttered and slapped a hand over his eye where a stray sequin had ricocheted off my flying blades.

'I am so fed up of being *disposed of*!' I snarled. 'I am *so fed up* of being taken for granted!'

Then I sank down onto the bed and groaned, because T-shirts took me ages, and this one had been a real corker.

'Bang goes a hundred quid,' said Nelson, gently picking a sequin off my damp forehead. 'Quite literally, as it turns out.'

I stared at the explosion of spangly particles around my room. That was the phone bill money.

And then the bloody phone rang in the hall, like I needed reminding.

Nelson answered it.

I was still staring at the debris, wondering if I could persuade Nelson to find me a job temping at his office, when he walked in with the cordless phone. I knew who was on the other end from one glance at his face, which had tightened and turned a funny shade of grey.

He offered the phone to me without speaking.

'Hello, Daddy!' I said in a derangedly cheerful voice. I couldn't help it. I was trained from an early age that it's polite for ladies to answer telephones as if the National Lottery were calling to offer one the jackpot.

'How's my little girl?' he demanded.

'Fine, thank you!'

Nelson looked astounded and tapped his forehead aggressively.

I glowered back. Like I was going to tell *my father* I'd just been sacked.

'You haven't called home for a while and your mother was wondering if you'd got yourself into trouble, so I said I'd ring up and find out.'

That was the automatic expectation, by the way. I was their only offspring with a functioning brain and a working knowledge of PAYE, and yet I was the one who was meant to be permanently teetering on the brink of disaster.

Nelson was now miming something very complex, so

I turned my back on him while I worked out what my best ploy was.

'Everything's fine,' I lied unconvincingly. 'But, do you know, Nelson was telling me that I'm coming up to the last moment to put some money in my pension and—'

'Let me stop you there, little lady!' My father has no qualms about interrupting. It's not an attractive trait. 'I hope you're not about to ask me for some money?'

'Well . . .'

'Because we know what happened last time I lent you some money, don't we?'

I shuffled over to the window so Nelson couldn't hear what I was saying. A heavy feeling was expanding in the pit of my stomach, like someone was inflating a balloon in there.

'I do know. And I've told you that I'll pay you back, every penny.'

'Where is he these days, that Perry character?'

I bit my tongue and tried to remain ladylike. 'He's set up a chalet rental agency in Switzerland. Just as he said he would.' I didn't know where, that was all. Or what his new mobile number was, now that the other one no longer worked.

'Skiing away on my assets, I daresay.' My father had the effrontery to guffaw like a horse, then he stopped abruptly. 'It's only because you *gave* him the money that I can't prosecute that bastard Perry Hamilton for theft, you realise, Melissa? Ten thousand pounds!' he roared.

As if he'd ever let me forget.

'I know that,' I replied heavily. 'But it was an excellent investment opportunity and I have complete faith that it's all a misunderstanding. He'll be on the phone to sort it out any day now.'

He cackled again and I made a very undignified face into the receiver. 'My dear girl, how many times have I told you that only men make business deals in bed!'

'We weren't in bed!' I yelled. Not that it was any of his business. My entire head was turning red now. 'We were never in bed! I don't . . . do that kind of thing!'

And I didn't, by the way. Appearances can be deceptive. Just because someone has a generous chest and a romantic nature doesn't mean they're easy. As Orlando found out when he tried to proposition me on our third date after no more than a Fiorentina and Diet Coke at Pucci Pizza.

My father was still cackling in an unpleasant Leslie Phillips manner. 'Your trouble is that you persist in thinking the best of everyone, my dear little Melissa. It's rather charming, but it's only charming up to a point.'

'Which point?' I asked frostily.

'The point at which you stop making a complete fool of yourself and find a nice man to take care of you and your congenital idiocy.'

I said nothing because I was focusing on not bursting into tears. My father knew exactly which buttons to press to inflict maximum torment. I supposed gloomily that it was his job.

'For most girls that's at the age of about twenty-one,' he added helpfully. 'And the idiocy comes from your mother's side.'

I was twenty-seven, and I had a diploma, I might add – not that he rated it much above a cycling proficiency certificate.

With a supreme effort, I managed to retort, 'Better to think well of everyone and be proved wrong on occasion than to go around like, like . . . like a suspicious old crone.'

'Only nuns and children can get away with simpleton behaviour, Melissa,' he snapped.

There didn't seem to be much reason to continue the conversation after that.

'Couldn't you have spoken to your mother?' asked Nelson as I pulled the velvet throw over my head on the sofa and sank into the fresh depths of misery the conversation had opened up to me.

'No. She wouldn't have been any help.' My mother spent half her existence organising my father's social life, and the other half recovering from it. In public, she was the epitome of the perfect politician's wife, all blow-dried blonde hair and tailored suits, but, well, it took a lot out of her. Little did she realise that being a Deb of the Year in 1969 would only qualify her for becoming Secretary of the Century for the rest of her life. From the cheerful sound of my father's voice, he'd already spent an agreeable afternoon reducing her to a quivering mousse of apology before he decided to start on me.

Nelson put his arms round me over the top of the throw and gave me a reassuring squeeze. 'Come on, Mel. You'll get another job. I'll help you. And for God's sake, what with all those mad school friends of yours you've got more contacts than MI5. The only people you don't know in London are the ones in witness protection programmes.'

I had to concede that was true. For one reason or another, I ended up going to four schools in all, all of which, in retrospect, were really just giant networking grounds. Taking into account school and friends and Mummy's endless parties – and the fact that I do enjoy meeting new people – I did rather know just about everyone, even if I didn't always like them very much. And, I reasoned privately, if some of the dozy girls I knew from school had managed to get jobs, there was absolutely no reason why I couldn't get one.

'Well?' said Nelson.

'Oh, let's face it, I wasn't a career estate agent,' I said, sitting up. I wiped my eyes and pulled myself together. 'No point getting on my high horse about it. Plenty more jobs out there.'

Nelson looked sympathetic, though I know he wasn't completely taken in by this show of bravado. He had, after all, seen it many times before.

'Why don't you go and have a nice long bath?' he suggested. 'Let's start the evening over again. I can knock up a chicken korma and we'll watch *Upstairs Downstairs* on UK Gold.'

I was in full agreement with this excellent plan and was washing that estate agency and my vile father right out of my hair when the phone rang.

I cursed and got a mouthful of shampoo. If it was Emery calling to chew over fresh plans for her ghastly wedding, I swore I'd drown myself in the bath. In a moment of unusual family warmth, I'd stupidly mentioned something about helping her with her wedding dress, as well as my own bridesmaid's dress, and she wouldn't let me forget it, claiming she'd already spent the money she'd saved on the wedding cake deposit. There's something of my father about that girl.

Then again, I reasoned with a lifting heart, it could be Orlando.

Nelson edged into the bathroom with the walk-around phone in one hand, and the other hand gallantly covering his eyes.

'Don't be an idiot!' I said, taking the phone and giving him a little push. 'You've seen it all before!'

'Not quite like that, I haven't,' he muttered and backed out of the room, closing the door behind him.

I sank back into the warm bath water and said, 'Hello?' into the phone. The acoustics of the bathroom seemed to make my voice sound rather sultry.

Unfortunately, it wasn't Orlando on the other end.

It was Gabi, and from the background noise it sounded as if she was calling from a bus. Gabi had no qualms about discussing her life at full volume in front of an audience of complete strangers, whereas I did.

'Hiya, Mel,' she said. 'How you bearing up?'

The sound of her voice reminded me of Dean & Daniels and the genius letter templates I'd finally perfected and being sacked, and my mood deflated like the bubbles in the very cheap bubble bath, revealing the dunes of my porcelain-pale tummy in all their undulating glory.

'I *was* fine,' I said, contemplating my navel. 'Now I'm not so sure.'

'Oh, don't be such a *wimp*!' bellowed Gabi. 'It's not like you! Come on out for a drink, and we can brainstorm what your next move should be.'

Even on a good day, much as I loved her, Gabi's brainstorms tended to involve a lot of imaginary violent behaviour and few realistically practical solutions, but of course I didn't tell her that because she must have been feeling terrible that she still had her job while I'd been made redundant.

'Come on out,' she wheedled. 'Come out, just for one drink. On me.'

'We-e-e-ell, OK,' I said, to be nice. 'Can Nelson come too?'

There was a faint noise on the line, which could well

have been Gabi swooning against the side of the bus. Despite her near-military campaign to get Aaron down the aisle, Gabi had something of a soft spot for Nelson. Presumably she'd given him a Posh Boy Exemption too, or else the fact that he worked for a charity rather than an estate agency swung the balance in his favour.

'Oh, if he must,' she said, pretending to sound reluctant. 'But get a move on. And don't bother getting dressed up. I don't want you overshadowing me if Nelson's coming.'

3

We went to the Bluebird on the King's Road because Gabi was paying and there was a bus Nelson and I could get there and back.

When we arrived, Gabi was already halfway down a large Cosmopolitan and was scanning the bar with a beady glare. With her dark hair, very bright red lipstick and what-is-this-peculiar-smell? expression, she could easily have passed for an unimpressed bar reviewer, although I guessed the real source of her irritation was the absurd number of thin blonde women dominating her line of sight.

Nelson and I made our way over to her table, while I checked to see if there was anyone around I knew. I'm a bit short-sighted, and when you know lots of people, it's so easy to offend swathes of your address book, just by leaving your specs in your bag.

'Is that Bobsy Parkin over there?' I muttered to Nelson.

'Bobsy what? You forget that I don't have the same glittering social circle as you do.'

I squinted. If it was Bobsy, she'd certainly smartened herself up since I last saw her. You certainly couldn't do highlights like that in your kitchen with some Loving Care and an old bathing cap.

'Bobsy Parkin. Parents live in Eaton Square. Not the brightest button in the box but very good with animals.

Had an allergy to ink that made her hands swell up like boxing gloves, so she did her GCSEs in pencil, or something.'

Nelson paused in his polite shoving to give me the full benefit of his incredulous expression. 'The more you tell me about your school, the more amazed I am that you're so normal.'

I shot him a hard look. Nelson's mother was a Labour County Councillor and made a big thing about not sending Nelson to private school. She made very sure they were living in the right catchment area for the grammar school though.

'Bobsy Parkin?' asked Gabi avidly, when we finally reached the table, still sniping at each other. 'Didn't you tell me about her? Is she the Bobsy Parkin who rode Jasper Attwell's Great Dane bareback round the Chelsea Arts Club? You have *so* got the best friends, Mel.'

Nelson groaned.

I made a mental note to edit what I told Gabi more carefully in future.

We squeezed around Gabi's table, and angled our chairs so she could sit very close to Nelson and I could look at Bobsy without drawing attention to myself. She was sitting at a corner table, having supper with her father. I guessed he was telling her some upsetting family news because he was stroking her hand in a consoling manner.

'How are you, Nelson?' cooed Gabi. 'When are you going to take me out sailing on that yacht of yours?'

'It's a very small one-seater racing dinghy. There's barely room for me on it. Can we focus on working out a job for Melissa, please?' said Nelson impatiently. 'Much as I adore her company, she has certain financial commitments to BT and London Electricity, which I am currently meeting for her. And there's about to be a catastrophic run on the Bank of Barber.'

Gabi's eyes went all glazed. I must admit that Nelson does suit a touch of impatience. And much as he thought she was a nice girl, Gabi did bring out the impatience in him.

'Yes,' she said. 'I've made a list.' And she got out a notebook. 'Sorry, Mel, I nicked it from work. I'll put a note in the stationery book.'

'Oh, forget it,' I said, with a pang for my immaculate stationery cupboard that would doubtless go to hell in a handcart now that Carolyn was in charge. 'It's not my responsibility any more.' But I couldn't stop looking at Bobsy long enough to care. She looked a lot better dressed than she did when I knew her at school.

'So listen, Mel, I've made a list of your skills and achievements, and another list of all the mad flakes you told me about who work in nice offices,' said Gabi in her best efficient manner. I'd only ever heard her use it on the phone when she was trying to negotiate her store card repayments. 'Shall we go through it? Starting with Poppy Sharpwell-Smith – according to you, she's got an au pair agency in Kensington but she's a total ditz who thought that fairy cakes were made by real fairies. You could organise her, no problem. Sounds like she needs it, if you ask me. Or there's Philly Bloom the florist, who you said you knew from your Scottish dancing club . . .'

Nelson looked pained. 'I've changed my mind. You two stay here and let me get another round in.'

I humoured Gabi for ten minutes, agreed that temping might suit my short attention span quite well, conceded that the bar was indeed full of Afghan hounds in human form, then I cracked and excused myself to help Nelson attract some attention at the bar. Getting served immediately in bars is one of those mysterious things I just seem to be able to do. I also felt the need for a large drink.

However, curiosity got the better of me en route, and I drifted by Bobsy's table, near enough for her to notice my big social smile.

Bobsy returned the big social smile, and I spotted the new improved teeth, but she didn't beckon me over to join her. Still, I thought, family news is family news.

The barman served me as soon as I leaned on the counter, much to Nelson's disgust, and so we knocked back a quick livener while we were there, before taking two rounds of Martinis to keep us going.

Suitably fortified, Gabi ran through the rest of her job-option list, which made me feel even more desperate. I made my excuses, and slipped off to the loo. I hadn't realised how much my job at Dean & Daniels had suited me until I didn't have it, and though I wouldn't have dreamed of saying so to Gabi, some of the girls she was talking about filled me with, well, horror. It was quite chilling seeing one's friends and acquaintances through Gabi's critical eyes.

Still, I was beginning to understand her constant surprise at how normal and down-to-earth I was.

It wasn't that I hadn't fitted in at school because I *had*: I'd been in all the teams, had gone to all the parties, and no one had ever actively bullied me. I just never made any bosom buddies. To cut a very long and embarrassing story short, I had to change schools first when my father was caught red-handed in a tax scandal, then again when he and Mummy moved to France for a few years, then again when they moved back, then finally because I insisted on going somewhere I could actually pass some A-levels. Even though everyone was terribly nice, for the first year at each place, I always had the feeling that conversations stopped whenever I walked in the room. And that went for the pupils too. Unfortunately, my father has a ghastly 'silver fox' sort of charm, and that, combined with a marked reluctance to pay taxes, kept him in one column or another of the papers – which naturally kept me top of the gossip pops.

My elder sister, Allegra, dyed her jet-black hair bright red, brazened it out and made scandal her big entrée into the cool girls' circle. Emery just floated through the education system as vaguely as she's floated through everything else since. But I was mortified for Daddy, and Mummy – and me – and though I made lots of friends, I was really, really careful never to do anything to draw attention to myself. I was so good at being nice to everyone that I never really made any special friends.

Daddy always insisted on the most expensive schools, so we'd 'forge our own social connections' – or so that everyone else's backgrounds would be as weird as ours, if you ask me – but unfortunately, whereas boys' schools forgive a lot on the rugby pitch, girls' schools don't.

Girls remember *everything*.

As I washed my hands and checked my nail varnish for chips, a familiar face emerged from a cubicle and loomed up behind me in the mirror. Bobsy, at least, had been some way below me in the pecking order, on account of the way she always smelled of pencil shavings and cat litter.

'Hello, Bobsy!' I exclaimed. Not an animal hair in sight. And just the one earring in each ear, both of them diamonds too. 'How are you?'

'Melissa, darling! I'm fine, thank you so much.' Her voice was much softer than I remember, as if it had been filed and polished. Maybe she wasn't yelling at horses so much these days. I noticed she still wore her 'trademark' hairclips (our Home Ec teacher, Mrs McKinnon, stressed the need for a lady to develop a chic trademark) – only now the large red camellia on the clip was definitely real Chanel and not the Top Shop knock-offs we'd all gone mad over at school.

I swallowed and wished I'd put on my better shoes.

Bobsy beamed broadly. 'You haven't changed at all. Still the same old sexy Melons. How are *you*?'

'I'm very well,' I replied, stoutly. Nearly everyone at school called me Melons – because I was so chunky, I guess. Even so, I did feel a little guilty, because although the school network was still operating at full strength (Christmas especially was exhausting – some old girls clearly roped off October onwards for writing cards), Bobsy had rather slipped through the net. I had absolutely no idea what she was doing, but she was looking very well on it.

'Are you still with that law firm?' she asked.

'Er, no. I've moved on from there.' That had been my first position, five jobs ago. As soon as I got a place ship-shape, I usually ended up being made redundant. Nelson said it was my own fault – being too organised just high-lighted the excess staff, and I was too nice, according to him, to fight dirty when it came to office politics.

'Really?' Bobsy raised her eyebrows in enquiry. They were very *groomed*.

'Actually, I'm between jobs right now,' I admitted in a rush of cocktail honesty. 'As of today, in fact. Any sugges-tions?'

'Oh, dear,' she said sympathetically. 'How annoying for you. Well. What sort of thing are you looking for?'

'Anything . . .' I was about to add 'at all' but managed to change it to '. . . new and exciting.'

Bobsy put a thoughtful finger to her lips. I noticed, with mounting approval, that it too was very nicely shaped. I liked to keep my nails polished too; stylish nails took my mind off typing. 'What would you say your skills were?' she asked.

'I'm very good with people,' I said immediately. 'You know, organising them, making sure they're happy. Smoothing out problems before they happen. And conversation. I'm awfully good at talking to the most tedious, difficult people.' And I bloody well should have been after twenty-seven years with my father. Then, just in case she could read my mind, I added, 'I've got excellent typing speeds and decent IT skills, and I'm terribly discreet.'

'Oh yes, discreet,' she said with a naughty smile. 'Well, you would be, what with your daddy's shenanigans!'

Hot beads of sweat prickled under my arms. I looked away, and caught sight of us in a mirror; Bobsy with her finger still on her perfectly lined, red lips and me with my chignon unravelling round my flushed face. Why was I standing here in the loos of the Bluebird being interviewed by Bobsy 'Pencils' Parkin? She was a lovely girl, but I didn't need a job in a poodle parlour, and certainly didn't want my father dragged into the conversation.

'Anyway,' I said, standing up straighter. 'It's lovely to see you, Bobsy, but I don't want to keep you from your dinner, gassing on here. We should meet up for lunch some time.'

She rubbed her nose with a more familiar horsey

gesture, and said, 'Absolutely. Yes.' She reached into her tiny handbag which was so tiny it couldn't be of any practical use, so I guessed it cost a fortune. I only had enough money to be stylish, not fashionable.

Bobsy dug about a bit in her bag, then handed me a little card. 'Listen, if you're looking for some part-time work, go and see Mrs McKinnon.'

My brow creased. 'Mrs McKinnon? The Home Ec teacher? From St Cathal's?'

Bobsy nodded. 'Call her, and say I spoke to you. She might be able to help your . . . job situation.'

'She's running a temping agency?'

Bobsy smiled and, really, she looked like a different girl. A woman, in fact. 'You could said that, yes.'

The card read simply 'Hildegarde McKinnon' with a Chelsea phone number, and it completely threw me. Home Ec was my favourite subject, and Mrs McKinnon was my favourite teacher, but she wasn't exactly the careers officer, unless you wanted to spend your working life as a party-planner. Which, come to think of it, my mother, also an Old Cathalian, has.

Mrs McKinnon's classes were supposed to cover such essential topics as ridding your surfaces properly of bacteria and devising delicious dinner-party menus for a Muslim, a vegan, a lactose intolerant and a pregnant woman; however, with a bit of prompting, she usually diverted into more arcane waters, such as how to eat lobsters without licking your fingers, or how best to decline a marriage proposal on a pheasant shoot. I adored her lessons.

Mrs McKinnon herself was something of an enigma. There was never a sign of Mr McKinnon. Rumour had it that he'd once asked her to pass him a serviette instead of a napkin, and had been summarily dismissed. Most of the girls were scared of her, but I was sort of fascinated by the obvious fire she had boiling away under her lint-free exterior. I mean, no one can get that exercised about fruit knives without concealing depths of extreme passion. And, on a personal level, Mrs McKinnon did spark off my interest in dress-making by persistently pulling me up on my ill-fitting school uniform and making me adjust my seams for needlework prep.

But with a final adjustment to the Chanel hairgrip keeping her glossy mane under control, Bobsy was off, before I could ask her how learning the correct way to dismount from a moped could possibly help me pay my substantial debt to British Telecom.

'So,' said Nelson wearily when I got back to the table, 'is it *the* Bobsy Parkin, or just a Bobsy-a-like?'

'No, it's her all right,' I said.

Nelson muttered something about horses, but I wasn't listening because it occurred to me that there was now a bottle of Krug on the table.

'Oh, you shouldn't have! That's so sweet but totally unnecessary!' I gasped. 'Which one of you . . .'

'Oh no, Melissa, we didn't buy it,' breathed Gabi. 'It just appeared. For you, the waiter said.'

'Did it?' I frowned. I told the man at the bar to send us the bill, not a bottle of champagne.

'While I slipped off to go to the loo,' said Nelson as if he should have stopped it arriving somehow.

The penny dropped, and I had to come clean. This wasn't the first time this had happened to me. In my limited experience, I'd discovered that there were some awful men out there who thought they could buy a lady's company – and more! – for a bottle of champagne. I always sent it back, though.

Nelson's jaw was jutting.

Gabi was touching the bottle reverently and looking pained, because none of us could possibly afford Krug and it's simply the best tonic for a bad mood. I must admit that even I found manners rather vexing at times.

But who had sent it? And was there any way of keeping it?

I looked around discreetly and spotted Bobsy's father beaming at me, his red face nearly split in two at his own cleverness.

'Oh, look,' I said, turning back to Gabi and Nelson with no little relief. 'It's Bobsy's father who's sent it over. How sweet. Bobsy must have told him about my bad day. How considerate – of them both!'

'Do you think so?' said Gabi doubtfully. 'She doesn't look that pleased.'

It was true – Bobsy was pouting like a trooper about something.

'Are you sure that's her father?' she added. 'I don't see a resemblance . . .'

'Um, yes,' I said. 'Well, I suppose it could be an uncle. Or a family friend? Very generous, anyway.'

I was about to go over there and thank him myself, when Nelson said, rather icily, 'And how was he meant to know about your bad day while you and Bobsy were chatting in the loos? Was your redundancy in the *Evening Standard* or is Bobsy's daddy a psychic counsellor?'

At this juncture, Gabi took it upon herself to open the bottle in a very practised manner and had three glasses poured out before I could digest what Nelson had said and stop her.

'Gabi!'

'Come on, Mel.' She'd already swigged half a glass.

'Sometimes a girl needs a glass of champagne, no matter where it's come from.'

'But Bobsy . . .' I wrestled with my conscience.

'Oh, for the love of God, Melissa,' said Nelson crossly. 'It's obvious to everyone in here apart from you that he can't possibly be Bobsy's father. He has his sweaty paw on her knee!'

Oh, yes. So he had. Urgh.

'Well, who is he then?' I demanded.

'How would *I* know?' Nelson looked askance. 'I would have said it's her boyfriend but it's stretching the terminology a bit too far.'

'Sugar daddy,' said Gabi knowledgeably.

I tried to angle my gaze so I could observe Bobsy and her sugar daddy but it was impossible without staring. So I stared anyway.

'Oh my God,' I said. Then I shut my mouth because I couldn't for the life of me think what to say next.

'Well done, Bobsy, I say,' said Gabi, refilling her glass. 'Wish I had a man who'd shower me in Krug. Aaron's a right tight git when it comes to champagne, even though he's coining it in at the moment.'

'I think you'll find *they're* drinking house white wine,' observed Nelson. 'Which may explain Bobsy's lemon-face. Mel, close your mouth and stop gawping. This isn't a motorway pile-up.'

I rearranged my face into a blasé expression, but I really couldn't hide the fact that I was shocked. Gabi and Nelson were always going on about how I was too easily shocked by things. I suppose I had a very sheltered child-hood; with the benefit of hindsight, of course, I realised my lack of exposure to television and the tabloid press had been because of the numerous scandals my father wished to keep from his family. And my mother had had plenty of things of her own she didn't want to talk about.

But even so, I thought, how *rude* of that man to send me a bottle of champagne while he was on a date with Bobsy! I'd be livid!

'I can't drink it,' I announced, pushing my glass away.

'Good for you,' said Gabi, finishing off her own glass and grabbing mine.

'Gabi, we have to leave right now.' I got my coat and started winding my scarf around my neck.

Why on earth had he sent it? Was it because I was looking over there at Bobsy? Did he think I was flirting with him?

A hot wash of shame ran over my skin. What kind of girl did I *look* like?

'Stay here and finish the bottle now it's opened,' said Nelson firmly. 'Then go over there, thank him for his kindness and wish the pair of them a happy evening. If you want, I'll pay for it at the bar for you, and you can pay me back.'

This was a very generous offer, since although Nelson earned more than me, he still didn't earn the kind of money you can chuck around on champagne.

'OK,' I said, with a massive effort. 'But you two can drink it. I couldn't possibly.'

The moment Gabi had drained her last glass – which wasn't long – I walked over to Bobsy's table and rushed through my thank you speech, blushing to the roots of my hair. I made myself meet her eye and hoped she could detect the unspoken apology on my face. I looked at *him* as little as was polite, and turned down his enthusiastic offer of another bottle at their table. Poor Bobsy, I thought. What a creep. I sincerely hoped he shelled out for a cab home for her.

After that, none of us was in the mood to go on elsewhere, and the prospect of Nelson's chicken korma and the sofa was more tempting than ever. Nelson and I decided to walk home since it was a mild evening, and Gabi decided to join us for some of the way as she, at least, was still full of champagne fizz.

I could have been drinking iced water for all the effect those cocktails had had on me, and Nelson had gone quiet, which was plain ominous.

Gabi put her arm in mine as we walked along, and bumped her hip against me companionably. Since I was a good four inches taller than her, I didn't bump back for fear of bumping her over.

'Poor Mel,' she said with her customary lack of tact. 'It's just not going your way at the moment, is it?'

'No, it's not,' I replied shortly.

'No job, no man . . . good thing she's got you, eh, Nelson?'

If this was a lame attempt to bring Nelson into the conversation, it failed.

'We need to get you out more,' said Gabi with a fresh squeeze. 'That's what we need to do. We'll have a girlie makeover evening, and hit the town.' She fluffed up my brown curls with her spare hand. 'Forget Orlando. You'll find another bloke in no time at all. One that sends champagne over to our table.' She paused, then added, 'Younger than that bloke, though, obviously.'

'How tacky,' spat Nelson.

'Yes,' I agreed. 'It's tacky.'

'Tacky, but cost-effective. And your love life needs a jump-start.'

My heart ached, hard, at the bleakness ahead of me. I had managed not to think about Orlando all evening, but now that Gabi had mentioned his name, the dull aching returned. I had only agreed to go to the Bluebird in part because it wasn't a bar that reminded me of him.

We usually seemed to meet in bars. My heart used to turn over when I saw Orlando perched on a stool, chatting away to the barman. He was so blond and handsome with long legs and the sort of half-smile that hinted at inner naughtiness – the complete storybook-hero package. I didn't care what the experts said, a broken heart doesn't heal with time. Mine was only suppurating. We would have been going out for two years in three days' time – well, two years, on and off.

Mainly off.

'Didn't you meet Orlando when he bought you a bottle of champagne in a club?' said Gabi.

'Well. Yes. But that was different.'

'*How* was it different?' asked Nelson. He'd never liked Orlando. When I told Nelson we were having a break, all he'd said was, 'Neck or leg?'

I bit my lip. 'That was Fate, not some sleazy chat-up line. He brought it to my table and asked if I'd like to share it with him. He'd been taking his mother out for dinner and she'd just had to run off to deal with an urgent family matter. What else could I do? It was going flat.'

I was appalled to see Gabi and Nelson roar with laughter.

'What?'

'I love it when you tell that story. Cracks me up every time.' Nelson wiped his eye with his sleeve. 'You are so gullible.'

'I am most certainly not,' I bristled. 'Ask Quentin.

There isn't an estate agent in that office who can get one over on me.'

'Not for want of trying,' snorted Gabi drunkenly and for some reason the pair of them were off again.

I didn't get the joke, but I didn't like to interrupt either, as it was obviously a bonding moment, but really, it was true: everyone said how efficient I was. Hughy frequently used to boast about the appalling liberties he took with his last PA, then wring his hands and claim he couldn't any more because I was just impossible to lie to.

I let them giggle and strode on down the street. It wasn't that I couldn't laugh at myself, but I was absolutely not in the mood that night. I didn't think I'd ever felt so low in my whole life: there was *nothing at all* there for me. When I lost my job at the law firm, I had Orlando to cheer me up, and when Orlando told me he wanted to have a break, that's when I threw myself into organising the huge Valentine's party at work. Now I didn't have either, plus I was more in contact with my draining family than ever, with Emery's wedding coming up.

I would have turned to drink if it didn't have such alarming effects on my personality. Too many glasses of wine and the sultry Sophia Loren persona, which I occasionally tried on along with my tighter dresses in the privacy of my own room, had a tendency to rise to the surface, all hips and hooded eyes. *Not* what I needed right now.

Footsteps scuttled behind me as Gabi and Nelson hurried to catch up.

'Blimey,' panted Gabi, 'you can certainly shift when you want to.'

'Sorry, Mel. We didn't mean to upset you.' Nelson slung his arm around my shoulder. 'You know, from behind you looked just like Marilyn Monroe wiggling down the platform in *Some Like It Hot.*'

'Thank you,' I said gratefully, as much for the comforting warmth of his big hand on my shoulder as for the compliment.

'*Mincing away* in a fit of rage,' he continued.

Gabi took my other arm, possibly to inveigle herself within reach of Nelson's hand. 'Sorry,' she said. 'It's just that you deserve to be happier, when you're so good at making life easier for everyone else.' She squeezed me against her own warm hip. 'Why are you so scared about putting yourself first for a change? You've got to stand up for yourself a bit more. Sod whether it's ladylike or not.'

My lip wobbled, and I let it. It was tough putting on a brave face all the time. At least with Gabi and Nelson I could admit that things weren't so great. That was something to be grateful for; you sometimes don't realise how a pair of shoes are crippling you, until you take them off and marvel at your bunions and blisters.

Well, that was one good thing. Just another two to go.

'Hey, Gabi, there's a cab,' said Nelson, pointing out a taxi with an orange light. 'Why don't you grab it and get home while there's still time for Aaron to buy you another drink?'

Gabi looked at me, torn with indecision. I knew there was nothing she'd like more than an evening at our house, scoffing curry and gazing at Nelson, but on the other hand, it was still only nine o'clock, and Aaron would be getting home from the trading floor with a fistful of cash. They got very little time together as it was, but I did sometimes wonder if Gabi preferred things that way.

Nelson solved Gabi's dilemma by flagging down the taxi, which pulled up next to us.

'Where to, mate?' said the driver.

'Mill Hill,' said Nelson, and before she could open her mouth, he opened the door for her and ushered her in.

Gabi gave me a tight hug. 'I'm leaving you in Nelson's capable hands,' she said, and pulled a comedy face of thwarted desire, for my eyes only. 'It'll all work out, Mel,' she shouted as the cab pulled away, and blew a tipsy kiss out of the window.

'Will it?' I said morosely, watching as it pulled away. 'I wouldn't bet on it.'

'It will, you moron,' said Nelson, putting his arm round my shoulder again as we set off. 'You just have to start valuing yourself a bit higher. And I don't just mean at work.'

'I know what you're hinting at, Nelson, and I *do*,' I protested. 'I've got very high standards.'

Nelson snorted.

'Don't be so critical! You just don't know Orlando the way I do.' As soon as the words left my lips, I realised my mistake, because Nelson had a charmless ability to make all Orlando's good points seem thoroughly . . . I don't know, *ordinary*. But I ploughed on regardless, if only because right at that moment, I needed to hear positive things about me and Orlando spoken aloud. Even if I had to do it myself.

'Orlando's everything I want in a man,' I insisted. 'He's romantic and creative, and he really cares about me. The *real* me.'

'So why did you split up?' said Nelson bluntly.

'We're on a break,' I faltered.

But as I said it, I knew I couldn't keep lying to myself any longer. We *had* split up. We'd been split up since the New Year. We'd been split up since he utterly failed to send me a Valentine's card or indeed even a text on my birthday.

Orlando and I were over, and there was no point pretending he was ever coming back. Suddenly I had no idea how I'd managed to convince myself otherwise for so long.

My legs stopped walking as the shock of it hit me like a bus.

'How is this different from the times you've had a break before?' Nelson asked, when I didn't go on. 'And are you allowed to start looking for a replacement while he decides? Mel? Why have you stopped walking?'

I barely heard him. It was as if a bright light was shining into all the dark corners of my life that I hadn't wanted to look at before. I blinked away a hot tear and rubbed my eyes furiously. Suddenly I felt so *lonely*. Stupid and lonely.

I didn't *want* a replacement. I wanted *Orlando*. Even though he clearly wasn't worth it.

As he couldn't see my face, Nelson mistook my sudden devastated silence as permission to carry on with his lecture.

'I don't understand why you waste your time with these flaky layabouts,' he tutted. 'You need someone sensible, who can support you, and look after you. You're an old-fashioned girl at heart, and, deep down, you're only going to feel cheated by anything less than unconditional devotion from a decent man who's worth devoting yourself to. You know, it really makes me angry, Mel, watching you throw yourself away on losers like Orlando. You're worth so much more than that.'

'Shut up, Nelson,' I said, biting my lip. 'You're not my dad.'

'More's the pity,' he retorted. 'That's precisely why your male-role-model pattern's well and truly screwed up. Talk about lowering the bar.'

At the mention of my bloody father for what felt like the millionth time that night, the floodgates finally crashed open and I burst into tears right there on the street.

Nelson stopped walking immediately and put his hands on my shaking shoulders so he could see my face, which was red and unattractively screwed up like a tantrumming toddler.

'Oh, Mel!' he said, sounding aghast. 'I'm *so* sorry. I didn't realise how . . . You just seem to take these things in your stride. I mean, you didn't seem that cut up about Orlando.'

'Well, I was! I *am*!' I sobbed, outraged by his insensitivity. 'Of *course* I'm *cut up* about Orlando! Just because I don't go on and on about it . . .'

It didn't mean I hadn't been praying every time the phone rang, or hanging around until the last minute so I could be there when the post arrived. Avoiding certain parts of town so I wouldn't have to be reminded of the good nights, and switching off the radio when certain songs came on, so I wouldn't have to be reminded of the bad ones.

'Dignity's about the only thing I have left!' I howled, ignoring the ominous build-up of snot in my nose.

Nelson enfolded me in a bearhug, and I buried my face in his shoulder gratefully.

'Go on, have a good cry,' he said into my hair.

I wept into his jacket for a bit, then felt Nelson shuffle us to the far side of the pavement so my back came into contact with the brick wall. I wondered for a moment what he was doing, then heard him say, 'No, honestly, she's fine,' to a passer-by, and realised he was trying to shield me from public gaze.

Was I fine? I wiped my eyes where my mascara must have smudged, and composed myself with a few deep breaths.

'Nelson,' I said, when I could trust myself to speak without hiccuping. 'Be honest with me. Have I made a complete fool of myself?'

'With Orlando?' He looked me straight in the eye. That was the thing about Nelson: he always told me the truth. Even when a white lie would have been kinder. 'Yes, you have a bit. But only because you're determined to see the best in people. That's not a crime. In his case, I'd say it was an achievement.'

'But I love him,' I whimpered.

Nelson gave me a hard look.

I corrected it to, 'Loved him,' and hated myself for caving in so quickly. But Nelson was right, and we both knew it.

'I know you loved him,' he said with a sigh. 'But, Mel – he wasn't right for you.'

'And I suppose you know who is?' I couldn't help feeling riled by the weary tone in his voice.

'No, I just think you're such a romantic that you made yourself ignore the obvious warning signs. Like his slip-on shoes. And his year-round tan, and . . .' Nelson saw my face and checked himself. 'Maybe it's about time you had a break from men altogether. Be single for a while. Appreciate yourself a bit more, since these revolting lounge lizards you end up with clearly don't. What is it your stupid magazines say? "Take time out to learn to love yourself."' Nelson rolled his eyes to indicate that although he endorsed the idea, he hadn't retracted his usual opinion of self-help jargon.

'Well, you've certainly taken enough time out,' I said tartly, before I could stop myself.

I adored Nelson, but it galled me to take drip-feed relationship advice from a man who hadn't had a snog since our Millennium Eve party, especially when it was delivered in such a patronising manner.

'OK, well, you're obviously fine now,' he huffed, and set off walking again.

I hurried to catch him up and slipped my arm through his. 'Sorry.'

Nelson made an indeterminate noise and we walked along in silence for a while, but by the time we turned into our street, he was happily discussing curry ingredients.

Half my brain was discussing curry ingredients along with him, but the other half was busy soothing the jagged edges of my heart, and wondering whether Nelson actually might have been right about taking a break from love altogether.

I hated it when he was right, but the more annoyed his advice made me, the more right I knew he was.

4

I woke up the next morning at the usual office time. The momentary pleasure of realising I didn't have to get up was swiftly replaced by twin dull thuds: one in my chest reminding me that I'd been made redundant by Dean & Daniels as well as by Orlando, and the other in my stomach reminding me why I should never eat mango chutney with Nelson's curries.

The combination pinned me firmly to the bed.

Before I could roll over and go back to sleep, Nelson knocked very gently and put his head round the door. 'I'm going to work now, but I've made you a pot of coffee. Very strong.'

The smell of the coffee went quite a way to waking me up, and his thoughtfulness was also soothing. I was so lucky to have a flatmate like Nelson.

'Thank you,' I mumbled. 'You're a doll.'

'And can you have a think about the phone bill, please.'

I pulled the covers back over my head.

'I'm not doing this because I want to be mean' – Nelson's voice drifted sternly through the goose-down – 'I just want you to sort yourself out. While you're still used to getting up before ten.'

I had to concede he had a point.

I wasn't brought up to sit around feeling sorry for myself, no matter how bad things were. When Nelson was safely out of the house, I hauled myself out of bed, drank the coffee, showered, got dressed, applied some artful make-up and put on my best clothes. Feeling better already, I phoned the number on Mrs McKinnon's card, made an appointment and obtained directions, then hopped on a bus to Chelsea.

Of course I didn't tell Nelson or Gabi where I was going. I was going to drag myself out of the doldrums first.

Mrs McKinnon's address was in a very smart street indeed, with more blue plaques than estate agents' boards. Her office was only a third-floor flat, but the front door was as shiny as red nail varnish and there were over-flowing hanging baskets of pansies outside.

I rang the brass bell and was buzzed in. The hall smelled of furniture polish and fresh flowers and daily cleaning, and there wasn't a single piece of junk mail lying around. I took off my shoes to tackle the three flights of stairs better, and paused halfway up the last flight, so I could replace them and catch my breath before arriving in elegant calm. No point in looking unfit and at a disadvantage.

I was expecting a secretary, but there didn't seem to be one in sight. Instead, Mrs McKinnon herself was perched on the edge of the reception desk.

'Good morning, Melissa,' she said, extending a hand. 'How are you?'

Mrs McKinnon's firm but friendly handshake was the template for mine, so it was no surprise to find it rather comforting. She always insisted on the importance of hand cream in making a really good first impression; she kept a nailbrush on her desk and wasn't afraid to use it on us. I think, in her head, she was teaching at a different school entirely. Perhaps even in a different century entirely.

'Very well, thank you,' I said, wondering if she would feel entitled to point out any shortcomings in my manicure now that I was grown up.

'I'm delighted to hear that. Do come in,' she said in her beautiful Edinburgh accent.

I followed her into the office, remaining a few paces behind so I could get a better look at the pictures on the wall. To my surprise, they were rather racy prints from some Victorian magazine.

Mrs McKinnon had not changed at all in the ten years since I'd last seen her. Her tweed skirt was perfectly pressed, her laced-up high heels were perfectly polished and, from this vantage point, I could see that the seams of her stockings were still perfectly straight.

She was never what you would call pretty, but there was definitely something rather attractive about the general aura she gave out, like discreet French perfume or lavender furniture polish.

'So, Melissa,' she said, taking a seat behind her desk. It was empty, apart from a cherry-red iMac, a leather-bound notebook and an orchid. 'What can I do for you?'

I slipped onto the leather-studded chair and took a deep breath. 'Well, I'm rather between jobs right now, and Bobsy Parkin suggested I give you a ring,' I said. It suddenly occurred to me that I had no idea whatsoever what I was meant to say next. Our conversation on the phone had extended only to time and place. I didn't even know what sort of temping agency this was, or whether I should have brought my typing certificates.

'Bobsy!' said Mrs McKinnon, wearily. 'I do tell her . . .

Dear me, Melissa, no one calls her Bobsy any more. She much prefers Eleanor these days.'

'I didn't even know that was her name,' I admitted.

'I wish you girls would embrace the grown-up world.' Mrs McKinnon looked pained and tapped her fountain pen against her notebook. 'After all I taught you about making a good impression.'

'Oh, but you did!' I exclaimed hurriedly. 'I carry hand cream, a whistle and a spare pair of tights in my bag at all times!'

She smiled, opened her book at a fresh page and leaned back a little in her chair. 'So, did Eleanor fill you in about my agency and its clients?'

I nodded, eager to please, out of habit. I didn't want Mrs McKinnon to think that Bobsy and I hadn't had a long and exciting chat about how great her job was. Even though we hadn't, exactly.

Mrs McKinnon examined me closely over the top of her glasses and I adjusted my nod to a vague shake of the head.

'She didn't really go into *details*,' I conceded. 'Just that she was having a fabulous time and getting a lot out of her work.'

'Did she now? Well, Eleanor rarely has ten minutes to herself these days. She is a very busy girl.'

I couldn't imagine Bobsy being busy. Unless she walked dogs as well as middle-aged men. I didn't say that, though. And I hoped it wasn't showing on my face.

'So what have you been doing with yourself since you graduated from art school?' asked Mrs McKinnon, changing tack.

'Um, I've been managing various offices for the last few years,' I said. I hated this pushy bit of interviews, even when it was disguised, as now, with friendly chit-chat. We never really did much interview practice at school, and boasting was, by and large, frowned upon.

I could practically hear Nelson yelling at me to stop being so self-deprecating, so I jutted my chin and pretended I was talking about someone else, instead of myself. 'I'm rather good at it, actually. I've been on three IT courses and I've got excellent typing speeds. In fact,' I added, seeing a chance to be ingratiating and truthful at the same time, 'a lot of my job involves the sort of things we used to talk about in Home Ec – you know, getting organised, being pleasant and stimulating company, putting people at their ease. Event-catering. That sort of thing.'

I paused and scrutinised her face for a reaction.

Mrs McKinnon rewarded me with a Sphinx-like smile. 'That's very interesting, Melissa,' she said smoothly. 'Well done. Now, I expect you're wondering what sort of agency I'm running here. So let me outline the nature of my work. As you know, I spent the best part of fifteen years teaching the girls at St Cathal's how to be charming and decorative young women, so you could go out and make hapless men good wives. I like to think that most of my pupils were actually *too* good for most men.' She adjusted the pearls around her neck. 'But a few years ago I had what you might call a damascene revelation and decided someone of my particular abilities was wasted in the field of education.'

A bell rang in my mind. Wasn't there a rumour that Mrs McKinnon was *sacked*? Must ask Bobsy, I thought.

I mean, Eleanor.

'So, to cut a long story short, I decided to eliminate the middle man.' She tapped her pen again. 'There is a distinct shortage in London of charm and intelligence. Most young women today are power-crazed and utterly superficial.'

I adored the way she could roll her rs like a V8 engine. It sounded so marrrrvellously disparrrrrraging.

'And yet, as I taught you at St Cathal's, old-fashioned as it may be, there remains nothing more attractive than a young woman able to converse fluently on a wide range of topics while maintaining an aura of elegance and feminine allure. Is there, Melissa?'

I nodded enthusiastically, but was thinking: surely that ruled Bobsy out? Attempting to pursue an intelligent conversation with Bobsy was always a bit like playing two-man Tag in Wembley stadium.

Mrs McKinnon was on an emotional roll, however, and working to a crescendo. 'It occurred to me, one parents' evening, that there was a burgeoning market out there, of men—' She leaned towards me, confidentially, and added, 'Especially, shall we say, older, *professional* men like your father, who are in great need of a little temporary charm in their lives, to alleviate the stress brought about by the pressure of business and high finance.'

Like my father? I was temporarily thrown. What could she mean?

And did I want to know?

'Men who, for one reason or another, are marooned in London without recourse to the restful company of their own wives, men who might appreciate a little discreet companionship and stimulating conversation, to ease the knots and troubles of the day. Provided by young ladies who are, I feel, utterly unappreciated by their own generation. Everyone benefits. I think of bringing the two groups together as not unlike a form of social work.' She paused for me to agree.

'Quite,' I said, but I must admit that my mind was now somewhat distracted – wandering all over the place, in fact. What on earth could Daddy have to do with this?

'I imagine you're a delightful dinner companion, Melissa,' she said.

'Well, yes, I am, actually,' I admitted. Because, without being vain, I was. You learn to keep chatting when your companion erroneously expects you to be supplying the dessert course. To *be* the dessert course, if you know what I mean. And I include Orlando in that.

'I realise that it's not exactly the temping you've been used to, but, if I can be utterly frank with you for a moment . . .' And Mrs McKinnon tipped her head in that heart-stoppingly intimate way she used to at school.

I must confess that I was *hugely* flattered at being taken into her confidence like this. All thoughts of Daddy flew out of my head.

'Melissa, my dear, you have a rare combination of beauty, common sense and charm that would keep you as busy as you liked. Even more so than darling Eleanor. I could guarantee you a few evenings' work that would leave you the rest of the week free for whatever other activities you wanted to do. And my clients enjoy frequenting the smartest restaurants. Claridges, Gordon Ramsay, the Savoy . . . It really is the most pleasant way of spending a few nights a week. You can be all done and ready to go home by eleven, unless . . .'

She paused and raised her eyebrow in a meaningful way.

'Unless what?' I asked boldly.

'Unless you and the client are having such an enjoyable

evening that you decide to extend the appointment. That, of course, is entirely at your discretion.'

Mrs McKinnon was looking at me as if she didn't expect to have to elaborate.

I must have looked a little shocked, because her expression softened and she quickly added, 'But of course, I only said this to cover all eventualities, Melissa. It remains absolutely in your hands, and if you wish, the possibility need never even be considered.' She flicked her hand in a dismissive gesture. 'Most of my clientele are in search purely of charming company and vivid conversation and I know you'll be more than capable of satisfying every requirement on that score.'

'I see,' I said.

Had I understood that right? Mrs McKinnon was running some kind of upmarket escort agency? Had the world gone completely mad?

A tiny frisson of excitement trembled through me and I suppressed it at once. It was, as she said, entirely at my discretion. Which meant not at all.

'I must stress, Melissa,' she said lightly, 'that there's nothing at all untoward going on.' She tilted her head persuasively. 'Let's just say it's a matter of matching up enchanting young ladies like you, with men who truly appreciate all you have to offer, and are willing to reward it accordingly. Exactly *what* you offer is your decision entirely.'

I nodded, slowly. I wasn't what you'd call a femme fatale. Despite all those flattering compliments she was scattering before me, even Mrs McKinnon must see that. Since I didn't offer a full menu to my boyfriends, there was no way on earth that any of her clients would be getting more than a bar snack.

Still, the voice of reason in my head was pointing out that at least I'd be in charge of what was on offer. Which was more than I'd felt on some dates.

'I see,' I said again, more confidently. 'It sounds very interesting.'

'I know. Isn't it just?' she said, and reached into her top desk drawer for a sheaf of papers. 'Let me give you this to read through. No, no,' she said, as I started to skim it, 'have a proper look at home and ring me if you have any queries. May I take your mobile phone number?'

I dutifully repeated my phone number and gave her my email address too, for good measure.

'Excellent.' Mrs McKinnon rose from her chair and extended her hand again. I could smell her perfume: Arpège. Just enough to float around her, not so much that it entered the room before she did. Spray here, here, and here, then walk into the cloud of fragrance.

Why couldn't I remember my Latin as well as that?

'Thank you so much for your time,' I said, politely.

'Thank *you*, Melissa,' she said, shaking my hand with just the right measure of enthusiasm. 'I do believe that this is the beginning of great things.'

To celebrate I bought myself a bunch of red tulips on the way home. There's nothing like flowers to cheer you up and with tulips you really don't have to spend a lot to make a nice display. I also relished the mental picture I presented of a smart young woman strolling through town with a bright bunch of flowers. Did she buy them herself? Were they a gift from a lover? Or did a flower salesman press them into her hands as she walked past the stall?

All this forward motion had given me quite an appetite

and I fell upon the fridge like a woman possessed, only to find the shelves emptier than Tesco's on Christmas Eve. Nelson was ruthless like that: he only bought organic and chucked everything out the second it passed its sell-by date. He had left a note on the fridge door, reminding me that it was my turn to cook, and the realisation that soon I'd be able to go to Waitrose with a light heart and open purse filled me with indescribable joy.

Ignoring my stomach's cries for a Hobnob, I settled down with one of Nelson's peppermint teas and put my glasses on to read through Mrs McKinnon's contract, Post-it notes and pencils at the ready in case of queries.

It was written in such vague terms that after ten minutes' close study, all I could establish was that the agency was called the Charming Company and that it wasn't based in the same place as Mrs McKinnon's office. Still, I'd read through enough estate agents' contracts not to be surprised by minor discrepancies like that.

What was more surprising was the list of particulars, starting off with a whole page just about dress. She obviously wasn't employing only Old Cathalians – as if she had to tell girls like me to wear smart suits, matching underwear, no gold jewellery and to have my hair done nicely! I didn't dress any other way.

Mrs McKinnon also suggested adopting a different name for professional use, '*so that charm and fun can remain uppermost in your mind at all times*'. I must admit this appealed to me, since I suddenly felt as if I could do with a spell off from being Melissa Romney-Jones.

'*Leave your mundane worries about council tax or dental appointments at home,*' she wrote, '*and remember to take a fresh and appealing new personality out to be dined!*'

The magical Cinderella effect was only a little spoiled

when she stated baldly, '*For reasons of legal and personal discretion, real names will not be used under any circumstances. Any employee found to be contravening this rule will be summarily discharged from the Charming Company.*'

Mrs McKinnon covered appropriate conversation, topics to avoid, names not to drop, and so on at mind-boggling length. There was even a sub-list of where the loos were in all the smart restaurants.

I was curious to know how much all this charm cost, and when I flicked through to the clauses about fees and commission and so on, my eyes popped. No wonder Bobsy's date could afford to throw champagne around. No wonder Bobsy herself was looking like she'd been overhauled by Gwyneth Paltrow's stylists. God, I thought, I really wouldn't have to do this for very long to get Daddy's loan paid back.

I leaned back in my chair and thought about exactly what it would mean to get that debt – and Daddy – off my back. It would be *wonderful*. No more snide comments that only he and I understood; no more tugging my strings to make me feel about two feet tall. But the biggest, most satisfying irony of all would be that in order to pay back that money, I'd be getting *paid* for using exactly those 'pointless finishing-school skills' he took for granted in my mother, and said were only good for finding husbands for my sisters. Me – unmarriageable Melissa.

That made me smile.

Yes, I thought, with a delicious bubble of excitement starting to rise in my stomach. Yes, I *could* do this.

Plus, I reasoned, warming to the idea, there were literally heaps of beautiful cocktail dresses in my wardrobe that never saw the light of day; dresses I'd made myself to fit in all the right places, and then had to wear to all

the wrong places. Though I'd never mark myself down
as a beauty, Gabi insisted that I scrubbed up all right,
and although I wasn't the sort of girl to chat up complete
strangers in a bar, I could certainly deal well with clients
when I was in my PA role at work.

The bubble sank a little at the thought of being eyed
up all night by a complete stranger, but I reminded myself
that this would be a role too, a job. Nothing I hadn't done
before, in different circumstances. And, I don't know,
maybe I could *help* them in some way. Eating out alone
is never much fun, even at the nicest restaurants.

I focused on the gratifying moment of triumph when
I could hand over that cheque to Daddy, and pushed any
doubts aside. Sometimes one just had to get on and *do*
things.

The final page was taken up with Mrs McKinnon's
Mission Statement. It made for stirring reading. Some of
it felt familiar – as though it might have been lifted from
a school song.

When I got to the lines about 'A smile is free and so
is charm / A kindly ear is heartache's balm' I realised it
was in fact *our* school song.

I was sitting there daydreaming about my new bill-
free, high-gloss personality, and what I'd order from the
Claridges sweet trolley, when the front door banged and
Nelson's briefcase hit the floor by the door.

'Hi, honey, I'm home!' he yelled from the hall. Just a
joke, honestly. Apart from the 'his and hers' bathrobes,
we weren't really like an old sitcom couple.

'Hi, honey!' I yelled back while he hung up his coat.
'Good day at work?'

'No, rubbish. Dinner in the dog, is it?'

Oops. I hadn't even thought about supper.

I looked down at the contract on the table in front of me and decided that Nelson didn't need to know about it just yet. But, I mused privately, Honey was a very good name, as courtesan stage names went. Flirty and feminine, like a James Bond girl. Plus, I was used to Nelson calling me honey now and again, so I wouldn't stare off into the distance wondering who Jennifer or Antonia was.

Hastily, I shoved the contract under the newspaper and distracted him with a couple of leading questions about his day at work, while I worked out what nutritious meal for two I could concoct from dry pasta, mustard and a tin of condensed milk.

5

I didn't have much time to dwell on my meeting with Mrs McKinnon because the next day I had to go home to measure up Emery for her wedding dress.

I phoned beforehand to let everyone know I was coming, but when I arrived, bearing flowers and chocolates for all, Daddy had gone off to Norway with some of his hunting buddies for some kind of extreme fishing weekend, and Mummy had installed herself in a rigorous Yorkshire health club.

'I'm joining her as soon as you're done,' Emery informed me, scoffing a truffle as I tried to get the tape measure around her tiny waist. 'Poor thing's worn to a frazzle – this month she's had to organise three cocktail parties, file Daddy's tax return with the accountant, hold a dinner for the council, *and* give a speech to the local WI about being in a photo-shoot for *Country Life*.'

I pursed my lips crossly. If my father had had to pay a professional to supply my mother's various services, he wouldn't have been able to afford her. Then again, at the back of my mind, I had a troubling feeling that he might once have been involved in some minor pay-roll scandal along exactly those lines.

'And you're going because . . . ?' I asked, pushing the thought away.

'Oh, I need to de-stress before I really start on the wedding plans.'

I failed to see how Emery could possibly need de-stressing. Emery was so vague that she once couldn't accurately describe her own toothache to the dentist and so had two completely healthy molars removed. If anyone needed de-stressing it was me, and any other mug she was employing to arrange her nuptials.

'I thought you were going to get a planner?' I asked suspiciously.

Emery sighed. 'I want to get one, but Daddy's being impossible, as usual. Apparently three hundred people isn't enough, but a wedding planner is a mad extravagance. Everyone else has one. Still,' she added, with a little more steel in her voice, 'I'm working on it . . .'

'Mmm. So no messages, then?' I asked hopefully. I was never going to get much in the way of moral guidance and/or support from either of my parents, but it would have been nice of them to *be* here to see me.

Emery paused and thought hard, her finger pressed on her lips to aid the process. 'Oh, yes, Daddy said to tell you he hasn't forgotten about Perry and the cash,' she said, while I was measuring her back. 'Whatever that means. He claims he's on an economy drive before my wedding. Don't know what he means by that either, but he did one of his ghastly just-out-of-the-coffin type laughs when he said it. Do you think I should go for something sort of more oysterish? You know, with puffy-ish . . . things?'

'Stop waving your arms about, please,' I said, and was glad that she couldn't see my face, which had tightened anew at the mention of Daddy's loan.

The three best things about Emery were that she was

so airy-fairy it wasn't easy to fall into an argument with
her, unlike the rest of the family; she had amazingly
straight nutmeg-coloured hair, exactly like old paintings
of the Virgin Mary; and she was quite kind, or at least
too self-involved to be intentionally rude.

This didn't mean she couldn't deliver some real
humdingers, though.

'Are you going to be bringing a plus one to the
wedding?' she asked. 'Only I need to know for my list.'

'Why?' I replied tetchily. 'It's ages off yet.'

'Not really. Shall I put you down for a plus one, then
if Orlando's dumped you again, you can always bring
Nelson instead?'

'If it makes it *easier* for you,' I seethed. 'Anyway, you
needn't concern yourself with Orlando. Orlando and I
are . . . not seeing each other any more.'

Emery sighed the wise sigh of the recently engaged.
'Oh, Mel, you need to hurry up and find a man,' she
said, shaking her curtains of hair reprovingly. 'Or there'll
only be divorced ones left.'

I ignored the fact that her own Prince Charming had
two ex-wives to date and wasn't yet forty. But I hadn't met
William, so didn't feel it was fair to comment. The only
facts I knew about him were that he was a partner in an
American law firm in the City, he was a fiercely compet-
itive sports enthusiast, he spent a good deal of time travelling, and that none of these gave him much time to spend
with Emery, a situation which suited both rather well.

From the pictures I'd seen he was reasonably good-
looking, in a glinty-eyed, jutty-jawed kind of way, and
Emery seemed pretty keen on him, but that wouldn't
have been enough for me. There had to be *some* romance
there.

'If the choice is between spinsterdom or life imprisonment with a man like Daddy, I know which I'd rather choose,' I said, measuring her neck rather more savagely than I intended.

Emery choked slightly. 'But Melissa . . .'

'I mean, who are you holding up as an example of marital bliss? Mummy, the unpaid housekeeper? Allegra, the largely ignored trophy wifelet?'

Allegra had been married to Lars, an Anglo-Swedish art dealer, who collected prehistoric arrowheads, for three years now. I didn't know if art was all he dealt in, because he was very rich and operatically moody. Though that could just have been the Swede in him. Allegra spent much of her life floating around galleries and private views like Elvira Munster, and was as much admired (and twice as flinty) as Lars's arrowheads.

'Allegra is very happy with Lars,' insisted Emery.

'Only because he can't spend more than forty days a year in England for tax reasons and she divides her time between a small mansion in Ham and a small palace outside Stockholm.'

'That might be it,' she agreed vaguely. 'Still . . .'

'Still . . .' was Emery's favoured conversational gambit. It conveyed agreement, mild disagreement and 'let's change the subject' all in one syllable.

I don't know why people make such a big deal about home comforts. My family home is one of the least comforting places I can think of.

Back in London, barely two days passed before I got a call from Mrs McKinnon. It came just after another ridiculous phone conversation with Emery about whether three hundred people could be sufficiently impressed with the release of one hundred doves on completion of her self-penned wedding vows. I regret to say that I had spoken my mind.

'Hello?' I said, all ready for Emery's apology for putting down the phone while I was still explaining why chucking partially suffocated birds over the congregation might be less than festive.

'Hello, Melissa,' said Mrs McKinnon. 'How are you fixed for tonight?'

I was tempted to remind her – jokily – of her instruction that a lady is never available at such short notice, but didn't think it would be a good start to our professional relationship.

'My diary is quite clear actually,' I said, quite truthfully. There was only Nelson's pub quiz on offer and I always felt such an idiot while he and his brainy mates were gaily scattering facts around like confetti.

'Excellent,' she said. 'If you hie yourself along to the Savoy at half past six, you'll meet the most charming man called Lord Armstrong-Siddeley who will be wearing a red silk hanky in his top pocket. He's interested in point-to-points, vintage cars and clay-pigeon shooting, and he'd love to take you out for dinner.'

'Is that his real name?' I asked. 'Good gracious – did his family design the motor car?'

'My dear, didn't you read the contract? We don't do real names,' she said, and there was a sliver of ice in her tone. 'And no.'

I blushed. Clearly I had a lot to practise.

'Wonderful!' I tried not to sound crushed. 'Clay-pigeon shooting, eh? That sounds wonderful!'

'Call me at eleven, just so I know how it's going and that you're . . . safe,' she said with more of that meaningful tone.

She needn't have worried on that score: I'd already decided that this date would be finishing dead on eleven.

I spent the rest of the morning calming the butterflies in my stomach by finishing off Gabi's T-shirt – she wanted something 'ladylike', so I was stitching seed pearls around the neckline to give the effect of piles and piles of tiny pearl necklaces. This was the third I'd made for her – if I didn't know better I'd swear she was selling them on somewhere. My mind welcomed the repetition of embroidering the beads because it was racing with all sorts of questions.

First of all, what if Lord Armstrong-Siddeley was someone Daddy knew? What if he recognised me from somewhere? Of course, it was perfectly innocent, just a little dinner and chit-chat, but I'd hate to . . . well, I'd hate anyone to get the wrong idea – like I'd done with Bobsy and her Dinner Date. But then hadn't I assumed they were father and daughter? And what could be more wholesome than that?

I'd been going over and over the whole situation, and although there was a part of me that shied away from the . . . well, *post-date* aspect of it, there was another part of me that thought the idea of being a modern-day geisha girl was eminently sensible. Mrs McKinnon wouldn't be involved in anything seedy; she was always far too protective of 'her girls' to have put me in any sort of danger.

It was, I reasoned to myself, just like temping, wasn't it – but on a social basis? Not everyone had the time or the inclination to deal with all the emotional stress that went with a relationship. I certainly didn't want another relationship, for instance, but that didn't mean I didn't want to go out and be entertained over a nice meal.

I snipped off a trailing thread with a certain satisfaction.

That's what I intended to tell Nelson. Eventually. I was going to give it a week or two to see if it worked out first, though. No sense in rocking the domestic boat for no good reason.

It wouldn't be me they were having dinner with, anyway, I told myself: they'd be dining with Honey. The more I thought about it, the more I liked the idea of inventing Honey; it relieved me from any personal responsibility and would probably mean I'd have more fun too. I just had to remind myself continually that Honey arrived when my dinner date walked into the restaurant and left immediately after coffee.

While I stitched on Gabi's faux pearl necklaces, I ran through Honey's background and personality, working out where she was meant to have gone to school and whether she had any brothers or sisters and how much sundry personal information we could safely share. I frowned. It could end up quite complicated. And then I had the most brilliant brainwave. If nothing else, it would remind me whether I was being Honey or Melissa.

The minute I finished the final strand, I got a bus into town and went to a tiny shop in Soho Granny once took me to when she was going through her Rita Hayworth redhead phase but didn't want to ruin her lovely hair with henna.

A wig: the quickest, simplest way to be two people at once! And I'd always wanted to be blonde; Nelson frequently said I had a blonde personality in a brunette's body. Whatever that meant.

There were loads of wigs to choose from, and I tried on nearly all of them – curly red hair, angelic Titian waves, scary jet-black Cleopatra bob – but as soon as I saw my own eyes looking back at me through a heavy fringe of real caramel-blonde hair, I knew I'd found the right one. It was me, but at the same time, it very much was not.

To be honest, I looked so amazing that for a moment or two I could barely breathe: I looked like a gorgeous, film-star version of myself. My skin glowed, my lips seemed poutier and there was a new flirty twinkle in my eye. The shimmering strands around my face transformed my outfit; my plain camel V-neck and jeans suddenly looked kittenish instead of smart casual. The mere thought of what I'd look like with the stockings and suspenders I'd planned to wear as ultra-feminine Honey made me blush to my naturally stitched, real-hair roots.

I stood there for nearly ten minutes, just marvelling at this sex bomb in the mirror, turning this way and that, putting the hair up, then down again. The sales assistant looked on and smiled patiently. I supposed she had to go through this rigmarole every day. It was almost a relief to take the wig off and see sensible Melissa there again.

It cost me every single penny left in my Emergencies Only account, but you get what you pay for, don't you? Miracles aren't cheap.

Lord Armstrong-Siddeley could have been one of two or three men sitting in the American bar at the Savoy. They were all wearing red hankies in their top pockets, and, to my mind, looked as if they were waiting for someone.

I tried making eye contact with the first man, but he sank behind his newspaper, and the second one winked at me in quite a game manner, but appeared to be with his wife, so it couldn't be him. There's only so long a girl can stand at the entrance to a lounge, so I went up to the bar and ordered a gin fizz. I don't normally drink much, but it was what Daddy ordered for us when we

were all out: a Scotch for him and gin fizzes for the little
ladies.

Naturally, he's never bothered to remember that I
loathe gin fizzes. I always order it if I need to have a
drink in front of me, but don't actually want to drink
anything.

'Honey?' said a low voice, somewhere around my ear.

I ignored it for a moment, until I realised that the voice
was talking to me. I swivelled around on my bar stool,
clamping my knees together so my skirt didn't ride up.

Suddenly I understood why sultry starlets always
looked so moodily preoccupied in their pictures; they
weren't dwelling on some good-for-nothin' man, they
were concerned about whether their good-for-nothin'
stockings were still in place and not on show.

'Oh, yes, hello!' I said.

Lord Armstrong-Siddeley, as I clearly couldn't call him
aloud, looked exactly like my granny's old Basset hound
and I took to him immediately. His eyes were rather blood-
shot and his country suit drooped, but in an expensive
manner.

He seemed about as nervous as I was, so I extended
a hand, and he shook it gratefully with a good honest
grip. A signet ring crushed into my fingers but I gave
him a reassuring smile.

'How are *you*?' I asked, since he appeared rather lost
for words. It was an odd situation all round, but nothing
that couldn't be soothed with a few thoughtful questions.
'Have you had a *very* tiring day?'

'Oh, um, yes.' He was staring at my legs.

'Are we going to have a drink first, or is the table
booked for seven?' I enquired, to distract him from my
discreet skirt rearrangements. It was riding up again.

'Seven thirty. Table for two. In the Grill.' He tugged at his collar, unable to meet my eyes.

I slid off the stool to prevent further distraction. I wasn't used to being ogled. 'It is quite hot in here, isn't it? Would you like something to drink to cool you down?'

That did the trick. Lord A-S turned to the barman and ordered a double Scotch, and I stuck with my gin fizz so I wouldn't be tempted to drink anything and get giddy.

Over several Scotches and gin fizzes (which I disposed of discreetly in the potted palms while he was blowing his red nose) we discussed his collection of pre-war farm vehicles. Well, I say 'discussed'; if there's one thing Mrs McKinnon drilled into us, it's that chatty girls are popular, but not as popular as good listeners. I knew that from the outside I appeared enthralled – regularly shifting expression, gentle nods of encouragement, faint hums of surprise – but internally I was wondering whether to have lamb or steak and also how exactly I could mention to Lord A-S that one can have nostril hair removed quite painlessly these days.

'So do you have a car of your own, my dear?' he asked eventually, catching me out by ending a sentence without starting a new one in the same breath.

'Oh, er, yes,' I said. 'I have a Subaru Forester.'

'Good God!' he exclaimed, choking on an ice cube. 'That's not a young lady's car, is it, my dear?'

'Isn't it?' I replied, surprised. Most of my friends had Golfs, which are OK, but I had had to buy my own car, and not request it as a birthday present. 'I bought it from my father's gamekeeper up in Scotland.' Which was semi-true – there was some mention of gambling debts, but on whose side I never worked out.

'I say, car like that – I bet you must be quite a handful, Honey. Well, I can see that already!' He smiled at me in a whisky-enhanced fashion and I am afraid to say a hint of a leer had entered those bloodshot eyes. 'Quite a lively young thing, are you? Quite . . . sporty?'

I remembered too late that Honey should probably drive a cute little Mini or a Ford Fiesta or somesuch. Damn.

'Sporty? Oh no,' I replied firmly, determined to get back onto safe fictional ground. 'I was quite the worst netball player *Surrey* ever saw. But I wasn't bad at hockey,' I conceded, seeing his obvious disappointment.

The effect was immediate. 'I bet you were. You have wonderful legs,' he dribbled. 'I can quite imagine you playing hockey, streaming down the wing in your gym skirt, fresh air in your lungs, chest heaving under your hockey shirt . . .'

Men have such romanticised ideas about school games – quite why, I will never know – so I tried to put him straight. 'Oh, yes. Shin pads chafing against sweaty shins, mud caking on one's frozen thighs, bruises forming all over one's weary body . . .'

Lord A-S leaned forward in high excitement. 'Do you have any of your games kit?'

'Good heavens!' I laughed. 'It's far too small for me now!'

'Nnngh,' he spluttered in response. 'How small?'

I was saved from having to find an answer to this bewildering question by the arrival of the waiter, who led us to our table.

I let Lord A-S order for me, as I'd always found that although men profess to prefer women who enjoy their food, the sight of them actually demanding three courses plus wine and cheese doesn't come over so well. Besides which, Lord A-S was clearly a man from my father's rigid mould, and I guessed (correctly) that any attempts to order my own food would be pretty futile.

Not that this bothered me, since he was paying, and we both happily ploughed into prawn cocktails, followed by steaks, washed down with claret for him and a Babycham for me.

By that point, I was warming to Lord A-S, despite his persistent interest in my games record at school and also my experience with horses.

'Those are horse-riding thighs, am I right?' he demanded unexpectedly, halfway through his crème brûlée.

I looked down to check my stockings weren't visible, then remembered that Mrs McKinnon had probably told him that Honey shared his interest in point-to-point. 'Oh, yes, indeed. I love a good ride!' I said cheerfully.

His eyes lit up – again, I seemed to have said exactly the wrong thing. 'Got a stallion at home, have you? Eh? A young stud?'

'No,' I lied, creatively. 'A pony, called, um, Babycham.'

'Oh, I can just picture you in jodhpurs, my dear,' he groaned. 'Streaked with mud after a hard day's chase, chest heaving under your riding jacket . . .'

My *chest* – again. I gave him a dark look. Was there a single leisure activity that wouldn't involve my chest heaving?

Still, I conceded, if he wanted to drool all the way back to his estate thinking about me flattening some poor horse, let him. He was clearly having a pretty good time and I'd barely had to break sweat conversationally. It made a pleasant change to discover that well-brought-up girls with wholesome hobbies were a big turn-on for some people.

In fact, I thought, savouring a mouthful of crème brûlée, if I *started* flirting the poor man would probably explode.

Just to see what would happen, I smiled across the table in a sultry fashion and was gratified to see Lord A-S whip out his red spotted handkerchief to mop up the beads of sweat on his brow.

Mind you, there was a limit to how much drooling a lady should encourage in the course of one meal.

'It *is* awfully warm in here,' I said briskly. 'Are you feeling well at the moment?' It's my fail-safe topic changer with men; there's nothing they like better than an exploration of possible symptoms, and no topic of conversation they won't abandon to do so to a sympathetic ear.

'Why?' he asked, looking alarmed. 'Is it the old trouble flaring up again?'

I didn't know what the old trouble was, but I nodded supportively. 'Are you under stress at the moment? You really ought to be taking care of yourself, you know.'

Lord A-S swigged the last of his wine disconsolately. 'You've hit the nail on the head, my dear. You really can read me like a book, can't you?'

Yes. It was a very simple leather-bound book with a lot of pictures and not many words.

'Why don't you tell me all about it?' I soothed, relieved to be out of the treacherous waters of innuendo. I didn't always get innuendo, by which time it was often too late and I found myself struggling in the whirlpool of proposition. 'And have a glass of water, for heaven's sake.'

Well, out it all came: the worries about the fishing rights, the funny twinges he was getting in his ear, the ghastly rash on his leg, the Ukrainian domestic who'd unwittingly destroyed his secret collection of Edwardian pornography, the son who was only hanging on at Ampleforth by a hair, the astrology-fixated daughter who was determined to go to New York to become a night-club singer despite never having left Bourton-on-the-Water. Worst of all, he confided, the mentally unstable wife who was bedridden and unable to accompany him on his sorties into town.

No wonder the poor man needed some restful and amusing company over dinner.

I had it all sorted out by the time we'd got on to our second round of crèmes brûlées.

'. . . so tell Rory that if he passes his GCSEs you'll give him four thousand pounds to spend on a car of his choice,' I finished up triumphantly.

'Four thousand pounds!' Lord A–S – or Lester, as he was now insisting I call him – looked utterly horrified.

I regarded him in what I hoped was a wise yet quizzical fashion over the top of my coffee cup. 'How much do you imagine a decent crammer costs these days, Lester? Hmm? Let me tell you, my sister Emery . . . I mean, Pomona, had to retake her A-levels four times at four different crammers and Daddy said he could have bought her a brain transplant more cheaply. I sometimes think he should have done,' I added.

The clouds lifted from his face. 'Well, yes, I see what you're getting at there. Jolly splendid idea! Bribery, what?' Lester looked like a very pleased, very overripe tomato. 'Good God, I wish I'd done this years ago! I had no idea girls like you could be so damned sensible!'

I elected to ignore the 'girls like you' bit. I didn't assume all blondes are dumb, even if Gabi did. And I was hoping my blonde mane was more St Tropez than the King's Road.

'Now then, Honey, what say we retire somewhere for a nightcap?' he suggested in a treacly voice. A hand snaked under the table and patted my knee.

I froze.

The hand stopped patting and twanged my suspender belt.

'Lester, please!' I said, firmly. 'That is most certainly not on the menu!'

'Oh, Honey!' he spluttered. 'There are so many other areas of my life that I need help with! Practical help!'

I smiled as politely and as maternally as I could. 'Then I suggest you contact a doctor, Lester. I'm hopelessly unqualified to advise you, and I'd feel terrible about putting you at risk from my inexperience.'

'I don't see you as an inexperienced girl, Honey!' he slavered, staring at me with a mixture of frustration and awe.

I could see that my protestations were cutting no ice. In fact, my nannyish tone seemed to be heating things up. Desperate measures were called for.

I swallowed and thought quickly. 'Do tell me, when's your birthday, Lester?' I asked.

'December. Twenty-eighth of December,' he replied, confused.

I pursed my lips and shook my head sadly. 'Oh dear, you're a Capricorn.' My eyes drifted into a distant, hippyish expression. 'The goat. I should have guessed from your clothes. I bet you're a martyr to your knees and lower limbs, aren't you? Varicose veins? Am I right?'

Lester's expression shifted noticeably. 'Well, yes. That's the kind of nonsense my Catriona's always coming out with.'

'Is it?' I said innocently. 'She sounds a very sensitive child to me. Rather innocent, and that's such a *precious* thing in a young woman, don't you agree?'

The hot hand retreated from my leg and he looked troubled. I could tell he was being uncomfortably reminded of his daughter. Good.

As soon as my leg was my own once more, I grabbed my bag from under the table, chattering away smoothly all the while. 'I'm a Cancerian, you know. Home-loving. Which reminds me, I really must rush back, before I turn into a pumpkin! Can you believe what time it is? Nearly eleven! How time flies when you're enjoying yourself.'

'But . . .'

I leaned over the table, taking care not to let my wig slip, so I could bestow a very daughterly kiss on his damp cheek. 'Lester, I've had a splendid evening. Thank you so much. Have a safe journey home, won't you?'

'I will,' he said faintly, and it was all I could do not to pat his head.

I slipped out of the Savoy, collecting my jacket from the cloakroom on the way, and leaving a generous tip for the attendant with a flourish and a smile.

It was a mild night, and as I walked down the Strand I could see the strings of lights glittering in the river along the Embankment. My heart felt quite floaty, although that may have been the cognac that Lester had pressed upon me over pudding – Gabi would have killed me if she knew he'd ordered the whole bottle to the table and I'd restricted myself to only one glass.

I examined the floatiness while I crossed my fingers and wished for a taxi. There was a little relief in there – OK, so Lester was a little saucy, but I'd dealt with worse – mixed with pride in a job well done. I had flirted, I had flattered and I had sorted out his immediate problems with tact and ingenuity. And he had certainly appreciated my company.

More to the point, I had done nothing that I would be ashamed to tell Nelson.

Not that I was going to tell Nelson just yet, though.

I shifted from foot to foot, scanning the crawling traffic for an orange taxi light, and it dawned on me that maybe some of the floatiness was down to the stockings. The sensation of taut silk straps rubbing on my thighs and the faint swish of friction every time I crossed my legs did make me feel more Honey than Melissa. To be honest, Honey was far more flirtatious than Melissa would ever have been. But then Honey didn't have to care about what her date thought of her, whether he'd heard of her father, or whether he'd want to call her again. In fact, Honey could *enjoy* wearing stockings because she knew the date was entirely under her control.

All Honey had to be was entertaining, and I had no problem whatsoever with that.

The ogling, though, would take some getting used to.

A black cab appeared out of nowhere, and I got into it with a light heart, knowing I could claim the fare back afterwards and not have to justify it to myself later.

I got in thankfully and closed my eyes as I sank into the seat. A wave of delayed relief washed over me. Now it was all over, I felt absolutely shattered.

6

Friday dawned bright and early and for the first time in ages, I woke up with a smile on my face.

Hughy had phoned me several days previously in a complete state about the drinks party Dean & Daniels were throwing to celebrate the opening of the new offices and the arrival of the new American agents. Carolyn was meant to be in charge, but her sudden absence from the office with 'food poisoning' (pre-American-arrival chin job, according to Gabi) revealed that she'd only got half the arrangements made. Well, not even half: she'd ordered some glasses and written the memo reminding everyone to be on their best behaviour.

For a very generous cash payment, but mainly as a favour to Hughy, I got on the phone and, in under three hours, had whipped up the necessary drinks, canapés, flowers, waiting staff and so on. There were some odd guidelines emailed over from the New York office, but it was far too late to chase up some of the requests. Some of Carolyn's ideas – a Frank Sinatra karaoke machine, for instance – I decided to ignore altogether.

It was a little galling creating a fabulous party for the very people who'd sacked me, but it was great to have some hard cash in my hand at last. Hard cash that I intended using to treat Nelson to a slap-up breakfast.

Without even noticing what time it was, I got up,

dressed, made the necessary adjustments to my face for leaving the house, and swung down to the corner shop for fresh milk and croissants. As a special treat, I bought a copy of *OK!* to read over breakfast. I was thinking of developing Honey's personality along the lines of society characters culled from its pages.

Nelson was up by the time I got back, standing by the counter in his boxer shorts and tartan dressing gown, staring blankly at the boiling kettle and mouthing to himself. He was a handsome man, but could look surprisingly tramp-like first thing.

'Morning!' I carolled gaily. 'Coffee and croissants for two!'

He spun round when he heard me, as if in surprise that someone else might live in his house. 'Oh, are you up already?'

'Indeed I am,' I replied, popping the fresh and warm croissants in a bowl. 'Why don't you just sit down and relax like the man of the house while I make you some breakfast?'

Nelson narrowed his sleepy eyes. 'Very wifely. I thought you didn't want to be someone's domestic servant.'

'This is friendship. I am paying you back for your many morning favours.'

Nelson muttered something I didn't catch and swiped my *OK!* to read.

'Didn't you get a proper paper?' he complained. 'I know more than enough about Jordan's breasts already.'

'Don't be a snob. Just think of all the lovely conversations you can start around the water cooler this morning,' I said, looking for the cafetière. 'Girls can only admire so much chit-chat about charity tax relief. Go on, read bits out to me while I make the coffee.'

There was a pause, and the flicking of glossy pages, then Nelson recited, dutifully, 'Prince Edward and his wife, Sophie, have a young daughter and a lovely house full of furniture. Victoria Beckham has bought a pair of shoes in Milan. Someone from *EastEnders* has had a swimming pool installed. But I think the story is really about the new boobs she's had installed at the same time.'

'Very good! You sound just like Gabi already!'

'Diana Ross has a new record out, and now looks like one of those washing-up brushes, all moulded plastic with a weird explosion of hair on top . . .'

I made the coffee properly, grinding the beans freshly, warming the pot, catching the kettle just before it boiled. I even got out the matching glass cups and saucers I bought at Portobello Market and put the milk in a jug, instead of dumping the carton on the table.

Nelson had stopped reading aloud.

'Well, go on,' I prompted him. 'Don't get distracted by the recipes. Flip through to the tacky parties.'

'Oh, there's nothing in it, it's a load of arrogant nobodies who mistakenly believe we care what happens in their empty lives,' he said abruptly and before I could stop him, he'd chucked my lovely brainless magazine in the bin.

'What are you doing?' I screeched. 'Don't start censoring my reading! You're not the editor of the *Guardian*!'

I dumped the cafetière and croissants on the table and scrabbled around to rescue *OK!* before Nelson could scrape his soggy cereal on top, as he was threatening to do.

An unseemly tussle ensued, and I regret to say I won it with a very unladylike jab in the crotch area.

'I don't know what your problem is,' I gasped, flattening out the pages. 'Just because you work in fund-raising doesn't mean to say you have to whip me with your social conscience in the comfort of my own home.'

Nelson was doubled up, speechless, so I took advantage of his silence, grabbed the biggest croissant and poured myself some coffee, flicking straight through to the social section, as is my wont, because sometimes I'd find pictures of one or two dreadful Hoorays from my past, celebrating their fourth 'twenty-fourth birthday' or the opening of their new scented-candle shop.

'Am I getting old,' I mused, 'or is everyone starting to look awfully familiar?' That blonde girl looked like at least four girls called Emma that I went to school with, and that oily sleaze there looked just like . . .

Orlando.

'No,' gasped Nelson, crawling along the floor to make one final grab at the magazine. 'Don't . . .'

I calmly lifted the pages just out of his reach and continued staring in horror at the caption. 'Orlando von Borsch shares a joke with Lady Tiziana Buckeridge on board her yacht the *Saucy Sue*, named after her successful libel action against the *Sun* newspaper.'

It wasn't a joke they were sharing. It was the same bloody air.

I wished I could cast the magazine aside in the manner of an ice-cool Grace Kelly but I couldn't. My eyes were glued to the brief copy above, which hinted at the 'blossoming close friendship between playboy playwright Orlando von Borsch and the thrice-divorced Lady Buckeridge, nicknamed Buckaroo by the tabloids for her habit of discarding husbands'.

It was a good job I'd made the decision to draw a line

under Orlando and move on with my life. Because, seeing this horror, I felt a dreadful numbness in my stomach, where I'd normally expect to feel agony and rage. I felt gutted, literally, like a salmon.

Well, OK, there was some rage there too.

Nelson sat back down with a thud and reached up to the table for a croissant. 'I didn't want you to see that,' he said with a note of resignation in his voice. 'I could have paraphrased it for you.'

'I'm not a baby,' I replied defiantly. 'It's much better to . . . see for myself.'

I mean, I didn't even know Orlando *was* a playboy. He drove a knackered Porsche 924, for God's sake. And the only creative writing he ever did was on his parking-ticket appeals. I seethed inwardly. The mercenary, sleazy, gold-digging *reptile*.

'I hope you're going to start listening to me about dating lounge lizards, Melissa,' snorted Nelson, unable to resist. 'Just because a man pays you attention doesn't mean you're somehow obliged to devote your life to him. You're worth more than that.'

But I wasn't listening any more. I was trying to coax the flame of anger into an inferno big enough to engulf the lingering memories of the happy times I'd had with Orlando.

Then the phone rang, and I grabbed it in case it was Emery, another regular *OK!* reader, calling to revoke her plus one wedding invitation. Or my father, calling to check I hadn't lent Orlando any money.

'*What?*' I spat into the receiver.

'Hello, Melissa,' said Mrs McKinnon. 'You sound agitated. What do we do before we answer the phone?'

'We think of our favourite thing and smile so the person

on the other end can tell how pleased we are to hear from them,' I parroted automatically.

How and where does this stuff lodge in your brain?

'That's right!' said Mrs McKinnon and, bizarrely, I felt much better. 'What are you up to for lunch?'

'Nothing,' I admitted.

'Excellent. I have a rather last-minute lunch date for you, if you're able to take it?'

'Why not?' I said, dully. Orlando and Buckaroo stared mockingly up at me from the kitchen table, all teeth and grease and tans. I slapped the magazine shut. 'Where is it?'

'The Lanesborough,' she said. There was the sound of perfectly manicured nails clattering over a keyboard. 'He's one of Eleanor's clients, but she's holidaying in the Med at the moment. His name is . . . Marcus Anthony and he's a businessman. I must confess, I haven't met him *in person* – he came to us via a personal recommendation, but Eleanor assures me he's exceedingly nice.'

'OK,' I said. Marcus Anthony. Classics expert, probably. Cords and a pipe, with an interest in tragic plays. No wonder he needed to arrange private-sector company. Still, a bit of flirty appreciation and a nice meal was just what I needed right now. 'What time?'

'Be there for twelve thirty,' she said. 'You are a very good girl, Melissa. A credit to the agency.'

I beamed, and replaced the receiver.

Nelson was staring at me over his croissant. 'Who was that?'

'Sorry?' I stalled. Oops. I'd totally forgotten he was there.

'Who was that?'

'Oh . . . that. Hughy. It was Hughy. He wants to run

through a couple of things about this party at Dean & Daniels. He's taking me out for lunch.'

You know, it truly disturbed me how good I'd got at lying. I never used to be able to lie like that. Maybe it was my paternal genes finally emerging.

Nelson narrowed his eyes again.

'Don't do that, darling,' I said, levering myself up. 'It'll become a habit and before you know it, your face will look like a tortoise.'

I swished out of the kitchen and shut myself in my bedroom where I focused on making myself look as beautiful as possible. And it did make me feel better to see how blue my eyes looked with fine brown eyeliner and how bright my skin seemed against Honey's golden mane. As I rolled on my black silk stockings and clipped them to the new suspender-belt I'd bought at Peter Jones, it felt like fastening on armour. Armour that only I could see.

Marcus Anthony was waiting in the bar at the Lanesborough, fiddling importantly with some Palm Pilot gadget.

I knew immediately why he'd chosen that particular name; if you squinted your eyes, he looked a little bit like Russell Crowe, circa *Gladiator*. Gabi thought Russell Crowe was God's gift and claimed she'd ditch Aaron like a week-old pizza for ten minutes alone with Russell in his little Roman skirt, but I didn't understand that surly charm thing. In fact, I thought surly charm was a contradiction in terms.

I didn't get a good feeling about Marcus, although I doubted it mattered, since he was clearly getting such a good feeling about himself already. His black shirt was unbuttoned one button too far for a lunch date and there was more than a suspicion of fake tan about his hairline.

Worse than that, he was wearing slip-on shoes and no socks, but I pushed my doubts aside and forced myself to be cordial. It was what I was there for, after all.

'Hello, Marcus,' I said politely. 'I'm Honey.'

'Well, hello,' he said, taking my outstretched hand and kissing it. His eyes flicked up to my face as he did so, as if he expected me to swoon at his feet. 'You really *are* a honey, aren't you?'

I removed my hand as graciously as I could and suppressed the urge to wipe it clean. 'It's lovely to meet you,' I said.

'The pleasure is all mine, believe you me. What can I get you to drink, Honey?'

'A sparkling mineral water, please,' I replied.

He summoned the waiter with a practised gesture. 'A bottle of Perrier, please, and a bottle of Krug – two glasses.' He looked back to me with a knowing smile playing around his wet lips. 'I'm sure the lady will change her mind.'

I forced out a tight smile to the waiter, and said, ironically, 'Well, that's what we ladies do, isn't it?'

Marcus guffawed. 'And that's why we men love them, eh?'

Fortunately, he was too busy throwing his head back to laugh at his own wit to notice my sub-glacial stare. The waiter saw, though, and moved his eyebrows in a barely perceptible display of sympathy.

I knew already that Marcus was an entirely different animal to the amiable Lester. And as the conversation began to flow like a mighty river – in one direction and with no apparent means of diversion – I sipped my water and wondered why Marcus had contacted Mrs McKinnon at all. He obviously thought he was God's gift to women, and probably spent most weekends trawling the bars of Fulham for underfed blonde teenagers to impress with his left-hand-drive Ferrari. He didn't need company. He didn't have a bed-bound wife, pretend or otherwise, and even though I thought he was a total sleaze, I was sure he was more than capable of finding his own dates.

He just didn't seem to be a typical Mrs McKinnon client. In fact, Marcus was exactly the sort of man she used to warn us off at school.

I glanced up to see him admiring himself in a knife, while continuing to reel off the story of his latest takeover battle.

But, I steeled myself, I wasn't here to marry him, I was here to provide entertaining and pleasant company. And provide it I would.

'So,' I said, 'do you have any recommendations for lunch?'

'I like a lady with an appetite!' he leered.

'Well, I always save room for pudding,' I replied, aiming for a sisterly tone. I didn't want to risk Honey-ish flirtation until I'd got a better grip of the situation, so I added, in a very unsexy, jolly hockey-sticks manner, 'As you can see from the size of my hips.'

His eyes bulged lasciviously, and I knew I'd said the wrong thing. 'They are delectable hips, Honey,' he oozed. 'Just . . . delectable.'

'I wouldn't say that.' I raised the menu to eye-level to study it so he wouldn't spot my blushes.

Was I imagining the sound of lip-smacking behind the cardboard?

We ordered – he insisted on my ordering from the à la carte menu and not the set lunch, even though I preferred what was on offer – and, fortunately for me, the food was so delicious it took my mind off Marcus's auto-monologue. Not that I attempted to stop him; after all, what is more relaxing and gratifying than a long discussion about oneself? It was, anyway, much easier than making conversation, and allowed me plenty of time to familiarise myself with the dining room of the Lanesborough, though I maintained a scintillating array of 'How fascinating!' 'No, really?' expressions.

Marcus ordered 'a tasting plate of your finest desserts' and watched me very closely as I picked self-consciously at the confections on offer.

'Honey by name, Honey by nature,' he mused stickily. 'Tell me, Honey, do your collar and cuffs match?'

It took me a moment to work out what he was on about. When the penny did drop, I blushed to the roots of my wig once more. But by now, I'd grown more inured to his flirtations, and with only twenty minutes of our lunch date to go, where was the harm in a little flirtation? I was about to bail out, after all.

'I can't imagine what you mean,' I murmured, but I couldn't stop the blush.

'Oh, I love a girl who blushes,' he crowed. 'It's so lady-like! And so rare these days! You really are a rare creature, aren't you, Honey? With your beautiful olde worlde manners and that wonderful Miss Marple accent. It's as though you've stepped out of an Alfred Hitchcock film! God, you could drive me wild.' He leaned in a little closer. 'You *are* driving me wild. I bet you're a little tiger between the sheets.'

By now, the only place I wanted to drive Marcus was over the edge of a cliff, but I smiled mysteriously.

To my surprise, I experienced a sudden thrill of satisfaction from knowing that my collar and cuffs certainly *didn't* match, but there was absolutely no way he was ever going to find out. And it wasn't as though I was leading him on, because I hadn't promised anything in the first place. Apart from Grade A fantasy material.

Thank God he can't tell I'm wearing stockings, I thought.

My smile increased.

Marcus downed the last of his champagne with a big gulp and signalled for a waiter to come over. 'Could you put this on my room tab, please?' he asked.

'Certainly, sir.'

'Room 316.'

'Lucky you, staying here,' I said, prepared to be chatty with the finishing line in sight. 'Are you here on business?'

He winked. 'You could say that.'

'Well, what sort of business?'

'Come up and find out.'

'I don't think so.' I checked my watch and conjured up a rueful expression from somewhere. 'I'm afraid I have to leave at half two.'

'No, you don't.' Marcus beamed. 'I've booked you for the whole afternoon.'

Booked me? Like he *booked* the room?

My face froze. 'Excuse me?'

'Come on.' Marcus urgently shrugged on his jacket as if the fire alarm had just gone off. 'I booked the room specially. And I don't think I can wait one more second to see those fabulous hips unveiled in all their peaches and cream glory.'

'What?' I spluttered. 'No, I'm sorry, but I think you must have misunderstood . . .'

'What's the problem?' Marcus's expression turned impatient, then lascivious. He slipped back into his seat. 'Oh, I get it. You want to play a bit harder to get. Well, I can live with that.' He leaned forward again, and this time, he slid a finger down my nose, and into my open mouth. 'That's even more of a turn-on, actually. The reluctant lady. I like it.'

I resisted the temptation to bite his finger off. My head was throbbing with embarrassment, and I knew I'd gone way beyond blushing. My face felt white-hot. 'There must have been some crossed wires somewhere, Marcus. I'm not . . .' I could barely bring myself to say it. 'I'm not a *call girl.*'

'Yes, you are.'

'No, I am not!' I glared into his stupid smug face. 'I most certainly am not.'

'Don't be a silly girl. Get real. You think I'd pay hundreds of pounds for a little lunchtime chit-chat? I mean, it's a charming way to combine foreplay and lunch, but . . . you know? Anyway, Eleanor was always more than happy to—'

'Well, I'm not Eleanor!' I snapped. 'Mrs McKinnon should have made that perfectly clear. I would never, ever . . .'

'Honey,' he drawled, 'if it looks like a call girl, talks like a call girl, and gets paid like a call g—'

I punched him, as hard as I could, smack on the jaw.

Marcus was thrown backwards by the unexpected power of my right hook, tipped over on his chair and, in falling, kicked over the table as well, dragging the table-cloth as he went, scattering cutlery, glassware and crockery everywhere. As he fell, I noticed, apparently in slow motion, that his fat face was frozen in a mask of utter bemusement.

That said, he wasn't nearly as surprised as I was.

Shaking with humiliation and rage, I spun on my heel and marched out of the restaurant, head held high. I refused to stop or look back until I was safely on Knightsbridge, hailing a taxi to Mrs McKinnon's office like a Valkyrie hailing a horse of war.

She was going to get a piece of my mind.

Unfortunately – or perhaps fortunately, I don't know – I never got as far as hailing a cab, because in my adrenalin-fuelled fury, I stormed right into someone outside the Lanesborough, nearly knocking him over.

As I started stammering my apologies, I realised I needn't have bothered. It was Nelson.

'What are you doing here?' I demanded, although I could guess exactly what he was doing. I struggled between relief at his familiar frame and horror that he was here to witness the messy aftermath of something I'd rather he'd never known about.

'Are you OK?' He looked concerned and touched my right hand. The knuckles were white but the skin around them was red raw.

'Of course I'm OK!' I spluttered. Now my momentum had been broken, the horrible reality of what I'd done was starting to dawn. 'I'm not some child who needs to be chaperoned everywhere! Did you follow me here? Did you?'

My heart was still hammering in my chest. I knew it wasn't on to take out my fury and self-loathing on Nelson, but I couldn't help it. It had to go somewhere.

'Calm down, Mel.' He put his hands on my shoulders and for a moment I longed to sink into his arms and be comforted, but I was twitching with rage and not entirely in control of my limbs.

Besides, this wasn't the place to linger. I didn't fancy the waiter materialising at the door and billing me for shattered crockery. And I definitely didn't want to see that sleazy creep, Marcus, who was exactly the type to sue first for assault and then non-delivery of goods.

I wrenched myself from Nelson's comforting hands, and began to march down Knightsbridge. There's something about marching in high heels that really stirs up your internal fire, and I'd been wearing heels so long I could practically triple jump in them.

I heard Nelson running down the road to catch up with me. 'Suppose you tell me what's going on?' he panted.

'No,' I hiccuped.

'Come on, Melissa!'

'No!'

'I insist,' said Nelson, and I could tell by his voice that he meant it.

A police car went by, sirens on, lights flashing, and I shrank against him.

Nelson gave me a strange look.

'Not here,' I whimpered.

'Oh, for God's sake.' He took my arm and steered me expertly into a coffee shop. I was powerless to resist: his forcefulness, the comforting smell of coffee and the abrupt jelly-ness of my knees now the adrenalin had worn off worked their magic on me and I sank into a booth.

Nelson leaned in very close and dropped his voice to a discreet level. 'Before I go and get the coffees,' he said, with a very serious expression on his face, 'how bad is the bad thing that's happened, on a scale of one to ten? Because anything above an eight and we don't have time to waste on espresso.'

A shiver of horrible realisation ran over my skin. I knew what he was thinking, and I was ashamed at my own foolishness. 'Seven,' I admitted. 'Six, maybe.'

He rolled his eyes, and said, 'Don't go anywhere.'

In the meantime I took deep breaths. Dignity. Calm. Poise.

Nelson was back in three minutes and placed a double espresso in front of me. 'So you've been working as an escort,' he said. 'Do you want to tell me why?'

I gaped at him. 'How did you know that?'

'Because I'm not an *idiot*, Mel,' he said, exasperated. 'I guessed what that Bobsy girl was up to and just put two and two together. And the way you snuck out of the house dressed as Minnie Mouse was a clue.'

'Did you follow me?' I demanded. I'd taken great pains to distract Nelson by telling him there was a suspicious-looking council worker hanging around the back yard.

'Of course I did!' Nelson looked affronted. 'You think I'd let you put yourself in danger like this and not follow you?' He pursed his lips. 'Don't wear shoes like that if you want to go undercover again. I could hear you clip-clopping three streets away.'

I put that to one side for a moment. 'Were you going to come *into* the Lanesborough?' I spluttered, my imagination bulging with mortifying scenes. 'Then what were you planning to do? What were you going to *say*?'

Nelson had the grace to look sheepish. 'I don't know. I hadn't quite got that far. I think I was going to claim you were my wife, or something, and drag you away . . . Anyway, more to the point, what the *hell* did you think you were doing? You of all people!'

'It wasn't what you think,' I said. 'I wasn't there to . . .' I dropped my voice discreetly '. . . *have sex.*'

Nelson's eyebrows shot up. 'Really? Which century are you living in?'

'It's not that kind of agency,' I insisted. But as I said it, even I was forced to acknowledge that it was, or else that creep wouldn't have booked a room ahead of time. My skin crawled with revulsion.

Nelson, meanwhile, was giving me his best You Silly Girl look. I had my pride. I tried to fix my own reasoning for taking the plunge in the forefront of my mind. 'It's about providing companionship, for men who appreciate good company. Mrs McKinnon runs it – our old Home Ec teacher. She's the most upright and well-mannered woman I know.'

Was she, though? Faced with the seedy reality now dawning on me, my rosy vision of Mrs McKinnon was slipping, and I didn't like what was underneath. She'd never even met that Marcus Anthony man. In fact, she was really taking *Bobsy*'s word for my safety. Bobsy, of all people! I was still of a mind to go round there and tell Mrs McKinnon how very, very disappointed I was in her.

'Oh, stop being so naïve!' Nelson jabbed his plastic spoon on the table in front of me to emphasise each word. 'I can't believe you're being so deliberately obtuse! She's running an escort agency!'

I glared at him. 'That's not what *I* was doing.'

'It might not be what you were offering, but that's what you were working for! How many girls on her books put the shutters up after coffee, do you think?'

I dragged my dignity up tall. 'It isn't always about sex, Nelson. Haven't I always told you, there are far more useful things a woman can offer a man than just sex? And since you ask, it made a nice change to feel appreciated for once. I'd rather get paid for being interesting company than be expected to put out for the price of a pizza.'

Nelson groaned. 'For God's sake, don't start defending it. Should I blame myself? Is this because I told you you needed a break from relationships? I mean, when I said you should value yourself a bit higher I didn't mean *literally*.'

'Believe it or not, this isn't about you,' I snapped. 'It's about *me*.'

We sat in silence and glowered at each other over our coffee cups while the freeform jazz burbled away in the background.

Nelson suddenly leaned forward and peered at me. 'Are you going to tell me why you're wearing that blonde wig?'

'So I can be a different person,' I said haughtily. 'I don't wish to be recognised.'

'I only recognised you because of that ridiculous wiggle you have when you walk,' he admitted. 'Especially in that skirt. It's like watching two big men wrestling in a small sack.'

'*Thanks.*'

Nelson half smiled, but his eyes were still flinty with anger. Then even the half-smile evaporated. 'Melissa, you have *got* to wise up. I worry about you.'

'You don't need to.' I was calming down now, and there was only a simmering disappointment coursing through my veins along with the espresso. It had been a horrendous day, all told. My cherished illusions about both Orlando and Mrs McKinnon had been shattered – as well as some illusions about myself. God, I felt so tired. The sooner I could climb into bed and forget today ever happened, the better.

Nelson, however, was only beginning. 'I mean, it's one thing trying to see the best in people, but not at the expense of ignoring other clanging great warning signs,' he started off. 'And then trying to persuade yourself the most unacceptable behaviour is reasonable . . . I mean, for crying out loud, Mel!'

'I'm not entirely stupid, Nelson,' I interrupted before he could get into a hectoring rhythm. 'I knew what the possibilities were, and I admit I was perhaps a little . . . naïve in imagining I could control the situation. But I won't let you make me feel small for trying to earn some money using the best of my abilities.'

'Your typing is just as good as your conversation,' he groaned.

'Yes, but my problem-solving is much better. And I'm never going to make a decent life for myself doing filing and selling the odd T-shirt, am I?'

I looked at him obstinately.

He looked back at me obstinately.

We remained locked in this cross stalemate until I cracked. I hated it when Nelson was mad with me.

Anyway, I thought, rallying, look on the bright side: first, at least I'd established that I definitely wasn't the sort of girl who could sell her body for cash; secondly, that sleaze Marcus would never be able to eat at the Lanesborough again; and, lastly, there was something very chic about being able to throw a punch hard enough to knock a grown man over. So that was two positive new discoveries I'd made about myself I wouldn't necessarily have realised under normal circumstances.

'I don't want to fall out about this, darling,' I said, grabbing Nelson's hand. 'It was very thoughtful of you to look after me like that, and I am grateful, honestly.'

Nelson sighed and ran his other hand through his hair. 'Listen, Mel, my brother Woolfe needs a new office manager. It's just part-time, but promise me you'll go and talk to him about it.'

'OK,' I said, with some reluctance. To be honest, the thought of yet another office that needed organising filled me with complete weariness.

'And promise me, on your honour, that you'll never, ever do anything like this again,' he added sternly.

'Nelson,' I said tetchily, 'you're not my father.'

'Promise me!'

If I hadn't been feeling so worn out and cross with myself and with the world, I might have fought more. But suddenly I didn't have any fight left, so I agreed, and let Nelson bundle me home in triumph on the bus.

7

By the time the bus lurched to a halt at our stop, we'd sulked our way to some kind of truce.

'You know what your problem is, Melissa? You've got floral wallpapered patches in your brain,' said Nelson as we walked down our road. He slung a comforting arm around my shoulder, in lieu of apology.

'I know,' I said, curling my own arm round his solid waist. 'It comes of being left on my own as a child. Too much Enid Blyton and not enough Jilly Cooper, that's my problem.'

'Yeah. You can spot a pirate or a rare-dog smuggler at a thousand paces, but not a double entendre.'

'Good job I have you, isn't it?' I added, with a squeeze.

Nelson grunted. 'Makes me wonder what I did in a previous life to be saddled with the responsibility.'

I could tell he was still cross, but was also trying very hard not to remind me of my idiocy. I was more touched by this Herculean effort than by his rescue attempt. Nelson loved being right. My forgetting to pay the Congestion Charge after he'd left a Post-it note on my dashboard could keep him chirpy for days.

When we got to our front door, he said, 'Listen, why don't you put the kettle on, and I'll go to the shops and get some food for supper? I fancy a nice quiet evening in, and obviously you're not safe to be let out on your own.'

The words might have been teasing, but Nelson's tone was kind. I knew he growled like a big bear, but he could be terribly protective and gentle too. My heart lifted a little. 'Lovely. Here,' I said, searching in my bag for my purse. 'Let me give you some . . .'

'No, thank you,' said Nelson airily. 'I'm not laundering the profits of prostitution.'

And he strode off before I could think of a good retort.

Inside, I took my Honey wig out of my bag, where Nelson had stuffed it crossly when we got on the bus, and I replaced it carefully on its stand on my dressing table, smoothing out the knots, until it sat there spreading a delicious pool of caramel-coloured curls around my various boxes and glass jars.

I'd miss being Honey, I thought. Just as I was starting to get to know her too. Still, she was a bit of a liability.

I peeled off my kept-for-best clothes slowly: the high heels, the soft cashmere jumper, the tailored skirt, the lace suspender-belt, the smoky-black stockings. They were my favourite wardrobe highlights but I'd never had the confidence to wear them all together like that before. Not out of the house, anyway. Maybe I should, I thought sadly. Then I had a shower, to wash off all the bad thoughts of the day, Honey's sultry Chanel No. 19 replaced with bracing grapefruit shower gel.

Usually, putting on my silky lounge pants felt like the ultimate in Hollywood style, but now it didn't. It felt somehow less glamorous.

To cheer myself up, I got the tub of ice cream I'd been eating one scoop at a time out of the freezer and curled up on the sofa with the remote control. I shouldn't really eat ice cream, what with my rollercoaster curves, but it cheered me up just like champagne, plus it was cheaper and not so likely to lead to indiscretions.

I'd hacked my way through a good two-thirds of the tub, and was feeling much more like my normal self when the front door opened and I heard Nelson come in.

'Hiya, handsome!' I yelled morosely, digging out a really big bit of chocolate. 'Kettle's on.'

There was no reply from Nelson, and I realised there was another set of shoes clumping very slowly down the hall behind his. A very distinctive set of footsteps.

Which could only mean that Roger Trumpet was with him.

Nelson's head popped round the door. 'Roger,' he mouthed, gesturing behind him.

Bloody *hell*.

I put the ice cream down, and hastily rearranged myself into a more ladylike pose, checking the radiators for any drying underwear or discarded stockings. My mind raced, searching in vain for something – anything – to talk to Roger about.

But it was too late. Roger shuffled into the room. 'H'lo, Melissa,' he said and threw himself into Nelson's chair.

Poor Roger. Nearly thirty and already preparing for a lifetime of confirmed bachelorhood. No woman, apart from Magda, his cleaning lady, had set foot in his flat for over three years, and that included me. Nelson had told me several nights ago that Roger had taken up pipe-smoking since his cat got run over by a cycle courier. I'd thought about suggesting that these dismal single-man habits may in fact have been perpetuating his single state, but Roger was such a sensitive soul and I feared chipping away the warty exterior to reveal the handsome prince beneath could be a lifetime's project.

'Hello, Roger!' I said brightly. 'You're looking well. How are things?'

'Oh, fine,' he said in a tone that suggested anything but.

His mood settled over the sitting room like a damp mist.

I could really have done without this. I was looking forward to an evening in, soothing my raw and aching soul with ice cream and junk television, not a sponsored silence with Chelsea's least eligible bachelor.

But it would have been deeply discourteous not to attempt to cheer Roger up a bit, so I dragged a smile onto my face and attempted to engage him in positive conversation.

'I heard you were going to Battersea Cats' Home to get another kitten,' I began. 'Did you find one?'

Nelson came in with the teapot and mugs and immediately made cut-throat gestures as best he could with both hands full.

'No,' said Roger. 'I couldn't.'

'Oh *dear*!' I sounded just like my mother. 'Why not?'

'Landlord's clamping down on pets. I think he wants us all to move out so he can knock the flats into one and make it into a warehouse conversion.'

'Warehouses? In Chelsea?'

'Really?' said Nelson, pouring the tea. 'I had no idea heavy industry ever penetrated that far. What'll they call it? The Old Pashmina Factory? The Old Sloanorium?'

'It's not funny,' whined Roger. 'I could be homeless.' He took a cup from Nelson and blew heavily onto it.

I bit my tongue about the tea-blowing. I wasn't against

it, per se, but Roger did have rather challenging breath. Anyway, Roger wasn't going to be homeless. His mother, Lady Trumpet, was loaded. 'You can get another moggy, though,' I said briskly. 'If you have to move.'

'Can't replace Liza,' he mumbled. Liza was his cat. After Liza Minnelli. A white cat, apart from two huge black patches around its eyes, it had spent most nights screeching its head off on Roger's balcony, entertaining its many admirers. All feline.

I could see the remaining ice cream melting just out of reach, but I seemed to have lost the will to lean over and get it. That's what Roger Trumpet could do. He was a one-man nerve-gas explosion.

'Still,' I said, 'if you do have to move out, you can always go and stay with your mum for a while. Surely she's got plenty of room?'

This time Nelson practically exploded with no-no-no hand gestures and eye-rolling. I didn't see why; Lady Trumpet was perfectly nice, if rather old-fashioned in her views, from what I'd gleaned from Roger and Nelson. Old-fashioned and keen to give Roger the benefit of her advice on all topics.

'Don't talk to me about . . . that woman!' spluttered Roger, and I was astounded by the degree of animation suddenly on show.

'Why ever not?' I make a point of disregarding any sentence that begins, 'Don't ask me about . . .' and so on. It's never true.

Roger seemed stricken with some paralysing nervous complaint, so Nelson explained, 'You know how Lady Trumpet is . . . quite keen for Roger to settle down and have a family of his own to take over the estate management?'

I nodded. Who wouldn't have been, with the prospect of a son like that returning home to haunt you for the rest of your merry widowhood?

'Well' – Nelson shot a few quick glances in Roger's direction, but he was still gazing twitchily into the middle distance like a thwarted badger – 'Roger's mother's told him that if he doesn't bring a partner of his own to her seventieth birthday, she's going to fix him up with . . .' He turned to Roger. 'Who was it she's going to fix you up with?'

'My cousin Celia.'

I frowned. 'Celia Minton? Wasn't she at school with my sister? In Malvern?'

Nelson gaped his fake gape at me. It was meant to indicate sarcasm and surprise, but it just made him look a bit cod-like. 'Is there anyone, I mean *anyone*, you don't know?'

'Oh, my sisters and I went to lots of schools between us.' But now I understood why Roger's face was so grey. Celia Minton came to our house once and managed to break every item of china put in front of her. She might even have shattered a glass at one point; she was singing duets with Emery when it happened, and either she shattered it or Daddy squeezed it so hard it broke – we never established which.

'Well, if it's so awful, why don't you find your own date?' I asked.

I knew the answer to this already, but sometimes it's better to flatter a man.

'Who said I actually *want* a date?' Roger said bitterly. 'Anyway, I don't think Magda works evenings.'

'Well, if you're contemplating *hiring* your partner . . . Mel, over to you,' said Nelson. 'I think this is more your field of expertise.'

I flushed bright red, and glowered at him. If I'd thought Nelson would be chivalrous and brush this under the carpet, I'd been wrong; I should have known he'd never let me forget it.

'Melissa can be your date for the evening,' said Nelson, with a very charming smile, 'but it'll cost you, I'm afraid.'

Roger nearly spilled his tea. 'What? You're an escort these days?'

For a moment, I felt very close to bursting into tears and running out of the room. It was almost worth storming out just to make Nelson realise he couldn't tease me like that. And, I thought bitterly, he'd look very ungallant for making terrible suggestions.

But then if I did, I'd have to sit in my room all night, unable to return until Roger had gone. Roger would spread it around that I was working at Raymond's Revue Bar, and I'd be damned if Nelson was going to make me feel ashamed of having an innocent approach to life.

'No, I'm *not* an escort,' I replied frostily. 'What Nelson means is that I've started my own freelance girlfriend agency, providing discreet social cover for the temporarily single. You know, widowers who need help organising a dinner party, or . . . or high-flying gay men who don't want to come out just yet, but need to take a partner to a business function. That sort of thing. All the comfort and efficiency of a girlfriend, without the sex. Or the demands for attention and flowers.'

I came to a stunned halt, amazed at my own eloquence. Really, the words were tripping off my tongue. OK, so this was the reasoning I'd used to convince myself that Mrs McKinnon was a legitimate quasi-social worker for the lonely and unpartnered. Still, if I found it convincing, Roger ought to.

'And what's it called, this agency of yours?' asked Nelson in an unnecessarily arch manner. 'I forget.'

I gave him my Grade One Death stare. But Roger was agog, so I couldn't back down now.

'Er . . .' My eyes raced round the room in search of inspiration. The Rosebud Agency? My Girl Friday?

On the bookshelf I spotted a picture of my parents at Allegra's wedding. Daddy was looking suave in his morning suit, beaming broadly, and my mother was looking Mogadoned in pistachio chiffon – as well she might, having just organised dinner for four hundred and fifty. All Daddy did was write the cheque, and he still made the most outrageously arrogant speech saying how glad he was to have got one daughter off his hands; his little girl was now someone else's little lady.

'It's called the Little Lady Agency,' I said, noticing for the first time how bizarre my mother's face looked: wrinkled in some areas and Botoxed-out in others. Like an aerial view of crop-rotation fields.

I will never let a man take me for granted, I vowed to myself. If I'm going to be someone's little lady, they can appreciate me properly, or bloody well pay for it.

'Really? Fantastic,' said Roger, and I could have sworn his face lit up for the first time ever.

Nelson's head swung round. 'What?' he said, caught off guard.

'That's the perfect solution!' Roger stirred himself sufficiently to dig out a tiny dog-eared diary from his back pocket. 'I don't *want* the palaver of a girlfriend, for heaven's sake. I'm quite happy as I am. But if it gets my mother off my case . . . It's a fortnight on Saturday. Out in Hereford. Can you make it?'

'I'll have to check with the appointments book at work,'

I lied. Did I want to do this? It was all very well winding Roger up, but . . .

'Melissa's agency is *terribly* exclusive,' said Nelson, helpfully. 'And her consultancy fees are simply *horrendous*.' He was using the Ghastly Fulham Voice he habitually adopted to take the piss out of my school friends. 'You might not want to book her when you hear how much she costs.' He glanced up at me to see if I'd spotted the lifeline he'd thrown me – very big of him, I didn't think.

But Roger looked so relieved I wasn't sure I could bear to let him down. It would be helping him out, I argued to myself; if his mother got off his case, he might be less stressed all round, and that might make him more relaxed with girls.

I didn't believe the bit about not wanting a girlfriend. It sounded like justification to me. Like men who claim they wouldn't give houseroom to a Picasso because the responsibility would be too dreadful and, besides, it wouldn't match the decor.

'God, the *money* doesn't matter,' he spluttered. 'I don't care what it *costs*.'

Nelson raised his eyebrows at me. Roger wasn't short of a bob or two, rented flat or not. His mother's family were big in cider and, quite apart from anything else, he spent nothing whatsoever on entertaining, cars, girlfriends, personal-hygiene products, drinking or drugs. Maybe he enjoyed living in squalor. Maybe he had a secret life working as a socialist activist.

They were both looking at me now.

'So?' asked Nelson in a funny voice. 'How much does an evening with Melissa Romney-Jones cost?'

I thought quickly. What would I charge to make a whole new outfit for someone?

Three hundred quid. No, not enough. Roger's personality was much harder work to alter and he was less conversational than my dress-making dummy.

Five hundred quid? Or was that taking advantage?

I was unpleasantly reminded of that Winston Churchill quote, the one about knowing what a woman was and just haggling over her price. Oh dear.

I was sorely tempted to say I'd do it for nothing, just to salve my conscience. After all, Roger was a friend, and I'd spent the last few years trying to help the rest of Nelson's mates to hone their social skills for free – editing their wardrobes, dragging them to proper hairdressers, explaining about PMT, and so on.

But then I thought of the ten thousand pounds I owed Daddy. If I didn't get that money paid back, he'd hold it over me for ever. And I didn't want to be his little girl any more, I wanted to show him that you didn't have to be brainless to be charming, and you didn't have to be a blue-stocking to be smart.

And I wanted to do it before Emery's wedding, so I could march in there with my head held high.

'The whole-day rate is six hundred pounds,' I heard myself say. 'And there's usually a surcharge for weekends, plus travel expenses and so on.'

Nelson's face! He looked as if he was in a wind tunnel.

Then I got a grip on myself. 'But since it's you, Roger, I'm sure I can arrange something around the eight-hundred-pound mark.'

'Fine,' he said, sounding unusually brisk. 'Just persuade my mother that I'm perfectly capable of finding my own bit of stuff, and it's money well spent.'

'And that is all that's on offer, Roger,' said Nelson, taking a Fair Trade Jaffa Cake to dunk in his tea. I could hear he was trying to be light, but there was a definite edge to his voice. He often used that tone when trying to explain pre-tax allowances to me. 'Mel's just going to *pretend* to be your girlfriend for that weekend.'

'Absolutely,' I said, looking serious. 'Any more dates and you'll have to pay for them. Up to but not including our wedding.'

Nelson almost choked on his Jaffa Cake.

Roger was smiling, though. Roger Trumpet was smiling, and, what do you know, it kind of suited him.

Mind you, I thought, it'll suit him better once I've persuaded him to get his teeth scaled.

8

Roger Trumpet's party went exceedingly well, if I say so myself. It didn't take much doing either. Propriety reigned in the Trumpet manor house, devoted girlfriend or not, so I was spared the horrors of Roger's morning toilette; I just had to remember to make my own bed very tightly in the morning so it looked as if I hadn't slept in it, and leave a lipstick behind his dressing table.

The funny thing was that once I was all dressed up in my Honey stockings and heels (which Roger liked a bit too much), a weird sort of objectivity took over. I was there to do a job, and seeing Roger through Honey's eyes instead of Melissa's made that easy. I surprised myself by spotting his good points – his dry wit, his broad shoulders – and he really did bloom when I told him about them in no uncertain terms. I got quite emphatic on the topic, in fact, since Roger was paying me for my expertise, and, more to the point, there was no way he could get the wrong idea.

I was wrong about one thing, though: Roger *really* didn't want a girlfriend. Which was rather unfortunate, as I'd succeeding in inflaming several other female guests over tea with judicious hints about his devilish charm, not to mention his considerable personal worth and the tragic hereditary disease that gave him such terrible breath.

'I'm perfectly happy as I am, Melissa,' he said to me while we were perched in a window seat during the birthday party, giving the impression, from a distance, that we were engaged in a romantic tête-à-tête. 'I know it's some kind of manic compulsion for you womenfolk to get everyone hooked up, but I *like* my own company. I just need someone to take to these shindigs once in a while, and I don't think it's fair to keep a girl hanging around for an annual Christmas dinner at home and the occasional wedding. It'd be like having a dog and only walking it on my birthday.'

'What a delightful analogy,' I replied, keeping my nose well down my champagne flute. Liberal applications of Acqua di Parma don't disguise all aromas, alas. That said, Roger's overnight transformation was pretty astonishing. Obviously the grooming and hygiene boot camp that I'd put the man through beforehand helped, but there was a new confidence about him – the confidence, perhaps, of getting one over on his dragon of a mother at last, or of knowing he had a dry wit and broad shoulders.

'Frankly, your agency is a genius idea,' he continued. 'Do you mind if I pass on your details to friends? I know of at least two who'd be most interested in renting a smart girlfriend. And they're all perfect gentlemen, you know. There'd be no funny business.'

'Er, fantastic,' I said, stunned. To be honest, I hadn't actually thought beyond the end of this date – a date I'd really only agreed to go on in order to wind up Nelson. Was this something I could actually *do*?

Then I heard my voice say, 'I'm, um, having some new cards made up, so can I send them on next week?'

'Splendid!' He was sufficiently emboldened to punch me matily on the arm.

'Um, Roger,' I added, struck by the sudden paralysing thought of what my father would say, should this ever get back to him, 'if you speak to your friends, do you mind terribly if you don't give them my name? It helps everyone all round if the Little Lady is anonymous.'

'I see!' he exclaimed, tapping his nose delightedly. 'Don't want to spot the same rental dog being walked by one's mates, eh?'

'Er, no.'

Then the Hon. Danae Courtley-Knowles hove into view with a very determined look in her eye, and insisted on Roger giving her a guided tour of the knot garden; that was the last I saw of him for the evening, although I did meet some very interesting single young men – while maintaining a vague air of distress about my missing *cher ami*.

Lady Trumpet was delighted by this dramatic turn-around in Roger's romantic life, and by the time I made my farewells, we were quite chummy. I had to remember to keep biting my lip and casting worried glances behind her head, to sow the seeds for mine and Roger's sorrowful parting, but I think that only increased her joy, knowing that her malodorous son was the cause of feminine turmoil.

I don't know how Roger coped with the subsequent onslaught of female attention, but, to be honest, that was overtime, and if he wanted me to sort it out, I'd have to invoice him.

I thought about the feasibility of the Little Lady Agency all the way back to London, speeding down the M40 with an invigorating sense of purpose. And the more I stretched the idea around in my mind, the more reasonable it started to seem. It would be less an escort agency, more a bridging service for men without girlfriends in their lives to sort them out. I could offer a sort of spring-cleaning for men like Roger, who'd benefited immeasurably from a quick tidy-up.

I'd have to set out on a very businesslike footing right from the start, though, I thought firmly. But if ridiculous airheads could start up businesses selling ethnic bags and hand-painted light bulbs on Northcote Road, there was absolutely no reason why I couldn't make a success of a proper service. If the worst came to the worst, I could turn it into a temp agency.

A very stringent one, mind you. Any temps would have to meet my standards.

By the time I was crawling through the outskirts of London, I'd got it planned in my head, right down to the headed notepaper. But I reined in my wilder fantasies of offices and staff; it would be more prudent to start off very simply, and see how it went. All I'd need would be business cards, some stationery, a couple of small ads in the right sort of magazine, a new phone and – since working from home was out of the question – somewhere stylish and discreet to hold meetings. All this was still going to cost money, though.

By the time I was parallel-parking outside the house, I was wrestling bravely with the dilemma of how I'd raise the capital to get started.

I didn't have any emergency money left – my savings had long gone on paying off my student loan, and the last few drops on my wig. I couldn't borrow any money from my family, obviously, and didn't want to get a loan from Nelson. If this project was going to be about earning back my independence, I couldn't start with another loan, even from an old friend like him. So, with a very, very heavy heart I decided to put my Subaru in *Autocar*. In the end, it was harder to fix a price for it than it was to fix a price for myself.

Fortunately, a man called Ed came round the very evening that it was in the small ads, and he snapped my hand off.

God, how it hurt.

I couldn't watch as he drove off, but I knew it was going to a good home; Ed seemed to know Nelson from somewhere, and Nelson's friends were all terribly nice. But even the promise that I could take cabs everywhere and bill them to my company didn't ease the stab of loss I felt as my lovely green Subaru – and my independence – rounded the corner in a throaty roar and disappeared.

'I'm going to make so much money I can track you down and buy you back,' I muttered, my hands balled into fists. I couldn't allow myself to contemplate the alternative.

I think Nelson overheard me, but he said nothing and merely proffered a chocolate biscuit. He was already at the limits of his patience in humouring me about the agency in the first place. Actually selling my car to go ahead with it seemed to have stunned him into temporary silence.

I thought long and hard about how to phrase the small ad for the agency, so as not to attract the wrong sort of interest. Or, indeed, run over into a more expensive box size. In the end, it read: Gentlemen! No Little Lady in Your Life? Call the Little Lady Agency: everything organised, from your home to your wardrobe, your social life to you. No funny business or laundry', followed by my new mobile phone number and an email address.

I reckoned that said enough. I didn't want to be too explicit, and I could always weed out time-wasters over the phone. Besides, I was still exploring the legal aspects of what I was doing.

I decided to keep my Honey wig – and personality – for agency purposes. As far as I could see, the work would divide into two broad categories: organisation and free-lance girlfriending. My own Melissa personality was fine for the organisation work, but I decided glumly that no one would pay to take Melissa out for dinner, so keeping Honey was best for everyone. I'd be able to salve my conscience by 'being' someone different, and the client would get a more flirty, better value companion who would have no qualms about setting her limits and sticking to them.

So, in that sense, Mrs McKinnon had been right about some things. Not many things, mind you. Nelson insisted that I resign from the Charming Company over the phone, rather than put anything in writing – thank God I hadn't had time to return my signed contract.

It was not an easy conversation.

'You astonish me,' he said, as I put the phone down with a shaking hand, my ears still ringing with Mrs McKinnon's acute froideur. 'You never thought at any point that it might end up in the papers? "Rogue MP's Daughter in Top Totty Escort Scandal"? Busty Melissa says, "I had him for dinner"?'

I shook my head woefully. 'No. God. It would have been horrible, wouldn't it?'

'And you think that your new little venture won't?' he added.

'There is nothing in my new little venture to be scan-dalous,' I insisted. 'Guide's honour.'

He snorted, but had the grace to leave it at that.

In stark contrast, Gabi was wildly enthusiastic about my new career, but then she was a stalwart friend and didn't know about the Mrs McKinnon fiasco. Nelson had agreed it should remain our never-to-be-mentioned-again secret.

I told Gabi everything else, though. She was particularly interested in the wig and insisted on trying it on herself when she came round to pick up her T-shirt. It made her look like a very small drag queen. The wig, not the T-shirt, I hasten to add.

'I hope this is going to make you realise what a fox you are,' she said reprovingly, when I finally persuaded her to take it off.

'What do you mean?'

'Demonstrating your abilities and charm to a parade of appreciative, well-to-do men.'

'Men who need help in the first place,' I reminded her. 'It's hardly sexy, is it?'

'Aren't all your boyfriends like that?'

I ignored the barb, though it stung. 'Anyway, I'm off romance for a while. It's all going to be purely professional.'

Gabi gave me a hard look. 'Just don't do your usual trick,' she warned.

'Which is?'

'Smartening slobby men up to their full potential then letting some other cow run off with them.' Obviously she could see from my abrupt blinking that she'd struck a nerve, because her expression softened and she asked quickly, 'Are you going to be doing party-planning? Like this party you've done for Dean & Daniels? You're so good at stuff like that. You could make a fortune.'

'I suppose,' I said, somewhat mollified. 'I'll do anything that comes up, really.'

Nelson sniggered from the sofa.

Gabi hid a smirk. 'Well, I've been telling everyone in the office what a great job *you* did. I don't want Carolyn passing off all that hard work as her own.'

I tucked in the tissue paper round her T-shirt. 'So what are they like?' I asked. 'Are you all-American now? Are there water coolers and stress counsellors everywhere?'

Gabi pulled a face. 'Something like that. They've sent over a new office manager and some American agents and their American assistants. I don't even have a desk any more. They want us to work in podular mode for greater company cohesion.'

I looked over at Nelson for clarification.

He looked blankly back. 'No idea.'

'But are they nice people?' I asked.

'No, not really.' Gabi's final shreds of tact gave way under the full force of what I sensed was personal outrage. 'Jonathan Riley' – she hooked her fingers into bunny rabbit ears for greater emphasis – 'or "Doctor No No No" as we like to call him, makes Quentin look like, like . . . Prince Charles. I've seen more compassionate traffic wardens. He's the Executive Relocation Co-Ordinator.'

My mind boggled.

'He's *what*?' demanded Nelson from the sofa. 'Are you making this up?'

'No,' spluttered Gabi. 'He's basically just the new London manager. He's about as much fun as the clap and half as sociable. You would not believe the hours we're all working these days. The only bright side I can see is that Carolyn really fancies him, for some reason, so she's grabbed most of the extra work he's loaded onto us, just so she can look all keen and make us look slack.'

Knowing how lazy Carolyn was, this impressed me more than anything.

'But if he's so horrible,' I asked, curiously, 'why does she fancy him?'

Gabi rolled her eyes and rubbed her fingers together. 'You know what she's like. That big house in Fulham isn't going to buy itself.'

True enough. That office had always been a bit of a hunting ground for girls after big houses, Gabi included. Still, I felt rather sad for Dean & Daniels. For all its flaws, it hadn't been a bad place to work. We'd always had cake on our birthdays. Well, I'd always gone out and got one, anyway.

'And, er, I suppose he has a certain flinty charm,' Gabi conceded reluctantly. 'Beneath the unpleasant manner and foul temper.'

'You women, you're all the same,' grunted Nelson. 'All this nonsense about wanting a man to be nice to you and you go for bastards every time.'

'Not any more!' I said, bouncing over to the sofa to give him a big hug. 'It's just kind, sympathetic, caring men for me from now on.'

Nelson made to push me off, but I knew he secretly liked a hug now and again. 'Wasn't it no men at all?'

'Oh, yes.'

Gabi was viewing us with a rather ambiguous expression. 'Please tell me you'll come to the welcome party?' she asked anxiously. 'There'll be loads of free drink.'

'I know. I ordered it.' I bit my lip. 'But, um, Gabi, maybe it's not a good idea.' I pulled an appealing face, which I hoped would convey what I didn't really want to

have to put into words. Carolyn was an avid reader of
OK! magazine, and she would doubtless take inordinate
pleasure in making some horrible remark about the whole
Orlando business.

'Why ever not?' she demanded.

'I just don't want to go,' I said in a rush. 'Personal reasons.'

Gabi looked at me, then looked at Nelson, who was
glowering meaningfully, and then muttered, 'Oh. Right,
fine. I see what you mean.'

None of us looked at the pile of glossy magazines on
the coffee table.

'Don't you want to go and enjoy your moment of
triumph when it's a massive success?' said Nelson. 'Surely
that's more important than some creepy freeloader with
slip-on shoes?'

'No, it's not.'

Gabi went silent, then pointed her finger at me. 'I've
got it! Wear the wig. Don't tell anyone it's you – I mean,
there'll be so many dumb blondes miling around the
place, another one won't make a difference. I'll just say
you're a PA from another estate agency. Then you can
see what a fabulous job you've done, and if you meet any
new people, you can give them your card and drum up
some party-planning business at the same time!'

I squinted at her doubtfully. 'What about Carolyn?'

Gabi snorted. 'Like she'll notice. She'll have her
Sloaney nose right up Jonathan's transatlantic passage,
believe me. And her Botox prevents her from making any
sudden neck movements, so as long as you avoid her line
of sight, she'll never know. Just wear your glasses or something.' She appealed to Nelson, flashing an inviting smile.
'You'll come too, won't you, Nelson? Please? I need
someone I can talk to.'

Nelson caught my eye and gave me his Grade Three Big Brother Warning look. Then he looked over at Gabi, rather more kindly. 'Believe me, Gabi, if she's wearing that wig, I am most certainly coming with her.'

In the end, I didn't stop at just the wig. If I was running the risk of facing out the Dean & Daniels lot, I needed to be fully prepared, so in addition to the wig, I was also wearing false eyelashes and a roll-on Girdle of Steel so stern I was able to squeeze into an old blue velvet cocktail dress a whole size smaller than normal.

Despite all that – or maybe because of it, actually – I felt distinctly glamorous. And about a million miles away from Melissa the PA of old. There was no way Hughy or Carolyn would recognise me dressed up like this; even Nelson could barely believe it was me.

'Bloody hell,' he said, when I finally emerged from my room. 'I thought you wanted to mingle inconspicuously!'

'You think it's too much?' Really, it was a very understated dress, very elegant, and I wasn't wearing any jewellery, just my long blonde hair in a low ponytail.

'No, no, it's not that,' he said, rather faintly. 'You don't look overdressed at all, you just look . . . rather nice.'

'Oh, listen, you don't have to worry about me making a fool of myself in this,' I interrupted. 'I can't actually eat or drink a thing. My bladder's being compressed into my lower intestine, along with all the surplus flab from my stomach and hip area.'

'Thank heaven for small mercies,' said Nelson drily. 'Come on, we're going to be late.'

Gabi had been quite right: a veritable swaying cornfield of spindly blonde women stretched out before us as we pushed our way into the crowded lobby. I, on the other hand, felt more like a corn on the cob.

'Oh, go on, Nelson, have just one glass of wine,' I wheedled. 'Gabi would be very hurt if you left immediately.'

'One glass.' He pointed a finger. 'Don't leave me alone with her for too long. I may be tempted to drink more.'

'You don't mean that!' I said.

'Don't I?' muttered Nelson, casting wary glances about him.

Gabi was in charge of the drinks table and was painstakingly stacking champagne coupes in a pyramid. It took her a few flattering moments to realise it was me.

'Wow, Mel!' she exclaimed when the penny finally dropped. 'Thank God you're here,' she added, in a lower tone. 'I'm going completely mad. Jonathan's already bollocked me for not folding the napkins in the designated manner.'

Nelson eyed the pyramid of glasses suspiciously. 'Tell me you're not going to have one of those tacky George Best champagne fountains. Mel, I thought you were meant to have organised this party with your famous taste?'

'There were some arrangements Carolyn had already made,' I replied, tight-lipped. 'I didn't have time to check all the details.'

Gabi started unscrewing some bottles of vodka. 'Beneath the surface sophistication, they're still estate agents. Anyway, behold the luge!'

Nelson and I watched in stunned silence as she poured the vodka over the two-feet-high ice house on the main table. It flowed in an icy stream down the chimney and out through the front door and lower windows.

'Another of Carolyn's arrangements,' I pointed out quickly. 'I saw Ice Luge on her list, but I assumed it would be a dolphin or something. And it was too late to cancel it.'

'Are you sure that's the image you want to project?' asked Nelson incredulously. 'Buy a house through us but make sure you get contents insurance at the same time?'

'Let me get you a glass of champagne, Nelson,' said Gabi.

'In a flute, please.'

'There should be two boxes under the table,' I added.

I left Gabi and Nelson arguing about the soft-drink provision – the upside of driving for Nelson was the opportunity to be saintly with a string of orange juices – while I had a quick nosey around the new offices. So far, there was no sign of Carolyn, but I had no doubt she'd pop up any moment, all teeth and foil highlights, to take the credit for the party and graciously accept the thank-you bouquet she'd probably have ordered for herself from Paula Pryke.

Looking around, it was no comfort to note that they'd clearly spent three times what they saved on my salary on refitting the place in the style of an American legal drama series; there were leather swivel chairs everywhere, and gleaming Apple Mac Powerbooks, and desks with ergonomical spaces cut out, and no sign of any framed family pics.

So this was podular working. 'Chuh,' I muttered under my breath. 'Where are the wastepaper bins?'

'You like the layout?' said an American voice behind me.

I swivelled round on my heel.

There was a man standing right behind me, wearing

the sort of smirky grin that Nelson persisted in wearing when he'd done something particularly bloke-ish and money-saving, like changed the oil in his car or unblocked a sink without calling out a plumber, as I'd have done. The self-satisfied expression alone was enough to unsettle any normal woman, but my eyes were instead drawn to his astonishing hair.

It was a vivid copper-red, the gleaming colour of a penny when you've left it overnight in Coke, and the faint wave in it was neatened to within an inch of its life, presumably to counteract the attention-grabbing colour.

He saw me gazing in wonder at his head and ran a hand through his hair self-consciously.

I shook myself. How rude of me. I got just as annoyed when people talked into my breasts instead of addressing my face.

'I was just wondering where one puts one's waste paper,' I said. My eyes slipped involuntarily back to the man's hair. It was actually rather gorgeous. But he was probably teased mercilessly at school about it, poor thing.

'We're still working towards an achievable paperless target. But I can see that we need to address the wastepaper situation,' he said, appearing genuinely agitated. He looked around the room and spotted Gabi refilling Hughy's half-pint glass with champagne. 'Hey! Abby? Ally?' he called, waving his hand in the air until she put down the bottle and came over. Hughy took the opportunity to refill a second glass next to him.

'It's Gabi,' said Gabi, through gritted teeth.

I flinched on her behalf.

'Yup. Gabi. Pardon me, Gabi. Make a note to get some wastepaper baskets. Stainless steel. Stylish. With large capacity.'

'I thought you wanted recycling bins,' she said.

'We need both! Maximum efficiency! But with style, OK? Conran Shop,' he added. 'Tomorrow. Thank you, Gabi.'

'No problem, *Jonathan*.' Gabi shot me a meaningful look, then shuffled backwards and tugged her forelock sarcastically once his back was turned.

I didn't quite know what to say. I was just surprised she hadn't given him a more Anglo-Saxon gesture.

A hand shot out from underneath a perfectly white cuff and I forced myself not to look for any evidence of ginger arm hair. 'Jonathan Riley. I've been overseeing this by video link,' he apologised. 'I've only been in the country for a short time and I guess there are elements which need fine-tuning. Excuse me while I post a reminder?'

He was so busy reminding himself on his little Dictaphone that he'd reminded Gabi about the bins, that I let the matter of my own name slip by. It didn't quite fool me, though: I sensed that he wasn't quite as naturally organised as he wanted to appear. People said I was very organised, but it was only because I constantly made myself to-do lists; if I didn't do that, I'd be a complete flake. Genuinely anal people simply remember everything naturally.

'You're the new managing director from New York?' I asked, though it was self-evident.

'I am, that's correct.' He plumped up his tie. 'The Executive Relocation Co-Ordinator, to be accurate.'

'Well, it all looks marvellous,' I said, which I thought was pretty generous of me, in the circumstances.

Still, I thought to myself, no point bearing a grudge, is there? And despite his appallingly uptight attitude, Jonathan Riley certainly had a rather more pleasing aspect than Quentin, with an immaculate front elevation and no need for renovation work at all. I reckoned him to be in his late thirties, with a few lines around the eyes, but with an assurance about his manner that I find only comes after you've bought a good few made-to-measure suits. He had very pale skin, with faint golden lashes, and unusual, piercing grey eyes. His eyebrows were a slightly deeper shade of copper, and flicked up and down in subtle punctuation to his conversation. Like eyebrow semaphore. He was, in all senses of the word, a bit of a fox.

Well, in theory, anyway. I was on a man detox. Carolyn was welcome to him.

'Isn't it an awesome event?' he said, breaking my train of thought. 'Have you had a canapé yet?'

'I don't eat standing up,' I lied. 'But they look *marvellous*. Did it take you long to put together such a wonderful party?' I added, slyly, just to see exactly how economical Carolyn had been with the truth. Hughy had, after all, asked me to keep quiet about my part in the arrangements tonight.

'No, no, I can't take the credit for it,' he admitted. 'It was organised in-house.'

I held my breath but praise was not forthcoming. Clearly he hadn't been informed *who* exactly had organised it in-house; I could just imagine Carolyn dropping her eyes modestly and accepting the compliments in not-actually-lying silence. I found this particularly annoying, and, I regret to say, felt a tingle of mischief run down my skin. Funnily enough, since I was here, clasped in a corset and tight dress, and not wearing my boring office outfit, I didn't feel the same obligation to be nice old Mel, especially not to an offish man who'd been so brusque with Gabi.

'Hey, like the cups?' he asked, raising his own glass. 'Now these I can take the credit for – I asked for old-fashioned coupes specially.'

I studied the glass in my hand. Actually, I didn't like them. They were the only jarring note I'd spotted – apart from the ice luge, of course. Coupes are all very well for Playboy bunnies, but I wasn't sure that they weren't a little, um . . .

'So clever of you to be ironic!' I said with a twinkle. 'I haven't seen champagne coupes used at a party for *ages*. Makes everyone knock it back faster, before the bubbles go completely flat.'

Jonathan's face seemed to freeze, as if I'd offended him badly. Oops. Had that sounded too rude? I felt a pang of guilt.

'But, you know, who needs to go by style guides? They can be rather chic,' I added, touching his arm briefly, before he could get his Dictaphone out and summon Gabi again. 'They can be rather, um, glamorous. In the right hands. And it's obviously working.' I nodded towards the tipsy conversations raging away behind us. 'I daresay a coupe holds a little more than a flute does too. Estate agents will appreciate that. But flutes are more of a classic choice, especially for a stylish relaunch like this!' I felt I should qualify this bossiness, so I added, 'I organise parties myself, you see. Well, as part of my business, anyway.'

He looked at me, straight in the eye. It was an unsettlingly direct gaze, but I held my ground. 'Really?' said Jonathan. 'And what else does your business do?'

'I run my own personal consulting agency,' I replied coolly. 'Problem-solving on a personal and social sort of level. If you have any more problems with your glassware,

maybe you should give me a call.' And I extracted a business card from the inner pocket of my bag, and handed
it over.

Inside, my heart was hammering away like a steam
engine. Where did all that spiel come from? It had just
flowed silkily off my tongue, as it had done that night
with Roger Trumpet. And normally I was such a rotten
liar. Were these my father's slippery genes emerging? I
held my breath while he read the card, convinced he was
about to burst out laughing.

Jonathan's expression changed very slightly; I thought
I could detect the tiniest hint of a smile in his eyes, but his
mouth remained straight and rather forbidding, so it might
just have been wishful thinking on my part. Or nerves.

'Maybe I will call you,' he said in his crisp American
accent, and tucked it into his inside pocket. 'I want everything to be just perfect here. It's an important move for
me. And for Kyrle & Pope,' he added quickly.

'It's so important to get things just right, isn't it?' I
heard myself say. 'I'm a perfectionist too.' Then my brain
kicked in, and rescued me in the nick of time. 'I know
you must be dying to circulate, Jonathan,' I said, resting
my hand very briefly on his sleeve, 'so I mustn't monop-
olise you.' And before he could say anything – and, more
to the point, before I could get intimidated and start
gabbling like a total fool – I flashed him a Hollywood
smile and slid away.

When I reached the drinks table, Gabi was subtly
stroking the small of Nelson's back and nodding while
he lectured her on why she should buy ethically sound
coffee for the office. Her face still bore traces of indignation, but Nelson's soothing presence was obviously
making up for Jonathan's earlier volley of orders. As I

approached, Nelson spun round to see who was stroking him, Gabi withdrew her hand as if it were on fire, and they both fiddled with the now partially derelict vodka luge-house.

'Ah, Melissa, time to go,' announced Nelson gratefully.

'Thanks!' said Gabi, looking hurt.

'It's not you, Gabi,' I explained, putting my arm around Nelson's waist. 'It's just his time of the month. Besides, I think I ought to go now too. Hughy's working his way round all the women in the room, as he always does, and I can't dodge him much longer.'

'So what do you think of Jonathan?' she asked, goggling her eyes. 'Were you more dazzled by his total lack of charm or by his girl's hair?'

'You didn't tell me about his hair,' I chided her. 'You might have said. I made a perfect idiot of myself, gawping at it.'

Gabi's face shone with glee. 'Didn't I say? Sorry.'

'Anyway, I don't think he's so bad,' I said, out of a sudden contrary impulse more than anything else. 'I've met ruder men than Mr Riley. I'm sure a lifetime of being teased about his hair's brought on a lot of his . . . brusqueness. Besides, I think it's rather . . . unusual.'

Gabi looked at me as if I'd gone mad. 'Freakish, more like. Why are you defending him? The man's a mini-dictator! He's banned trainers from the office – even for the PAs!'

'Good,' I said. 'About time too.'

Nelson yawned. 'Can you two save your chit-chat for tomorrow's email? There's a programme about naval archaeology I want to watch at half ten.'

'I'm *so* sorry about him,' I said, kissing Gabi good-night.

'Don't be,' she replied, extending her cheek in Nelson's direction. 'Goodnight and thank you for coming, Nelson.'

'Oh, er, yes. Night, Gabi.' He gave her a swift peck on the cheek that made her blush (totally uncharacteristically) under her blusher, then with one quick backward glance at Jonathan Riley, I was whisked away yet again by Nelson.

9

To be honest, I had expected to spend my first month or so hanging around the kitchen, praying for my new pink mobile phone to ring, but as it turned out, after the initial lull, which had my nails in tatters, the enquiries, then appointments began to trickle in.

The adverts generated a number of calls, not all of which were entirely appropriate, but even the seedy enquiries gave me excellent practice at pretending to be my own courteous but chilly PA. I put the word around my own school acquaintances as well as Nelson's, and talked a friend of a friend into making an oblique reference to the 'homme improvement' skills of the Little Lady Agency in the grooming pages of her internet shopping guide. But my first clients were word-of-mouth – from the now really quite fragrant Roger Trumpet.

As soon as I had my cards ready, I posted one to Roger with a friendly note, and two days later he called to make an appointment. He wanted me to help sort him out with some new clothes, having finally moved into a new block of flats and hence no longer wishing to sport the ragged-trousered-cider-heir look. Our mission went so well that three more of his badly dressed friends called me soon after, to be nagged and flattered around the department stores of London, either to suit their mothers, to suit themselves, or to suit sisters who simply couldn't face the prospect of seven hours in Selfridges with a clothes-phobic who still pushed his jacket sleeves up like Don Johnson in *Miami Vice*.

Those were just clothes enquiries. Mind you, I'd already come to realise that clothes were usually just the tip of the iceberg. Once I'd proved I could deal with the clothes, all the other issues tumbled out like so much badly packed shopping.

Take Jeremy Wilde, for instance, younger brother of Cora Wilde, an old schoolmate whose Belgian mother ran off with a tennis coach and thus bonded Cora and me in our shared scandalous gloom. Jeremy was a semi-professional surfer, fulltime scarecrow, and utterly unable to talk to women without hyuk-hyuking nervously to himself every third sentence. He was lounging in front of me in the airy surrounds of One Aldwych, making the fashionable minimalist chair look positively fragile.

The surroundings weren't helping. To disguise the fact that I didn't have an office, I held my appointments in a variety of hotel lounges, and I tried to match the location to the client, so they'd feel at ease and also be obliged to behave well. As I'd shaken Jeremy's hand, with the doorman's eyes still trained on what appeared to be a vagrant being treated to a cup of tea, I knew I'd have to find some 'school day room' option too.

Cora had told me that her father's constant attempts to smarten Jeremy up were driving everyone in the family insane, and frankly I could see why. He was wearing a zip-up Lycra cycling shirt, a pair of fraying cords and shoes that I couldn't even begin to describe. OK, I'll try – they looked as though he'd inserted each foot into a Cornish pasty, then run carelessly through a field. Where did these boys get their clothes, I wondered. Did they select them from the abandoned remnants in the school laundry-room, then commit to them for life?

'So you can come in and sort out my whole wardrobe?' he was saying with studied indifference.

I nodded. 'We might have to be ruthless.'

'That's OK,' he said. 'I'm not really into clothes.' Jeremy scratched his ear and hyuked to himself. It might have been his ear, anyway. It was hard to tell under his blond afro.

'We can pop in somewhere for a haircut too, if you like,' I suggested.

'And when we've done the clothes, can you, er, sort out some music for me?'

I peered at him over my glasses. I'd added glasses to Honey's wardrobe: tortoiseshell 1950s originals that swept up at the sides like cat's eyes.

Despite my initial decision to reserve Honey for dates, I found she was creeping into every aspect of the business. For one thing, making Honey the 'face' of the Little Lady Agency made me feel as though Melissa was still private property, like taking off a uniform and slipping back into comfy lounge pants at the end of the day. And for another thing, Honey wasn't afraid to speak her mind; I realised pretty quickly that my own 'softly softly' approach was wasted on most clients, whose ears were tone deaf to female tact. Honey's frankness saved us all a lot of time.

Moreover – and this was something I'd never have told Nelson in a million years – I was rather enjoying wearing Honey's clothes to work. I tried it as an experiment one day, to see if it would help me be more assertive with new clients and did it ever! The stockings, the 'best' clothes, the sexy hair: it added up to a far more powerful,

interesting woman than mousy old Melissa. I didn't feel
the need to disguise my hips as I normally did, because
I was dressing up as someone else, a confident woman
who filled out her pencil skirt fearlessly, and who wasn't
ashamed to admit she knew the best places to get men's
shirts tailor-made.

And, OK, I enjoyed wearing the blonde wig. Both up in
a glamorous chignon and down in a tumble of golden curls.

Needless to say, though, on this particular occasion,
Jeremy was getting a very low-fat version of Honey. He'd
have hyuked himself into an accident otherwise.

'Music?' I said, puzzled. 'But, Jeremy, you must know
what music you like?'

He frowned. 'I do. I mean, like, chick music? The last
girl I brought home refused to put out when I put the
Dead Kennedys on? Said it made her feel like she was
being shouted at? Made me phone for a taxi!'

I wrote down HMV under Hackett, Nick Ashley and
Reiss. 'Don't say chick, Jeremy. At least, not when you're
talking to another chick.'

'Ho, then?'

'No.'

'Bitch?'

'No!'

'Female?'

'Lady is just fine. It may be old-fashioned but it's
always flattering.'

'Chuh!' he said in his plummy drone. 'I don't want a
lady! Hyuk hyuk!'

I removed my glasses and blocked off the whole of
Friday for Jeremy in my desk diary. If he was as chronic
a case as I suspected he was, I might need to bring in
Gabi, the heavy artillery.

As Jeremy and I were wrangling over whether eat-all-you-can-for-a-fiver Chinese restaurants were an adequate first-date venue, my work mobile phone rang in my bag.

I knew I should have switched it off, but Jeremy had overrun and I needed to check some messages.

'Read this,' I said to him, and thrust a copy of *Elle* into his hands. 'I'll be back in a moment.'

I smoothed down my skirt, swallowed the big-sister tone I'd been taking with Jeremy, and walked through to the foyer where it was quiet.

Then I imagined a creamy hot chocolate in a pure white bone-china cup, picked up the phone, and said, 'Good morning, the Little Lady Agency, Fiona speaking.'

I'd get a receptionist eventually. She would just have to have a stage name too.

'Hello?' said a familiar American voice. 'I'd like to make an appointment with your boss. I didn't catch her name.'

The hot chocolate in my imagination vanished, and was instantly replaced with a coupe of dry champagne. It was Jonathan Riley. His voice was brisk but assured and sounded far more at home at One Aldwych than Jeremy's did.

And after ninety minutes of Jeremy and his faux surf-dude drawl that kept slipping to reveal Eton vowels, I must admit I found the clipped novelty of Jonathan's accent rather sexy too.

I swallowed, and wondered if there was any point in adopting a whole new voice. He'd see through it immediately. 'I'm afraid Honey is with a client at the moment, but I can have her call you back . . .'

'I'll hold,' he said.

What could I do? 'Thank you so much. Let me transfer you.' I pressed the silence button a few times, waited a second or two, then unhooked the call and said, in a marginally posher voice. 'Hello, Jonathan! How delightful to hear from you again!'

'Honey – as I now find I should call you,' he said. His tone was suddenly much flirtier – significantly flirtier than it had been when we'd met the other night. Maybe he was one of those men who was better over the phone than in person. And I reminded myself that Jonathan was an estate agent: mini-Hitler or not, I'd never met one who couldn't turn on the charm like a warm tap. 'How delightful to hear someone say delightful,' he went on. 'You sound just like Mary Poppins.'

'You'd be surprised how handy that can be.'

He laughed, a quick, dark sound, with just a hint of barkiness. 'Listen, you must think me very dumb for not getting your name at a party that was all about networking, huh?'

'Not at all,' I replied. 'My fault for not networking properly myself.'

'But my loss. Anyway, about what you were saying at the party – I was wondering if I could make an appointment to see you? I think I might have a project for you.'

'Of course.' I felt a faint twinge of nervousness in my stomach; there could be no amateurism at work with Jonathan. He was a smart guy. This would be a proper test.

'What day were you thinking of?' I asked, looking at my diary. There were significant chunks of it blocked off already: Jeremy W, shopping and grooming on Friday; Philip R, Habitat on Thursday morning; Bill P, parental visit to bachelor pad, Wednesday lunch . . .

'Today would be good.'

'Today?' I mused thoughtfully, as if wondering where

I could fit him in. Today was in fact clear after I'd disposed
of Jeremy, but Jonathan didn't need to know that. 'What
about three o'clock? I can squeeze you in for an hour?'

'That sounds ideal. Do you serve English afternoon
tea to your clients?'

His telephone manner really was rather charming.
'Only the ones that have been *very* good,' I said, matching
his bantering tone without thinking.

'And if they haven't?' joked Jonathan.

When I realised what I'd said, my face went crimson
with embarrassment, but I told myself that it was *good*
– Honey was meant to be confident and, um, a bit
saucy.

'Then they get sent . . .' I was about to say 'straight to
bed with no supper', but this time I bottled out, and
instead said, 'out to the patisserie to buy their own.'

Jonathan laughed again and I let out a silent sigh of
relief, and tried not to notice how attractive his laugh was.
It was hard to equate that laugh with Gabi's whip-cracking
uber-boss.

Not that I found *him* attractive. Just his voice.

'Well, that's excellent,' I said briskly. 'I'll see you at
three then.'

'Isn't there something you've forgotten?'

My mind went blank. 'Um, I'm looking forward to
seeing you?'

'Well, so am I, but I really meant where's your office?'
said Jonathan.

Dur. I blushed. 'My office?'

'Your office, yes,' said Jonathan impatiently. 'Don't tell
me you hold meetings in Starbucks.'

Well, it wasn't going to be *Starbucks* but . . .

'Oh, yes, of course,' I said, my brain racing. Where

could I take him? Not home, obviously, and the only other
place I knew in London was . . .

My father's pied à terre flat in Dolphin Square. Which
he wasn't in this week, because he was on some freebie
constituency trip to a cheese factory outside Brussels.

I had a bad feeling about involving my father, however
indirectly, in all this, but decided that making the right
impression with Jonathan was critical. And it would only
be this once.

I prayed silently that Daddy's cheese trip wasn't an
elaborate cover for a dirty week in London with some
bimbo PPA.

'It's not up to Kyrle & Pope standards, I'm afraid,' I
said breezily, 'but I'm based in Dolphin Square. It's a
large block of flats, on the Embankment, quite near
Whitehall. Do you know how to get there?'

He didn't, so I gave him directions.

'I look forward to seeing you later,' he said, most courteously. 'Honey.'

A shiver went through me at the casual way his accent
wrapped itself round the little endearment, and I gave
myself a real shake. I was going to have to get used to
men calling me Honey. And I was going to have to get
used to differentiating 'work' charm from simply being
nice myself. Jonathan was an estate agent; he was practised at this easy professional charm, knowing it didn't
mean anything. I could do it too, with men like Jeremy
or Roger, where I knew where I stood, but Jonathan wasn't
the sort of man I was used to dealing with.

He was no Quentin, no Nelson, and he was certainly
no Orlando. Which left me with very little to go on.

Back in One Aldwych, Jeremy had hooked a long leg
over the arm of the chair, exposing the patchy crotch of

his cords which was worn like an old teddy bear, and was snickering over some lingerie spread in *Elle*. As I walked in, he slipped a hand down the back of his waistband, scratched himself like a monkey, then examined his finger-nails. I had no compunction whatsoever about booking him in for an expensive session of date-behaviour coaching later on in the month. Then I packed him off at high speed, so I could prepare myself – and my father's flat – for Jonathan's appointment.

Daddy's flat used to belong to my grandmother when she still lived in town. Now Granny was ensconced in Brighton, Daddy used it during the week when Parliament was in session, and had unceremoniously banned anyone else from having the keys, even for overnight theatre stays and so on. I only had a set because he frequently took advantage of my proximity to phone me at all hours with instructions to 'let the plumber in' or, on one memorable occasion, 'sort out the fumigation people'.

The porter at the front desk greeted me with a big smile as I walked in. Jim and I had spent many a happy hour dealing with Daddy's imperious instructions, and I made sure the porters were all well tipped at Christmas, even if he didn't.

'Mr Romney-Jones still away then?' he asked.

I nodded. That was good. There were hundreds of flats in the building, but the porters had a magical recall of everyone's whereabouts, and if Jim thought Daddy was away, then he was. 'Just popping in to meet a, um, an interior designer,' I said. 'Sorry, can't stop!'

Jim waved me through graciously.

I put the key in the lock and crossed my fingers. 'Hello,

Daddy!' I called out, ready with my story about hunting for a missing bag, just in case.

But there was no sound and I let myself in with a grateful exhalation of breath.

It wasn't a large flat: there was a spacious sitting area, with cream sofas at one end and a dining table at the other, a compact galley kitchen, bathroom and double bedroom. However, the fondant colours and streamlined Art Deco style (organised by me, with Granny's assistance) made it seem much bigger than it was, and the view over the Thames from the large windows was marvellous.

I sighed. I'd have loved to live here. Granny had told me such marvellous stories about chilling magnums of champagne in the bath, and running around the Embankment in bare feet after fancy-dress balls in town, and all the fun she'd had with her string of bizarre friends.

But there wasn't time for any of that. I opened my big fake Kelly bag on the coffee table and took out the bunch of flowers I'd brought with me, plus my desk diary, a pint of milk, some biscuits I'd packed for my lunch and my smart shoes that I couldn't actually walk in but which looked divine for sitting around in.

Daddy used the flat mainly as an office, so there was enough hardware around for it to look genuine; I just had to hope no one called him while we were here. I didn't even have to run round removing family photographs, since there wasn't a single one on display.

That, in itself, made me feel much less guilty about borrowing the place.

The intercom buzzed dead on three, just as I was giving the room a quick hoover round and I composed myself to let Jonathan in.

I hoped he could find his way through the maze of

corridors: I'd given him very specific instructions so he wouldn't have to enquire at the front desk for Melissa Romney-Jones. My eye skated around the room, looking for last-minute giveaways. I couldn't see any, and then there was a knock on the door.

I took a deep breath, steeled myself and turned the handle.

'Hello again,' Jonathan said, and politely held out a hand for me to shake. He was wearing a very well-cut navy suit, with a sharp white shirt underneath and a lilac silk tie in a perfect Windsor knot. His hair gleamed in the sunlight; Gabi had been wrong – there was nothing freakish about it whatsoever. Jonathan had lovely hair.

I almost wished we'd met at One Aldwych so I could have demonstrated to Jeremy how a man should dress.

'No Fiona?' he said, with a trace of a smile.

'Fiona?' My mind went blank. Oh yes, my secretary. 'Dental appointment,' I said breezily. 'Will you come through? Excuse the informality, but I didn't think a tower-block office would be conducive to business.'

'It's an awesome apartment. I'm impressed. Tell me,' he said, following me and taking the sofa opposite mine, 'what is it that's different about you today?'

I smiled and pushed my horn-rimmed specs up my nose. 'I'm wearing my glasses, and not my contact lenses.'

'That must be it.' There was a momentary pause, then he sat back and crossed his legs. I noticed he was wearing black silk socks and well-polished shoes, and I had to suppress a sigh of approval.

'So, what can I do for you?' I asked, briskly. 'Your . . . project?'

'I think I need to engage some professional help,' he said seriously.

'For Kyrle & Pope?' I wondered if that sly Quentin had suggested my idea for helping clueless homeowners furnish their new houses, and passed it off as his own.

'No, for me.' Jonathan adjusted his cuff and paused, as if marshalling his thoughts. 'I hope I've read your agency right, anyway.' He laughed nervously. 'I hope you'll pardon me if I haven't?'

I smiled, but said nothing, just in case he *had* read my agency wrong. I wasn't quite sure what he meant, but couldn't imagine him at Mrs McKinnon's in a million years.

I hoped, anyway.

Jonathan fiddled with his cuffs again, then looked up, all business. 'It's a rather tedious story,' he began, 'but I think I can rely on you to be discreet?'

I nodded, as if anything else was unthinkable.

'OK. It's like this. I was meant to be moving over here with my wife, Cindy. Regrettably, Cindy didn't wish to move with me, and has decided to remain in New York.'

'Oh dear,' I sympathised. 'But maybe when she sees the lovely house you have here in London . . . ?'

'I don't think so.' Jonathan pulled a quick grimace. 'She's moved in with someone else.'

'Oh. Oh dear.'

'My brother, Eamon.'

'Oh *dear*.'

'To have their baby. Anyway,' he continued quickly, as if he hadn't meant to say so much, 'I'm happy for Cindy to follow the life course she and her analyst feel is most appropriate for her, but it's put me in rather a difficult situation. I'm not familiar with England at all – this is only my second time in London. I need to do a lot of entertaining, and obviously I'd like to meet as many of the right folk as possible, and have as interesting a social life as time permits. I don't, on the other hand, have a wife to arrange it, nor do I want to load it onto my PA at work, or embark on a relationship with a young lady.' He paused. 'I'm not in that space right now, and I don't think it would be – what's that terribly British expression I've heard them use at the office? It wouldn't be *on*?'

I nodded and his eyes lit up. Part of Jonathan seemed itching to jot it down in a vocab notebook. Again, I got the distinct impression that he had a terrible fear of doing the wrong thing – it was one of my own little foibles, and rather painful to see in someone else.

'No, indeed,' I murmured reassuringly, getting the picture at once. He obviously didn't want to go into details. 'So you'd like me to act as a buffer between you and the match-makers, and a freelance social negotiator while you settle in? Parties, introductions, interpretations of local customs, but without any emotional complications . . .'

He smiled, clicked his fingers and pointed at me. 'You got it.'

'Don't do that,' I snapped automatically.

Jonathan clasped his hands and looked a little shocked.

'Sorry, sorry.' I touched my fingers to my mouth and made an apologetic face. 'Force of habit. English men of a certain background tend to respond well to nannying. Saves time. But I'll try to be more diplomatic.'

'No, no,' he said faintly, 'you just do what you do.'

'Teatime!' I carolled.

Damn. I sounded just like my mother.

To buy myself a little thinking time, I made a pot of tea and put some shortbread on a plate for him.

I wasn't sure what to make of Jonathan Riley at all. On the one hand, he seemed immaculately self-contained: well-dressed, dry and professional, and, as I'd experienced on the phone, quite charming. A proper grown-up, in other words. And yet there was that faint fidgetiness about him, just a hint of nerves that could snap out into a brusque series of orders at any time.

I was usually so good at summing people up but for some reason, Jonathan had me rather stumped. Which is probably exactly what he wanted.

When I went back with the tray, he was staring out of the window at the Thames. Well, either that, or he was checking the windows for signs of deterioration. I wondered if he was valuing my flat.

Daddy's flat.

'How do you take your tea?' I asked, teapot poised.

'Oh, y'know, I don't know yet,' he said, returning to the sofa. 'I've never really taken tea before. I normally drink coffee.'

'Gosh, I'm sorry,' I said, feeling a bit told-off. 'I should have asked. Would you like me to make you . . . ?'

'No, no, no.' He settled in his chair, and helped himself to some shortbread. 'When in Rome. I want to learn good native habits. The girls in the office are so eager to make me feel at home. Carolyn keeps appearing in my office with takeaway sushi and memos about local slang in case I get confused.'

He gave me an odd look. 'Come to think of it, one of the girls in the office says she knows you – Gabi Shapiro? You know her?'

I swallowed my mouthful of tea the wrong way and spluttered for a second. 'I do know Gabi, yes,' I said. 'She's an old friend. And an excellent PA,' I added.

'Well, she speaks very highly of you. Honey by name, Honey by nature was how she put it.'

'How sweet of her.' My mind raced. Gabi had offered to talk up Honey's agency to appropriate people through work contacts, but I'd told her at least five times that on no account was she to mention my real name. If Gabi was going to start feeding Jonathan details about 'her friend Honey' – details that were actually based on her real-life friend Melissa – it was all going to unravel in a very messy manner indeed.

'You got any special tea manners I should know about?' he asked, half seriously.

'Not really.' I poured him a cup with a splash of milk and handed it over. 'Add sugar, if you want,' I said. 'Just don't blow on it.'

He was too busy scoffing his biscuit to reply for a moment.

'Where do you get this stuff?' he asked eventually, waving a second shortbread finger around. 'It's fabulous! We need some of this for the clients at the office.'

'Oh, I make it myself. Terribly easy.' I sipped my tea modestly. 'I tell all my male clients how to throw it together, then all they need to do is buy in a decent take-away, get some good ice cream and serve it up with their home-made shortbread. Result: girls think they're Jamie Oliver.'

'Your own recipe?' he asked. The earlier nerves had vanished and he sounded much more like the charmer I'd spoken to on the phone.

I couldn't tell a lie. 'No, my flatmate's.'

'She's a great cook.'

'*He's* excellent, yes.'

Jonathan raised his eyebrows. 'I see.'

'No, you don't,' I replied, a little tetchily.

He made a small 'back off' gesture, but I didn't rise to it. 'Tell me,' he said instead, his voice more serious again. 'How do you work this?'

'Work what?'

'Work this whole Little Lady girlfriend thing? I mean, are you going to be booking your time exclusively for me?'

'No. That would be very expensive indeed.'

'Well, I could afford it.'

'I wouldn't do that anyway,' I said. 'I like being free-lance, sorting out lots of individual problems.'

'But London isn't that big – won't people recognise you if you're out one night with me and then somewhere else the next night with another man?'

I topped up my teacup while I considered my answer. This had occurred to me before, but the more I thought about it, the less of a problem it was really.

Most of my work seemed to be coming from drastic wardrobe makeovers, and I could easily pass for a personal shopper if we bumped into an acquaintance of the client's. In the temporary girlfriend aspect of things – well, I intended to be very selective about those dates; not do too many too often. And as Gabi would have pointed out had she been there, there was something inherently interchangeable anyway about the innocuous blonde arm-candy men seemed to want. I didn't have to draw special attention to myself, just be there and be amusing.

In any case, I reasoned, there were always different-coloured wigs. Different ways of wearing my hair, different dresses, different personalities to adopt . . .

It was really rather exhilarating, realising I could make

up the rules as I went along, and not necessarily be wrong.

Jonathan was looking at me quizzically and I snapped back to attention.

'Oh, discretion cuts both ways, I find,' I said as if I'd been doing it for years. 'It's as much in a client's interest to be vague about what exactly I am as it is for me. We're still quite old-fashioned here in London – no one sees anything wrong in a man having good girl friends that organise his life right up to his wedding to someone else. I've got a lot of friends, and they have a lot of friends . . .'

I let my voice trail away, crossed my legs in what I realised was a very Honey and not-at-all Melissa manner, then added, 'Besides, if no one asks whether you're an item, then there's absolutely no need to say. And they don't often ask in London.' I peered at him over my glasses. 'Which doesn't mean they don't discuss it, though.'

'I love that!' said Jonathan and he was about to snap and point, but remembered and stopped himself.

I smiled and offered him another biscuit.

He took one with a wry expression. 'You got me trained already,' he said. 'Rewarding me with cookies when I get it right.'

'Nooo,' I said, and blushed. 'I wouldn't dream of it.'

This time it was definitely Melissa blushing. That wasn't Honey. Honey didn't blush.

'So where does your own life fit into this?' he asked. 'I mean, that flatmate of yours' – the eyebrow hooked upwards ironically – 'does he live here?'

'No, he doesn't,' I replied truthfully. I wasn't sure I wanted to get into the minefield of whose flat this was. 'This is my office – I don't live here.'

'OK, I get it.' Jonathan gave me a 'say no more' look. 'And does he mind you hiring out your services?'

'Not at all,' I replied, cursing myself for mentioning Nelson and his bloody biscuits in the first place. 'He's my *flatmate*.'

'Just your flatmate?' There it was again: the dry twinkle that probably had New York housebuyers writing out cheques faster than you could say damp course.

'Just my flatmate, yes.'

Warning bells were clanging away in my head. I'd devised three golden rules for making this work: don't reveal *any* private details; don't form crushes on clients (not hard, so far); and don't say things that are blatantly, completely untrue, no matter how much better it might make the client feel.

Anyway, this wasn't meant to be about *me*. It was meant to be about *Jonathan*. And I shouldn't even have admitted that I had a flatmate, come to think of it, not when I should be focused on thinking like Honey. Honey would be living in a smart mews house. Paying all her bills *on her own*.

'Nelson is an old family friend. So, have you made a plan for your house-warming?' I asked, changing the subject. 'You are an estate agent, after all. You want people to see your house.'

'No, I hadn't made plans,' he repeated, amused.

'Then let's talk about throwing a party!' I said. 'How about a themed one? So the girls can wear something fun?'

'You just changed the subject,' Jonathan pointed out.

I gave him my best 'MP's daughter' smile. 'Yes, I did, didn't I?'

Then, just as I thought I could relax, the phone rang.

My grandmother had had her old Bakelite phones converted to modern sockets and the bell pealed unmistakably through the flat.

Jonathan jumped at the harsh sound and spilled his tea into his saucer, splashing his trousers, making him jump again as the hot liquid soaked through.

I leaped forward as he whipped a white handkerchief out of his pocket and started mopping the spreading stain on the sofa.

Aargh. The cream sofa. His new suit. The cream sofa. His new suit. I hesitated with my napkin.

'Go get your phone,' said Jonathan, mopping frantically.

'Oh, I'll leave it,' I said, trying not to let my concern for the soft furnishings override my concern for my client. 'The machine can get it. Are you scalded?'

What if he was one of those suing Americans, I wondered in panic. What if this was going to close me down before I started? His splash was in quite a personal area too, too personal for me to mop without taking our professional relationship a step too far.

'No, no, I'm fine,' he insisted, crossly.

I suddenly remembered that my father was too mean to pay for a 'modern' answering machine and had one of those clunking eighties ones – which would play his out-going message aloud if I let it get to the pips.

'Um, actually, I'd better take it. You'll have to excuse me,' I said hastily. 'It's terribly rude, I know, but, er, the machine's playing up. Do have another cup of tea . . .'

I scuttled across the room and grabbed the phone.

'Can I speak to Martin Romney-Jones?' said a man's voice.

'Oh, er, I'm afraid he's . . .' *He's*! I screwed up my face and hoped Jonathan hadn't heard, then focused every scrap of concentration into a snooty Carolyn impression. 'I'm afraid that's not possible. Whom did you say you were calling for again?'

'Martin Romney-Jones. My name's Alastair Miller, from the constituency office of . . .'

'Oh dear, I think you must have the wrong number. *So* sorry!' I trilled, then hung up. As a precaution, I pulled the phone lead out of the socket.

I gave Jonathan a few extra seconds to tidy himself up, guessing he'd already be unsettled by the loss of control, then I shimmied back across the room and settled myself into the sofa again. 'Do you know, I think this must be the same number as some very dubious gentleman?' I said confidentially, pouring milk into my tea. 'I get the *oddest* calls . . .'

Jonathan raised his eyebrow in query and I shot him a naughty 'I couldn't possibly say' look from beneath my tortoiseshell rims.

Then we both looked down to hide a smile.

We discussed terms (very favourable) and times, and he gave me all his details, which I copied into my desk diary. We discussed his likes and dislikes and which papers had the best property coverage. It turned out he was an avid viewer of both *Location Location Location* and *Ground Force* which were shown on PBS.

I assumed he was being ironic again, but it was very hard to tell.

I promised to introduce him to Kirstie Allsopp and Alan Titchmarsh, nonetheless. Friends of friends come in handy.

We were getting on splendidly, with very little sign at

all of the rudeness I'd seen at the party, when at four thirty, Jonathan's phone rang. He rolled his eyes apologetically as he took a call from the office.

'Sorry. I have to go,' he said. 'I've got two viewings this evening. Big houses. Lovely gardens. Please excuse me.'

I realised then that I should have shooed him away at four, but it was hard to be nannyish with a professional man who wasn't old enough to be my doting father and too old to be bossed around like a younger brother.

'Not at all,' I said, standing up. I'd pushed my luck in this flat long enough and my nerves were starting to wear through. Every time I heard a footstep in the corridor, my ears twitched like a nervous cat's.

We moved to the door, and I concentrated on not shoving him out too forcefully.

'Oh, by the way,' he said, his hand caressing the Bakelite doorknob approvingly, 'I hope you don't mind me asking, but Honey – is that your real name?'

'No,' I said. 'Of course not. I rely on an element of discretion and anonymity here, you know.'

A hint of a smile touched the corners of his lips. 'I see. I guess it helps those men amongst us who aren't so good with names.'

I nodded. 'Absolutely. Honey this, Honey that. Or you can just refer to me as the Little Lady. Lots of men do. Hence the name of the agency. You know . . .' I pulled a face. '"I'll have to ask the Little Lady if we're around for bridge tomorrow night." Or "The Little Lady made these delightful shortbread biscuits." It's why the English used to be so good at affairs. Fewer names to get wrong.'

'I get it.' Jonathan put his hands in his trouser pockets, and suddenly looked much younger. Boyish, nearly. 'But

I feel a little odd, calling you a stage name. And I can't say, "Hey, Little Lady, pass me a cashew," can I?'

'You could if you wanted. I know some men who do exactly that already and I don't even work for them.'

'C'mon,' he said, teasingly. 'Give me a name.'

'No, sorry.' I leaned against the back of a chair and crossed my feet neatly. I wasn't sure how the atmosphere had suddenly got so flirty, but it had, and it was oddly exciting. 'A girl has to have a private life. To you, Jonathan, I'm plain old Honey Blennerhesket.'

He shrugged, in a hey-I-tried way. '*How* do you pronounce that last one again?'

'Blen-ner-hes-ket,' I repeated slowly. It was my grandmother's maiden name, actually, though I didn't tell him that.

'OK, then, Honey.' He winked at me, then his face sobered. 'No winking either, right?'

'No,' I said sternly. 'Only when people are watching us.'

'And even then you'll pull me up for winking at you in public?'

I nodded. He was quick. 'But I'll pull you up in a different way entirely. More girlfriend-ly. You might like it.'

Jonathan laughed; it was a brief, contained laugh, as if he daren't let too much out. Then, abruptly, the glimmer of flirtatiousness vanished and he was back to sternness again.

'I'll call you to arrange another meeting about this party,' he said. 'I've got a feeling it'll be great.' He nodded a goodbye, and turned to walk down the hall.

I couldn't stop myself shouting, 'Goodbye, Jonathan,' after him.

He raised a hand without turning round. 'Be seeing you, Honey,' floated back up the stairwell.

I was left watching Jonathan's navy rear view disappear while my heart rate began to return to normal. Then I went back into the flat, plugged the phone back in, and with trembling hands cleared away every last sign that I'd been there.

My gamble had come off, but my nerves were jangling, and not just because of Jonathan. Thank God he hadn't needed to visit the bathroom – it would have been full of Daddy's shaving stuff! I couldn't *ever* risk doing this again. Even though he wasn't here, my father was still managing to complicate my affairs and wind me up into a state of hypertension.

Still, I thought, as I sponged the sofa clean, I'd pulled it off pretty well so far. I smiled, then quickly crossed my fingers so as not to jinx myself.

There was something about Jonathan Riley that made it very easy for me to play the confident, flirtatious, capable Honey role – but at the same time, really rather complicated.

IO

Since half my days were spent hauling scruff-bags round the centre of London and the other half setting up those meetings, I soon got very good at spinning out cappuccinos in cafés while I worked on my file cards and made calls. There was no point going home, because I only had to pop out again straight away, and besides, while Nelson wasn't actively dissuading me, he wasn't trying to hide his disapproval of my new career either.

All that Honey-Melissa double-think was absolutely exhausting, especially since I was switching between one and the other all day long, depending on which of my phones was ringing. Once or twice I forgot which I was, and gave Nelson quite a shock when he called to ask what we were doing for supper.

Thankfully, I was never tempted to be Melissa with Jonathan, which was just as well. In his first few weeks in London he called me non-stop, wanting advice about restaurants and where to get his hair cut and the like. I supposed Cindy had done that kind of thing for him in the past, so I patiently reeled off everything he wanted to know, while he made humming noises and took notes. Before long, I was seeing him several times a week for coffee and informal seminars on various aspects of London life.

Being Melissa simply wouldn't have cut it with Jonathan: bar the occasional flash of tension, he was a model of professional control. It made me want to be professional and controlled too, even when I'd just squeezed my feet into Honey's stilettos and wiggled all the way down Knightsbridge because the stupid bus stopped in the wrong place.

The only downside of self-employment, I soon found, was that I really did miss the office: the gossip and the teasing and the free coffee and email. Mind you, Gabi was on the phone so often that we might as well have been in the same room. She certainly had a lot to get off her chest since the merger. We started meeting for lunch in Green Park since it was only a ten-minute walk from Camp Kyrle, as she'd taken to calling it.

If Jonathan was brisk but courteous with me, he didn't seem to be quite so much fun around the office. Quite the reverse.

'It's just no fun without you there,' she said, stabbing her fork into a Pret a Manger pasta salad. 'There's no one to take the piss out of people with. They're either too po-faced or too brown-nosed. And half of them don't even realise when you're taking the piss in the first place.'

'Oh dear,' I said automatically. I was in the middle of sorting out my file cards – one card just wasn't enough for some clients.

'I thought the Sloaney pony-girls were bad,' Gabi continued. 'But they're nothing on the new American PA Jonathan's brought over. Nothing! Patrice, her name is. You know how the King's Road lot smiled at you because they didn't get the joke? Well, this one smiles, even though she *does* get the joke, and you can see it going on her mental checklist of reasons to hate you.'

I jotted 'Patrice' on Jonathan's card, then stopped filing abruptly and checked my watch.

Gabi waved a chunk of pasta at me. 'And you know what the worst thing of all is?'

'What? Actually, hang on a second, just something I have to do.' I flicked through the cards and dialled a number.

'Can I come and work for you?' pleaded Gabi. 'Please? You so need a secretary. You're dead busy!'

'I am, yes. Would you excuse me a moment?' I said, squashing the phone into my neck while it rang.

Gabi popped the pasta into her mouth and chewed it unhappily.

'Hello? Is that Warick?' I barked, when the call was picked up at the other end. 'It is? Well, get those fingers out of your mouth this moment! Yes, right now! Do you want to get infected cuticles?'

Then I hung up and put the phone back in my bag, so I could give Gabi my full attention. 'Sorry,' I apologised, 'what were you saying?'

She looked stunned. 'Who was that?'

'Warick Howard. Have you met him? He's a friend of Tassie Morley, from school. Been trying to stop biting his nails for years, so now I'm phoning him at random, twelve times a day, to remind him to stop. Apparently frightening him is the only way.'

'And you just yell at him and hang up?'

'Yes.'

'And he's paying you to do it?'

'His girlfriend is. Very well, actually. I'm thinking of offering it as a new package – nail-biting, smoking, nervous eating . . . That sort of thing.'

'Wow,' said Gabi, raising her eyebrows and digging into her pasta again.

I had reached Jonathan's section in my index. He

already had three full cards packed with details, including two mobile phone numbers, various nuggets of food information and a cryptically abbreviated family tree. He'd had such a tough time that I was determined not to put my foot in it.

'How's Jonathan settling in with the boys?' I asked, as casually as I could manage.

'You tell me, *girlfriend*,' replied Gabi, sliding her head from side to side like a Ricki Lake guest. She had many enviable TV-learned skills.

'I'm not his girlfriend,' I said, shuffling his three file cards awkwardly. 'Honey is. I need to talk to you about that, anyway.'

'Yeah, right, you're not his girlfriend.' Gabi looked frankly disbelieving. 'I doubt the man's capable of forming lasting human bonds. Which is a shame, since I can see how, if you just saw a *picture* of him, you might think he was quite a dish, in a stony-faced sort of way. Tragically, he has the warmth and interpersonal skills of Joseph Stalin. Can you work on that? I could tell him you're a trained horse whisperer.'

'No. Absolutely not. Listen, Gabi, you must stop telling him stuff about me,' I said firmly. 'He doesn't know *me*. He only knows Honey, and that's the way I want it to stay. The less he knows about my real life, the better.' I gave her a stern look. 'Repeat after me, Gabi: Jonathan is seeing a woman called *Honey*.'

'Yeah, yeah. They're all talking about it, you know,' she cackled. 'Jonathan's mystery woman. Mainly Carolyn, as it happens. I have to warn you, she is not one happy bunny about it.'

'And that's another thing. No one at work must even suspect that it's *me* – it'll ruin everything!'

'Why?'

Really, Gabi could be very dense sometimes. 'Well, if everyone at work knows it's *me* he's dating, they'll realise it's all a big front! And they'll let the cat out of the bag completely – you know what Hughy's like with gossip. I once *mentioned in passing* that Charles was flogging a mews house in Chelsea, and three hours later Carolyn's demanding to know about this S&M brothel on our books! No, the whole *idea* is that they have to believe he's got some gorgeous, out-of-their-league blonde so no one'll try to set him up with anyone else.'

Gabi gave me one of her dark looks. 'There are self-flagellating monks in Tibet with higher self-esteem than you. I don't know why you bother with this Honey stuff. You know you're everything a man like Jonathan would want?' Gabi waved her fork at me. 'English rose, well-connected background, keen on horses, good with feeble-minded relatives . . .'

I turned red and nearly choked on my sandwich at the thought of Jonathan finding out about my father, not to mention my mother's spell in the clinic, or Allegra and Lars's internet art experiments. 'Well, precisely! I *especially* don't want Jonathan to know about my feeble-minded relatives. Or my chequered past. Or—'

Gabi sighed. 'You're a fool to yourself, Mel. Can I have the tiniest taste of Nelson's apple pie, please?'

I handed over the Tupperware, my appetite severely checked.

Jonathan and I had a meeting the next day to discuss his Welcome to London party. My father had returned from his Euro cheese freebie and although he wasn't in town – as far as I knew – I didn't want to risk another meeting in Dolphin Square. Jonathan had demonstrated a marked (professional) interest in my prime Embankment location, but I'd manged to keep him away by insisting that meetings taken near *his* office, in delis and coffee shops, would fuel the rumours about his new girlfriend.

Our appointment was in Harvey Nichols' fifth-floor restaurant, somewhere I'd been dying to try for ages. I'd pretended I could just squeeze him in if we made it a lunch, then cursed my own stupidity, and spent the next twelve hours panicking that I'd be expected to pay and, if so, would I have enough credit left on my Visa card.

As it turned out I didn't need the sixty quid cash I'd coaxed from Nelson because Jonathan insisted on paying from the moment we sat down. My coat (vintage belted macintosh, to go with the rest of my Young Miss Marple look) had barely been taken before he was scanning the menu and brushing aside my polite murmurs about who should 'host' the bill.

'No, really,' he stressed as I attempted to insist in an unconvincing manner. 'You're tax-deductible. It's essential to my business life that my private life is professionally managed, so I'll be claiming all this back.'

'Oh,' I said. 'How romantic!'

He gave me an unsettling direct look. 'If only all women could be so cost-effective.'

Obviously the flirty mood wasn't on the menu today.

I clamped down on the flutter of disappointment and I reminded myself that this would make everything much easier.

Jonathan dispatched his carpaccio and a glass of mineral water, then got straight down to the agenda for today.

'I took a call this morning from an old girlfriend of

my mother's who lives in Holland Park – she wants me
to go round for dinner because she's got some god-
daughter who'd love to introduce me to London life.' He
tapped his fork handle on the table tetchily. 'This match-
making nightmare's started sooner than I'd hoped and I
need to get this party in motion so we can nip it in the
bud, yes? ASAP.'

I stopped playing with my asparagus. The galling thing
about eating out in a nice place with Jonathan was that
my appetite seemed to vanish. Normally I rampaged
through a menu like a ravening wildebeest but when I
was being Honey I didn't seem to put away food in quite
the same hearty manner, even though I always ate at
places I could never afford otherwise. It was a skill I
wished I could transfer to my real-life dates.

'Well, quite,' I said, running through my mental party
checklist. 'Did you have some dates in mind? You'll have
to give people a little notice at this time of year.'

'I was thinking next Saturday.'

'Oh?' I swallowed. Jonathan's face had assumed a non-
negotiable expression, the strong lines around his mouth
tightening. I took out my new notebook and wrote the
date carefully at the top of the page. 'Um, that's quite
soon, Jonathan. You might find people can't make arrangements that quickly, what with holidays and such like.'

'Can't they? Surely they're either free or they're not?'

I acknowledged that this was true. 'OK, then. How
about an afternoon do? That way you're not competing
with prior evening engagements and you can give it a
lovely English afternoon tea theme?'

Jonathan nodded. 'Sounds fine.'

'And you'll have it at your house?' Jonathan had moved
into one of the nicest rentals Dean & Daniels had ever

had on its books: a riverside property in Barnes with a magnificent sweeping lawn.

'I think so, yes. Might as well get some publicity for Kyrle & Pope, don't you reckon?' He gave me a brief flash of his dazzling American dentistry, but it vanished before I could smile back and his usual, slightly stony air reappeared. Jonathan had an unfortunately grim resting expression.

He broke up some bread as if he'd lost interest in the topic. 'I'll leave the details to you, if that's all right. It's not my area of expertise. Guest list, food, drinks, you know. Whatever. You've got my address book, haven't you? Charge what you want, but don't bother me with napkin details.' He ran a hand through his hair, ruffling it up. I noticed it had a bit of a curl to it, something he must work hard at taming. Then he smoothed it down again, absent-mindedly. 'Just make sure it's perfect, OK. I don't want any screw-ups.'

'Is business very hectic?' I asked, wanting to nudge him onto more comfortable conversational ground. 'You must be rushed off your feet.'

He looked up, as if surprised that I'd noticed. 'Yeah. Yeah, it is. I seem to be on call twenty-four-seven.'

Jonathan came alive much more when he was talking about his reorganisation of Dean & Daniels. Getting everything in smooth working order was obviously something of a mission for him. But though I kept up a steady stream of light chit-chat about resident parking restrictions around Wimbledon and where to take clients for drinks after the corporate hospitality stuff, the Rolodex in my head was whirring round, thinking of interesting people I could invite for Jonathan to meet: friends of friends, old clients, party acquaintances, work colleagues . . .

Work colleagues. I stared blankly at the halibut that had arrived in front of me.

How was I going to get away with being Jonathan's on-show girlfriend if the entire Kyrle & Pope/Dean & Daniels entourage was going to be there? If the point of the party was to show Honey off to everyone, then I'd have to meet Hughy and Carolyn and Quentin.

'You'll be inviting everyone from your office, I suppose?' I ventured.

Jonathan was already halfway down his dish of mussels. He stared at me, his chunk of rye bread suspended in mid-air. 'Yes, I will. Don't you think? Show them I'm human, fill them with free drink, that sort of thing? Isn't that good politics?'

'Yes. Yes, of course it is.' I made a conscious effort to rein myself in. What were you going to say next, I chided myself. Don't invite Carolyn? She's a cow? I wasn't even meant to know who she was!

No, of course they all had to be there, and so had I. I took a deep breath. I was just going to have to be clever. And so glamorous that they wouldn't recognise me if I wore a T-shirt with my name and address on it.

'Lovely,' I said, with more conviction than I felt. 'Well, on the invitations, I'm going to suggest that everyone brings you a little present to welcome you to London – that always focuses people's minds for a party – and we'll serve strawberries and cream, with champagne and Pimms. I know the best little string quartet, an old school friend runs it, does all the nice Cambridge balls. We'll just have to pray for a fine afternoon.'

'You can't organise that too?' he asked drily.

'I can have a word.' Jonathan had very stern grey eyes, but I was determined not to be fazed. I'd seen scarier appearances than that over the breakfast table, at home with my parents. Plus I had a very confidence-inspiring tummy-flattening suspender-belt on. 'You are asking to be welcomed to London, after all. And a spot of rain does get a party going. We can always play sardines in that huge house of yours!'

'Honey, I haven't the faintest idea what that is, but coming from you it sounds almost enticing,' said Jonathan – finally with a little more charm. He popped the last piece of bread in his mouth, swept the napkin off his lap and mopped the corners of his lips with it. Then he scrumpled it onto his plate and motioned for the bill. 'Listen, sorry to eat and run, but I've got to shoot, got a viewing in Brompton Cross. You stay here and have a coffee, some dessert. I'll settle up with the maître d'.

'I'm sorry to cut it short.' He made an apologetic grimace. 'See? We're like a married couple already.'

I smiled. 'Almost.'

'Call me if you hit any snags.' He leaned over the table to sign the credit card slip and I got a good whiff of his cologne. Creed. The one Cary Grant wore. I was impressed.

'Invite some cool people,' Jonathan instructed, adjusting his tie, 'but no one that'll expect me to join their social circus. I've done all that and I don't have time to do it again here. Especially not here.'

I looked at him curiously. His words were rather harsh, but the expression on his face, which I could just about see while he bent over the bill, was sad. Sad, and definitely not so tough.

How miserable it must have been for him, to come here on his own and start again, I thought suddenly. Marriage break-ups were grim all round. And just when he needed real friends, he was having to make brand new, almost pretend ones, starting with a pretend girlfriend he was having to pay, and staff who already hated him for being a tough cookie.

I wasn't so sure about the tough cookie thing myself, despite Gabi's continued grumblings.

'Jonathan, I will make sure that come what may, you'll have a very pleasant afternoon,' I said fervently, and I meant it.

He looked up, surprised. 'Thank you,' he said. 'I hope we will.'

When Jonathan's back view was gliding safely out of sight on the escalator I ordered a double espresso and a chocolate mousse, and consumed them both slowly, and with great relish. It felt rather naughty, sitting in Harvey Nichols wearing silk stockings, eating a chocolate mousse paid for by someone else. And I really felt I'd earned it, cracking Jonathan's stern exterior, even just a little.

Then I got a grip, ordered a peppermint tea for my digestion, and started making a list of things to do.

'You did all this?' breathed Gabi, struggling to balance a glass of Pimms with a plastic plate of strawberries and the mini Yorkshire pudding she'd grabbed as it went past. 'Bloody hell. I knew you were efficient, but I didn't realise you had super powers.'

'Jonathan has a lovely house and garden,' I said serenely, waving a vague hand at the pretty chairs and casual flower arrangements I'd been up since five in the morning sorting out. 'All I did was . . . enhance it and book some caterers. And listen, Gabi, can you please start pretending you don't know me.'

'I'm not sure I *do* know you,' said Gabi. 'Have you bleached your eyebrows?'

'Shh.' I had gone to some pains, it was true, to be as blonde as possible so as to avoid detection by the Dean & Daniels contingent. And I was almost satisfied that with my big garden party hat, my enormous sunglasses and, above all, my new halter-neck sundress complete with integral bra support, I'd be heaps more Honey than Melissa.

'You have, haven't you? Let me have a look.' She started to remove my shades when I spotted Hughy staggering down the steps into the sunken rose garden, heading our way. He too was laden down with food, bearing two plates that were piled with almost architectural care; I wondered nostalgically if his new PA was taking such cunning steps to reduce his cholesterol as I used to. His straining red weekend jeans suggested not.

'Oh, Gabi! You should have heard Jonathan singing your praises this morning,' I said in a loud voice, for Hughy's benefit. He was hovering in a not-so-subtle way three feet behind her, waiting to break into the conversation. 'He says you're the most marvellous PA they have and that they're not paying you nearly enough!'

Fortunately Gabi had her back to Hughy, or else he'd have spotted the look of extreme incredulity that crossed her face.

'Ah, hello there,' I said over her shoulder, adopting a slightly posher accent than usual. Hughy would be a big test; he wasn't the most observant of employers, but even so, I had to tackle this head-on.

Hughy smiled at me in a dopey fashion. 'Hello, yourself.'

Gabi widened her eyes in silent protest, turned round

and introduced us. 'Honey, this is Hugh Jerrard, another colleague of Jonathan's at Dean & Daniels. Hughy, this is Honey Blennerhesket, Jonathan's . . . um, Jonathan's . . .'

'Jonathan's friend,' I said smoothly, offering my hand to shake. 'Would you mind terribly if I didn't remove my sunglasses? I've got awful hayfever.'

'Not at all, not at all.' Hughy grasped my hand and shook it like a Labrador finally locating a missing bone. 'Well! Well, Jonathan mentioned that he'd started seeing a local girl, but I had no idea he'd managed to find such a stunner . . . The jammy bloody Yank, um, sod.'

I smiled kittenishly. After my sisterly relationship with the agents at Dean & Daniels, it was most unsettling to have Hughy now eyeing me with undisguised approval, but at least this would ensure Jonathan's non-single status would get round the whole network faster than if we'd been caught in flagrante on his desk.

Not that that was an option.

'Shall I leave you to chat about Jonathan while I replenish my plate?' suggested Gabi, to Hughy's apparent delight.

'No!' I said, a bit too quickly, grabbing her arm. The shades were helping my undercover look, but Hughy wasn't totally stupid. 'No, um, do stay and, er, tell me what you brought Jonathan for his Welcome to London gift!'

Gabi flashed me another dark look.

'Let me tell you what I got him,' interrupted Hughy, touching me none-too-subtly on the arm. 'It's a corker. I got him a lap-dance voucher for Spearmint Rhino, then we're going to take him to the dog-racing in Wimbledon.'

'From one dog-house to another, then back to your own!' said Gabi brightly. 'How very English!'

'You can get *vouchers* for Spearmint Rhino?' I asked.

Hughy nodded happily then looked guilty. 'Actually, probably shouldn't have told you that. Eh?'

I made an airy gesture with my hand. 'Oh, I'm terribly broad-minded, you know. Jonathan's his own man!'

Hughy gulped visibly.

'How about you, Gabi?' I asked.

'I brought him a pound of jellied eels. They're in the fridge, if you'd like to try them later,' she said. 'As I told Jonathan, in some parts of London they're widely held to have aphrodisiac properties.'

'Are they?' Hughy looked fascinated.

Gabi nodded. 'You should give it a go.' Then her face clouded. 'Shit. Here comes Patrice.' She grabbed Hughy's arm as he made to slide off. 'You're not leaving me with Patrice. She's still after me about those expense forms you made me lose.'

A tall, very coiffed brunette stalked up and shot out a hand like a piston in my direction. 'Hi,' she snapped. 'Patrice Canterello. Jonathan's PA. You must be Honey. Pleased to meet you.'

'Hello, Patrice. How well informed you are,' I said. 'I can see why Jonathan finds you so very indispensable.'

Jonathan, in fact, had never even mentioned Patrice, which only made me more astonished that she knew who I was. For the first time in my life I felt a faint glimmer of sympathy for Carolyn. Patrice was clearly a proper PA, the sort of gimlet-eyed control freak who'd twig me in about three seconds, even though she'd never met me before.

'Will you excuse me?' I murmured apologetically. 'I need to have a word with the caterers . . .'

'Thanks!' hissed Gabi, as Patrice began to buttonhole Hughy about his excessive and receipt-less use of taxis.

I walked across Jonathan's lovely lawn as elegantly as I could in high heels, flashing 'Hello there!' smiles hither and thither to give the general impression that I knew everyone and they knew me.

Despite the somewhat eclectic mix of guests, the party seemed to be going well, with plenty of animated little knots of chatter around the garden and inside the cooler conservatory where the string quartet was playing. The warm sunshine and plentiful champagne was helping a good deal too.

I accepted a refill of champagne from one of the wine waiters and scanned the garden for Jonathan and Nelson. I'd invited Nelson for some moral support – and also because Gabi had insisted he be there to 'save her from estate agent overdose'. I couldn't see either of them, which I supposed was a good thing.

I sipped my champagne then discreetly tipped half of it into a flowerbed. I couldn't afford to get drunk and slip over on the grass: Honey's dress, for one thing, depended on my staying upright to remain decent, and for another thing, I needed all my wits about me to negotiate the Dean & Daniels minefield.

And there was something about Jonathan, his grown-upness, maybe, or his need for everything to be just so, that made it impossible for me to relax. His perfectionism was infectious. I stepped nearer a rose bush for cover and eased my aching right foot out of my stilettos and onto the soft grass.

Now I'd encountered Hughy successfully I wasn't quite so uptight about avoiding the rest of the Dean & Daniels staff, but at the same time I was trying to remain out of reach of Carolyn. Not because she was a good deal more observant than Hughy but because she had the ability to rattle me, and I didn't want any tell-tale Melissa nervous gabblings to break through and spoil the glossy Honey effect.

I swapped feet so my left foot got a chance to cool off. Over by the swanky Portaloo (created in ivory and gold plastic and apparently hired for most of Elton John's parties), Nelson was rescuing Gabi from the gesticulating clutches of Patrice. I was about to go over and say something when Jonathan waved at me from behind the drinks chiller. He was surrounded by some red-faced estate agents from Martingales, Dean & Daniels' biggest rival in the Chelsea market, and seemed anxious to escape. He said something I couldn't hear to the man next to him, who slapped him on the back with a hearty Brompton Road guffaw, and started walking over.

In the rush of organisation that morning, most of which Jonathan had spent holed up in his study making phone calls, I hadn't really had time to admire his outfit but, safely behind my sunglasses, I gave him full marks for his linen suit and cream shirt, unbuttoned just the right amount and not at all creased. He looked just as well-dressed off duty as on. Most men of my acquaintance seemed to think smart casual meant a polo shirt with their school sweatpants. Jonathan, on the other hand, looked like an advert for expensive aftershave.

Slipping my foot hastily back into the shoe, I reapplied Honey's crimson lipgloss to compose myself. But as I looked up from the compact, I spotted Carolyn. And she was heading my way.

I glanced anxiously between Jonathan and Carolyn, wondering who was going to reach me first. Carolyn must have been biding her time, like some kind of basking shark, waiting till I was on my own and defenceless, just like she used to do at work . . .

Calm down, I told myself. Why would she think it's you? She's not expecting to see you here.

Carolyn was mincing closer and closer, taking quicker steps as she got near me, casting swift little glances towards Jonathan's trajectory. Anyone would have thought she was trying to get to me before he did.

'Hello,' she bellowed from twenty feet away, still mincing briskly. 'I'm Carolyn Harker, Jonathan's Girl Friday! You must be the lovely Honey we've heard so much about.'

I smiled tightly. Unlike Patrice's machine-gun information assault, Carolyn managed to make it seem as though *she*'d invited *me* to the party.

'Hello.' I grabbed her hand, knowing of old that shaking hands with Carolyn was like squeezing out a used J-cloth. Nothing had changed.

'Now, where do I know you from?' she said at once, putting a finger to her lips. Her mouth, I noticed, had a curious, set expression to it. Emery's Home Ec blanc-manges used to be like that – very heavy-handed with the gelatine. 'You're awfully familiar!'

I laughed in a tinkly fashion. 'How funny! Everyone says that! Apparently I'm the spitting image of Sophie Dahl!'

'Really?' said Carolyn. 'That must be it! A couple of years ago, though, perhaps? She's really quite thin these days . . .'

I tinkled again. The cow.

'Perhaps if you take off your sunnies?' she suggested. Bugger.

'Do you know, I'd love to,' I said in a confidential

manner, 'but I simply can't? I have the most frightful hayfever, and much as I adore Jonathan's roses, they're making my eyes stream. I'd scare you all to death if I took my sunglasses off.'

'Poor you,' said Carolyn. 'But you don't seem very sniffly.'

'No, curious, isn't it?' I looked anxiously for Jonathan who had been waylaid by a guest. I wasn't so sure I wanted him to talk to me now. Carolyn would be on full alert for any signs of unconvincing behaviour.

'How long have you and Jonathan been seeing each other? Don't you find him a real sweetie? He must be terribly well-off, is he? Is it true that his wife ran off with his father?' rattled Carolyn, with a quick glance over her shoulder. Jonathan had freed himself and was heading our way.

Too late. 'Jonathan!' I said, relief flooding over me. 'Where've you been all afternoon!'

'Circulating, Honey,' he said, slipping an easy arm around my shoulder. 'Just like you told me to.'

As his warm fingers touched my bare skin I realised I'd never actually considered how we'd negotiate the physical side of our pretend relationship. An embarrassing shiver ran over my skin as his palm touched the exposed skin on my back and his fingers curled round my shoulder. Jonathan had good hands, my brain noted automatically, not too soft and girlish, but no hard skin.

I reminded myself that whatever the impression we were trying to give, it was all acting. Even if it all seemed to be getting a bit Method.

'Ah, how sweet!' said Carolyn as my face turned crimson. I couldn't help it. 'The first blush of romance!'

Jonathan squeezed my shoulder. 'I love the way Honey blushes. She's a real English rose, isn't she?'

The snappy managing director vanished and the smooth-talking estate agent took over in a dizzying haze of charm.

Carolyn tensed her mouth into something almost resembling a smile.

'Have you met lots of nice people?' I squeaked, trying not to sound like myself. My voice was getting more and more like Liz Hurley's. But at the same time, a cool, logical voice in my head noted that if I wanted to put my arm around Jonathan's waist and squeeze it, I could. In fact, I was meant to.

So I did. I felt him flinch a little in surprise but he relaxed against me and we leaned together, almost exactly like a proper couple.

He had rather toned stomach muscles, I noticed, through the crisp linen of his shirt. Obliques, according to my twice-viewed yoga video.

My own stomach was fluttering badly.

'I've met some great folk,' replied Jonathan, showing no signs of nerves whatsoever. 'Lovely people. But more to the point, who have you been meeting? No one wants to hear about me. I am old news, let me tell you.'

'Honey's made a big impression on the boys from work,' said Carolyn before I could say a word. 'I've just been having a chat with Hughy and Charlie and they can't talk about anything else. But then they've always been like that. Pushovers for a decent pair of pins!' She brayed loudly to indicate this was really a joke, then spoiled the effect by adding, 'They used to be absolutely *ridiculous* about Melissa. Mel this and Mel that . . .'

Jonathan raised his eyebrow. 'Really? Melissa who ran the office? I begin to wish Quentin hadn't let her go, this paragon of virtue.'

I daren't open my mouth. Apart from anything else, Jonathan's arm had slid down my back and was now around my waist, playing with the tie of my wrap dress. I could see Carolyn had noticed too.

'I wouldn't say that Melissa *ran* the office . . .' she began tetchily.

'Carolyn, would you mind if I had a few moments with Honey?' he asked, sweetly. 'I want to thank her for making such a wonderful job of this party.' And as if to emphasise exactly how he wanted to thank me, he pulled me a little tighter against him so my right side, including my not-very-tethered breast, pressed against his jacket, so closely I could feel the slight roughness of the linen.

My insides were fizzing like an Alka-Seltzer. My heart was thudding in my chest and every time the breeze caught the silk of my dress the skin above my stocking-tops tingled. I was an embarrassing mass of reactions. This was quite a lot further than I let my own boyfriends go on a first date – and Jonathan hadn't even checked first! I knew I should be hopping mad, but to be honest, I wasn't really quite sure what I felt.

'Well, Honey, I hope we'll catch up later,' said Carolyn. 'And Jonathan, I must steal a quick word with you before I go!' She smiled, or as near to smiling as her Botox would allow, and stalked off.

I stayed stock-still while she walked away, not wanting Jonathan to move his hand, but at the same time not wanting to make him think I was, well, enjoying it. That would be very unprofessional.

'So, how's it going?' said Jonathan in his normal brisk tone. He abruptly removed his arm from my waist and adjusted his jacket. 'You think she got all that?'

I nodded, trying not to look disappointed. 'Oh yes, it'll be round the office in no time.'

'I sincerely apologise for the contact there,' said Jonathan, formally. 'My fault for not establishing the parameters this morning. I appreciate that we should have agreed some kind of code beforehand, but I saw the opportunity.' He shrugged. 'I thought it would look a little odd if I asked permission to put my arm around my own girlfriend.'

'Oh, quite,' I said.

'You're not offended?'

'Hardly!' I realised I was still talking in the ultra-posh voice. It seemed I couldn't stop. 'I mean, it has to look convincing, doesn't it?'

'Precisely. Good job for us that the bounds of English good taste protect us from any outré displays of affection! Particularly outdoors!'

Was it my imagination or was Jonathan now talking in a posh American accent?

There was a brief pause in which I could hear the string quartet embark on the theme tune from *Inspector Morse*.

'Excellent,' I said, taking a definite step away from him. It occurred to me that perhaps we should arrange some kind of code, but now was not really the time. When I was a bit more composed, perhaps.

'I've been having a very interesting chat with Gabi and that great big room-mate of yours,' said Jonathan. 'Still not going to tell me your real name?'

'No,' I said. I felt a little more in control at last and new confidence surged through me. 'Please don't ask me again.'

Jonathan raised his eyebrow. 'OK, Cinderella.' He made

a sweeping gesture towards the garden. 'You think it's going OK?'

'I think it's going marvellously.' Over by the drinks table, Hughy and Quentin seemed to be getting into a heated discussion with the Martingales agents, and Gabi was nowhere to be seen.

Neither was Nelson.

Maybe it was all going a bit too marvellously . . .

'Now,' I said, 'because we said "drinks from three to five" on the invitations, you're perfectly at liberty to start kicking people out – politely, of course – at quarter to.'

Jonathan looked uncomfortable. 'Isn't that a bit . . . rude?'

'No, no. Guests like to be told what's going on. It gives them a sense of purpose, otherwise they'll get too drunk and start arguing, or they'll carry on grazing on canapés and ruin their diets. Anyway, you don't have to usher them out, the staff will. And I did think it might be a problem, so I got you these,' I added, and reached into my bag for the envelope.

Jonathan regarded it suspiciously. 'What's this? Your invoice?'

'No!' I said. 'It's your Welcome to London present. I just hope no one else has thought of it first.'

Jonathan seemed touched. 'Oh, hey, you didn't have to . . .' Then his face went mock-stern and he wagged the envelope at me. 'Listen, tell me now if it's more tickets to *The Lion King*. Or *Mamma* goddamn *Mia*. Or what's that thing with the midgets? The Reduced Shakespeare Company? Is that all you Brits do in the evenings? Go to the theatre?'

Lastminute.com had obviously done well out of Jonathan's guests.

'No, it's not,' I said. 'We watch television mainly, but it would have been rude to give you a TV licence. Anyway, think yourself lucky you didn't end up with a pile of plastic Beefeaters and pre-paid Congestion Charge vouchers.'

'No, I got those, from Quentin,' said Jonathan. 'He's pretty sore about that, hey? But, thanks for this. You shouldn't have.' He fiddled with the envelope and extracted the tickets. 'So, what we got here . . . ? Two tickets for . . . the London Eye? That Ferris wheel thing?'

I nodded. 'You can tell everyone they're timed tickets and we have to be there by six. Then they'll have to leave, so we can.'

'And we can drive into town and stand on a big Ferris wheel with a bunch of tourists?'

'Not necessarily.' I bridled to disguise the unexpected jolt of embarrassment; I should have guessed Mr Stand-Offish wouldn't want to mingle with the common tourist. 'They're not really timed. You can take them any time you want.'

'Only kidding,' he said, doing his annoying pointing thing. 'That sounds like a really cool thing to do.'

'Mmm.' Sometimes Jonathan could be incredibly formal and distant, and at other times he could seem positively high school. Like now. I didn't pick him up on the pointing thing because the discussion at the drinks table had gone beyond heated and now Carolyn was moving in, her hands held up in a conciliatory fashion – which could only make things worse.

'Jonathan,' I said, trying to keep the concern out of my voice, 'I think we should perhaps have a word with—'

Suddenly he clasped me to his chest in a big bearhug

and my nose filled up with the smell of Creed and warm male skin.

'Now then, Patrice,' I heard him say over my head, 'don't I get a moment's privacy?'

My first thought was: has he been drinking?

My second thought was: oh my God, he smells divine.

And when I struggled to get free and saw Patrice's thunderous face, my third thought was: oh great, now Patrice hates me, as well as Carolyn.

'Pardon me,' said Patrice, icily. 'But I need to talk to you about Monday's meeting with Henderson Corshaw.'

'Patrice, your job is to arrange those meetings and let me know time, place and agenda,' Jonathan snapped testily. 'That's what I pay you for. I don't want to have to think about it during my minimal time off, OK?'

Patrice reeled slightly. 'But I need to . . .'

'Please, Patrice! Not now, OK?'

My attention, however, was elsewhere.

'Good God!' I exclaimed, pointing at the fractious scene unfolding by the huge bucket of ice. 'I knew we should have stopped serving Pimms at four! Aren't they *awful*?'

'What the hell is going on?' Jonathan spat, sounding deeply annoyed. 'Jesus. Can't you English go anywhere without having a fight? Can't you just go to the gym more often?'

My mood, which had been turning quite mellow, dissolved into panic. I tried to explain that the estate agents I knew would probably have heart attacks should they look at an exercise bike too quickly, but Jonathan's flash of annoyance froze the words in my throat.

So this was the office Stalin Gabi had been talking about.

'Don't worry about it,' I began weakly. 'I'm sure they're just bickering . . .'

As I spoke, Hughy started windmilling his arms at a lettings agent from Battersea and I knew we were in for trouble.

Jonathan and Patrice immediately set off at a gym-honed trot to break up the schoolboy pushing and shoving that was sending guests scattering like frightened ducks off a pond. I could have told them that, traditionally, tipsy alpha male public-school boys indulge in meaningless shoving at most social events and that it was highly unlikely to turn into anything else – but, in these shoes, I couldn't get across the lawn fast enough to do that.

As Jonathan approached, one of the Martingales lot gave Hughy a shove which momentum turned into a barrelling stagger; he crashed into the table, bringing it down on top of him, whereupon Quentin, emboldened by Pimms, punched the offender, then ducked out of the way before the return punch could land on him. It landed instead on Carolyn, who went down vertically like one of Fred Dibnah's tower demolitions, knees first.

Well, I did what any self-respecting hostess would do, seeing her beautiful, elegant garden party degenerate into a free-for-all.

I set off the nearest intruder alarm.

11

'What did you say to the police?' demanded Gabi when we met up for our picnic lunch in the park the Tuesday after. 'I don't expect they get many house break-ins attended by a hundred people in garden party outfits, accompanied by a string quartet.'

As it turned out, the aftermath of the party hadn't been as challenging as I'd anticipated, since most middle-class people rather enjoy seeing a policeman in action. The local guests, in particular, left with a warm glow about the prompt response times of the Barnes constabulary. Well, that and the Pimms.

'Oh, I told them it was a faulty alarm and plied them with strawberry tartlets,' I said, upending a sachet of brown sugar into my cappuccino.

'Hmm,' said Gabi. 'And what did you tell Jonathan's guests?'

'Well, you know. I sort of managed to persuade most of them that it was part of the Welcome to London theme. "Our famous boys in blue" and all that, just making sure they all got home safely, without drinking and driving.'

'And Jonathan? Did he see the funny side? Or did he go off on one?' Gabi's incredulous expression told me exactly where she'd put her money.

'Well . . . we laughed about it eventually.' I bit my lip. Jonathan hadn't seen the funny side at all, in fact. He hadn't exactly blamed me, but I'd got a real broadside of office brusqueness that chilled me to the marrow.

It had been particularly unpleasant, coming after that rather enjoyable display of 'affection'; if I'd had any illusions about what was real and what was faked with Jonathan, they'd certainly been cleared up now.

'And did he enjoy himself?' asked Gabi, raising her eyebrow suggestively. 'Because it looked that way from where I was standing. I've never seen him so amused. Well, until the police rocked up.'

'Oh, yes, I think so. By the time I'd ushered everyone out and got the police settled, he was running late for his tennis trainer and had to leave in a hurry.'

'Still, you made an impression.' She eyed me curiously. 'The office is abuzz, as Carolyn would say.'

'Mmm,' I agreed, trying not to let my disappointment about the debacle show. Instead of a pleasant post-mortem à deux, I'd been left to deal with the largely non-English-speaking hired staff, none of whom seemed to understand about washing glasses properly. Not even any flowers to say sorry. Or thank you.

I rallied myself. This wasn't the point, and anyway, he didn't have my address. 'Yes, indeed. Mission accomplished on that front.'

'See what a moody arsehole he is now?' she added, with a distinct trace of gloat.

I lifted my chin. 'I imagine he's trying to establish his authority. I'm sure he'll relax into his role once he's more settled.'

'Yeah, right. And you say Carolyn got whacked in the eye?' Gabi asked gleefully, for the second time.

'Full on. Like something from a kung-fu film, only with real sound effects.'

Gabi snorted uncharitably. 'No wonder she's taken some time off. What a waste of her fake tan!' she snickered. 'God, I'm sorry to have missed that.'

'Yes,' I said, turning to look her in the face. 'Where *did* you get to? I tried to find you but you'd vanished.'

Gabi had the grace to turn red and miss a bit of pasta salad with her fork. 'I was talking to Nelson in the conservatory. About charity work,' she added, as if that made it better. 'With the lead piping.'

'*Gabi.*' I attempted to look disapproving – not hard, since for once I really was. I liked Aaron – he was hardworking and cheerful, but I had my doubts about Gabi's somewhat businesslike approach to their relationship. I'd never seen her go fluttery when she talked about him, the way she did whenever Nelson was around.

'Nothing happened!' she protested, unnecessarily.

'Too right! Oh, Gabi. I thought you and Aaron were getting on better. What about your weekend break? At Champneys?'

'It was OK.' Gabi had been nagging Aaron about minibreaks for ages. They were the currency of romance for her.

'And?'

'And nothing.' She examined her beautiful French manicure, and twisted the platinum band Aaron had given her for her birthday. Most girls would have been thrilled with a platinum band, but for Gabi it lacked a certain something. Like a massive diamond solitaire. 'We had a nice time.'

'Just a nice time?'

'*We had a nice time.* He played golf and I had three consecutive reiki massages. *What?* Don't look at me like that!'

I sighed. I wasn't London's Greatest Romantic by any stretch of the imagination, but I just didn't believe Gabi's 'kissing doesn't last as long as his'n'hers Rolexes' view of romance. She couldn't be that hard-nosed, and still fancy a do-gooder like Nelson. 'Gabi, if Aaron has nothing else to offer you besides your own set of matching store cards, then don't you think maybe you should be looking else-where? Where's the love? The romance? I mean, is it fair on Aaron, for a start?'

'No. Oh no. I've heard your Marry for Love lecture too many times before, Mel,' she said, bundling her empty plastic containers into the paper Pret bag. 'And we're not going to have it again. Me and Aaron, we understand each other. We're a good team. And believe me, I'm a lot nicer to be around when I know the bills are all paid.' She gave me a 'that's the end of that' look, and went on, 'Tell me about Jonathan instead. I was dying to get inside the house and nose around. Why did you let him keep all the doors locked? What is he, Bluebeard?' She eyed me, hungry for gossip, and leaned in closer. 'What's his bedroom like? You must have had a sneaky peek.'

'I didn't go in his bedroom,' I spluttered, thrown off balance by the force of Gabi's curiosity.

'Well, what about his bathroom? Has he got fabulous toiletries?' She looked wistful. 'You always know when Jonathan's in the office, because the place smells sexy, instead of reeking of stale wine and old socks.'

I turned to look at her. 'Sexy? I thought you all loathed and detested him?' I asked, curious. 'Are you sure he isn't starting to defrost, now he's got you all under control?'

'Chuh! Some hope. He's stepped up his campaign, if anything. We've got motivation charts and God knows what else to fill in. But . . .' Gabi pulled her sympathetic face. 'Apparently, there's a rumour that he came to London to escape some terrible heartbreak in New York. So now we all think, well, we *hope*, it's all to compensate for his inner turmoil and not just because he's a total bastard.' She peered at me. 'Is it? Can you find out?'

'No, I cannot,' I protested. 'Jonathan's never even mentioned his . . . *situation.*'

'So why are you pretending to be his girlfriend?' she demanded.

'He's . . . busy.' My mind whirred, trying to be discreet but at the same time give Gabi sufficient information to satisfy the roaring flames of her nosiness. She wouldn't let it lie otherwise. 'He needs someone to organise his personal life, but hasn't got time for a real girlfriend.'

She pointed at me. 'Is he gay?'

'No,' I said firmly.

'Is there a vengeful ex in the picture?'

'Gabi, this isn't Twenty Questions!' I snapped. I was starting to see why Jonathan was so buttoned-up at work with gossip-hounds like Gabi slavering for details of his painful personal life.

Besides, he hadn't mentioned Cindy, the ex-wife, since our initial meeting. I hadn't asked, but that wasn't to say I wasn't starting to get curious.

'Hmm. I can't imagine him with a woman. She'd have to be extraordinarily patient and thick-skinned.' Gabi put her finger on her lips. 'If there *was* ever a woman at all . . . God, I wish I'd been able to have a quick shufty round his house! He does play things very close to his chest. We've all noticed that. No pictures in his office. Kyrle & Pope screen-saver. A bit secretive. Enigmatic. Would you say? Is that fair?'

'Gabi, it's called being professional!' I exclaimed,

inching back a little on the bench. I felt a protectiveness towards Jonathan that I'd never have dreamed possible.

'Do you have his card there?' asked Gabi innocently. 'Just a quick look and I could silence all manner of inaccurate gossip at work . . .'

I shuffled back, but not quick enough to stop her lurching for the file cards on my knee.

'Gabi, no!' I screeched, trying to knock her hands away, but I managed only to upend the box, spilling cards all over the path. 'Oh, shit!' I wailed, scrabbling around to pick them up before the wind got them.

We got on our knees and grabbed wildly, much to the amusement of some kids on the benches opposite.

'Royston Pilling: needs chiropody. Destroy "snuggly". Aries?' read Gabi.

'Give me that,' I said, snatching the cards off her.

'This isn't what you'd call secure, is it?' she said, as I managed to seize Jeremy Wilde's card from the duck pond in the nick of time. 'Carrying everyone's details around with you in a bag. What if you were mugged? Do your clients know how vulnerable their social defects are?'

'I can't afford an office and I can't work from home.'

'Can't you?' mused Gabi. 'Does Nelson not approve?'

'No, he doesn't.'

'He's so principled, you know,' she said, a dreamy look spreading over her face. 'Such high standards.'

'I know,' I snapped, shaking grass cuttings off Jeremy's card. 'But either you're with Aaron or you're not. You can't be in love with two people at once. Gabi, you mustn't marry someone you don't love.' I could see she was about to kick off, so I patted her on the knee. 'Now, let's not talk about this any more. I have to go home this weekend to show Emery her toile, and I can't afford to lose a gram of positivity.'

As I said this a passing pigeon pooed on Barnaby Mulligan's file card, the only one that hadn't fallen out of the box.

'The natural world has spoken,' said Gabi, returning to her normal beady-eyed state. 'You've got to get an office. I'm going to start looking for you at work, and we'll worry about how to pay for it later.'

There were four cars parked outside my parents' house when the taxi from the station dropped me off, and I immediately felt the pain of my pedestrian state.

Cars were a big deal in our family, representing, as they did, independence, money, and the power to run things over. My father had a large black Jaguar XJS, my mother had a Mercedes estate ('for the dogs'), Emery had a dilapidated old Beetle and my grandmother had a little red Alfa Romeo sports car. I was especially pleased to see that parked outside, even if it was blocking in my father's Jag.

'Hello, darling,' said Granny when I walked into the kitchen.

She was the only one who acknowledged my arrival; my parents didn't even break off from the hissed argument they were conducting over the table.

'You tell her!' hissed my mother.

'No, you can tell her!' my father hissed back. 'I can't deal with Emery. It's like talking to you, but under general bloody anaesthetic. She's your daughter, you tell her.'

'You are such a manipulative swine, Martin!'

'At least I'm not half-witted, unlike the female members of this family!'

'Is this about Emery's wedding?' I guessed.

Granny poured me a cup of tea. 'In a way. Your father isn't keen to pay for the fleet of Rolls-Royces for the bridal party.'

'But he paid for Allegra to have nine cars. Even the vicar arrived in a Roller.'

'Well, he did and he didn't, darling,' whispered Granny, as though she was updating a late-comer at the theatre. 'It *seems* your father did some deal with a friend of his who runs a top-end car-fleet business. They made some murky pact, by all accounts, something to do with getting publicity in the constituency. But now they've fallen out and so the cars are no-go.'

'I see.'

My mother let out a frustrated squeal of annoyance and hurled a plate of salad at my father.

'Do you *want* to be detoxed next month, you raddled old soak?' he demanded, picking tomato off his shirt. 'Or are you working up to being entirely pickled for the wedding? Like Lord Nelson but in a seven-hundred-quid hat and Teflon corselette?'

'Emer-eeeeee!' wailed my mother. 'Your father wants you to arrive at the church in a *Ford Granada*!'

'Shall we go for a turn about the grounds?' suggested Granny cheerfully, then added, 'There's something you and I need to talk about,' in an undertone.

We walked round the apple orchard, arm-in-arm, and not for the first time I decided that home would be almost bearable if it was just Granny living there. She was the only member of the family I actually felt related to, although her imperial cheekbones and cat-like eyes had gone to Emery and Allegra and not me. Granny was like the calm in the storm, a fresh breeze in a sulky atmosphere.

She never asked me whether I'd met anyone nice; instead she sort of intimated that, like hers, my life must be too full for words, which was awfully flattering, if not exactly true.

My father liked to mutter that she lived in a fantasy world and had been an appalling mother, but as far as I was concerned her sole error seemed to be that she'd allowed her daughter to marry a bounder like him. Besides, when it came to parenting skills he was hardly qualified to judge.

After some gossip about the wedding – Emery's sports-mad fiancé, William, including shooting lessons and season tickets on their wedding list, Mummy wanting a low-carb croquembouche and so on – she asked, 'How's that adorable Nelson?' Granny had a soft spot for Nelson and Woolfe. Most people did.

'He's fine, thank you.'

'Still no plans to find somewhere of your own?'

I shook my head. 'I *like* living with him. It's like flat-sharing with Jamie Oliver and the Dalai Lama.'

'Damn,' said Granny, crossly.

'What?'

'Well, it's . . . oh, rather delicate, really.' She stopped walking and sighed. 'I had a little windfall on the horses on Ladies' Day' – Granny knew someone who knew one of the Queen's trainers, as you do – 'and I want to get rid of it before your father finds out and demands that I pay for Emery's ring cushions or some other horror. He really is a *dreadful* man, Melissa.'

She let out another deep sigh of resignation and plucked at a magenta rhododendron. 'Grab, grab, grab. You'd think he was fund-raising for some disaster appeal, not paying for his daughter's wedding.'

'You could always buy some of Lars's spearheads?' I suggested. 'I hear he has a new consignment coming in.'

Granny looked coyly at her rhododendron. 'Well, I was rather hoping I could persuade you to launder it for me.'

'Me?'

Launder it?

'Well, the bet was sort of, um, in your name. Oh, just a silly loophole,' she added, in response to my aghast expression. 'Tax, or something. I was going to give it to you for Christmas. But, listen, darling, I thought you could use it as a deposit on a flat?'

'That's very kind of you,' I said stoutly. God, did everyone take advantage of me – even when I wasn't there? 'But I like living with Nelson, and you know how I feel about handouts.'

'Oh, it's not a handout, darling!' she exclaimed. 'It's an . . . under-handout!'

'I couldn't possibly,' I insisted. 'I'm an independent girl, and if you must know things are going quite well at the moment . . .' Then an idea came to me, cutting straight through my usual warm fog of principles. It startled me with its Honey-ness.

'You know what, Granny?' I said. 'Can I make you a business proposition?'

Granny actually clapped her hands with glee when I told her about the agency. Well, the edited highlights of it. I swore her to hand-on-heart secrecy, of course, and made her draw up a little 'between us' agreement, so I'd be paying her back at a decent rate of interest once I started making a profit. She wanted to lend me double, just to annoy my father, I think, but I refused. Her loan was enough for a deposit on a very, very small rented office, but somewhere smart, and that was all I needed.

'Melissa, darling, I'm so proud of you. You're a chip off the old block,' she said, and that made the loan feel less like a debt and more like an advance.

Unfortunately, she drove off home to Brighton soon afterwards, and by the time I got back to London on Monday night I felt utterly washed out. Emery's toile was 'all wrong, totally wrong. Oh God, Mel, you've got to start all over again!' She had lost more weight and yet her arms now seemed to be three inches longer, which she put down to Pilates. I put it down to her innate ability to make my life complicated.

On the bright side, my father disappeared after lunch on Sunday, saying he had to get back to London 'for a meeting'. He didn't, however, offer to drive me back, although I was grateful. If he was shaking Granny down for cash for Emery's wedding, I had to be next on his 'debts to call in' list.

Gabi was as good as her word and within a matter of days she had found me a small office in a quiet street near Victoria Station above a very discreet beauty salon that looked more like a solicitors' from the outside. I'll draw a veil over how she negotiated such a cheap rent from the landlord, but suffice to say, it involved her famous Carolyn Harker impression and some sweet-talking from me.

I also had to explain my move to Jonathan, who swallowed my witterings about 'proximity to public transport' and 'period charm' with little or no incredulity. He was an estate agent, though.

'Obviously I should be charging you more rent,'

grumbled Nelson as he grappled with a roller. We were painting the main sitting room – now my office – a soothing shade of lavender that Nelson claimed reminded him of the school san.

'Listen, I thought getting you to do my books would put your mind at rest, not give you more ammunition to hurl at me,' I protested, hurt.

'Oh, the figures add up,' he said. 'I just didn't realise I was harbouring such a devious little businesswoman.'

I'd had to come clean to Nelson about the deposit from Granny. And he'd seen the new leaflets I'd had printed, complete with lists of Homme Improvement packages and a few charmingly worded testimonies from satisfied clients, identified only by discreet initials. Reluctantly, he'd had to agree that it all looked pretty smart.

'Well, make up your mind,' I huffed. 'Either the business is a go-er or it's not.'

Nelson said nothing and eliminated another section of slurry-brown wall. Nelson saying nothing was worse than a lecture.

For once, though, I refused to be cowed. I'd had a very productive day: an easy morning's work helping a charming but taste-free IT whizz-kid friend of Aaron's buy a pair of glasses (which turned into a quick trip around the shops for a matching date outfit for him), followed by an afternoon chatting with my contact at *South West Property Now* magazine. I was writing a feature for them about adding the woman's touch to a bachelor flat and I had my fingers crossed that if I did it well enough, I could pitch for it to be a regular Little Lady advice series.

The day had been rounded off in splendid fashion by an after-work drink with Jonathan and some interior decorators who were competing for the Dean & Daniels' rental refurbishment contract. It had been especially flattering because he'd deferred to my opinion several times during the meeting, claiming that I was a freelance interiors expert. He'd also given me a very friendly squeeze on the way out, which might have been for the benefit of his contacts, but was rather nice all the same.

I paused and reminded myself that I definitely didn't want to start fancying Jonathan just because there were no other men on the scene. Mind you, there was something rather sexy about men who knew what they were talking about. Men who might not be conventionally attractive, but who were obviously highly competent at their jobs. And I was beginning to think that Jonathan's terseness was largely for the sake of office appearance: I noticed he was perfectly courteous to waitresses and always tipped taxi drivers lavishly.

'Stop it,' said Nelson.

'Stop what?' I blushed.

'I know what you're thinking about.'

'No, you don't,' I said, immediately filling my mind with a wall of iMacs and laser printers.

Nelson put down his roller and wiped the lavender paint off his hands. His hair was liberally speckled with it already. 'Oh, yes, I do.'

'Ohhhh, no, you don't,' I said, then regretted it because Nelson didn't look as if he was in a pantomime mood.

'It's behind you?' I tried.

'Stop it,' said Nelson.

'No, really.' I'd just spotted Gabi pulling up outside in Aaron's Audi TT. Aaron's fifteen-hour day in the City meant Gabi drove it more than he did – which suited her fine. 'Gabi. She's just behind you.'

Nelson swore under his breath, looked ashamed, then went into the kitchen to make a pot of tea.

Within moments, Gabi's feet were thundering up the stairs. 'Wow!' she said, bursting through the door. 'Someone's been busy!'

'Someone has been busy,' said Nelson, emerging with a tray of mugs and a packet of chocolate digestives. 'Mainly me, with back-up from Lots Road auction house, Busy Bee Electricians of Parson's Green, Dial-a-Granny Financial Brokers and IKEA of Croydon. Mel has also popped in to offer advice. And now you're here to help test-run the refreshment facilities!'

Gabi stared at him and smiled goofily.

It was not her best look.

'Tea?' I said, perhaps a little too loud.

She nodded, and I sloshed out strong tea for the three of us. You really would have thought the plain white cups and saucers had come from Heals, not IKEA. I hadn't got the furniture from there though – I wanted the office to have a warm, reassuring feel, so we'd scoured Lots Road for old-fashioned heavy furniture: a big desk for me, some squishy red leather armchairs, brass desk lights and the pièce de résistance, floor-to-ceiling bookshelves that Nelson and Woolfe had made for me at the weekend from MDF, then stained to look like solid mahogany.

It was now an office that Mary Poppins *and* Sherlock Holmes would be proud of.

'Nelson has been an absolute star,' I said, giving him a big hug before handing him his tea. 'My gratitude knows no bounds, but he knows that already.'

He grunted, but I spotted a trace of pleasure under his grumpy expression. 'I still say why not put a rocking horse in here and be done with it?'

'What do you mean by that?' demanded Gabi.

'Well . . .' Nelson waved an airy hand around. 'The pretty colours, the Enid Blyton books on the shelves, the comfy chairs . . .'

Gabi looked at him mistily. 'Did you have a nursery, Nelson? Did you have a nanny?'

'Melissa . . .' Nelson appealed to me.

I didn't say anything, because there *had* been a rather lovely old rocking horse in the auction that I'd seriously thought of buying. I'd read somewhere that rocking could be therapeutic too. But I'd keep that to myself for the time being.

'Look, Gabi,' I said, 'do you like the sign?'

I pointed to the newly painted sign, now ready to be hung up on the bracket outside where the London Violin Academy sign had once peeled in the breeze. I'd designed it myself: a silhouette of a woman clad in a full New Look skirt, juggling a tray of cocktails, a ribbon-wrapped present, a stack of papers, a diary and a birthday cake. 'The Little Lady Agency' curled around it in italic script.

'He-e-e-ey,' cooed Gabi, 'I like that! Especially the bomb!'

'It's a birthday present,' said Nelson. 'Though a bomb wouldn't be inappropriate for some of Melissa's clients.'

'Whatever,' she said. 'It's making me want to walk in and spend money. And I don't even need your services!'

'Don't say that yet,' observed Nelson, dunking his biscuit. 'None of us ever knows when we might need Mel at an hourly rate.'

'For you, Nelson darling, it would be free,' I said blithely and helped myself to another biscuit.

'I've got to hand it to you, Melissa,' said Gabi, patting my knee. 'You're a real pro now!'

'Thank you,' I said. 'I *feel* like a real pro!'

She and Nelson sniggered – another of their private jokes, I supposed.

I just smiled and sat there, sipping my tea, looking around my new premises, and felt a warm glow of satisfaction. It might not be completely finished just yet, but the Little Lady Agency was definitely on the way.

12

When Emery phoned up the following week to cancel her dress so 'we could start all over again with more of a medieval feel', I tried really hard to think of three positive things.

After a good deal of effort, I could come up with only two.

One: I wasn't really up for the forty-two thousand beads she wanted embroidered all over the original design, and if she'd actually thought about how heavy that would make it, she wouldn't have been so keen either.

Two: to be honest, I wasn't quite as far along with it as I'd claimed.

In fact, I'd barely even thought about buying the material. The toile – the trial-run version I'd made to get the measurements right – was still on the dummy in the spare room in my office where I'd left it, lending a spooky Miss Haversham feel to the place. I hadn't even got round to unpinning it.

I just didn't seem to have the energy. Since I'd stopped running around town like a mad thing and started sticking to a routine, I was getting twice as much done, but by the time I got home my brain seemed to cut out entirely. It was as much as I could do to help Nelson rustle up some supper, then sink in front of the television with him. I was so bushed one night that I even sat through a whole episode of *Das Boot* without registering it was in German.

Or that Nelson had finally got his way and watched *Das Boot* instead of *Coronation Street*.

'Do you think you're overdoing it?' he'd asked, prodding me occasionally to check I hadn't slipped into a trance state.

I shook my head. It was a blessed relief to be Melissa and not have to come up with some bright and articulate response. It was also nice to give my body a rest from the slinky clothes too: I was slumped in a pair of tracksuit bottoms, an old Pony Club T-shirt and Nelson's slippers, while my work clothes hung behind the door in my bedroom, still neat and curvy, unlike me.

'Mel?'

Not that I resented it. In fact, I surprised myself with how decisive and practical I could be. But I had to keep reminding myself that Honey wasn't really me, and that I needed to keep her out of my house.

Our house.

Thank God I lived with a man who didn't care what I looked like of an evening.

'Mel?'

I could hear Nelson somewhere far off in the distance, but I was too comfy where I was to reply. Then I fell asleep and apparently dribbled onto his shoulder for two hours.

Nelson, being a complete sweetheart, didn't move me.

Still, I firmly believe that if you look for those three positive things, eventually they'll all turn up.

Lovely Madeleine at *South West Property Now* magazine had liked my advice feature so much that the following month she'd asked me to write an etiquette agony column for them. I had to make up my own letters, but since I spent most of my working day explaining what men should wear to weddings, or how to tackle unhygienic flatmates, I didn't need to stretch my imagination too far. I was at my desk on Friday afternoon, finishing off the reply to my final Little Lady letter (how to deal with annoying group email jokes without alienating people you don't even know) when the phone rang.

I was hoping it would be Jonathan. We were meant to be working our way through his Welcome to London theatre tickets, and I was in the mood for something involving dancing, theatrical dialogue and bright lights. He had become rather tedious on the subject of how much better these things played on Broadway, but always remembered to pre-order drinks for the intervals which more than made up for it.

'Hello, is that the, er, Little Lady Agency?'

I could tell at once from the extreme reluctance in the caller's voice that he half wanted me to say no.

'It is,' I said in a friendly, encouraging tone. 'How can I help you?' I reached for my notebook and gazed at the tree outside my window. If Jonathan couldn't make the theatre, I wondered about suggesting the London Eye. As far as I knew he still hadn't used the tickets I'd given him.

'Oh. Um, I read about you in *South West Property Now*.'

'Good!' I replied brightly. Not that anyone would see us on the London Eye, so strictly speaking it wouldn't be a business date. More of a 'getting to know you' sort of date. I wasn't nosey, but there were one or two things that were starting to pique my curiosity.

'I need you to dump my girlfriend for me.'

'Right.' That snapped my mind back into focus.

'I mean, she's not really my girlfriend,' he amended quickly.

Really, I thought wearily. How many times had I heard this? There's a certain breed of young men who would secretly prefer girlfriends to come with a licence, like cars or shotguns, to save confusion.

'Are you sure about that?' I said. It wasn't nice being dumped. Even all these months after the event, I still had hot and cold flushes, thinking about Orlando and how frightfully it had turned out. If I could come up with a kinder way for some other girl, it could only be a good thing.

'I mean,' I added, 'if she's not really your girlfriend, then perhaps you just need to be rather firm and . . .'

There was a faint, frustrated groaning from the other end. 'No, you don't get it. I've *tried* being firm. She just decided we were going out and that was it. I've tried talking to her but she just doesn't want to hear. And now . . .' The voice trailed off disconsolately.

'I see,' I said, tersely. Some men were frustratingly vague about their intentions. I checked my desk diary, which was looking quite full for the following week. 'Why don't you come into the office and we can discuss it? I could see you on Wednesday afternoon?'

'No, no,' he said. 'It's urgent. I need you to help me dump her this afternoon.'

'This afternoon?'

'Yes!' he squeaked. Then he added, 'I'm outside! Can I come in?'

I peered out of the window. There was indeed a nervous chap hopping from one foot to the other on my doorstep. One of the beauty therapists from downstairs was sneaking a cigarette break and staring at him, in the same way a garage mechanic looks at a clapped-out Vauxhall Nova.

Oh, why not, I thought. He's probably the one who needs a stiff talking-to, not his poor deluded girlfriend.

'Come on up,' I said, adjusting my wig and slipping my stilettos back on underneath the desk.

'Are you telling me everything, Bryan?' I asked, giving him a firm look. '*Absolutely* everything?'

Bryan Birkett nodded unhappily. 'I know I should have told her from the start. I mean, it was a nice dinner and everything, and I know it wasn't very gentlemanly to take advantage, but I didn't think we'd end up . . . like this.' His voice, which had been rising hysterically, dropped at the end and he gazed at his feet.

I put the cap back on my fountain pen and pushed the horn-rimmed glasses up the bridge of my nose. There was something else underneath all this, but he wasn't going to admit it. 'And this dinner was what? Eleven months ago? And you've been trying to split up with her since then?'

He nodded again and slurped at his coffee. 'She just refuses to let go. She won't listen to anything I say, just keeps on talking about where we could send the kids to school.'

'Right.' This wasn't so unusual. I knew plenty of married couples who'd been snogging casually at a school reunion dinner one minute then trailing round Peter Jones making a wedding list the next, without any active memory of how they'd gone from one state to the other. Or at least, the groom had no active memory of it.

More to the point, I knew plenty of girls who weren't

above using all their powers of bamboozlement to cling limpet-like to a relationship, particularly with an easy-to-manipulate specimen like the one cringing before me.

It spoke of a certain lack of ambition to me, but who was I to judge?

'Can you help?' he pleaded. 'I mean, can you talk to her?'

I looked at his hopeful little face. To Bryan, the whole sphere of womanhood was clearly a mystery, requiring the intervention of an interpreter: mother, sister, nanny . . . me. I think he liked it that way. He certainly didn't look as if he wanted to tackle the rocky path to enlightenment.

'I prefer action, Bryan,' I said as kindly as I could. 'Sometimes getting straight down to business saves an awful lot of time and effort.'

He gulped his coffee. I shifted in my seat so his gaze wasn't quite so firmly fixed on my chest.

By the time I'd calmed him down, and he'd hoovered up a whole plate of ginger biscuits, it was gone three thirty, so I suggested he give me a lift to West Kensington, and I'd get a cab home from there.

'Do you mind if I bring this with me?' I asked, shoving the bag with Emery's toile into the boot of his car. I knew it basically fitted her, so I could always take it home and repin it around her. In fact, if she thought about how much work was involved, it might trigger a rare guilt trip. Stranger things had happened.

As we drove through London, fragments of new information began to emerge about Bryan and Camilla's complicated relationship. Complicated in that he'd tried to escape more times than Houdini, and she'd thwarted him at every turn. I was beginning to wonder what hidden talents this man must have for Camilla to want to hang on to him quite so tenaciously.

'I don't think I've ever heard of anyone being dumped by FedEx before,' I mused.

'I wanted to be sure she got the bloody letter,' he groaned. 'While I was safely out of the country. I didn't know her flatmate was going to sign for it, then leave it under the Yellow Pages for five months, did I?'

I agreed that absent-minded flatmates could be a terrible curse on a relationship. Fortunately, Nelson practically policed my post, especially red bills.

We pulled up outside his house, and immediately Bryan turned a clammy shade of white.

'Oh, shit, shit, shit, shit, shit. There's her car, parking at the top of the road,' he muttered hysterically.

'OK,' I replied calmly. 'I'll talk to Camilla and you can—'

'I don't mean Camilla,' he whispered, now almost paralysed with fear. 'I mean her *mother*.'

'Bryan!' I snapped, turning to him. 'Now is the time to come clean! What haven't you told me?'

'We're meant to be announcing our engagement,' he gabbled. 'Today, her mother, coming round, Camilla making cakes and everything, talking about wedding planners, I have no idea, *no idea*, shit, shit, shit.'

'Why didn't you tell me that to begin with, for heaven's sake?' I said crossly.

'If I said it aloud it would be *real*!' he wailed.

'Don't panic,' I said, laying a hand on his flailing arm. 'Leave it with me.'

We made it into the house as Camilla's mother finally got her car wedged into a surprisingly small space. From my

vantage point behind the curtains in Bryan's room, I saw
Camilla emerging from the passenger side. I had seen her
type before, at the various horsey events Allegra used to
drag me to: the sort of girl who would cling onto the
reins with her teeth, rather than stop to have her broken
arm set.

'Pooky!' she bellowed as she let herself in. 'We're here!'

Bryan shot me a panicked look.

I ruffled his hair and undid the top six buttons on his
shirt, then did them up again the wrong way.

'What are you . . .' he started.

I put my fingers to my lips to shut him up, undid his
belt, then pressed my mouth against his neck so my pale
pink lipstick smeared a little on his skin.

I was somewhat taken aback when he grabbed me and
tried to kiss me for real; I got a brief insight – I think –
into what might have made him such a catch.

'No!' I hissed, giving him a hard shove.

Bryan looked disappointed.

God, some men, I thought. No sense of occasion.

'Get downstairs, and look confused,' I ordered. 'Offer
to make her some tea.' I was about to add 'act nervous',
but that wasn't really necessary.

As Bryan left, I gave his belt a tug, so he nearly fell
down the stairs trying to do it up.

Originally, I'd simply planned to be the Other
Woman, but if half of what he'd told me about Camilla
was true, then I needed to step things up a bit. It was
drastic, but . . .

I slipped off my pencil skirt and unbuttoned my blouse,
stuffing them in my big handbag. Then, with no small
effort, I wriggled into Emery's toile. Emery was at least
two sizes smaller than me, but the lace-up feature of her

dress allowed me to wedge most of my ample bosom in, if I held my breath. I couldn't do it up, which meant that my bra was very much in evidence.

I examined myself in the mirror. At least I'd got my glamorous new balconet bra on. Black wasn't the ideal choice for bridal underwear, but the stocking tops showing through the skirt did give me a usefully vampish look. I adjusted my wig so it looked ruffled, but not too wig-like, then walked downstairs very carefully.

The whinneys of rage and complaint emanating from the sitting room made me feel even more sorry for Bryan than before. I was beginning to see why he might prefer to live in his own fantasy world than deal with real life.

'What sort of tart wears cheap lipgloss like that?' Camilla was honking. 'You're covered in it! You pig! By rights I should walk out of this door right now and leave you to her!'

There was a hopeful pause from Bryan, then she yelled, 'Not on your life, Bryan! I'm not leaving here until you're jolly sorry you ever looked at another woman! Sit down! Where do you think you're going? Mummy! Sit down too!'

I left my bag by the door for ease of get-away, then shimmied into the room.

Camilla and her mother turned and stared at me, their mouths temporarily frozen.

I pretended not to see them. 'Bryan, darling, I know it's terribly bad luck, but I thought you'd want to see the sort of thing I was . . . Oh, hello! Are you the wedding planners?' I asked.

'No!' gasped Camilla's mother. 'No, we're . . .'

'Oops,' I said, covering my exposed bosom with a hand. I'd remembered to swap my signet ring onto my engagement finger on the way downstairs and I made sure Camilla got a good look at it. 'Sorry about this. We're planning a renewal of vows ceremony, and I wanted to have the dress I never had first time round.'

'The dress you never had,' repeated Camilla, stunned.

'Mmm,' I nodded. 'Bry and I were married on the beach in Thailand, weren't we, darling, and I always said that after I'd got rid of the baby weight, and Bryan had got over his illness, we'd have the wedding of our dreams. It's been hard, what with me being posted abroad for so long, but now I'm home and everything's in full swing! It's been wonderful, hasn't it, darling? We've been courting all over again!' I gave him a hug for emphasis.

He hugged me back, weakly.

'You're very quiet, big man,' I said, huskily. 'Cat got your tongue?'

'Cat'll get more than his tongue!' roared Camilla, suddenly springing to life.

I was relieved to see her mother sink onto Bryan's sofa with a deep sigh of confusion. She had the look of a woman who'd played a lot of lacrosse in her youth and I didn't fancy my chances if she got pushy.

'Oh, he's not . . .' I turned to Bryan sternly. 'You haven't been up to your old tricks, have you? I can see you have. You naughty boy.' I wagged my finger at him, indulgently. 'He hasn't asked you to marry him, has he? Oh, *Bryan.*'

'*Yes, he has!*' Camilla's eyes were furious, rather than tear-filled, I noticed. 'How the hell are you so calm about it?'

I smiled the smile of the MP's patient wife and put on a patronising expression of forgiveness. 'Married life is all about working through problems, don't you think?

Don't feel bad, darling, you're not the first to be taken in by that boyish vulnerability. Bad, Bryan!'

Camilla spluttered something unintelligible, but the wind left her sails as quickly as it had arrived and she looked as if she was about to burst into tears of frustration.

'Can I get you a cup of sweet tea, Mrs, er—' I began, turning politely to her mother, who averted her eyes at the sight of my exposed bosom. 'This must have come as quite a shock.'

I was surprised to find I was almost enjoying myself. It was quite a novelty to be the one causing the disruption, rather than having to sort it all out.

Fortunately, her mother suddenly came to life. 'Camilla, I think we should leave! While we all still have some dignity.'

She gave me a very pointed look as she said that.

'I'm so sorry,' I said, offering a hand to shake. 'Bryan, say something.'

'Sorry,' mumbled Bryan, looking shell-shocked.

Camilla swept past him without saying a word. As they left, I distinctly heard her mother whisper, 'Not *again*, Cammy! This must stop!'

'Bye-bye!' I shouted after them. My heart was pounding so hard I was sure it must be visible through my chest.

'Where did all that come from?' demanded Bryan in an undertone. 'You didn't say you were going to do anything like that.' He'd appeared behind me, peering over my shoulder to check, I think, that Camilla had really gone.

'It just . . . comes,' I whispered back.

'You were magnificent,' he whispered. 'Really . . . amazing.'

'She's gone, Bryan,' I whispered. 'I think we can stop whispering.'

We both stood there, breathing hard, watching the Volvo estate disappear round the corner.

Then I became aware of how close Bryan was standing to me and took a definite step sideways.

'You were amazing,' he said again, this time more suavely. 'Can I take you out for a drink?'

'Bryan, I think you would benefit from some time on your own, don't you?' I said sternly. 'Now, I need to get out of this dress. *On my own.*'

I virtually had to push him to one side to get to the stairs.

As with most situations in my life, Emery's dress was much harder to get out of than it had been to get into. The annoying thing about mentally transforming myself into Honey was that, like Superman, the effect wore off after a while, and I'd have hoped to have been free of Bryan's house and well on the way home by this stage. As it was, I had one arm out of the bodice and was seriously considering biting the remaining stitches with my teeth to free myself when my mobile rang.

'Hello?' I said, trying hard to sound professional despite being practically nude on top and clad in my sister's wedding dress below.

'It's Jonathan. Where are you?'

'I'm actually in a meeting,' I said. 'I shouldn't have answered my phone.'

'Oh, sorry,' said Jonathan, not sounding particularly sorry. 'But it's kind of urgent. I need your company for a very, very important meeting. Tonight. Can you make it – it's drinks after work?'

With some effort, I looked at my watch. Half past four

already. Nelson had muttered something about wild trout for supper, there was a whole raft of soap operas on and it was my night for the hot water.

'Please?' said Jonathan, with some effort.

'Oh, go on,' I said, unable to resist.

13

Jonathan was standing by the door of the Oxo Tower, looking at his watch as if it were one of those *Mission Impossible* watches that would issue him with instructions. His face was even more guarded than normal, but as I approached he gave me a quick nod, and a smile that didn't quite reach his eyes. I noticed his pale skin looked stressed with the bright sunlight that had started to warm up the London air.

'Hello,' I said cheerily. 'You look smart. New suit?'

He just grunted, which was unusual, because normally Jonathan was well-mannered enough to trade compliment for compliment, a trait I had come to appreciate very much.

'What took you so long?' he demanded, raking a hand through his hair, which gleamed luxuriantly in the sun. 'I thought you said you'd be half an hour. And what the hell's that?'

He gestured to the bag with Emery's toile in it. I'd stuffed it into a smaller bag for portability, but tell-tale puffs of material were escaping.

I took a deep breath and counted to ten, so as not to be rude. But I wasn't going to let him order me around the way he ordered people round at Dean & Daniels. It wasn't that kind of arrangement.

'Jonathan,' I said, 'might I remind you that you called

at very short notice, while I was dealing with another client? I came as quickly as I could. Regrettably, I have some baggage.'

Jonathan snorted. 'Don't we all?'

'I'm going to go to the ladies' over there, freshen up and come back. And we'll start again, shall we?' I gave him a dark look. 'Jonathan?'

This was the first time I'd had the nerve to return his own professional brusqueness – or rather, the first time I'd been too cross to censor myself or feel intimidated by his manner.

For a brief moment, Jonathan looked as though he were about to yell at me. His eyes glinted and a muscle on his jaw twitched. He was obviously in a much worse mood than I was. But I refused to lower my glare, and after a second or two, he had the grace to look shame-faced.

'OK,' he said, letting out his pent-up breath. He rubbed his chin ruefully, where tiny prickles of ginger stubble were beginning to show. 'Pardon me.'

'Thank you. I'll be two minutes.' I walked to the ladies' as carefully as I could. My suspenders had gone slack and I could feel the thin layer of London grubbiness on my skin. So far, the choice bits of my own wardrobe had been fine for a tepid early summer, but I had a feeling some re-investment would be needed to keep Honey looking elegant and cool during summer.

Safely inside the ladies', I splashed my wrists with cold water, readjusted my stockings, shook out my wig and replaced it, and spritzed myself (and the inside of my high heels) with cologne. Then I blotted my shiny nose, reapplied my lipstick, checked my teeth for debris, took a deep breath and walked back out, a new woman.

Jonathan had an apology ready at once.

'Listen, I'm sorry,' he said, blinking rapidly. 'I was out of line there. I should have filled you in – these people we're meeting, they're old friends of mine and Cindy's. They're in London for a few days, and called me this morning to see if I was around for a drink. I meant to call you earlier, but I've been out at viewings all morning, and, well . . .' His voice trailed off and he shrugged. He was trying to be cool about it, but I could see the tension in his face, deepening the lines around his eyes and nose. I could see he was terribly on edge. It was unlike him to be rude; brisk, yes, and sometimes a bit distant, but I knew he was a very courteous man.

'To be honest? I didn't want to see them, but I felt ambushed,' he explained awkwardly.

'I understand,' I said. 'There's no need to apologise.' I patted his arm. 'Do you want to freshen up too before we take the lift?' I dug around in my bag and offered him my Rescue Remedy spray.

Jonathan smiled. Wearily. 'Does it work?'

'Works for me. One quick squirt on the tongue. Two for driving tests and "We're going to have to let you go" interviews.'

Jonathan gave himself three short squirts, then squeezed his eyes shut. 'Thanks,' he croaked.

'OK!' I said, a little surprised by this glimpse of vulner-ability but determined not to let him see. 'Tally ho!'

As we soared up in the lift, he rattled off a briefing about his friends: 'Kurt and Bonnie Hegel. He's a lawyer, she's a life coach. She knew Cindy from college, they lived near us in New York. Nice enough, but they always took Cindy's side, you know? Both crazy about England – Bonnie reckons she can trace her ancestry back to the

Mayflower. I very much doubt that, but humour her OK?'

'Right!' I said. 'Do they know anything about me?'

'No.'

'And do they still talk to Cindy?'

'All the time.'

'I see,' I said, and glanced at Jonathan. I'd have loved to ask more about Cindy, but this wasn't the time. His jaw was set, and now a little muscle was twitching in his forehead. He probably thought he was hiding his nerves well but I had had plenty of practice at seeing through tough fronts.

I wanted to say, 'Don't worry,' but I've always thought that's an annoyingly pointless thing to say when there's clearly lots to worry about. Friends of exes were just the worst. Instead I focused on being as glamorous as I could possibly manage, if only to prove to them that Jonathan didn't need their sympathy.

We walked across the crowded bar and Jonathan enquired about the table we'd reserved at the balcony. It seemed the Hegels had beaten us to it. I tried to step back a little so Jonathan could lead the way over there, but he shoved me, none too subtly, in the back, and I was forced to shimmy round the tables, deranged smile fixed on my face all the while.

The Hegels rose, but didn't remove their shades.

'Hel-*lo*!' I said when we finally reach them, leaning over the table and offering my hand to shake.

'Hey, *you*!' said Bonnie Hegel in a very life-coaching manner. I 'took agin her', as my granny would say, immediately, and not just because of her Gucci shades.

To my surprise, both she and her husband embraced me warmly, then embraced Jonathan.

I don't like being hugged by people I don't know, and to be honest, once Bonnie and Kurt had finished with me I felt as if I'd just been inducted into some kind of cult.

'Honey, may I introduce Bonnie and Kurt Hegel?' said Jonathan in a very formal voice, emerging from Bonnie's bird-like grasp. 'Kurt, Bonnie, this is Honey Blennerhesket.'

I couldn't very well shake hands after being pressed so intimately and recently against Bonnie's skinny chest, so I was reduced to raising my hand in a weak salute towards both of them.

How annoying to be out-foxed so early on, I thought crossly. I put a hand in my bag to retrieve my own sunglasses, hesitated, since it *was* rude, then got them out anyway, and pointedly put them on my head.

'Let's get some champagne!' cried Kurt, waving at the waiter. 'It's a champagne moment!'

'Is it?' said Jonathan.

'Oh, it is, Jonathan,' replied Bonnie, covering Jonathan's hand with hers. 'It's so good to see you, and looking so . . . centred.'

I wondered what sort of state he'd been in when they last saw him. I, of all people, could imagine how horrible his marriage break-up must have been, but even so it was impossible to imagine poker-faced Jonathan crying himself to sleep over a bottle of Baileys and wearing the same pyjamas for four days. Besides which, surely it was rather ghastly to refer to his recent traumas in front of his new girlfriend?

'And great to see you in such vivacious company!' she added, with a distinctly ambiguous glance at me. 'You're moving on at last!'

I wasn't at all sure how I was meant to respond to that. Or, indeed, how Jonathan was meant to.

Jonathan, however, stepped in straight away. 'Well, thank you. And she's come straight from work, haven't you, Honey?' His voice was very crisp and if I was meant to glean clues from his expression, then there wasn't a lot to go on.

'Yes, you'll have to excuse me,' I said. 'I'm a bit *distrait.*'

I felt I had to add this since Bonnie was a vision in creaseless greige linen. How had she done that, I wondered crossly. I only had to *look* at a linen skirt to turn it into an unflattering concertina.

'No, no. I adore that . . . eclectic London style you have going on,' said Bonnie. 'It's extraordinary what you English girls can carry off.'

I straightened my spine and pulled in my stomach; the button on my fitted jacket was already under severe strain. 'Thank you!' I said. 'It's vintage.'

'Fabulous,' said Bonnie. 'Well done.'

Jonathan coughed nervously. 'Kurt? Here's the waiter, what'll you have?'

'A bottle of champagne, please,' Kurt instructed the waiter, keeping his eyes on me as he said it. 'I think we should celebrate this glorious summer day, and all that goes with it!'

I smiled and wondered whether they'd been sent here specifically by Cindy. Then I wondered what sort of report Jonathan wanted them to go back with. Was I meant to be cute, or professional, or sexy, or what? Really, I did wish he'd give me some sort of written agenda before these meetings.

'So, are you here on holiday?' I asked.

'Well, yes, I guess we are, although we don't consider

London to be a foreign country any more. We are head over heels in love with the UK,' confided Bonnie. 'We're thinking of buying a flat here. I mean, it would make sense, financially. And we prefer to get local flavour, instead of camping out in hotels all the time. They get so dull.'

'How nice,' I said politely. 'Jonathan's your man for that, aren't you, darling? Do you have Kurt and Bonnie on your books?'

'I do indeed,' said Jonathan.

'We're thinking about the Notting Hill area,' confided Bonnie as the champagne arrived. 'We're cool about getting something compact, but really nothing smaller than two bedrooms, because it's just like living in a box, you know? I mean, I need somewhere for my yoga practice, we both need an office, and Kurt simply cannot live without a *small* garden at least . . .'

Now I was really struggling not to take agin them.

'Jonathan's been handling some wonderful properties,' I said. 'But he's nabbed the nicest house for himself, haven't you?'

'Yes, I think I have,' said Jonathan, at the same moment that Bonnie put her hand on her upper chest and said, 'Oh, Jonathan, is it as nice as that amazing summer house you and Cindy had in Massachusetts? Oh, we had some fun times there! Do you remember? When Cindy set the garden alight on Hallowe'en, with the paper pumpkins, and you had to stamp them all out?'

She and Kurt hooted with laughter.

I noticed that Jonathan managed a small tight smile, but his eyes weren't laughing.

'Mind you,' Kurt said, pointing at Jonathan, jokily, 'mind you, she did that on the balcony of your New York apartment as well, didn't she?'

'Oh my God!' Bonnie was gulping with laughter. 'She did too! Those firemen! Were they pissed!'

Jonathan's smile evaporated altogether.

'Cindy sounds quite the pyromaniac!' I observed brightly. 'You didn't mention that, Jonathan.'

Kurt stopped laughing abruptly and gave Bonnie a noticeable nudge under the table.

'What? Oh, sorry.' She put her hand over her mouth. 'Sorry! Sorry, Jonathan. I just keep . . .'

Kurt turned to me and said, 'We have so many happy memories of Cindy and Jonathan. We're extremely fond of the both of them.' He spoke very solemnly, as if he were narrating a documentary about their divorce. 'Their separation doesn't change that.'

'I'm sure you have some wonderful memories,' I said warmly. 'Now then, Bonnie, how *do* you manage to look so fresh in this heat? Tell me your secret, *please* . . .'

The conversation rambled on, taking lengthy detours along Kurt's ascent to partnership and Bonnie's revolutionary visualisation techniques, but noticeably avoiding the thorny area of the divorce. Every time we approached it, I sensed Jonathan stiffen with tension, Kurt and Bonnie exchanged guilty looks and the conversation was swung away into safer waters of London house prices and the like. But like an iceberg, it was always there. Bonnie and Kurt just pretended not to notice it.

Jonathan was doing pretty well, making chatty conversation, but I could sense a strain about him that only increased the more he drank. And he was drinking faster than I'd ever seen him.

Eventually, I decided there was no point encouraging them. They might have thought they were being kind by not discussing Jonathan's troubles, but swerving round the topic the whole time just made it a million times more obvious. It wasn't really any of my business but I was damned if I was going to let them sit there tormenting him with politeness, then go home and report that he didn't give a toss.

'So, Bonnie, how is everything going with Cindy's pregnancy?' I asked.

Jonathan made a faint choking sound.

Bonnie looked aghast. Really, I expected a life coach to have a bit more go about her.

I raised my eyebrows enquiringly. 'Jonathan explained that Cindy is expecting a baby. And it can't be very easy for her, having to deal with such a major uprooting as well. I hope she's not having too tough a time of it?'

There was a brief moment of horror, then Kurt said, 'Yes. Yes, I think she's, um, being looked after OK.'

'That's good news,' I said, and put my hand over Jonathan's, partly to stop him breaking the cocktail stick he was fiddling with. By now I didn't care what sort of tongue-lashing I might get afterwards from him; if I was there as his pretend girlfriend, I intended to defend him exactly as I would if I were his real one. 'Do excuse my directness, but I really don't see the point in beating about the bush when it comes to family. It's so important to be open, if you want to make a fresh start. I mean, our past is very much to do with who we are in the present. Isn't that right?' I directed that at Bonnie.

She nodded rapidly.

'Jonathan's very lucky to have found such an understanding woman,' intoned Kurt, still in his documentary tone.

'Well, I'm not saying I understand how Cindy could have let such a wonderful man go!' I replied. 'But I hope

I'd never wish bad things on her when her . . . her *decision*'s brought Jonathan my way? I really do hope she has an easy pregnancy. I'm sure she has quite enough on her plate already.'

I put a hand over my glass as the waiter topped up our champagne, and changed the subject swiftly. 'But, Kurt, you were telling me about those wonderful shoes of yours. Did you say you had them hand-made? I've been looking for something similar for my father . . .'

Kurt grabbed this opportunity and sprinted with it, reeling off a whole list of ridiculously expensive shoe-makers, some of which I mentally noted for future reference.

Jonathan's hand twitched underneath mine, and I squeezed it back. I shot a quick look at him while Kurt was flicking through his personal organiser in search of a phone number, and he managed a brief, wry smile in return. It wasn't much, just a quick shrug of the lips, but for a second it broke the tension on his taut face, and it was real.

Poor Jonathan. He needed someone in his corner, no matter how tough he thought he was. I smiled back, reassuringly.

'Ah, cute,' said Bonnie. 'More champagne, Jonathan?'

Half an hour later, Jonathan sliced through Kurt's epic account of Great Fish We Have Known by saying, 'Listen, Kurt, I hate to cut the party short, but Honey and I really have to shoot. She's given me timed tickets for the London Eye and it'll take us a few minutes to get down there.'

Quick learner, I thought, approvingly. I caught his eye, but his expression was very straight.

For a hideous moment, I thought they were going to

decide to join us, but they seemed to have seen enough. I felt rather sorry for them, to be honest – being friends with both halves of a separated couple is such a nightmare.

'Goodbye, Honey,' said Bonnie, embracing me again. 'I've got to be straight with you, I came here hoping to hate your guts, but you know, I can't. I hope you'll make Jonathan very happy. He deserves it.'

'Er, thank you,' I said. 'I think so too.'

Bonnie carried on gazing at me with a thoughtful expression that I knew – from Emery – could lead only to a woundingly personal comment. Kurt and Jonathan were deep in some manly discussion about the shocking cost of 'gas' in London, so there was no chance of rescue there.

'You know, maybe it's a good thing that Jonathan's making all these radical changes to his life,' she began. 'Not just London, of course.'

'Really?' I said. 'What sort of changes?'

'You, for a start.' Bonnie nodded. 'You're absolutely so not his type? Which in this instance is maybe a healing thing?'

'And what is Jonathan's type?' I enquired, so overcome by curiosity that I nearly missed the barb.

'Oh, you know . . .' She made vague gestures. 'Dark, intense, intellectual rather than showy . . .'

'I don't think I have a type, Bonnie,' said a warning voice over my shoulder. 'I don't think one girlfriend in sixteen years can really count as a whole *type*.'

Bonnie had the grace to flush. 'Oh, Jonathan, you know what I mean.'

Jonathan put his arm round me. 'Honey is very much *my type*,' he said. 'She's never set fire to anything in my presence and she listens to conversations instead of treating me like a dry run for the high-school debating society.'

'Goodbye, Honey.' Before Bonnie could respond, Kurt clasped me in a bearhug. 'Hope to see you again soon. I do. I mean that.'

Jonathan was clasped twice, and then we left, holding hands. It felt very natural, and he didn't drop it once we were out of sight. I supposed it was his way of saying thank you, without actually having to say anything. And I was rather touched.

'Where are we going?' I asked, eventually. I wasn't sure what sort of mood Jonathan was in now. He'd gone quiet, but it felt more intimate than if he'd been making small-talk about the weather.

'The London Eye, of course,' he said, dropping my hand to check his watch. 'Where did you think we were going? You want to go someplace else?'

'No, no, that's fine.'

Secretly, though, I was quite pleased, both for the silence and for the excursion. Seeing Jonathan's discomfort at the memory of Cindy's betrayal had stirred up lingering memories of Orlando, and how I'd felt when I discovered how he'd betrayed me. I didn't want to go home with those unpleasant feelings still churning about, since virtually any innocuous household item could, with some prompting, remind me of him. Photos, coffee mugs, hair brushes . . .

The queue for the Eye was short, and Jonathan surprised me by having his tickets ready in his wallet. I wondered if he'd been carrying them round since I'd given them to him, or if he'd remembered them specially.

I opened my mouth to ask him, in a jokey way, and something in his face stopped me. I knew well enough by now that Jonathan's moods were unpredictable: he seemed to swing between charming estate agent flirting when we were together in public (and sometimes in the cab home too, if the evening had gone well), which I knew didn't mean much, and, when we were alone, deep silences, which no amount of prodding could dispel. If he'd been my real boyfriend he'd have been very hard work indeed, but I'd had enough practice with impenetrable bosses to know when to leave well alone. I did sometimes wonder if the silences were his way of reminding me that the flirting bits weren't real.

We stood in line behind a crowd of giggling French schoolkids brandishing London Aquarium bags and enormous rucksacks. My head and my feet both started to ache at the same time.

'Thanks for the tip,' he said gruffly.

'Sorry?'

He waved the tickets. 'Your cover-all excuse.'

'Oh, that. Happy to help.'

Then, courtesy fulfilled, he lapsed back into a brooding silence.

I sighed soundlessly. The prospect of Nelson's cooking and a gin and tonic had rarely seemed so attractive.

In the end, we only had to wait a few minutes, and when we got to the front the attendant winked at me, and gave us our own capsule.

Slowly, we rose into the evening sky, and beneath us the first few lights shone brightly out of the dulling background. I was always surprised and delighted by aerial views of London streets; on ground level it all seemed so solid and regimented, but from high up, you could see curves and whorls and swirls, spreading across the city like fingerprints.

I recalled miserably that I'd planned to take Orlando on the London Eye for an anniversary treat. We'd never got round to it.

I wished I hadn't drunk. One glass of champagne is never enough for me – it's either none at all, or the whole bottle. One glass makes me tediously melancholy. Two make me a party animal, and a whole bottle . . . Well, *apparently*, it's highly entertaining.

Jonathan, too, seemed lost in thought, and I didn't like to disturb him. His eyes were far away, and he clenched the metal viewing bar until his knuckles were white.

Silence in any relationship is an undervalued gift, I told myself. Business or personal. It demonstrates trust.

'Thank you,' he said eventually, when we were halfway up.

'What for?' I said. 'Look, there're the Houses of Parliament. Can you see?'

'Yeah. No, thank you for this afternoon. For coming out at short notice. For being so nice to Bonnie when she was being a bitch.' He paused and bit his lip, turning his tough face into something approaching boyishness. 'Thanks for dealing with . . . the whole Cindy issue. That was above and beyond. I apologise if it was embarrassing for you.'

'Not at all. I know they're your friends, but I didn't like their attitude,' I said, watching three red buses cross Waterloo Bridge in a line. Three shiny ladybirds. 'They wanted to know how you felt without helping you deal with it. Of *course* you want to know how Cindy is. You just don't want to have to ask. Mind you, to be fair, they probably didn't want to have to tell you.'

'I guess that's about the size of it,' sighed Jonathan. He took off his jacket and sank his forearms onto the viewing bar. His shirt-sleeves rode up and I could see the fine golden hairs glinting in the light. Without his jacket, he suddenly looked like any other young man, not some scary managing director with an efficiency fixation.

He stared out at London. 'To be honest, the weirdest thing is that I don't actually *care* how Cindy is. She's kind of faded away. I can remember exactly what she was like when we first met, what we did, what perfume she used to wear, but if you asked me what she thought about, I don't know, *the death penalty* now, I couldn't tell you. Sixteen years.' He put his head on his arms, then looked out bleakly towards the City. 'How come people change like that? How do they turn into someone you don't even know? And you think you're watching them all the time.'

'I know exactly,' I said quietly, wanting to match his frankness. 'You feel such a fool. It's bad enough that they've hurt you, but to make you feel so *stupid* for letting them . . . That's the worst thing. You blame yourself for not noticing.'

We were temporarily silenced, taken aback a little by each other's honesty. I wondered if I'd gone too far, then Jonathan plunged on. 'I mean, I can deal with the breaking up, but I hate having to write off all the years we had together. They just don't mean anything to me any more, because she obviously wasn't who I thought she was. I can't look back at those times now without thinking, Jeez, how could you be so dumb?'

I thought about the number of miserable nights I'd insisted to Nelson that Orlando was on holiday, or away on business, or concentrating on some project. And all the times Nelson had yelled at me to stop being so wilfully stupid.

'I don't think being smart or dumb comes into it, unfortunately,' I said, swallowing a sudden lump in my throat. 'I hope not, anyway.'

'No, I think it does. Either she changed, or I was too dumb to see something that was there all along.' Jonathan sighed. I wondered how much he'd drunk, to be telling me all this. 'I'm not a complicated guy. I like to know exactly where I am with people. I like them to be who they say they are.'

I raised an eyebrow. 'Well, apart from me.'

'What?'

'I'm not exactly who I say I am, am I? I'm not even who you're telling people I am.'

It occurred to me that these days *I* wasn't even sure who I was from one moment to the next. Even the wig wasn't always a fail-safe guide. Right now I was showing Jonathan the real me – he thought he was with feisty Honey, and had no idea that actually he was talking to Melissa Romney-Jones, Pony Club frump and fulltime sucker.

I ignored the alarm bells going off in my head. OK, so it went against all my rules, but it had felt more honest, and quite natural, to share a little of my own misery, when Jonathan was being so open about his.

God, it was complicated. Complicated, but actually quite exhilarating. In a weird way, I felt I could be more honest with Jonathan than with anyone else, *because* he didn't know me. How could he judge me when he had no idea who I was?

I sank my own arms onto the viewing bar.

'You might be right,' said Jonathan, 'but I feel I know

exactly where I am when I'm with you. You don't know what a relief that is some days. Being able to switch off and be myself. Not have to get results, or prove a point. I can just have some fun without feeling guilty or feeling I need to justify myself in any way.'

I looked sideways at him. This was the first real conversation we'd had, even though we'd been 'together' for some weeks now. There was an intimacy about being so honest that I actually found quite, well, attractive.

Much more attractive than his estate agent hot and cold running charm.

'*Do* you have fun?' I asked. He had a funny way of showing it if he did.

He smiled to himself, directing it out towards the river bank. 'Yes, I do.' He paused, then added, a little tentatively, 'Do you?'

'I do, yes,' I replied, honestly. For much the same reason, I added in my head: I have nothing to live up to, except my own rules. 'You don't strike me as being someone who switches off very often.'

Jonathan tore his gaze away from the skyline. 'What do you mean?' he said, sounding surprised.

'Well' – I wondered how to put it without being rude – 'you're quite self-contained, aren't you? Conscious of how you appear to other people. If you didn't worry so much about it, you wouldn't get so stressed. Really,' I said, touching him on the arm, 'you're doing fine.'

'You think?' Jonathan seemed to consider this. 'I guess I'm quite shy. Maybe it comes across badly. I just don't have your confidence in social settings. Business, now that's different. I know what I'm talking about there. And I've got notes, figures, background . . . But I couldn't just go in and meet people the way you charmed the pants off Bonnie and Kurt. Maybe I need to take lessons from you in that.'

I laughed out loud. Me, confident! What a difference a wig made.

'What?' demanded Jonathan.

'Oh, nothing,' I said. 'You could say I'm much better at business meetings too.'

We were at the top of the giant Ferris wheel now, looking down on the whole of London, curling and spreading out from the banks of the grey river.

'Look,' I said, overcome with pride for the glittering, surging city, 'see Battersea power station there? The building that looks like a table upside down with the white legs?' I pointed. 'Well, if you follow the line of sight along there . . .' I moved my finger towards Pimlico. 'That's my house!'

'Wow,' said Jonathan. 'Great location.'

I realised I'd just broken *another* of my rules, by telling him where I lived. Still, I rationalised, it wasn't like he could actually tell where it was. Even a red-hot estate agent like Jonathan couldn't narrow down a postcode from pointing at a distance of two miles.

As we descended, Jonathan slipped back into his own thoughts, and though we weren't speaking, a sort of companionable silence enveloped us as we both contemplated the steaming wreckage of our love lives.

I wondered if Cindy had been the life and soul of the party, leaving Jonathan trapped in the kitchen with the IT geek, the way I always seemed to get trapped while Orlando showed off elsewhere, resigned to being the last ones to leave, resigned to smiling politely, just out of Cindy's limelight.

There was so much I itched to ask him. What had

brought them together? How long had she played both men off? I wondered how she'd told him about her affair, how his parents were dealing with their sons' soap-opera problem, how he felt leaving every photograph album behind.

Poor Jonathan, I thought, looking at his lips tighten in deep thought. No wonder he was so detached, and so determined to plunge himself into his work. I wondered what he would look like laughing on a picnic, or dancing in a club. I tried hard but couldn't picture either. Even when I'd seen him 'off duty' at his own party he'd seemed on edge. At work.

Maybe the kindest thing I could do would be not to ask a thing, and leave our appointments a little oasis for him.

The pod finally approached the disembarkation platform and we did the little running-to-get-off thing in perfect unison, like a pair of tap-dancers, which raised a smile from Jonathan, at least.

'Very Fred and Ginger,' he said, taking my arm to help me off.

'I'm more of a Gene Kelly girl myself,' I replied archly.

Jonathan pulled a face. 'Oh, I know your sort. Don't tell me, you like a man to be a man even when he's doing pirouettes?'

'*Especially* when he's doing pirouettes.'

We walked over to the coffee stand, and Jonathan bought us both an espresso, then I went over to pick up Emery's dress from the Left Luggage counter.

'I've been meaning to ask you,' Jonathan said when I collected my bag. 'What *is* that in there?'

'My sister's wedding dress,' I said without thinking.

He flashed me his dry grin. His serious mood had

vanished like dew in the morning, and he was back to the professional charm. It was a relief in one way, and a slight disappointment in another. 'Now that is one complicated story, huh?'

'Oh, I don't know,' I said. 'After I stopped my sister's wedding because I was in love with her fiancé, my therapist made me carry it around to remind me that getting married is just another avenue for shopping, but without the potential for sale or return.'

Jonathan stopped walking and looked at me seriously.

'Really?' he said. 'You should have mentioned that to Bonnie. She's really into these alternative therapy techniques. Is it working for you?'

Good God, was there nothing this man wouldn't believe?

'For heaven's sake, Jonathan! Of course it's not!' I laughed, and walked on. 'I don't need to carry a dress around to know that getting married is a massive waste of time and energy. Although, if you ask me, trussing the bride up in a long frock she can't walk in, in a colour that makes her look two sizes bigger than normal, and then haranguing her about how much it costs is a pretty good metaphor for married life.'

I was about to add that my private life was out of bounds, but realised it was a bit late for that. Still, I reminded myself, no more information.

'You're not keen on getting hitched yourself then?' he asked, deadpan.

'No, I am not.'

'Really?'

'*Really.*'

'So, the dress . . . ?'

'My sister's,' I repeated. OK, but absolutely no more.

'You're carrying your sister's wedding gown around town in a Marks & Spencer's carrier bag?' he spluttered. 'Is that some kind of bizarre British tradition or something? Doesn't she *mind*?'

'Not at all,' I said, losing patience. 'My sister's getting married, I'm making her dress. This is her toile – the trial-run dress before I cut into real fabric – which she now wants altered completely.'

Too late. I'd missed Jonathan's trap completely and walked straight into it.

'You have a sister!' He did his pointing thing and I was in too kind a mood with him to pull him up on it. Then his face went dark. 'I think Bonnie saw it. It'll be all round Manhattan.'

'Good,' I said. 'Let it be all round Manhattan. I can email her, if you want, and explain about my therapist?'

'That would be great,' he said, checking his watch. 'Listen, I should go. I've got a stack of emails waiting for me back at the office. Can I put you in a taxi home?'

'That would be nice.' I could see a black cab at the end of the street. Miraculously, it had an orange light on and I waved at it. 'How are you going to get back?'

'I could do with the walk.' Jonathan looked at his feet, then looked at me, a serious expression in his eyes. 'Listen, what I'd really like to do is take you out for dinner. To say thank you for this afternoon.'

'You don't need to do that,' I said, embarrassed.

'No, really,' he insisted. 'I'd been dreading seeing Kurt and Bonnie again. I thought it would be a trial. Instead I feel kinda . . . good.' He grimaced and amended himself, 'Good in a way. And that's because of you.' He touched my arm. 'I shouldn't have dumped all that on you, up there on the wheel. It was out of line. But thank you for listening, all the same. You're a very good listener. I appreciate it.'

My stomach fluttered with butterflies. Jonathan looked so sweet and serious and far away from his scary persona that it was hard not to want to slide my arms around his neck and give him a big comforting hug. He'd loosened his tie, undoing the top button of his shirt, and suddenly I wished the taxi was another mile away. Three or four sentences away, at least.

But, I reminded myself sternly, that's not what he's paying you for! And how wrong would it be to start flirting with a man still aching so obviously? There was a reason he was hiring me after all: I was the protective screen over that broken heart!

No, I thought. I had to remain professional, uninvolved, completely Honey, the companion he was hiring for her wit and detachment. The moment I started blurring the lines between Melissa and Honey, it would all be over, in a variety of awkward ways.

Anyway, he was far too grown-up for me.

'Well, it's all part of the service!' I said. 'I had a lovely time. I'm just pleased it wasn't raining. Although that would have been a more representative view of London.'

Jonathan grinned. 'I've been here long enough to know that. So listen, we'll put that dinner in the diary some time?' he said. 'I so wish it could be tonight but . . .' He shrugged.

'Oh, absolutely,' I agreed. 'Just as soon as you clear that stack of emails, eh?'

The taxi pulled up next to me. For a moment Jonathan looked as if he was about to wave it away, but then he opened the door and turned back to me. 'So, are you going to tell the cabbie where to go?' His expression was neutral, but this time I spotted the tease. If he wanted to dig up information about the real me, he was going to have to try a lot harder than that.

'Trafalgar Square, please,' I said to the driver.

Jonathan laughed, took out his wallet, and gave the man a twenty-pound note.

'I'll call you,' he said, closing the door and making a phone gesture to his ear.

For five self-indulgent minutes, crawling through the evening traffic, I let myself pretend he was talking about a real date, not an appointment for a pretend one. Then I wound my imagination back in, and directed the driver to Nelson's house.

14

As May turned into June, then July, and the hospitality season gathered pace, I maintained my steady stream of bookings, and bought a large desk fan for the office and a sexy summer wardrobe for Honey. Usually I hated buying clothes, but I had no qualms whatsoever about splashing out on pretty tea-dresses and ribboned cardigans; I felt so much more confident when I was in her push-up bras and hold-ups that somehow everything just seemed to work better.

Nelson resumed his seasonal whingeing about the blight of corporate hospitality ruining sport (he used to camp out in a sleeping bag before Wimbledon to get tickets) but since I was getting a decent view of Centre Court and Ascot for the first time in my life, in return for making light conversation with bankers, I wasn't complaining. I had no time for needlework now, and having a free evening to relax and eat supper at home with my feet up on Nelson's lap was getting to be a real treat.

I didn't tell Nelson that. I didn't want him getting an even bigger head.

Cracking the whip at work kept him too busy to go out much at first, but eventually Jonathan's social life began to pick up, and he started to come out of himself a little more. According to Gabi, he was still the Demon

Headmaster in the office, but more reports were seeping back, to her astonishment, about his popularity with female buyers.

'I *cannot* understand it!' she would fume over lunch in the park. 'He spent fifteen minutes yesterday lecturing me about the' – sarcastic bunny ears – '"unmotivational manner" in which I answer my telephone. How on earth is that sexy?'

I merely nodded and said nothing, because I knew Gabi wouldn't believe me if I told her how charming Jonathan could be – under the right circumstances.

Jonathan was much more complicated than I'd first realised, and his moods changed like the London weather. I still wasn't quite sure who was in charge: him or Honey. Not that I minded – it certainly kept me on my toes in a way that bossing surfer dudes around didn't.

'I'm going to be away for a fortnight,' he informed me, dropping into the office unannounced one warm evening in early August. He claimed he was on the way back to the office after a viewing in Belgravia, but he didn't seem in much of a rush.

'Oh?' I said, coolly finishing off a letter on my computer. 'Going somewhere nice?'

Jonathan was perched on the edge of my desk, swinging his feet. He looked relaxed and was clearly in an excellent mood.

'Going somewhere *very* nice,' he said. 'A series of wonderful hotels in Italy. Plus I've lined up a selection of interesting tours – ancient ruins, churches, a couple of vineyards . . .' His hand traced an imaginary horizon in the air. 'Wish you were coming too?'

I looked up. One eyebrow was cocked in question, but I couldn't tell whether he was teasing or not. 'Jonathan, you're not my only client,' I replied evenly. 'Educational though your holiday sounds.'

'Honey, you know I could change that if you wanted. Put you on a retainer?'

'I don't want.' I sent the letter to the printer. 'I couldn't keep it up fulltime.'

'I'm sure you could,' he said, sounding amused.

I wondered, from the expression on his face, if I'd said something amusing, but ignored it, to be on the safe side. I took the letter out of the printer, enjoying the feel of the thick paper. Having the right kind of notepaper was a small daily pleasure.

'So I can't tempt you?' he added. 'Call it a bonus?'

The idea of going on holiday with Jonathan was quite surreal, and I had no idea why he was even suggesting it.

'Jonathan, look at my engagement book,' I said, gesturing towards my desk diary. 'I couldn't just drop everything.'

'Not even for your best client?'

I gave him a disbelieving look. A definite smile was twitching at the corners of his mouth. It wasn't like him to be so obviously flirtatious. I wondered if he'd been drinking over lunch. 'All my clients mean a great deal to me.' I signed the letter, then looked up at him over the top of my tortoise-shell glasses. 'Anyway, what would be the point of coming on holiday with you? You're going on your own, aren't you? Who's to see who you're with?'

My heart beat a bit faster in my chest as I said this, but I tried not to let it show.

'You're quite right,' he said seriously. 'As ever.'

My heart sank, despite itself.

'I *should* go on my own,' he went on, 'then I'll only appreciate your company more when I come back.'

'There's no need to be gallant,' I said, a little more crisply than I meant to. 'No one's listening.'

Jonathan sighed. 'I'm not being gallant. I'm only telling you how I enjoy your company.'

What with his deadpan expression and my habitual assumption that all compliments were jokes, we weren't exactly Bogart and Bacall.

'It'll be good for you to take a break, you've been working so hard! Are you all packed?' I said, attempting to sound light, but succeeding only in sounding nanny-ish. 'Got all your arrangements made?'

'Yup. Patrice's done everything but pack my bag.' Jonathan stopped examining his nails and looked up at me. 'Between you two, my life is completely planned out. All I have to do is turn up when you tell me to.'

'How neat.' I returned his deadpan look. 'Business and pleasure, both beautifully organised.'

'Indeed.' Jonathan fumbled in his pocket. 'OK, listen, since you've blown me out on the offer of a romantic Italian sojourn, I thought I'd offer you an alternative holiday bonus.'

He dropped a set of keys on the desk in front of me.

I was reminded unpleasantly of my father leaving me the keys to his Dolphin Square flat prior to some dubious housekeeping task.

'Please don't tell me you need me to let your cleaner in,' I said.

Jonathan looked as if the idea hadn't occurred to him. 'Would you do that? You don't have to. She comes on a Monday and a Thursday morning. No, they're my car keys. Have my car for the fortnight, go for a drive, enjoy yourself in it, whatever. The insurance is very comprehensive.'

I looked at them, then back up at him. Jonathan had a beautiful silver Mercedes SL. He couldn't have given me a nicer bonus.

'I remember you saying how much you missed your own car,' he explained. 'Thought you'd appreciate having a ride of your own for a while.'

'Thank you,' I said, scooping up the keys with a broad smile. 'Every smart girl needs a decent ride, as Granny always used to say.'

Having wheels again was fabulous, and having Jonathan out of the country thinned my appointments down so I had time to use them. I was gazing out of my office window the next afternoon, daydreaming about how I could surprise Nelson the gourmet fish-fiend with a cockle-happy day out in Whitstable when Gabi burst into the office, a look of supreme triumph illuminating her face.

Without even pausing for niceties like 'Hello' or 'Are you busy?' she shoved her hand under my nose, nearly causing me to inhale the massive diamond glittering on her engagement-ring finger.

'Look!' she screeched unnecessarily.

I didn't need to ask what it was, and despite myself, I was quite impressed. The diamond was about the same size as a sugar lump.

Gabi threw herself into the chair opposite mine and reangled my desk lamp so it shone directly on her new ring. She turned her hand this way and that, in the manner of a QVC jewellery model, while pretending to be unaware of the dazzling refractions coming from her left hand.

'Congratulations!' I said. A funny sensation settled in my stomach like indigestion. 'Um, I take it Aaron's proposed? Or is this another "commitment gift" like your platinum ring?'

'Melissa!' Gabi chided. 'Don't be snotty. I don't wanna be hearin' any hatin'.' She did her horizontal Ricki Lake head movement, as much for the accompanying flashing hand gestures as for any dramatic emphasis. 'I thought you'd be happy for me,' she added, looking a little wounded.

'Oh, God, I'm sorry,' I said, getting up from my chair to give her a big hug. I didn't like sounding so old-maidish and really wished I could summon up some genuine excitement. I scrabbled urgently for three good things: Gabi had got what she always wanted; I could help out with the wedding; Aaron already knew what he was in for.

Even I wasn't convinced by that little lot, but fortunately she couldn't see my face over her shoulder.

After some squealing (from her) and hugging (from me), we disengaged and Gabi helped herself to some iced tea and biscuits. Very slowly and with maximum ring-display.

'So, how did he propose?' I asked. 'Spare me no details.'

'*Well*,' said Gabi, breaking her biscuit into frugal quarters, 'last night, I got home and Aaron was already there, which was weird to begin with, because as you know, normally he works till late.' She sipped her tea, obviously settling herself in for a long story. 'Anyway, Aaron says, "Why don't we go out for a drive, babe?" And I was like, "Why?"'

'You thought it was going to be the car sex thing again, didn't you?' I asked sympathetically. Aaron had gone through a phase of adventurous manoeuvres inspired by some feature in *Loaded*, and also by his intense passion for his Audi TT.

Gabi nodded. 'Yeah. Especially when he wouldn't say where we were going. Anyway, he wouldn't take no for an answer, so we get in the car and set off, and head onto the M1. You know what Aaron's like – we hit Mach Four within about ten seconds, overtaking everyone, and then suddenly, without warning, he slams on the brakes and swerves in front of this lorry!'

I covered my face with my hand.

'I thought, this is it! Oh. My. God. It's some kind of death pact!' continued Gabi. 'But no, we're sandwiched between two lorries, and they're honking, and Aaron's swearing and everything, and suddenly we're lurching off at the next exit, going round the roundabout, down the other way, back off at the exit we came on at, round the roundabout then down the M1 again!'

I was beginning to wonder where this was going. Much like Gabi last night, I guessed.

'So, anyway, this time he drives really slowly, and I can tell it's killing him, doing fifty, but he stays in the middle lane, then suddenly he goes into the slow lane and there it was!'

Gabi's eyes shone.

'There what was?' I prompted.

'A sign, saying "Will you",' beamed Gabi.

'OK . . .'

'Aaron's like, "Ooh, look at that! I wonder what it means?" And I said, "I don't know, Aaron, but I'm starving. Can we get some supper?" So we come off at that twenty-four-hour McDonalds, you know the one?'

I didn't, but nodded anyway.

'And he gets out – which was weird too, because normally we just drive-thru – and when he comes back, he's got my Big Mac meal, but he tells me not to open it till we get there, so I don't get grease on his upholstery. Which made sense, because he won't even let me put lipstick on while he's driving in case I slip. *Anyway*, we set off again, and after a mile, Aaron hits the brakes, nearly crashes into some four-by-four, and there it is – a sign saying "Marry Me". Just above the "Tiredness kills – take a break" sign.'

'How romantic!' I said. Actually, I was more intrigued by how Aaron had managed to get the signs up without being stopped by the Highways Agency.

'No, no, that's not the end!' Gabi put her cup down to prevent excited spillage. 'I didn't want to draw attention to it, in case Aaron thought I was hinting, so I just went, "Aaah, bless!" And Aaron acted all casual, like it wasn't anything to do with him! He just put the CD player on, and it was playing our song . . .'

'"Every Breath You Take" by the Police,' I supplied.

'Yeah!' Gabi's eyes widened. 'So, I've got my hand in the chips, and we have a couple of chips each, and I can tell Aaron's stressed about something, but I assume it's the grease getting on his steering wheel, then I feel something hard in the chips and guess what it is?'

'A human finger?' I joked. I had a vague feeling of foreboding in my stomach that I couldn't quite pinpoint.

'*Noooo!*' said Gabi. '*Mel!* It's a diamond ring! And suddenly, there it was, underneath the Services board, in huge letters – Gabi Shapiro!' Gabi looked unbelievably proud. 'I've never seen my name that big! Can you imagine how many people on their way home saw that "Will you marry me, Gabi Shapiro?" on the MI?'

'It's certainly something that would stick in the mind,' I agreed, trying to ignore the voice in my head demanding to know exactly when she'd get round to telling me how much she realised she loved Aaron.

'Anyway, I'm all over the place, and just before Scratchwood, there it was again, all in one, massive letters, "Will you marry me, Gabi Shapiro?" I suppose he put it there again, in case an articulated lorry got in the way of part of the message and I missed a bit,' she mused. 'He's very thorough, is Aaron. God love him.'

Gabi's eyes were now shining with triumph, and I realised that I was crying, despite myself. There was something about weddings that just set me off like a tap.

'But are you *happy*, Gabi?' I gulped.

'I'm *so* happy, Mel!' she beamed. 'I'm going to have the wedding Victoria Beckham could only dream of! And Dean & Daniels will never ruin my Christmas with their stingy bonuses again!'

It wasn't quite the romantic declaration I'd hoped for, but I got up and ran round the desk and hugged her again, hating myself for being such a suspicious, mean cow.

'Have you seen the ring?' she went on, talking into my shoulder as I clutched her tightly. 'It's exactly like the one Catherine Zeta Jones has! And it's from Tiffany! I made him keep the box!'

'It's beautiful,' I sniffed. 'Have you set a date?'

'No.' Gabi was radiating the sort of exhilarated excitement normally seen only on Olympic podia. 'Not yet. There's so much to do! Will you help me?'

'Of course. Have you thought much about what you want?'

Ask a stupid question.

'I just want something very simple but elegant,' she said briskly, patting my shoulder and reaching for her handbag. 'Themed around Tiffany blue and silver, I reckon. For about two hundred people. Maybe two-fifty. How many is Emery having?'

'It changes all the time. Three hundred at the last count,' I said, wiping my eyes with the back of my hand and sinking back down into my chair. For a single girl, I seemed to attract an inordinate amount of matrimonial activity.

I looked over at Gabi, who had whipped out two wedding magazines and a highlighter pen. Not once had she mentioned loving Aaron, or wanting to make him happy. Instead she looked worryingly like a woman embarking on the trolley dash of a lifetime.

The heavy feeling in my stomach intensified and I slid open the top drawer of my desk for my Rennies. While I was at it, I had a quick squirt of Rescue Remedy too.

Gabi's announcement solved one of my immediate dilemmas though: she was definitely unavailable for our day-trip to Whitstable, since she and her mum were going to Liberty to start searching for The Dress.

'Isn't this fun?' I roared at Nelson as we sped along the A-roads to the east coast. I'd let him plan the route, on condition that we took Jonathan's car, and he claimed fear had steered him away from motorways and known accident blackspots.

Nelson looked at me from the passenger seat. He had insisted on wearing a bobble hat to keep his head warm, baseball caps in sports cars being totally verboten. My own head was wrapped in an old silk headscarf, printed with scenes of Italian palazzos and held on by nineteen Kirby grips. It wasn't completely practical, I admit, but I wanted to wear it.

'If I said I felt sick, would you stop?' he yelled back.

'No!'

'OK then,' he replied and dug himself in deeper.

We spent an hour or so wandering around the town then, sight-seeing obligations fulfilled, hit the seafood stalls. Nelson loved nothing better than stuffing himself with obscure rubbery bits of phlegm. He was in seventh heaven, picking through the salty offerings. I stuck to the potted shrimps and we set off along the shore.

It *was* August and technically the sun was shining, but there was a stiff breeze blowing all but the most hardy souls off the beach.

'I love English beaches!' I shouted above the wind. 'We haven't done this for ages, have we?'

There was a time when Nelson and I, plus Gabi, Roger, Woolfe or whichever of Nelson's other unattached friends were about, would regularly pile in the car and go to Brighton for the day. Obviously, time had erased the slippery pebbles, cold weather and upset stomachs from my mind, but I had fond memories of driving back in contented silence, full of chips, surrounded by friends falling asleep on each other. Happy days.

It was ages since we'd had a day off together, just me and Nelson. I put my arm round his waist and gave him a squeeze.

Nelson responded by slinging his arm round my shoulder for about nine strides, then removing it to get back to his winkles.

'I should bring Jonathan here,' I said. 'He'd love it! Totally English and uncomfortable.'

'Are you actually *going out* with Jonathan now?' Nelson demanded with a snort.

'No,' I said, quickly. 'Of course not. But you know how he sometimes asks me to take him to interesting places in London, so he can get to know it. I thought I might suggest a day-trip to the good old English seaside, that's all. Nothing's changed. Why do you ask?'

Nelson gave me a funny look. 'Because you're starting to sound as though you're his real girlfriend, not his pretend one. Jonathan this, Jonathan that . . .'

I blushed, but fortunately my face was already wind-chapped, so I doubted Nelson could tell. 'Well, I suppose now I've got to know him, and we spend quite a bit of time together, we're on a more friendly basis than I am with my other clients. But there's nothing fishy going on. He still doesn't know my real name. I mean, come on, he probably still thinks I'm a natural blonde!'

Nelson ditched his tub of winkles in a bin and moved on to his whelks. 'Is Honey really so different from Melissa?'

'Oh, yes, definitely,' I assured him. 'Honey's appallingly cheeky and wears her clothes far too tight. Besides, only *you* get to see the real off-duty, warts-and-all Melissa.'

'Do I?' said Nelson. 'Then I'm a very lucky man. Remind me to tell Jonathan about your disgusting face packs next time I see him. I'm sure he'll have lots to say about setting an alarm clock to maximise face-pack development time.'

'Don't be mean. He's not like that.' I gave Nelson a playful push and he pretended to stagger under the impact. 'It's bad enough persuading Gabi that he isn't some kind of robot.'

'Ah, Gabi,' said Nelson, spearing three whelks in a row. 'How is the Imelda Marcos of Mill Hill?'

Nelson had always tolerated Gabi's shameless flirting with good grace, and I was fairly sure that was as far as it went, but you never could tell. People could change, after all.

'Well, the thing is, Nelson,' I said, carefully, 'she's, er . . . Aaron's proposed. They're getting married.'

Nelson laughed out loud. 'The wedding list of the century! Peter Jones must be celebrating!'

'Don't you mind?'

'No! I'm really thrilled for her. Isn't that what she's been angling for for years? To be a lady who lunches? No, Gabi's a great girl and she'll have a fantastic wedding. Good luck to Aaron, I say . . . Why?' He looked at me closely. '*Isn't* it good news?'

I sighed. He hadn't mentioned anything about love either. 'Yes. I suppose it is.'

'You don't sound too happy about that.'

'Well . . . I'm not really.' I bit my lip, trying to be loyal and not discuss it.

'Why?'

I wanted to say, it's totally hypocritical because she never looks at Aaron the way she looks at you, but I hated sounding like such a prig. 'Because . . . I don't know if her heart's in it?'

'I can't see Gabi doing anything she doesn't want to, can you?' replied Nelson evenly.

'No, but . . .' I felt his solid warmth next to me and couldn't help feeling reassured. Temporarily anyway.

'You can't worry about everyone, Melissa.' Nelson ditched his empty shellfish carton in a bin and put his arm round my shoulders. 'Just because *you*'ve had a bit of a rough ride doesn't mean that Gabi's going to. And you don't know that she doesn't love him, deep down. People have funny ways of showing how they feel.'

He squeezed my shoulder and took my hand to wrap it round his waist. 'It can be hard to let other people know how you feel,' he went on, more seriously. 'I mean, sometimes it's just easier to make a joke out of things than to expose yourself to, er, ridicule.'

We stopped walking.

'I know,' I said, biting my lip, 'but . . .'

My phone rang in my pocket.

'Sorry, Nelson,' I said and fished it out. The number was withheld, which meant it was either the tax people, the mobile-phone people, or a member of my family. None of which options filled me with joy.

'Hello?' I said tentatively.

'Ah, Melissa!' It was Daddy.

'Hello, Daddy.' My blood ran cold at the sound of his voice. I *knew* everything had all been going too well! A slide show of nightmares whipped through my mind: did he want that blasted loan money? Had he found out about the agency? Or was it some fresh horror?

'Are you having a nice day?' he enquired.

'Yes, I am, thank you,' I replied, caught off guard by his civility. I stepped away from Nelson and immediately felt cold, inside and out.

'Good. Because we're not. We're having a complete bloody crisis. So stop what you're doing and get yourself back here. You're needed at home.'

'But, Daddy, I'm . . .'

'Melissa!' Then he rang off.

I put the phone back in my pocket.

'Nelson,' I said unhappily, 'whelk time's over. I have to go.'

15

The gravel parking circle outside the house was full of cars, which didn't bode well. I took three long deep breaths, vowed I wouldn't let them get to me, then rang the bell.

Emery came to the door. She was looking even more wraith-like than usual, with huge dark circles round her eyes and the sort of shattered expression one only tends to see on recently released hostages.

'Oh my God, Em,' I exclaimed. 'What's happened?'

'Daddy.' She drew in a shuddering breath. 'Daddy has *ruined* my wedding.'

'Already?' I said, taking her by the shoulders. 'Now, buck up, Emery. Has he really? Or have you just fallen out about the guest list again? You know, most people only have a hundred or so people at their wedding. It's not compulsory to invite everyone Daddy's ever met. You don't have to write off *all* Mummy's social debts, you know.'

Emery shook her head. 'No, it's just . . .' She waved her hand hopelessly. 'Just . . . You know.' Her head dropped and she let out a small sob. 'William says . . .'

It would have been nice if Golf-Boy William were showing any sign of participation in his own wedding, other than actually instigating it, but so far he was claiming that work and client management (i.e. golf and squash) had him booked right up, leaving Emery in sole charge of their nuptials. I could see I wasn't going to get any sense out of her, and with dread building in my heart, I pushed her spindly frame ahead of me, through into the kitchen.

My mother, father and grandmother were sitting around the table, which was piled high with brochures, paperwork, coffee cups, an overflowing ashtray, shredded tissues, and a smashed plate. The atmosphere was thick with cigarette smoke and bad temper.

'Melissa! Darling!' gasped Mummy, stubbing out her cigarette and lighting another. 'I'm so glad you're here!'

I ignored this, since what she really meant was 'I'm so glad you're here to deflect some of Daddy's wrath.'

'Hello, Melissa,' said my father. His eyes glinted dangerously and I had the abrupt, paralysing sensation that he knew everything. Not that this was anything new or even necessarily significant: he'd been able to make me feel guilt on demand since I was old enough to sneak biscuits.

'Melissa!' said my grandmother, rising from her seat as if to leave. 'Thank God you're here to talk sense into everyone.'

'Sit down, Dilys!' snapped Daddy. 'You're not going anywhere.'

Granny compromised by getting up but going only as far as the drinks cabinet, where she poured herself a large gin and tonic. My mother's eyes followed her movements longingly, but she tore her gaze away and puffed hard on her cigarette.

'I wish you would give up, darling,' said Granny, vaguely. 'I did. It gives one terrible *lines* . . .'

'What's happened?' I asked.

'That bloody Gwen Morrison . . .' my mother began, then paused dramatically, 'has resigned.'

Daddy had finally caved in under serious pressure and Gwen Morrison had been engaged as Emery's designated wedding planner from Town and Country Weddings: a nice, efficient girl who'd been at school with Allegra, and was therefore completely used to dealing with crisis after crisis. I'd met her only in passing, but she looked the sort to thrive on impossibilities and stress. She wore one of those upside-down nurse's watches on her jacket lapel.

I furrowed my brow. 'Hadn't you just taken her on?'

Emery shot Daddy a surprisingly poisonous glare. 'Taken her on, or just . . . *taken* her?'

My mother flinched. 'Emery!'

I stared at Emery, unsure of what she meant, exactly. 'Taken her where?'

'There was a misunderstanding,' Daddy responded smoothly. 'I don't think Gwen was quite up to the task in hand, so we decided to let her go.'

'Martin, my dear, she is threatening to sue you!' exclaimed Granny in a sunny voice.

'OK, OK,' I said, before my mother could chime in, or faint, or do whatever it was she was psyching herself up to do. 'But the wedding isn't until December, and you've been planning this for simply ages. Isn't it just a case of, um, chasing up the canapés?'

As I said this I knew it wouldn't be. Emery's face and my mother's clenched fists confirmed it.

Daddy, though, looked delighted. 'Well, quite. I knew we should have called Melissa. Jolly good, sweetheart. That settles it.'

My father never called me sweetheart. Ever.

Besides, it settled *what*?

'But, no, hang on,' I stuttered. 'Listen, I'm happy to help out, but I, um, I can't . . .'

'Can't what, Melissa?' demanded my father, turning all Jeremy Paxman. 'Can't help your own sister organise the wedding of her dreams?'

'Well . . .' I struggled to find some vestiges of resistance, but it was impossible. He was giving me his specially destructive stare.

'Can't make a few calls? To save your poor mother from a nervous breakdown?' he continued, appalled. 'Can't be bothered to give up a precious morning to address invitations?'

'Of course I want to *help* but I just don't have enough hours in the day!' I protested, seeing weeks of complete misery shimmer up before me like a nasty mirage. 'I mean, honestly, I'm run off my feet as it is!'

That, of course, was exactly what he wanted me to say. Daddy's thin mouth contorted into a curve of sheer delight, then frowned deliberately.

'But what time do you finish at that *estate agency*? Five, isn't it?' His eyes twinkled nastily. 'Plenty of time in the evenings.'

'I'm, um . . .' I could feel the heat creep up and over my face. Everyone was looking at me, their finely tuned trouble-sonars swivelling. I'd managed to keep my change of occupation from them until now and wasn't exactly planning to enlighten them completely anyway. But Daddy had that look in his eye. Was this one of his double bluffs?

I couldn't risk it.

'I'm not working at Dean & Daniels any more,' I admitted.

'You're not?' exclaimed my father in mock shock.

'What happened? Did they have to' – he contorted his face into an unconvincing expression of sympathy – '"let you go"?'

'Martin!' snapped my mother. 'Don't patronise her! If Melissa was sacked, then let her be sacked!'

'Yes, they did have to "let me go",' I said, jutting my chin. 'They were being taken over by an American firm, so there were redundancies. And I was one of them. It happens sometimes.'

'You're getting to be the most redundant girl in Chelsea,' observed Daddy. 'So what are you doing now?'

'Temping,' I said and prayed Granny wouldn't take it upon herself to assist me in my fibbing. Her lies tended to be rather baroque and I found it very counter-productive trying to keep up with her.

'Temping, eh?' Daddy raised his eyebrows, and I started to panic.

It could be that he didn't know anything whatsoever.

It could be that he knew everything, and didn't want to play his hand so soon.

It could be that he knew a fragment of something and was waiting for me to oblige by confessing the balance.

Honey wouldn't do that. Not in a million years.

I clenched my teeth together.

'Temping,' I repeated with a forced smile, which came out more as a snarl.

He gave me a long 'This is only half-time, Melissa' look, but I was pleased to spot a shadow of surprise cross his face.

However, before he could gather himself for a new attack, my mother surprised everyone by entering the arena. 'Well, in that case you'll have plenty of time to help me out! I'm sure Daddy will compensate you for your time, won't you, Martin? What's your hourly rate for your temping agency, darling?'

I didn't like to tell her it was currently averaging out at around a hundred pounds an hour.

'Belinda, are you *mad*? I most certainly will not compensate her!' Daddy roared. 'Do you have *any* idea how much this is all costing me? Thank God Melissa's embraced career spinsterhood – we'd be on the streets!'

Really. How can a girl not feel special when her own father talks about her in such adoring terms?

I looked over at Emery. She was hunched over her cup of tea, and flinched every time my parents yelled at each other. I suddenly felt very sorry for her. It was meant to be the happiest day of her life, after all.

I thought quickly. Jonathan was away for another ten days, which meant that I had fewer demands on my time than usual: just a few wardrobe overhauls and a small birthday party to arrange. If I really got my skates on, I could sort out the majority of the logistical problems for Emery and make some kind of plan for her to follow on her own as it got nearer the time.

December. It was quite a while away. Would I still be working for Jonathan then? I swallowed as a confusing blend of feelings swirled round in my head.

'Melissa! I want a word with you in my study,' Daddy said, and stalked out.

'It'll just be the old family responsibility lecture,' said my grandmother, getting up to put the kettle back on the Aga. 'I wouldn't worry. We've all had it today already.'

'Oh, God,' muttered Mummy to herself, and lit another cigarette.

I gave Emery a pat on the shoulder. Vagueness was all very well for slipping under the radar, but it would be tough to vague out of her own wedding day. 'Don't worry,' I soothed. 'We'll soon sort it out.'

'Gwen took the files,' said Emery dully. 'It took me weeks to narrow down the colour schemes.'

I looked at the three of them.

Mummy chain-smoking and muttering distractedly to herself; Granny singing under her breath and looking troublesome; Emery rocking gently in her chair, apparently tranquillised.

Daddy, William and Grandad all highly conspicuous by their absence.

Single life had never seemed so appealing.

By the time I'd walked through the house to my father's study, he was already seated behind his desk and had assumed his preferred headmasterly pose. I cursed myself for allowing him to gain this tactical advantage so cheaply, but felt a familiar wobble of trepidation all the same.

Daddy's study was the scene of all school-report dissection, uncomfortable debriefs about newspaper allegations, and other happy family events. It was dark and lined with bookshelves filled with old copies of Hansard and leather-bound books purchased from house sales. A large portrait of him in oils hung above the fireplace, while a beautiful black and white photograph of my mother at her coming-out party dominated the mantelpiece. There were no grand ancestral portraits because my grandfather had sold some to have the roof fixed and destroyed the rest in a fit of rage – the reason lost in the mists of time.

I leaned against the chair opposite him, rather than sitting down in it. 'How can I help you?' I said, with more bravado than I felt.

'Sit down, Melissa,' he said tersely. 'I don't think either of us have time to play games, do you?'

I sat down.

'Now, you're going to arrange this wedding of your sister's,' he informed me. 'Don't annoy me by arguing. You're going to do it for a number of reasons. One, there is no way that idiot child can do it herself and I'm damned if I'm going to let Belinda loose with my chequebook. Two, since this wedding is already costing me an arm and a leg I can scarcely afford, we're going to have to economise.'

His mouth twitched as he said this. It usually came back to money in the end.

'Surely hiring another wedding planner would be a sensible economy?' I asked. 'She could negotiate better deals than me.'

Daddy didn't even dignify this with a response. 'Three, I don't want some sneaky bitch coming in here and snooping about, selling details of my private life to the gutter press and generally poking around in my business.'

As if anyone was that interested in him! Revealing embarrassing details about wedding car deals and other cheapskate tactics, more like.

'And four . . .' He put his hands on the desk and let a smirk play across his face. 'How to put this? I believe you owe me some money, Melissa.'

Damn. I knew he'd gone too quiet about the loan. He'd been quick enough to offer the money when he thought it would make him a few bob, though. I wriggled in my seat. 'Yes, well, I hadn't forgotten about that . . .'

'I should hope not, little lady!'

My head snapped up as he said that, but my father's expression was a mask of smiling concern. 'It's not good for a child to be in debt at your age, really. And I've let this debt ride for quite some time now.'

'No, I *want* to pay it back,' I agreed, spotting a way out. Talking business reminded me that I'd done some fairly nifty deals while in Honey's stiletto slingbacks, which in turn made me sit up straight and concentrate on not getting rolled over by my father, as usual. 'So if I organise Emery's wedding, you'll write off part of the debt, instead of paying for a wedding planner?'

Daddy threw his head back and guffawed with laughter, then fixed me with an unsmiling gaze.

'No,' he said. 'But if you decide you're *too busy* to organise the wedding, we may have to . . . ah . . . discuss the rate of interest on your outstanding debt. I do need that money, Melissa. Marquees don't grow on trees.'

'Oh,' I said, feeling thoroughly boxed in. I reminded myself that I'd more or less decided to do it anyway, but my goodwill feelings towards Emery were beginning to evaporate.

'But I can't do it for nothing! I just don't have time! Surely there has to be *something* in it for me?' I suggested, clinging onto the last remaining shreds of my Honey attitude. I didn't want to be completely under obligation.

'Of course,' oozed my father. 'You can come to the wedding and bring anyone you like. Now, if you don't mind, I have some phone calls to make.'

I stood up. Granny was right, he was a really very unpleasant man. But he had the knack of making me feel dreadfully disloyal for not bending to his will like a dutiful daughter should. King Lear had nothing on my father.

I supposed that was what made him such an unshiftable local MP.

I lingered in the hall long enough to hear him get

through to Simon, his solicitor, and yell, 'No, no, no, no! I don't want to pay her off, Simon! I did nothing, and, anyway, it's her word against mine . . .'

Then he poked the door shut with the snooker cue he kept behind his desk, and I went back into the kitchen to begin the long metaphorical trek to the church door with Emery.

The next morning, after a fitful night's sleep in my old room, I forced Emery, my grandmother and my mother into Mummy's car and drove them to a nearby tea shop where we ploughed through a list of things to do. I didn't want to take Mummy to a pub and have her drown her sorrows, and I didn't want my father dropping in and distracting us.

His influence was all over the plans as it was.

'So, the cars are sorted out?' I asked.

'No cars.' Emery shook her head. 'Horse and carriage, from the Green Energy people. They're constituents. Daddy says they'll let us have that and five electric cars as long as I mention them in any publicity.'

'Right.' I made a note. 'Cake?'

'Local bakery is honoured to provide it.'

'Do you have to be photographed with the baker?' I asked sarcastically.

Emery shook her head, swinging her shiny curtains of hair from side to side. 'Um, no. I don't think so, anyway.'

'Dress?'

'You're making that,' Granny reminded me.

'Oh, yes.'

Oh bugger, more like. I underlined dress on my list. It had rather slipped down my to-do list, what with Jonathan's social demands expanding to weekends.

'What about invitations?' I asked. 'Do you have a list of guests? Have you chosen your stationery?'

Emery looked as if she was about to dissolve into tears.

'OK,' I said quickly. 'We'll have to sort that out.' I made a note and forced a smile onto my face. 'See, Em? It's not that hard! We'll get there.'

'I'm so glad you're here, darling,' said Granny, helping herself to the last éclair.

I beamed at her. Actually, if Granny were on the scene too, then it might just be bearable.

'It makes me feel so much less guilty about the cruise,' she went on, biting into her cake.

I stared at her. 'What?'

'Cruise,' she said, through a mouthful of choux pastry. 'Treating myself.'

Granny's finances were shrouded in mystery. She always seemed to be well-off, despite not having had a job since the late fifties, when she had a brief but frightfully glamorous career as a nightclub singer, much to the horror of her family. It seemed to have made her a lot of money of her own, too. Mummy usually muttered something about 'royalties on a record' and closed the subject fast.

'You're going on a cruise,' I repeated dully. 'Thanks a lot.'

She winked at me and whispered, 'More than one way to skin a cat, darling.'

I seethed and reflected that while everyone else in the family was an expert skinner, it always seemed to be me they ended up skinning.

I wasn't in the best of moods when I got back to London. Nelson knew how I'd be feeling after I'd spent the weekend up at home. When I got in, the kitchen was filled with the most delicious aroma of roast chicken and mashed potatoes and I was so grateful for his thoughtfulness that I could have burst into tears on the spot.

'You look terrible,' he said from the couch. He was watching a sailing video and eating Pringles from the tube.

'Thanks,' I said. I looked in the hall mirror. Did I look terrible? I did, really. My complexion wasn't nearly as radiant as it was in my Honey wig. And maybe I took a bit more trouble doing my Honey make-up, since I had to adjust it all for caramel-blonde hair, instead of whisking on my usual quick flash of rosy blusher and lick of mascara.

It's true, I thought bitterly. Honey's just an all-round better bet than Melissa. No one at home had even considered that it might be *painful* for an unmarried sister to be arranging a younger sibling's wedding. Honey would have pointed that out straight away and negotiated a consultancy fee.

That hadn't occurred to me until now, and I let a fresh wave of misery wash over me.

'Gabi phoned for you,' Nelson went on. 'She's coming over later to discuss her bridesmaids' dresses.'

'Oh.' I shuffled over to the sofa and threw myself down at the other end, putting my feet on Nelson's lap so he could rub them for me. 'Great.'

Nelson gave me a good hard look, and said, 'You know, you don't look so terrible now I see you in the light.'

'Too late,' I said, hugging a cushion. 'Damage is done. Will you do that magic reflexology rubbish on my feet, please? I'm a bag of nerves.'

'You don't mind if I watch this at the same time?' he

asked politely, starting to apply pressure to my big toes. 'I'm on it somewhere, apparently.'

'No, no.' Already the tension was ebbing from my body. Nelson really did have lovely strong hands. 'Watch whatever you like.'

Secretly, I quite liked watching Nelson sailing. It was nice to see him being rugged and practical, instead of spouting endlessly about sustainable developments and Gift Aid. He pointed out various sailing nuances that I pretended to understand while floating away on waves of foot-related bliss, and we were slumped there quite companionably, until the doorbell rang.

I looked at Nelson, peeved. 'That'll be Gabi.'

'Don't worry,' he said, failing to read my mind for once. 'I made extra mash. You're not going to be short-changed on the supper front.'

'I'll let her in,' I said, swinging my feet off his lap and shuffling to the front door, fighting back incipient resentment.

'Hello!' Gabi gave me a cursory hug, then bounded into the sitting room. 'Hello, Nelson!' I heard her coo.

I shut the door and marvelled that even as she was coming round here to discuss her wedding, she still bothered to get dressed up in her best clothes and full make-up in order to impress my flatmate.

'Ooh,' she was gasping. 'Is that you, Nelson? Sailing?'

'Yes,' he said, turning off the video. 'Supper's just ready. Do you want to open some wine, Mel?'

'He's amazing,' she whispered to me as I searched for the corkscrew. 'How lucky are you?'

'Pack it in, Gabi,' I said, trying to sound friendly. 'You're preaching to the converted.'

'I bet he's dead good at knots,' she continued dreamily.

'I *said* pack it in, Gabi,' I repeated, less friendly.

'Why? Are you jealous?'

'Are you *engaged*?' I hissed.

'Temper, temper,' she said, lifting her hands.

Over supper we talked about Emery's wedding – or rather, I unloaded all my rage about being duped into arranging it, and they agreed that I'd been stitched up like a kipper. I had to omit certain details, like the money I owed to Daddy, and Granny's hot horse-racing tip. It was getting exhausting these days, remembering who knew what and what had to be kept from whom.

Strangely, Gabi seemed unwilling to discuss her own plans.

'Oh, that's boring girls' talk,' she laughed, with a sideways glance at Nelson when I asked about her ideas for the reception. 'We can talk about that later!'

'Talk about it now,' said Nelson, pushing his chair from the table. 'I'm off for a long bath while there's still hot water left.' He picked up a copy of *Practical Boat Owner* from the coffee table and tapped me playfully on the head with it. 'Don't disturb me, madam. Night, Gabi.'

'Night, Nelson,' she cooed.

'Don't use up all the hot water,' I yelled at his departing back. 'And keep your hands off my bath milk!'

The bathroom door slammed and the pipes started clanking.

Gabi sank her chin onto her hands and smiled into the middle distance.

'Stop it,' I said, crossly. 'Stop flirting with him.'

'Oh, don't be such a spoilsport,' she said. 'He's lovely, Nelson. You don't know how lucky you are, having him doting on you the whole time.'

'I know!' I shouted, unable to contain myself any longer. 'I know he is! He's a *wonderful* man! But if *you* think he is, why are you getting married to Aaron?'

Gabi looked at me as if I were very slow. 'That's a whole different ball game, Mel.'

'No, it's not!' I'd had a long day and my patience was filo-thin. 'Gabi, you can't ask me to be a brides-maid and have me stand there while you get married to Aaron, knowing all the while that you'd rather be . . . rather be . . .'

'Shagging Nelson?' she finished.

I turned bright, bright red. 'Well, yes,' I spluttered. 'Yes, if you want to put it like that.'

'Don't be such a prude. There's nothing wrong with fancying people – it's perfectly normal. I told you before,' she said patiently, 'Aaron can give me the sort of life that—'

'No!' I said, losing my temper. 'No, don't give me all that cynical nonsense about partnerships and financial security! I can't believe anyone could be that shallow or that mercenary! Are you telling me that if Aaron lost all his money, you'd just walk out?'

'Um, that's not going to happen.'

'How do you know? You can't promise to spend your life with someone just because they're going to pay your bills! What does that make you?'

'About the same as what your job makes you, I'd say,' replied Gabi, nastily.

'But it's a job!' I snapped back. 'And I'm not confusing it with love!'

We both sat back, temporarily stung.

An awkward silence filled the kitchen, and I knew I couldn't take back what I'd said. It was a bit like waking up on a lilo and realising the shore is suddenly a lot further away than you remembered.

'Gabi, be honest with me,' I pleaded. 'If Aaron lost his job, if the TT had to go back to the garage, would you call off the engagement? Could you really do that? Is it really just his money that you love? Because if it is, *please* don't go any further with this.'

'Mel, you're being melodramatic,' said Gabi confidently. 'Even if he did lose his job, Aaron's not the sort of bloke to sit about waiting for handouts. He's a grafter. And I like that. It makes me feel secure.'

'And what does Nelson make you feel?'

Her confidence faltered. 'Nelson's different.'

'How?'

Gabi twisted her wine glass. 'Look, Aaron understands me. We're the same sort of people. Nelson's . . . well, he's . . . different.'

'In what way?'

'Look, Mel,' she started, then stopped. 'Oh, you wouldn't understand.'

That really riled me. *Wouldn't* I understand? But I bit my lip and tried to keep my temper.

'Nelson *is* lovely,' I said, 'but you're just using him to compensate for the complete lack of romance with Aaron! You can't be in love with a fantasy of someone!' It was pouring out of me now. 'It's totally self-delusional.'

'Oh, so says the great self-deluder!' Gabi snorted.

'What do you mean by that?' I demanded.

'Oh, I'm not in love with Jonathan Riley!' she said, in a hoity-toity posh voice. 'Oh no, it's just for work! I mean, yes, I talk about him constantly and yes, he's a *total* sweetie when he's with me, and yes, I'm always planning fun things to do and see, but it's OK for me to flirt with him, because *I'm* not falling in love, honestly! I know what I'm doing! I'm always in charge and in control and able to cope with everything life throws at me because I'm just a can-do kind of Home Counties gel!'

I looked at Gabi in horror as her voice rose hysterically. I couldn't remember us ever having a row before. And I couldn't believe she thought I talked like that.

'Jonathan's all you ever talk about. It's even worse than Orlando,' she steamed on. 'And it's not just him that's totally different out of the office, it's you too! It's as if this Honey personality has a licence to do whatever the hell she likes while nice sweet Melissa remains the same as ever. So you can flirt and carry on with Mr Grown-Up Bastard Estate Agent, and have the time of your life falling for a man you secretly don't think you should have. You want to have a close look at yourself, "Honey", because I'm not the self-deluding one here!'

I gaped at her. 'That's *not true.*'

'Isn't it?' she demanded. 'You don't fancy Jonathan?'

'Well, no, it's not . . .' I blustered. 'It's *work*. He doesn't want a girlfriend, that's the whole point. I mean, Jonathan just deals with Honey and, I mean, that's not really the way I am so . . .'

Gabi did her Ricki Lake side-to-side head-shaking thing – without a shred of irony. 'For crying out loud, Mel, listen to yourself!'

I took a couple of deep breaths. There was some truth, I had to acknowledge, in what she was saying. It was flattering that Jonathan could relax with me, and yes, it was nice to flirt with him, a man totally out of my league, but I knew it was just his professional charm. He made me flirt well, in the same way that playing tennis with an expert improves your own game. But at the bottom of it all, what kept it all safe, was the simple fact that all the flirting was Honey. Jonathan didn't know me. He wasn't ever going to know *me*.

Was he?

Gabi and I looked at each other over the debris of the supper, and, all of a sudden, I felt terribly, terribly gloomy.

'Oh, Gabi, I don't want us to fall out,' I said, taking Gabi's hand. 'I don't mean to sound negative. It's just that . . . you're my best friend and I don't want to see you make yourself unhappy. Money isn't everything, you know.'

I didn't add that I couldn't believe someone as nice as her could be so calculating.

'Believe me, Melissa,' said Gabi, 'I *refuse* to be unhappy. I'm just not so sure about you.'

I didn't think it was that simple, but in the interest of our friendship, I kept that to myself for the time being.

16

Some of the Little Lady's services were easier than others. I preferred the assignments that gave instant results: the hairdressing, the wardrobe adjustments, the confidence-boosting pep-talks. It really was gratifying to see the improvements one could wreak in only a few hours, just by encouraging and flattering where encouragement and flattery had never ventured before.

I wasn't so keen on the jobs that required me to be a bit unpleasant – although, as Nelson kept reminding me, if I could practise my self-assertion at work, it might help me stop being such a pushover at home. One job I seemed to be doing over and over again, as word spread through the south-west London bachelor community, was vetting domestics.

'I'm too scared to sack her' was the most common problem, closely followed by 'I can't tell when she's been'. 'I don't know if she has a visa' was another popular one, but I tried to steer clear of actual legal issues.

My tactics varied, according to the client and the slacking levels of the cleaner. Posing as a house-proud new girlfriend, popping in unexpectedly during their alleged hours, was one; setting burglar alarms to make sure they'd been was another. If that failed, Nelson had passed on a real corker, which I was using now, in a far-from-spotless kitchen in Battersea Rise.

'So you see, you'll be on the internet!' I explained cheerfully to the horrified cleaner currently trying to conceal a
procession of ants on Linus Coren's kitchen bar. She thought
I was Linus's bossy sister; she had already met Linus, an
IT specialist who modelled himself on Derren Brown, and
so posing as his girlfriend would have pushed the bounds
of credibility too far. 'All day! Isn't it marvellous?'

'Internet?'

I nodded. Rosella was charging Linus nearly forty quid
a week, every week, for moving the *Star Trek* action figures
around on his mantelpiece and not much else. 'Linus has
his own website, Linus On-Line, and there are webcams
in every room, you see, so one can log on and just watch
what's happening in the house. I know, it sounds terribly
boring,' I confided, woman to woman, 'but apparently
people go mad for this sort of thing. Obviously, it's a bit
of an intrusion for you, so Linus says he'll up your wages
by a pound an hour. But just think, Rosella! You could
be an internet star!'

'Cameras? Watching me all day?'

'Yes!' I sipped my coffee and beamed at her. The wage
increase had been my idea: I had some sympathy for the
cleaners, disinfecting pigsties, day in, day out. 'So we'll
all know when you're dusting and when you're putting
your feet up and eating Linus's chocolate digestives!' I
laughed heartily to show I was joking.

Rosella managed a weak smile.

'Biscuit?' I said, offering her the packet.

She went to take one, then looked guilty and grabbed
her duster.

When I got back to the office, Gabi was waiting on the
bench outside, her lunch in a bag on her knee. Since our

row we'd both been extra-careful to be nice to each other. I hated falling out with my friends, especially when it was only my worry for her that caused the argument. I'd decided to hold my tongue about Aaron until she got bored with planning her dream wedding; once the intoxication of buying stuff wore off, I was confident that she'd look at the long-term situation more rationally.

Which wasn't to say that my heart didn't plunge when I saw she had a whole armful of wedding magazines.

'Where've you been?' she asked, following me up the stairs.

'Chasing lazy cleaning ladies.'

There was a pile of post on the mat and I began sorting through it, while Gabi opened the windows and let some fresh air into the office. The final days of August had turned hotter than ever, and the roses on my desk were drooping in the heat.

'Now that's an agency you should start,' said Gabi, settling herself into my leather armchair with her bagel and *Cosmopolitan Bride*. 'Maybe I should leave Dean & Daniels and set up a sister agency with yours. The Little Lady Agency, in partnership with the, er, Helping Hands Agency.'

'I don't think so,' I said. To be honest, it did rather annoy me, the way Nelson and Gabi still seemed to treat the business as a bit of a joke. They simply refused to believe that being nice, or firm, or flirtatious, or helpful, or mysterious *to order* could be in any way taxing.

'Can I help myself to some Diet Coke?' she asked, opening the fridge.

'Please do,' I said absently, spotting a postcard from Verona, which read 'Been to Juliet's balcony – nice first-floor apt, city views, stunning elevation, family oriented neighbourhood, no chain. Offers? JR.'

Jonathan had good handwriting for a man, I thought. That very American handwriting, that managed to look masculine and feminine at the same time. Firm but neat, and not without style.

'Mel?' said Gabi. 'Why have you gone all pink?'

'Hot,' I said, fanning myself unconvincingly with the post. 'Very hot in here.'

The card had taken well over a week to get to London. I looked at the date again. He'd sent it the day he'd arrived. Very efficient.

'Mel!' said Gabi. 'You're flushed. Here, have a cool drink.'

She passed me a glass of water and snatched the post off me as I stupidly put it on the table to take the glass. 'Ah ha! A postcard from Jonathan!' She read it, and gave me a knowing look. 'Hmm, cryptic – and yet possibly romantic at the same time! Now I understand!'

'You don't,' I said stoutly, but as a sop to our spirit of cordiality, I let her debate the tackiness or otherwise of scratch-card wedding favours (in specially embossed gift envelopes) for the rest of lunch.

'I'd better go,' she sighed as two o'clock approached. 'Patrice watches that door like a hawk. She's got eyes in the back of her head. Mind you, that's what happens when you have your face lifted as often as her.'

'Bye, Gabi,' I said, getting up to kiss her goodbye.

'When are you going to come over and discuss bridesmaids' dresses with me?' she said, holding me at arm's length, the better to fix me with her best beseeching look.

'Um, I could maybe do Friday evening,' I said, ignoring the little voice of reason screeching furiously in my head. 'Let me just check . . .'

I flicked through my desk diary, and the phone rang.

'Stay there, I'll just get this,' I said, picking it up. 'Hello?'

'Honey! Guess who's back?'

OK, I had to admit it to myself: After not hearing it for a couple of weeks, it was a pleasant surprise to be reminded just how sexy Jonathan's voice was.

I swallowed hard and tried to remain cool.

'Jonathan!' I said. 'How was your holiday?'

By the door, Gabi was making silent film-heroine swooning faces. I turned away so she couldn't see me.

'You didn't get my postcard?' He sounded disappointed.

'No.' Why was I lying? Because I was paranoid about misinterpreting the card, I reasoned.

'Oh, well, I sent you one. Two, actually. European post's a nightmare. Listen, I'm back in the office right now, and I, um, have a very short-notice invitation for you, which I really hope you're going to be able to make.'

'Well, as luck would have it, my diary is open in front of me,' I said, scanning the different coloured inks that denoted parties, clothes shopping or consultations.

'How are you fixed for the end of the week?' he asked.

'Well, I'm pretty busy, but for you, Jonathan . . .' I said, letting my voice trail off flirtatiously.

Gabi made a faint choking noise and I checked myself, horrifed.

'Fantastic. Could you face coming to a charity benevolent ball with me? It's the, um . . .' I could hear him flicking through the papers in his in-tray. 'Can't find the damn invite. Anyway, it's some charity we're supporting and I've got a table of clients and important bigwigs to schmooze, you know the deal. At the Dorchester?'

'Marvellous!' I said, struggling to keep the excitement from my voice. 'I think I could make that. Is it black tie?'

'Guess so. I'll have to call to check unless the invitation turns up . . .' There was some muffled speaking. 'Oh, thank you, Patrice. Patrice's got the invitation right here.'

I could just imagine Patrice's tightened face, handing over that invitation.

'Yeah, it's Friday night. And black tie. There'll be *scads* of estate agents, I'm afraid,' he went on. 'But I guess there'll be other compensations. And I hear they serve their champagne in the correct glasses.'

'I should hope so too.' I ran a finger across my eyebrow, smoothing it down. 'So what time shall I meet you?'

'How about eight? In the bar?'

'Eight. Fine. I'll look forward to that very much.'

'I will too,' said Jonathan. 'And, by the way, thanks for leaving my car outside the house. Not a scratch on it, and a full tank of gas! Guess it's not true what the guys in the office say about lady drivers.'

'The guys in the office are probably just intimidated by a lady who can drive at all,' I said, thinking of Hughy's running repair bills at the local garage. The man couldn't park on a rugby pitch without denting something.

'Hey, don't you go including me in that,' said Jonathan. 'There's something very sexy about lady drivers. Don't tell me – you have your own little driving shoes for the car, right?'

'I do indeed,' I replied, because I did. Now, was he trying to extend the conversation here, or was he just being polite? 'Bright pink suede, since you ask.'

'Honey, you remind me more of Penelope Pitstop every day,' said Jonathan, and laughed darkly.

Prickles of sweat sprang underneath my arms, and I rushed to get off the phone before I could make a fool of myself.

'No way was that Jonathan,' said Gabi. 'I could definitely hear laughing from the other end of the phone. I
cannot believe you're blowing me out for Dr No,' she
howled. 'I'd rather have an evening in bleaching my mous-
tache than endure ten seconds of Jonathan Riley out of
office hours!'

'Sorry. But, you know, *work*.' I spread my hands in
apology.

She shook her head. 'It must be.' She wagged her
rolled-up bridal magazines in my direction. 'Whatever
he's paying you, it's not enough. Oh . . . shit!'

'What?'

'Jonathan's in the *office*!' Gabi turned tail and thundered down the stairs, screeching something unpleasant
about Patrice as she went.

I can't pretend that I didn't look forward to Friday enormously. I didn't have time to diet myself into svelte dinner-
dance elegance in forty-eight hours, so instead I withdrew
some money from my replenished emergencies account
and bought a truly miraculous corset from Rigby & Peller.
It gave me a wasp waist, and the sort of bosom you normally
saw only on milkmaids and Bavarian bierkeller women.

With this structural assistance, I decanted myself into
an old cocktail dress of Granny's: a gorgeous blood-red
sheath with a sweetheart neckline, which masked some
of the cleavage and skimmed discreetly over my curves.
I washed and dressed my wig into a sophisticated up-do
and spent quite a long time perfecting my Audrey
Hepburn make-up face.

It would have been nice to have had Nelson's seal of
approval on this glamorous and very un-me outfit, but
he'd left the house by the time I emerged, pink and

steaming, from the bath. He and Roger Trumpet had planned a weekend at sea in Nelson's dad's boat, and they'd gone out for an early steak supper in preparation for catching a very late tide.

Still, I thought, hailing a taxi to the hotel, maybe it's for the best. When I'd told him my Friday plans, Nelson had made more than a few snide comments about Jonathan – recently, with Gabi's gleeful encouragement, he'd taken to referring to him as Remington Steele or the Gay Divorcee. Since he'd only met him at formal occasions, when Jonathan was in his buttoned-up, paranoid office mode, I didn't think Nelson was being very fair. And I did wonder if there was just a tiny hint of jealousy there too: Nelson had been the only man in my life for so long, and now there was another handsome, opinionated grump on the block.

Nelson and Jonathan had a fair bit in common, come to think of it. I suspected that that was why Nelson had taken agin him.

Jonathan was standing at the bar, browsing a cocktail list and looking impatient but immaculate in his dinner jacket. His black silk bow tie was a proper one, not a pre-tied monstrosity, and his shoes shone like jet. Even in the dim light, I could tell the fortnight in Italy had given his pale skin a golden glow and he must have had his hair cut, because it was shorter than normal, cropped close over his temples and gleaming like polished bronze.

My breath caught in my throat. He looked so unbelievably grown-up and self-possessed that for a moment I was too scared to approach him.

He shot back his sleeve to check the time and saw me hovering at the entrance. A broad smile spread over his face, displaying his beautiful square teeth, and I couldn't help but smile back.

I walked over, feeling self-conscious.

Well, I didn't walk. To be honest, I shimmied. It was something to do with the corset and the high heels.

'Honey,' said Jonathan, stretching out his hands. 'Wow. You look absolutely stunning.'

'Thank you.' I was trying very hard to be casual. 'You look very smart yourself.'

Jonathan took my hands, raised the right one to his lips and kissed my knuckles. It was an old-fashioned gesture, but it suited him, and the setting. My stomach fluttered beneath the whalebones.

'What a gorgeous dress!' he said, looking me up and down approvingly. 'Where do you find all these wonderful clothes?'

I made a 'this-old-thing' gesture, but felt as though a million bubbles were jetting through my veins. 'It belonged to my grandmother,' I said. 'She used to sing in nightclubs in the fifties. Very upmarket ones, too, I might add.'

'Well, she can't have looked more show-stopping than you do in it. You carry off that vintage look so well.' He gave me a modified wink.

'That's very kind of you to say so,' I said, loosening my hands before they started perspiring, and deliberately looking around the bar so I wouldn't have to meet his eye and make a fool of myself.

Then I thought, why not?

I lifted my chin and gazed straight into Jonathan's grey eyes. 'I sometimes think I'm a vintage girl. A proper 1950s woman's woman.'

Jonathan's eyebrows twitched. 'A proper 1950s *man's* woman, if you don't mind me saying. What can I get the proper woman to drink?'

Mindful of my complicated underpinnings, and the even more complicated situation, I told myself firmly to insist on a gin fizz. But I heard my voice say, 'A Martini, please.'

'OK,' said Jonathan. He turned round and ordered it, with a Scotch for himself.

One Martini. Just one Martini to get me in the mood, then it was straight back onto the gin fizzes, and back onto the straight and narrow, I told myself.

'So,' said Jonathan, guiding me gently to a table with his hand just touching the small of my back, 'were you very busy while I was away? Or did it feel kind of quiet without me?'

'I had a lot more time on my hands,' I said, slipping into a booth. 'But I made a lot of scruffy young men less scruffy and very happy.'

'Oh, damn,' sighed Jonathan. 'There I was, hoping you'd been sitting twiddling your thumbs without me.'

He gave me a solemn look. Dinner jackets clearly brought out the James Bond in him. I sipped my drink and smiled with my eyes over the rim of the glass.

There's something about cocktail glasses that just makes a girl feel flirty, don't you think? Something about the rather saucy way you have to cradle them in your hand.

'There was no one there to remind me when I was being crass,' he went on, 'no one to tell me off for pointing at stuff, and no one to glare at the bella mammas when they tried to hit on me.'

Ouch. Did I do that? I wasn't sure what he meant by it – seeing off bella mammas was what he was engaging me for, after all. I assumed he was trying to get a rise out of me, so I let it go, rather than make myself look stupid.

'Who are we meeting for drinks?' I asked.

'Where?'

'Here. In the bar.'

Jonathan looked surprised. 'No one.'

'Oh,' I said, confused. 'I thought . . .'

I wasn't sure what I thought. Suddenly I wasn't sure of very much.

'Can't I take you for a drink on your own?' he asked, with a more familiar edge of uncertainty in his voice.

'Of course you can,' I said quickly. 'But if you want me to deflect women for you, there aren't many in here. And I don't see you pointing at anything so far.'

Jonathan laughed. 'That's what I missed. Can I get you another?'

To my surprise, my glass was empty, bar one small olive.

'Just one,' I said, holding up one finger for emphasis.

Three Martinis made the dinner part of the evening swing past in a very amusing blur. I was seated between an estate agent and a fundraiser, both of whom were terribly interesting, and very keen to talk about something – anything – other than estate agency and fundraising. Consequently I picked up some very handy fishing tips and several recommendations for health spas in Turkey, which I seem to remember writing down on a napkin, although I never subsequently found where I put it.

I was planning to sit out most of the dancing, since I'd had a couple of glasses of wine with the meal. Nelson had slipped a little card in my handbag, which read: 'Two drinks, charming; Three drinks, philosophical; Four drinks, dancing on the table; Five drinks, Orlando von Borsch.' I reckoned, with the food, I was approaching the wild dancing stage, so when the band struck up, I deliberately started a new conversation about the London Underground with the man opposite; since his last rant had been about how the cab drivers were basically running London, I reckoned he'd keep me anchored to my seat until at least one glass of wine had worn off.

I was nodding my head and trying to focus on something other than his quite remarkable nostril hair when I felt a hand on my bare shoulder.

Tiny electric shocks tingled all the way down my back.

'Honey,' said a voice above my head. 'Do you mind if I steal her away, Edward?'

My companion looked rather narked – he had, after all, just worked up a healthy head of steam about bus lanes – but before he could even open his mouth, Jonathan had led me by the hand onto the dance floor.

'I'm not fit to dance,' I protested as he slipped his arm round my waist and began to guide me expertly in the limited space available.

'I prefer my partners a little tipsy,' he said, turning me round with just the tiniest pressure on my back. 'Makes them more manoeuvrable.'

I could see what he meant. My arms had gone a bit loose and were draping themselves in apparent elegance round his neck, while my feet, usually four seconds behind my brain, were moving in close harmony with his. We moved around our allotted space rather gracefully. Jonathan's buttoned-up exterior hadn't hinted at rhythm like this. He danced with a nonchalance that made his easy steps even more impressive.

'Hey, you're good at this!' he said.

'Not as good as you.'

'Maybe you're only good when you're dancing with me.' He arched his eyebrow cheesily – presumably because his hands weren't free to do his click and point thing.

This was a whole new level of charm that I wasn't really prepared for, and even though I knew it was purely chat, my heart flipped.

'Is that a line from a film?' I enquired, trying to sound unimpressed.

Jonathan grinned. 'Hey, sassy.'

'Shh,' I said. 'I'm enjoying myself.'

'String of Pearls' turned into 'I Get a Kick Out of You', and we shimmered around the floor like a couple from the Peggy Spencer School of Dance, Penge. Actually, it wasn't so much like *Come Dancing*, as something from a black and white romantic comedy. My feet seemed to go wherever Jonathan wanted them to, and for once I wasn't even counting in my head. There were never enough boys to go round at my dancing class, so I often ended up being the man, since I was taller than most girls – taller than most of the boys, actually – so I did have a dreadful residual habit of leading. But tonight I was floating lighter than the feathers on Ginger Rogers' hem.

I was dancing like Honey. I felt like Honey.

I *was* Honey.

The band played 'Chattanooga Choo Choo' and 'Cheek to Cheek' and as I whirled round I couldn't help basking in the admiring glances. If the staff of Dean & Daniels could have seen anal-retentive Jonathan and frumpy Melissa now, they wouldn't have believed their own eyes. Then the tempo slowed, and I recognised the smoochy opening bars of 'Moonlight Serenade'.

I didn't want to sit down now, but a slow dance?

Jonathan sensed the abrupt stiffness in my back and spread his fingers wide along the base of my spine, reaching from my tail bone up to my waist. There was a layer of dress and a layer of good old-fashioned corsetry between his hand and my bare skin, but I could almost feel the heat of his fingers.

'Should we stop here?' he murmured in my ear, and his voice sounded so husky I went hot and cold and hot again.

'I don't want to,' he added.

I didn't trust myself to speak, so I nodded slightly and sank a little closer into his arms, close enough to feel the warmth of his neck when I breathed in.

It was without a doubt the most thrilling, dreamlike experience of my whole life up to that point, moving slowly, instinctively around the darkened dance floor in his arms. Even though I knew it was a corny thing to be thinking, I didn't want the song to come to a close. But it did, the final chords faded away in a ripple of applause, and at once I felt deflated.

After lingering for a tantalising couple of seconds, Jonathan's hand left my back, and he took my hand to lead me off the dance floor. As we approached our table, I could see several conversations stop and I braced myself for re-entry into the real world. However, just as I was making polite pre-conversation eye contact with my hairy-nosed lawyer, I felt Jonathan guiding me away from the table, towards the door.

'We need a little fresh air!' Jonathan was saying in a general table direction, loosening his bow tie and picking up a bottle of champagne and two flutes as we passed. 'Guess we overdid it! Would you excuse us?'

I just smiled and let myself be led out.

'What was that for?' I murmured out of the side of my mouth as we wove through the tables.

'Well, we've just given an exhibition foxtrot display, and I guess everyone will be expecting me to take you somewhere private – so I can let you know how admiring I am of your backwards dancing,' he said.

'What lengths you go to in order to be convincing,' I murmured.

Jonathan gave me a sideways, rather quizzical look. 'Plus, I'm hot and I need some air.'

'Me too,' I said, quickly.

In the corridor we passed one of the female guests from our table, and Jonathan paused to greet her.

'Hello, Sophie,' he said. 'Are you enjoying yourself?'

'Awfully much, thank you. You made such a gorgeous couple on the dance floor!' she gushed. 'Fred and Ginger all over again!'

'Why, thank you,' said Jonathan. 'But I flatter myself I'm more like Gene Kelly. My partner here prefers her dancers more muscular.'

I smiled at him, tingling with delight that he'd remembered, but his face was completely straight.

Sophie looked as though she was about to swoon. I'd never seen Jonathan have that effect on anyone at work, but in black tie he was a whole other proposition. 'Oh, yes,' she nodded a bit too enthusiastically. 'I can see that. You were both wonderful! So in tune with each other! It must be that couples' chemistry!'

'Will you excuse us?' Jonathan drifted us off down the corridor, walking away from the noise and the heat of the ballroom until we reached a secluded window, looking out onto Hyde Park.

'I've had a lovely evening,' he said, taking my hand

and looking at me very seriously. 'Thank you for coming.'

My heart had just about recovered from the dancing, but suddenly it felt as if it had stopped completely. The way he was looking at me, all serious and attentive, was more flattering than any compliment I'd ever had. Jonathan had such perfect manners, but he managed to make them seem so natural and spontaneous.

'Thank *you* so much for inviting me,' I said.

'The pleasure's all mine,' he said. 'Would you hold these?' He held out the flutes.

I took them, and he filled them carefully with champagne.

'To Honey Blennerhesket,' he said, propping the bottle on a nearby flower display. 'The woman who helped me start over.' And he clinked his glass against mine.

The breath caught in my throat. I smiled, and Jonathan smiled back, a little wonkily, and suppressed a hiccup.

Oh, he's *drunk*, I thought and a cold thud of disappointment hit me.

But hang on, said a small voice in my head: if he *is* drunk, it would be OK for me to play along with his romantic night-out behaviour – after all, I argued with myself, how much would I have given, after Orlando dumped me, to have a night of consequence-free flirting with a compliant partner?

Besides, there was something about Jonathan that made me want to flirt back. I couldn't help it.

'I can honestly say that yours isn't the only life Honey has changed,' I said, sipping my champagne and flashing a flirty look at him through my sooty lashes.

Jonathan leaned back against the alcove and held out his arm, so I could lean against him and look out of the window too. It was the kind of affectionate brotherly gesture Nelson often made after a couple of pints. I hesitated for a moment, then took a step nearer to him.

'You know, Honey, when I first engaged you, I used to dread our appointments,' he said, as I leaned tentatively against his side. 'It meant I had to go out, meet new people. Be on show. But now . . .' He let out a long breath. 'Now, *for some reason*, you don't know how much I look forward to them. You know, I never thought I'd say that. When Cindy and I split I thought I'd never . . .' He paused and corrected himself. 'No, I used to dread going out even when I was *with* Cindy. You're so different. You don't make judgements, you don't make demands, you don't take sides. You just make me feel like a million dollars.'

'Good,' I said. 'You make me feel like at least half a million pounds.'

Jonathan laughed and I could feel the vibrations of his laughter through the thin cotton of his dress shirt.

I swallowed.

'You're worth double,' he said. 'Triple. You know, Honey Blennerhesket is just the sort of woman every man wants on his arm. Witty, independent, decisive, practical.' He sighed. 'Not to mention beautiful. And you won't even let me have exclusivity during work hours.'

I closed my eyes with pleasure, then snapped them open as the shock of what he'd said cut through the pleasure like cold water. He didn't mean *me*, Melissa. He meant made-up, fictional Honey. Honey he was paying for.

I should have stopped there, but the champagne running through my bloodstream fought against the disappointment.

So what if he means Honey, I argued. You're here tonight *as* Honey, aren't you? And you're here now. You work hard enough living up to her standards, why not reap some of the rewards? You can't afford to pass up fabulously romantic opportunities like this . . .

I luxuriated in our reflection in the dark window. That woman in the corridor was right: we did make a very handsome couple. And if I was playing a role, pretending to be someone I wasn't, then so was he. He was pretending to be un-heartbroken, available, the courteous all-American gentleman. We were about as real as Fred and Ginger. Or Gene Kelly and Cyd Charisse.

'Honey,' Jonathan began, turning me gently towards him, as skilfully as he'd turned me on the dance floor. 'Honey, there's something I must say to you . . .'

I breathed in the musky smell of his Creed, and the warm woollen smell of his dinner jacket, and felt distinctly dizzy.

'It's about you and me . . .' Jonathan suddenly clapped a hand to his chest and twisted up his face. 'Oh, shit.'

'Jonathan!' I said, putting my glass down. 'Jonathan, are you all right . . . ?'

But Jonathan slipped a hand in his inner pocket, pulled a face and withdrew his mobile phone. 'Jonathan Riley?' he said, putting a finger in the opposite ear and turning away to talk.

I picked up my champagne glass as casually as I could, although my hands were shaking with adrenalin and delayed embarrassment.

'OK.' Jonathan clicked his phone shut with a big sigh and looked at me with an expression of extreme regret. 'Listen, you're going to hate me. Work. Client in New

York who will not stop pestering me about her stupid goddamn house. I have to call in at the office.'

'The penalties for being in demand,' I said, trying to sound light and unconcerned when in fact my stomach was doing cartwheels.

Jonathan took the glass out of my hand and put it on the floral arrangement. 'Honey, if she wasn't a major, major client, I would tell her that I was at a ball, at the Dorchester, with the most beautiful woman in London. But she is a major, major client. So I have to go.' He took my hand and raised it to his lips. 'But you're welcome to stay if you want.'

She was a major client? A cynical voice in my head wondered if it was actually *Cindy* on the other end of the line.

What with my corset, and the pressure of his lips on my knuckles, and the champagne, I was having great difficulty breathing normally.

'Why would I want to stay if you're not here?' I demanded breathlessly. 'What would be the fun in that?'

'Ah, that's what I hoped you'd say,' he replied with a wicked grin. 'Come on, let's get a cab out of here.'

We made our excuses – which everyone seemed to understand perfectly from all the winks and nodding that flashed around the table – and got into a black cab, hailed by the doorman outside the hotel.

In the back of the taxi, Jonathan took my hand and held it. Since it was his romantic evening, I didn't see why I shouldn't let him.

Annoyingly, Dean & Daniels was only around the corner from the Dorchester, and Jonathan quickly fell into one of his thoughtful silences.

'Are you all right?' I enquired. If I was being completely

honest, I was aching with curiosity to know what it was he was about to tell me before his phone rang.

'Just happy,' said Jonathan and squeezed my hand.

That was when I knew I had no right to spoil his evening by inflicting my own confusion on him. Instead I watched the buildings flashing past and enjoyed the feeling of being alone in the taxi with him.

'Are *you* happy?' he asked, out of the blue.

'I am,' I answered, truthfully. Because if he was enjoying being with Honey, I was definitely enjoying *being* her.

And then we were outside his office.

Jonathan fumbled in his jacket for his wallet, and got out of the taxi to pay.

'Here,' he said to the driver, shoving notes at him. 'And can you take the lady wherever she wants to go, please?'

'Jonathan, are you, um, OK to go back to work?' I enquired discreetly.

He leaned into the cab, screwing up his face in mock outrage. 'Honey, what are you suggesting? I'm very sober indeed.'

Now he mentioned it, I couldn't smell any alcohol on his breath. I blushed. That rather put paid to my 'he's drunk, so don't take him seriously' rationale.

'Goodnight, Honey,' he said softly and leaned over until his nose was level with mine. Then he leaned a little further and touched his lips against my cheek, then pressed a little harder, pausing with his mouth a few millimetres from my skin, so I could feel his breath on my cheek.

'Goodnight,' I whispered, breathing in the clean fragrance of his hair.

'Wow,' he said so close to my ear that I could feel his

whisper. 'You smell fabulous. Just like a real, old-fashioned, blonde bombshell should smell.'

Oh my God, I thought, throwing all caution and reason to the winds. He's going to kiss me, he's going to kiss me!

Then, while my eyes were still closed, waiting for his kiss, he was gone.

I sat there, unable to move or speak, while the driver restarted the cab and set off again. It was several minutes before I could drag myself back down to earth to tell him where to go.

If this wasn't falling in love, I didn't know what was.

Oh dear.

17

Outside our front door the lavender window boxes were bushy and fragrant and I sank my nose into the cushion of purple heads, breathing in the glorious scent until I felt dizzy. Only the distant noise of traffic spoiled the absolute peacefulness. London could be so lovely, between late night and early morning, I thought, with a burst of affection for the place. Then I slipped my key into the lock before I caught sight of any dog poo or wheel clamps, and let myself in.

I wasn't prepared for the scene that greeted me in the sitting room. I wasn't even prepared for all the lights to be on. Blinking in the brightness, I tried to absorb the bizarre tableau: Gabi, on the sofa, sobbing her eyes out; Nelson, in his yellow waterproof sailing jacket, automatically passing her tissues; Roger Trumpet, also in full sailing gear, twitching in embarrassment and fiddling with a sequinned cushion.

In turn, when they heard my entrance, all three looked up and gaped at me in my evening dress, blonde tendrils falling down round my face, slingbacks in one hand, gold clutch bag in the other.

There was a brief pause, then Gabi resumed her wailing with renewed vigour. I could just about make out the odd word: 'your fault', 'lucky bitch' and, oddly, 'forensics'.

'Well, thank God you're back at last,' said Nelson, making to get up.

It seemed to me that every time I arrived anywhere these days, people said, 'Thank God you're here' and abandoned me to whatever crisis they'd just initiated.

Roger also scrambled to his feet. 'Where've you been?' he demanded. '*Stars in their Eyes?*'

I put up my hand to stop the boys in their tracks. 'I've been to a dinner-dance at the Dorchester. Would you mind telling me what's happened?' I asked, and nodded towards Gabi.

'Gabi? Do you want *me* to tell her?' Nelson asked. His voice was tired, but full of kindness.

Gabi hiccuped, nodded and reached for another hanky. Then reached for a biscuit from the half-eaten family packet of Jaffa Cakes in front of her.

'Well. It seems Aaron and Gabi have had a, um, row, because Aaron wants to give up his spread-betting job and have a, um, a career change,' said Nelson tactfully.

'He wants to retrain as a forensic pathologist!' bawled Gabi, spraying biscuit crumbs onto the sofa. 'He wants to go back to college and all that guff about wanting to get married was just so that I'd have to support him through his bloody course! The bastard!'

Nelson and Roger exchanged ambiguous looks.

'Right,' I said.

'It's good that you're getting *angry* now,' said Roger, helpfully. 'When you arrived, you weren't quite so positive, were you? It's good to move on to anger. Much more cleansing.'

'Thank you, Roger,' I said with a warning tone. 'Don't you have a tide to catch?' Since his successful rebranding as a New Bachelor, Roger had taken to pontificating on relationship matters with all the profundity of an *Esquire* letters page.

'We'll go in a minute. Why don't you get changed?' said Nelson. He cast a meaningful look at my billowing cleavage. 'Into something less formal, maybe.'

'Good idea. Two minutes, Gabi!' I said brightly. 'Roger, why don't you put the kettle on?'

In my room, I stripped off my dress and set about unfastening the black silk clips and ties of my stockings and corset. It wasn't the glamorous disrobing I'd planned in the taxi on my way home; I'd imagined myself rolling the stockings down my legs, pretending Jonathan's strong fingers were flicking the fabric out of the clips. My skin had shivered deliciously, thinking about the long, slow way I'd unhook the corset, his seductively hooked eyebrow at the forefront of my mind's eye.

And yet, I reflected, as my fingers clumsily hurried over the fastenings, I'd gone from femme fatale to Brown Owl the moment I'd walked into the sitting room. So my sexy lingerie didn't have quite the magical spell I'd thought it had.

I shook my head in an effort to dispel the leaden anti-climax spreading through me. There was no point taking it out on Gabi – it wasn't her fault. I pulled on my black lounge pants and a jumper, and set my wig back on its stand, where it spooled out over my dressing table in sexy caramel waves. I made a mental note to give it a good wash. My own hair was a bit flat from being in a cap all night but I shook it out as best as I could, and pulled it into a high ponytail.

'That's more like it!' said Roger when I went back in. 'Much more comfy, eh?'

I ignored him.

'Tea?' said Nelson, wielding the pot.

I nodded and cast a worried glance at Gabi, who was clutching her knees and rocking backwards and forwards like a distraught Weeble. 'Why don't you two get away now, and leave us to it?'

'Maybe after a cup of tea,' said Roger. Clearly now I was here, the prospect of listening to an expert interviewer extract the full drama of Gabi's mercy dash was more appealing than just passing her hankies while she sobbed incoherently into Nelson's shoulder.

'No, we should go now,' said Nelson firmly. 'I don't want to miss the tide. Roger, can you put the bags in the car?'

Roger got up with visible reluctance and shouldered the kit bag.

Nelson drew me tactfully into the kitchen. 'I don't know exactly what's happened,' he murmured, 'but go easy on her, will you? She's really upset.'

'Of course I'm going to go easy on her!' I exclaimed, hurt. 'What else would I do?'

He gave me one of his annoyingly superior looks. 'What I meant was, this is *not* the time to discuss your romantic evening with Remington Steele, or give her one of your speeches about how marriage just turns women into Stepford wives.'

'As if!'

Really, Nelson could be so off sometimes. And since when had he been Gabi's Father Confessor anyway?

'I defrosted one of my shepherd's pies – she couldn't face it, but maybe now you're here it might be a good idea to get some food into her.' Nelson pulled a face. 'Poor Gabi. I hope he's worth it.'

I bundled him and Roger out of the house and put

the shepherd's pie in the oven. Never mind Gabi, suddenly I was ravenous.

'Supper'll be in twenty minutes,' I said, slipping onto the sofa next to her. 'So that gives you time to tell me what's happened.'

'I can do that in six words,' she said, holding up her fingers to count off. Her massive engagement ring was conspicuous by its absence. 'Aaron. And. I. Have. Split. Up.'

'Not. Necessarily,' I replied, counting with my fingers. 'You. Can. Always. Make. It. Up.'

'We can't. Not now.'

'Gabi, it's gone two o'clock,' I sighed, picking up my mug of tea. 'Just tell me what happened.'

Gabi drew in a shuddering breath. 'You know you blew me out for discussing bridesmaids' dresses tonight?' she began.

'Mmm,' I said, cautiously.

'Well, instead, I asked Aaron if he'd come with me to try out a restaurant I was thinking of, if we had a morning wedding, you know, with a lunch reception.' Her face creased. 'Aaron got really narky and said we should be trying to economise, not spend thousands on the wedding. And I told him not to be so tight, when he had a big bonus coming, and he . . .' Gabi bit her lip.

I took her hand and squeezed it. 'What did he say?'

'He said he wouldn't be *getting* the bonus. He told me that now he knew he'd have me by his side, he could make the biggest decision of his life, and give up the City job to retrain as a lousy forensic pathologist!'

'But, Gabi, that's a jolly noble thing to want to do,' I said, racking my brains for three positives. 'The police need brainy types like Aaron and, um, it's a secure job, isn't it?'

Gabi let rip with a howl of sheer frustration. 'I know! I know it's frigging *noble*! But why does he have to do it? Why can't he carry out a public service by earning lots of money and paying top-rate tax!'

There was no unsanctimonious answer to this. So I gathered my courage in both hands, and offered the sanctimonious one.

'Gabi, maybe Aaron feels there's more to life than money. Maybe he wants to do something more rewarding?'

'Maybe he just watches too much *Silent* bloody *Witness*!'

We sat in silence for several minutes while I wondered what to say next. I had a sinking suspicion that all this was somehow my fault.

'It's your fault,' she said, as if she could read my mind. 'You put all those doubts in my head.'

Doubts? *Doubts?*

'Oh, now, come on . . .' I began.

Gabi turned to look at me. Her face was red and streaky, like a frustrated toddler's. 'Wasn't it you who said that I should leave him if I was only in it for the Audi? Wasn't it?'

'Well, yes,' I said, horrified. 'But I was hoping you were joking. And that deep down you actually loved him for something other than his bank account. I didn't think you *meant* it.'

Gabi broke down into fierce sobs. 'Oh, Mel! It's not his fault. Or yours. It's all *mine*. I hate myself! I'm such a cow!' she wailed, pummelling her knees with her clenched fists. 'I'm the worst kind of bitch! What am I going to do?'

I couldn't bear to hear her so unhappy, even if she was

liable to turn violent. I flung my arms round her, hugging her face into my ample chest.

'You're not horrible,' I soothed. 'If you were a real money-grabbing cow you'd just walk away and not feel bad at all. I mean, it's a *good* sign that you feel so guilty and revolted with yourself.'

'Oh, Mel,' she hiccuped. 'I thought I had it all sussed, I thought as long as I had enough money I could make the rest come later.' Tears were running down her face. 'But Aaron *loves* me! I never realised just how . . . Oh, God, his *face* when he said he could manage anything as long as I was there with him! I wanted to die. But I just couldn't walk out like you said! He doesn't deserve to be screwed like this. So now I feel I've got to marry him, even though I know I like him, but I don't love him. Oh God!' she sobbed, 'I'm such a bi-i-i-i-itch!'

Actually, I wasn't sure Aaron was being quite as noble as he'd like to think, and if he was half the operator I thought he was, this was a rather smart move on his part. But I was too tired to come up with useful advice, so I just let her cry herself out until the oven timer pinged.

'Now then,' I said in a reassuring, nanny-ish voice. 'Let's have some supper.' I glanced at the clock – ten to three.

Ten to *three*!

I dished up the shepherd's pie into large bowls, which I've always found more comforting than plates in dark times, then squirted tomato sauce liberally over the mash, and we sat down at the table to eat. After several restorative mouthfuls, a weird second wind overtook me, and I no longer felt tired.

Gabi too seemed to recover somewhat, and shovelled forkfuls of mince into her mouth with an enthusiasm I hadn't seen since she embarked on her pre-Vera Wang diet.

'Mel, I'm so sorry,' she said when her bowl was clean. 'You're a good friend and I shouldn't dump on you. Everyone else does, and it's not fair.' Her face creased. 'That's *another* horrible thing I've done.'

I patted her hand. 'I've got broad shoulders. Anyway, it's better that you get this sorted out now, isn't it? No point leading Aaron on if you don't love him enough.'

Gabi stuck her hands in her hair and put her elbows on the table. 'Ohhhh. When you put it like that . . . I'm so angry at myself.' She looked at me from under her thick fringe. 'I was fine about this until I started talking to you. Am I the most wicked person you know? Tell me honestly now.'

'You're no worse than several members of my family,' I said sadly, thinking of Allegra's shameless totting-up of Lars's off-shore assets the night before the wedding.

'That's what I'm worried about.' Gabi scraped some crusty bits off the dish. 'But if I didn't feel something for Aaron, would I feel so terrible now? What if I could persuade him not to pack his job in?'

'Honestly, Gabi,' I said quickly, 'you need more than money to make a marriage work.' I thought about the marriages I knew well – Allegra's, my parents, Emery's. Jonathan's. They all had plenty of cash, and look where it had got them. Jonathan didn't even get to keep his old life, let alone his assets.

An image of Jonathan in his sexy dinner jacket floated into my mind, and I pushed it away. I wasn't going to think about Jonathan now.

'So what *do* you need?' demanded Gabi. 'And can you try not to sound so much like a Relate counsellor, please.'

'Well, you need a bit of independence. And respect. And some shared interests. Um, the same sort of sense of humour helps.' I thought hard, trying to pin down what I'd want in a husband. 'You need to be able to live together, and understand each other. Know when to give each other some space, and when to be close.' Actually, now I'd started, the words were tumbling out. 'You want a partner who can make you feel secure, and loved, so you can reach your full potential, someone who can inspire you, and encourage you to try again if things don't work out. Someone who loves you for who you are, not who you might turn into, or who you once were.'

Gabi looked at me with narrowed eyes. 'So why don't you marry him then?'

'Sorry?' I blinked.

She gave up picking daintily at the crusts and slopped a second helping of shepherd's pie into her bowl with more force than was necessary. 'You've just described your relationship with Nelson.'

I laughed out loud. 'Don't be *silly*!'

'Why not? He does all those things for you, and he clearly adores you. You make marriage sound like being permanent flatmates.'

'Oh, but I didn't mean to!' I protested. 'There has to be romance there as well! It's just that people think it should *all* be romance, and . . .' The poor stifled butterflies released at Allegra's wedding sprang unfortunately to mind. 'I think that's just asking for disappointment, really. I blame big white weddings. They only set you up for a lifetime of anticlimax. The dress that costs more than your car, your family gathered together on best behaviour, the idea that if you tick every box on the check-list, you'll have a perfect day . . .'

'Oh, Mel!' Gabi gave me a scornful look. 'Do *not* tell me you wouldn't have a big white wedding if the right man came along.'

I shrugged. I did occasionally allow myself a daydream about Welsh gold rings, and bowers of flowers, but why set yourself up to be let down?

'Were you always so horribly pragmatic?' demanded Gabi. 'I mean, is this all a result of dating sleazers like Orlando, or is it because of your dad?'

'A bit of both,' I said stiffly. 'Anyway, it's true. From what I've seen of married life, both parties have to love each other a lot, just to see them through your basic daily horrors, let alone major crises.'

Gabi mashed tomato sauce glumly into her shepherd's pie. 'So what should I do? Am I being selfish?' she asked. 'Should I just let Aaron find someone nicer?'

I drew in a deep breath. Gabi was a terrible fisher of compliments, and I wasn't going to indulge her on this occasion. 'That depends.'

'On what?'

'Well, can you tell me three great things about Aaron? That don't involve his car or his salary?'

Gabi screwed up her eyes and thought for a few painful moments. Eventually, she came up with, 'He's not the jealous type, he works really hard . . . Um, he knows how to fix electrical stuff?'

'That's not necessarily as great as you think,' I interrupted. 'Nelson's good with electrical stuff, but he uses it as an underhand negotiating tool.'

'*Nelson.*' Gabi sighed. 'There you go again. When are you two going to realise you're made for each other and spare me the agony of unrequited love?'

'Now, come on, Gabi,' I said firmly, determined not

to be sidetracked, even though the prospect of hearing her evidence for that was intriguing. 'Don't you think it would be better to have a complete break and sort out what you really *want* from a relationship?'

She slumped back in her seat. 'I wish you weren't so right all the time. Maybe it would be safer to do what you're doing,' she said. 'Audition lots of eligible men who don't have girlfriends, then persuade them that they need a real one.'

'No, I don't think it would be safer. At all.'

Gabi looked at me with renewed interest in her blood-shot, mascara-ringed eyes. 'Why not?'

I don't know if it was the late hour, or the comforting warmth of the shepherd's pie in my stomach, or just an impulse to confide in someone, but caution deserted me. 'Oh, because you end up falling in love with something you can't have.'

'You're in love with Jonathan Riley!' she crowed. 'I knew it!'

'I didn't say that exactly,' I added hastily. 'What I meant was, it would be very easy to fall in . . .'

Gabi fixed me with a look.

'OK,' I admitted, 'but it's probably one of those passing hormonal things. *Like you and Nelson.* I mean, Jonathan's way out of my league. He's a proper person, not a useless little boy. And he's had an awful time with his divorce, you know. He's definitely not looking for a relationship – that's why he hired me in the first place! And,' I concluded miserably, 'he doesn't know the first thing about me.'

'Don't be stupid,' retorted Gabi. 'Of course he does. He sees you about three times a week, minimum.'

'No. He sees Honey,' I corrected her. 'He sees this

confident, sexy blonde with no baggage, no embarrassing family, no visible panty-line and no hang-ups. If he saw me now, he wouldn't recognise me. And he certainly wouldn't want to date me.'

'I doubt that,' said Gabi. 'He might even prefer the real you.'

'Look, I know best, OK?'

'Have you . . . you know?' Gabi twitched her eyebrows suggestively.

The blood rushed into my face. 'No!'

'Would you?'

'The situation wouldn't arise,' I said haughtily, trying to ignore the shiver tingling over my skin.

'Come on,' she snorted. 'I know he's chronically charm-deficient, but even I have to concede that Jonathan's a good-looking man in the prime of his life. He must be getting it somewhere. Unless that's the reason he's such a grumpy bastard in the office.' She looked thoughtful. 'He does work very long hours. No,' she decided, 'no, Patrice would be enough to cool anyone's ardour. And, to be fair, he's been marginally less arsey since he came back from Italy. Slightly more mellow, even.'

'Good,' I said, and shivered inside.

'You know your trouble,' said Gabi, sounding much more like herself now we'd sidestepped onto my problems, 'you do your job too well. If you carry on the way you are, Jonathan's going to be so well settled in, and his broken heart will be so well healed that the next thing he'll be doing is asking you to line up a real girlfriend for him. Then how will you feel?'

I stared at her. I hadn't put the thought in so many words, but it had occurred to me. If it had occurred to Gabi, then surely it must have occurred to Jonathan too.

How long *would* it be? He already had two gym memberships and invitations for dinner two months in advance. And if he was thawing in the office too . . .

'You might want to be a bit less professional,' she suggested.

'I can't!' I wailed, horrified. 'He *expects* me to be professional! It's one of the things he likes most about me. He said so.'

'He's been telling you the things he *likes* about you?'

I blushed. 'In a sort of informal appraisal sense.'

Gabi rolled her eyes. 'You are in a *right* old mess, Mel.'

'I know.' I sank my chin onto my hands. How had we gone from discussing Gabi's mess to mine?

'You know the really annoying thing?' I moaned. 'Jonathan is exactly the sort of man Nelson's always telling me I should go for. Independent, successful, well-balanced, ambitious – but in a good way. I've never met a man like that before. And the one time I do meet one, I'm not even me! If I were me I'd be too scared to even make conversation with him!'

'Oh no. No, no. *That*'s not the really annoying thing,' replied Gabi. She sank her chin onto her hands too, so our eyes were level. Her brown eyes, normally sparkling with barely suppressed badness, were very sad. 'If we're being really honest here . . .' She hesitated for a second, then sighed. 'No, the *really* annoying thing is that Nelson is probably in love with you, and is only describing *himself* to try to get you to think of him as boyfriend material.'

I met Gabi's gaze with some amusement. 'Oh, Gabi, stop fishing.'

'I'm not fishing,' said Gabi, looking wounded. 'It's true. What's the point in me . . . *having feelings* for Nelson when it's obvious to everyone else that he's mad about you?'

'Look, I know he's terribly affectionate, but you're wrong.' I nudged her. 'Come on. You're just doing it to make me say he's in love with you.'

'I'm not,' she protested. 'I wish I were. Think about it. He spends all his time with you, he's endlessly patient with you whereas he's totally dismissive of everyone else, he's always cooking you supper and rubbing your bloody horrible feet. You even go on holiday together, for God's sake. Wake up, Mel! Why else would he put up with all your nonsense? Haven't you *seen Emma*?'

I looked at her and blinked. Well, gosh. Nelson did have a certain Mr Knightley-esque rudeness, come to think of it. I rolled the idea round in my head, testing it out. Nelson and I *were* awfully close, and he was far more affectionate to me than any member of my immediate family. Everyone liked him, and he made me feel, well, comfortable. And he did sometimes . . .

'Don't be silly!' I said. 'That's utterly ridiculous!'

Gabi shook her head and looked martyred. 'It's true, Mel. Believe me, I wish I didn't think so.'

'Well, I still think you're wrong,' I insisted. But I did love him enormously, and, if I were being brutally honest, he was quite handsome, in a windblown, seafaring way.

'Melissa, he's already your boyfriend in all but the bedroom area of things.' She twinkled, despite herself. 'And I bet he's just as strong and masterful there as he is everywhere else.'

'Shut up, Gabi,' I said, raising my hands. 'Too much information.'

I got up and boiled the kettle for a pot of tea. Suddenly I felt dog-tired. Was it only a few hours since Jonathan

and I had been whirling around the ballroom at the
Dorchester? It seemed like weeks ago.

'You're so lucky, Mel,' said Gabi, unexpectedly. 'I wish
I were more like you.'

'Good God, no, you don't,' I said.

'OK, I wish I were more like Honey then.'

I put a cup of tea down in front of her and said, 'That
makes two of us.'

I made Gabi comfortable on the sofa bed in the living
room, then turned in myself. The morning light had
started to creep round the edge of the curtains, and I
couldn't drop off, not even with my eye mask on.

I kept thinking about what Gabi had said. Maybe she
was right: maybe I should be with Nelson. It would make
so much more sense than this pointless chasing after
Jonathan, a man way out of my field of experience, who
would probably be horrified to see what Honey's feet
really looked like, under the stilettos, let alone rub them
better.

And Nelson and I did get on so well, persisted the
little voice in my head, and hadn't I just told her that
marriage should be about getting on with each other, not
wild unbridled passion?

I thought of my parents, constantly sniping away at
each other. I didn't want a marriage like that. I wanted a
marriage where my husband would look after me, and
respect me and make me laugh. Just like Nelson did.

I rolled over, trying to find a cool patch of pillow.

But even if it did make sense, getting together with
Nelson would make me a lousy friend. Despite her protestations, I could tell that Gabi was genuinely keen on
him.

But who wouldn't be? He was a real catch: handsome, kind, successful, principled.

How weird to think of him like that.

Thoughts flashed quickly in and out of my mind like trout in a stream, one after the other, each more unsettling than the last.

Nothing changed the grim truth that I had a terrible crush on Jonathan, though. Admitting it to Gabi had been weird, like taking a weight off my mind. But surely that would pass with time. Actually, it would pass the day he asked me to find him a girlfriend.

Or the day he saw me not being Honey.

Maybe it was time to cut my losses there, and concentrate on making *Melissa* happy – and who was better to do that than Nelson?

I carried on rolling over and over until it was time to get up.

18

Accompanying Jonathan to social dinners slowly began to take second place to accompanying Jonathan, full stop. Mid-week, I'd get a studiedly offhand phone call – 'Have you heard of Borough Market? Would you take me there?' – and off we'd go, to sip freshly roasted coffee and buy organic meat that I seriously doubted he'd cook in that huge kitchen in Barnes. I'd feel a little sorry for him, wanting to fill in his weekends with me, instead of doing the familiar married things he was probably used to. Then when I got there, Jonathan would be such excellent company that it was impossible to imagine him being lonely at all.

And so as September stretched into October, and the trees outside my office turned bright copper and gold and bronze, I started to see more of London than I'd ever thought possible. I did wonder if Jonathan had acquired a Victorian Guide to England, since most of the things he insisted we visit, I'd never heard of. Debtors' prisons, sites of ancient nunneries, shops that had supplied apricot creams to Queen Anne, you know the sort of thing. Doubtless hoping for hog roasts and urchins in knee-breeches, Jonathan had been on at me for ages to take him to a 'proper' Bonfire Night – so much so that I was beginning to dread it on behalf of Wandsworth Borough Council.

He absolutely insisted on coming with me to whichever 'local' fireworks event I was planning to attend – 'to get a real flavour of London life'. I wasn't sure what sort of display I'd take him to otherwise: a private one in the back garden at Buckingham Palace, maybe, with the Queen doling out the Roman candles from a biscuit tin, and screeching at Prince Andrew not to keep running back to check the blue touch paper. Nelson and I usually went to the big display in Battersea Park: it was close to home and Nelson knew some good free parking spots.

Jonathan claimed it was perfect. I told him to get a cab there and not to bring any valuables.

On Bonfire Night, Nelson and I arranged to meet Gabi in the Prince of Wales for a pre-display blood-warmer. Gabi was a rather more subdued girl of late: she and Aaron had, tearfully, agreed to spend two months apart, to work out what each really wanted from their relationship, and consequently she was spending more and more time round at our flat, to the point where Roger Trumpet was considering asking her to join his pub quiz team. And if that didn't focus Gabi's mind on her future, I didn't know what would.

Nelson parked and checked each door lock several times before we were allowed to set off for the Prince of Wales. We were in good time, but already the pub was heaving with pink-cheeked men bulging out of their jumbo cords, braying at girls in ski-wear. To the delight of my ever-rumbling stomach, there was a tempting hog roast going on outside.

'So what do you want to drink? Mel? Mel! What are you looking around for now?' asked Nelson as we struggled towards the bar.

'Um, mulled wine.' I hadn't actually told Nelson I was

meeting Jonathan. He'd been very snippy on the topic of Jonathan lately, which made me wonder afresh if Gabi was right about him being, well, fonder of me than he let on. I'd been waiting for the right moment to tell Nelson I'd be slipping off to be with Jonathan for an hour or so, but it hadn't yet arrived. Now I suspected that Jonathan would arrive before the right moment would.

While Nelson was at the bar, Gabi rushed in, looking flushed with excitement. 'Mel!' she said, breathlessly, pulling off her gloves. 'Have I got some gossip for you!'

'Did you leave the office at the same time as Jonathan?' I demanded. I couldn't risk Jonathan seeing me with Gabi; she was bound to call me Mel by mistake, and quite honestly, I didn't think I could throw myself into being Honey with those two knocking around in the back-ground. 'Is he on his way?'

Gabi looked confused. 'No, he was still there when I left. Why? Listen, you won't believe . . .'

'As long as he didn't see you coming here. He's coming here tonight to see the fireworks. So remember,' I said firmly, 'when he arrives, kindly make yourself scarce. You'll put me off.'

Gabi looked around for Nelson, saw he was at the bar, turned back to me and hissed, 'You want Jonathan on your own, don't you?' She rolled her eyes at me. 'I know you. You just don't want us around to spot you making cow eyes at him. You don't want a lecture from Nelson about getting the hots for your client.'

'Absolutely not,' I spluttered. Something had certainly cheered her up, and no mistake. But there was a tiny shred of truth in what she'd said. 'Where's Nelson with that drink?' I added nervously.

'Well, fine with me,' said Gabi, arching her eyebrows

at me. 'I am quite happy to be left alone with Nelson. It'll give us a chance to chat. You know, he's been really sensitive about all this business with Aaron. He's offered me his shoulder to cry on any time.'

Before I could address my misgivings about that, Nelson was back, pressing two hot plastic cups of mulled wine into my hands. 'I got two each,' he said, juggling the squashy cups. 'The crush at the bar is obscene. I've had less intimate encounters with *girlfriends*. Oh, er, hello, Gabi,' he said.

'Hello, Nelson.'

I looked between Nelson and Gabi quickly. Did I detect a frisson there? Or was it just my paranoid imagination?

'Did Mel tell you she's working tonight?' Gabi enquired, taking his spare cup of mulled wine.

'No, she did not.' Nelson glared at me.

'You and I have to make ourselves scarce for the duration of the display,' she went on. 'I might have to hang on to your scarf so we don't get separated.'

'Mel!' snapped Nelson. 'Why didn't you say? Who is it? Remington Steele, I suppose?'

'Oh, come on,' I protested. 'Jonathan wanted to see a bonfire, and I don't have any other free nights this week, and I thought since we were already coming to this one . . .' I flushed. 'Sorry. It was a planning error. You know I don't like mixing up work with my private life.'

'Oh, *we're* the problem! I *thought* you were getting a bit overdressed for Battersea Park.' Nelson nodded at my new coat and red leather gloves, both Outdoor Honey acquisitions. 'What if Gabi and I wore disguises too?' he enquired sarcastically. 'Would it be OK to join you then? I could be your brother, Silas, and Gabi could put on your ridiculous hat and pretend to be a Russian émigré duchess.'

I touched my hat self-consciously. It was a large fake-fur trapper hat that had made perfect sense in the shop, but now seemed a tiny bit *de trop*. It was definitely more Honey than Melissa. I'd put it on before Nelson got ready, partly so he wouldn't notice I was also wearing my blonde wig beneath.

'Don't take that off too quickly,' Nelson said, darkly. 'You don't want to take your *hair* off at the same time.'

'Thank you for your thoughtful words of advice,' I retorted, with a glare. 'Look, Jonathan'll probably just stay for the display. He normally rushes away from evening dates. We can still meet up for supper afterwards.'

'I don't know where we're going for supper,' replied Nelson loftily. 'Gabi? Did you have supper plans?'

'That depends. Ooh, look, there's Remington now.' Gabi nodded towards the door. 'Can't say he looks thrilled to be here. Still, when does he ever?'

Jonathan was attempting to stand still in the slowly heaving tide of people, casting urgent glances round for me. He looked a little out of place, but in a good way: his overcoat was dark cashmere instead of Musto sailing yellow, he wore a sheepskin winter hat, even though it wasn't that cold, and had a bright red scarf wrapped round his neck. Gabi was right, though: he did look a bit on edge.

'I'll see you later,' I said, my voice somewhat higher than normal.

'Maybe,' said Nelson and Gabi at the same time.

I started to slither through the throng, very conscious of the hot wine in my hands, and the large hat on my head. It was nice, watching Jonathan look for me, and when he finally spotted me, his face lit up and he looked much younger than he had done standing at the door, where he'd looked somewhat haggard. But then standing next to a wall of flushed rugger-buggers washes anyone out.

'Honey!' he said, as I struggled to his side. 'My God! What a hat!'

'Thank you,' I said, returning a random elbow in the ribs, with interest. 'Have a glass of mulled wine.'

Jonathan accepted the plastic cup with justifiable suspicion. 'What's in this?'

'Red wine? Oranges? Um, exotic spices? Drink it, it'll make you feel less annoyed with the crowds,' I advised.

'I don't think even Mogadon could do that,' he said evenly, as a conga line of young men in full cricket kit ploughed towards the bar with brutal efficiency.

Outside, we furnished ourselves with floury rolls full of roasted hog and apple sauce, which met even Jonathan's high critical standards, and we began to wander over to the fireworks. I paid for us to get in.

'No, really,' I said as Jonathan attempted to extract his wallet. 'Let me be responsible for the short-comings of English fireworks. I've already paid lots of council tax towards this. And finish your drink, because you can't take alcohol in with you.'

'OK,' he said, then leaned forward, and lifted up the earflap of my hat to whisper in my ear, 'Don't tell the guy on the door, but I never come to events like this without emergency supplies.' And he patted his inside pocket with a stage wink.

His breath was hot against my suddenly chilly ear and I shivered.

'Well done,' I said, keeping my voice level with some effort. 'Let's go and have a look at the bonfire before it gets out of control.'

'That happen often?' asked Jonathan, eagerly.

There were already several thousand people on the common, all doing that frustrated aimless wandering English people do at events where there is no clear 'best place' to grab. Most were on their phones arguing with friends in a 'better place' on the other side of the park. We picked our way through until we were a few metres away from the bonfire.

I was proud to see that it was a real corker: very big, with beautiful red and yellow flames, no visible sofas or toxic plastics in the pyre, and with a proper guy on top, dressed in what looked like a Harlequins rugby shirt.

'See?' I said to Jonathan, my face glowing from the intense heat. 'Isn't it great?'

'It's fantastic. Shall we step away?' asked Jonathan courteously. 'I'd hate that hat of yours to burst into flames.' He put his hand on the small of my back and we strolled towards the makeshift ropes, marking out the firework viewing area.

'I realise it's not proper animal fur,' I said defensively, 'but I'm not into wearing dead animals, especially on my head. Anyway, it keeps me warm.' I realised as I said it, that this was exactly the sort of defensive comment my mother made when criticised about her wardrobe.

'You're cold?' asked Jonathan, solicitously.

'Um, sort of.'

'Here,' said Jonathan. 'This should warm you up.' He reached into his overcoat and withdrew a silver hipflask. We came to a pause by a large oak tree.

'What's in there?' I asked as he unscrewed the cap.

'Whisky.' He passed it to me, then added, as I hesitated, 'Don't tell me it should be in a brown paper bag.'

'No, no,' I said. Hipflasks of whisky always reminded

me unpleasantly of the shoots I'd been press-ganged into as a teenager. Since I refused to shoot, I had to beat, and spent most of the time trying to shoo the birds horizontally to freedom.

Still, there was something chic about women who could drink whisky so I persevered with it. Now, I took a deep breath and sipped a small mouthful. It trickled down the back of my throat, leaving a smoky, burning trail.

The hipflask, I noted, was inscribed with Jonathan's initials and a date. I wondered if it was a wedding present.

I passed it back quickly. Jonathan took a long swig, then another. Then he made a 'gahhh' face.

'Dear me,' I said. 'Things that bad?'

He grimaced wryly. 'I guess it depends what you mean. I had a call from Cindy's divorce brief this afternoon, wanting to open the horse-trading before we get to court.'

'Oh,' I said. He had gone quite quiet of late on that topic, and I had begun to wonder, rather nervously, if there was a chance of them patching things up. 'It's going to court then?' I added, trying not to sound too interested.

'From the smart way she's reckoning up my assets, I'd say so.'

'I'm so sorry to hear that,' I said, meaning it.

'Are you?' Jonathan gave me one of his unreadable looks.

'Yes, I am,' I said. Then, in case this was overstepping the mark, I added, flippantly, 'Clearly word has got back to her about your fabulous new woman, and she's decided she's not up to the fight. A woman with no fighting spirit is hardly worth your time.'

'Something like that,' he said, but he didn't laugh, and

I realised he probably wasn't quite as over her as he liked to think.

I cursed my stupidity. I, of all people, should have known better than to take that detachment at face value! Just because I wanted him to be over her . . . Or did I? I pushed that thought away.

'I *am* sorry, Jonathan,' I said, tucking my arm into his for a friendly squeeze. 'It must be a miserable time for you.'

'It certainly is,' he said, taking another swig of whisky. Then he shook his head as if he were trying to shake the mental pictures away. 'I feel like I'm being asset-stripped – of all the stuff we bought to make our home together. Stuff we were given by friends. Stuff she gave me as presents! But, you know, it's all just . . . stuff!' He sighed. 'I just want to walk away from it. Put it all behind me. Jesus, this isn't a cheery conversation to be having. Can we talk about something else, please?'

'OK, then – tell me about work?' I asked, reasoning that at least there he'd be hitting targets and generally being indispensable. 'Found Bonnie and Kurt a house yet?'

'I've found them several houses,' said Jonathan. 'None of which are *quite* right.' He blinked rapidly, and put a finger up to his eye. 'Sorry,' he said. 'Contact lens. No, I seem to be working London hours *and* New York hours at the moment. Damn phone never stops ringing.'

'Then you shouldn't be so good at your job,' I replied. I liked the idea of Jonathan having lenses. It made him a little less perfect. 'Wouldn't it be boring if you had nothing to do?

'It's certainly never dull,' he conceded. 'And your friend Gabi is a tremendous asset in that department,' he said with a sly look.

'Gabi?' I affected mild confusion.

'Gabi Shapiro.'

'Oh *that* Gabi,' I said, scanning the crowd anxiously in case he'd spotted her and Nelson.

'Yes,' he went on, 'she keeps me up with all the gossip. Dean & Daniels is quite a hotbed of scandal.'

'Really?' I said, disbelievingly.

'Oh, yes,' nodded Jonathan, offering me the hipflask again and pursing his lips in pretend outrage. 'One of our senior agents . . . and his PA, would you believe!'

'*Who?*' I asked, curiosity getting the better of me.

Jonathan gave me an amused look. 'Does it matter, if you don't know them?'

I remembered that I had, of course, 'met' Carolyn and Hugh at the garden party.

'I know *of* them,' I said and nonchalantly took a large sip of whisky. 'Through Gabi.' I had to swallow several times to counteract the burning sensation in my chest.

'*Well,*' said Jonathan, with a man's fascination for gossip, 'Gabi was getting one of our new meeting rooms ready at short notice for a client consultation, but when she went up to put the flowers and coffee and so on in there, the door was locked from the inside!'

'Really? So what did she do?' I said, letting him think I was coaxing the information out of him.

'Very sensibly she alerted me, I gave her the master key and who did she find in there but Hugh Gerrard! One of our senior agents,' he added, by way of explanation. 'You may recall him from your garden party. Red pants.'

I contained my shock and horror, quite successfully, I thought. 'Gosh. With his PA, did you say?'

Jonathan nodded.

But *I'd* been Hughy's PA. Who had replaced me? I racked my brains but couldn't think.

'Who's that?' I asked innocently.

'A lady called Carolyn Harker,' said Jonathan, giving me an odd look. 'Again, you met her?'

'Carolyn! And Hughy?' I exclaimed. Then I added, 'As he asked me to call him at the party.'

Jonathan took his hipflask out of my gloved hands and knocked back a quick swig, rather more stylishly than I had. 'Indeed.'

I couldn't help myself. Carolyn – effectively demoted! 'And what were they doing?'

Jonathan feigned shock. 'What do you think they were doing?'

'To be perfectly frank, I can't imagine either of them doing that.'

Jonathan's face twisted into a wicked smile. 'Checking for damp?' he suggested innocently. 'Inspecting cracks in the foundations?'

'But it's a new building!' I said, thoroughly confused.

Jonathan roared with laughter, and I smiled politely, none the wiser. Still, it was nice to see him laughing. He looked like a different person when he smiled. I wished Gabi and Nelson could have seen him.

No, I didn't.

'Put it like this, Carolyn was on the desk, taking something down, like the good PA she is,' he said, with a solemn face.

'Goodness me.' It was hard enough to imagine Carolyn being swept away on a tide of passion; harder still to imagine Hughy instigating one. It would have to be one hell of a tide. I began to wonder if Gabi had been winding Jonathan up.

'Is she sure?' I asked, carefully. 'I find that extremely hard to believe. From, um, what I saw of Carolyn, she seemed rather . . . respectable.'

'Well, these office flings happen,' said Jonathan. 'Not that I think it's a very good idea though.'

'No?' My father seemed to take it as a perk of his job.

'No,' insisted Jonathan. 'It's very easy to imagine that just because your PA listens to you and indulges your every need at work, that she actually cares about you. I mean,' he added, 'obviously a good PA is in tune with her boss, but the relationships you have in the office aren't the same as the ones you have at home, are they?'

He shrugged.

Daddy was still very much at the forefront of my mind. And with him came an unwelcome reminder of several unpleasant scenes I had unwittingly stumbled into before we moved back to England.

'Oh, yes, I agree,' I said. 'Then when it all goes wrong – and it always does – you never get your photocopying done properly again because all the girls hate you, and everyone in the office knows about your intimate dermatitis.'

I was thinking more of Quentin there. He'd famously had a run-in with my predecessor, Tanya. Hell hath no fury like a woman scorn'd by a man with a flaky back and athlete's foot.

'Something like that,' said Jonathan, in a funny voice. 'But I guess some successful relationships have to start at work. You have to make sure to take the relationship out of the professional environment. Would you like some cotton candy?'

Was that a deliberate change of subject?

The loudspeakers near us crackled into life before I

could examine it further, and I stepped back as it blared in my ear. 'Ladies and gentlemen, the display will commence in five minutes' time. Five minutes' time.'

There was a sudden stampede in various 'good place' directions, and instinctively, I found myself walking away from the tree and towards the centre of the park.

'Where are you going?' demanded Jonathan. 'What's wrong with where we are?'

Before I could answer, his phone rang. Jonathan grimaced, took his tiny mobile phone out of his pocket, glanced at the number, then, with a great flourish, turned it off. 'Look!' he said.

'Look at what?' I asked, hoping I wasn't about to get a lecture about some tedious new DVD-player-phone.

'I have switched my cell off,' he announced with a big smile.

'Well, thank you,' I said.

'This is now leisure time,' he added, in case I'd missed the emphasis.

Did that mean he was treating this as no longer a work situation? And if he was treating this as leisure time, did he still expect me to be Honey?

I suddenly felt extremely vulnerable, all alone in the dark park, with a grown-up, soon-to-be-divorced man I really fancied, a tissue of lies I wasn't sure I understood properly, and a hat that could catch light at the merest twitch of a careless sparkler.

My blood ran cold with nerves, while my face went hot.

Jonathan looked closely at me. 'I'm switching my cell phone off,' he repeated, 'so I can give you my undivided attention. The impatient homebuyers of New York will just have to speak after the tone.'

'That's very sweet of you,' I said carefully. 'Would you like me to switch off mine?'

'That depends on whether you consider you're working or not.'

Our eyes met and I racked my brains for something clever to say while my heart pounded at the serious look on his face. I got the distinct impression that there was some subliminal message here I was meant to respond to, something probably very obvious, but in my panic, I couldn't work out what he wanted me to say: yes, or no.

Jonathan's eyebrows crooked sexily, and a smile flickered round the corners of his mouth.

If I *wasn't* working, then I was pretending to be someone I wasn't, someone who was up to this level of sophisticated banter. I could only carry it off when I was pretending to be Honey.

But hadn't he just told me how stupid it was to have affairs with people you work with?

He definitely *had* said that: in fact, hadn't he introduced the gossip about two people I wasn't meant to know well specifically to make that point? Was this just a way to catch me out, to get me to admit my feelings so he could let me down gently?

My spirits sank.

Then with a deafening roar of trumpets, the firework display started and we turned instinctively to the explosion of white light in the sky. Red, silver and blue chrysanthemums boomed and glittered in the inky darkness while selections from Wagner and Led Zeppelin boomed forth from the loudspeakers.

There are few things in life that make you feel quite so at one with humanity as joining in ritual responses with thousands of people at the same time. I suppose it's

why line-dancing and Moonyism are so popular. But my
mind refused to take it in, going round and round in
circles, wishing I had the courage to do what I wanted,
instead of what was right.

The noise from the fireworks and the musical accom-
paniment was so loud that there was no point talking. In
the general crush forward, Jonathan and I had ended up
standing quite close together, and I could feel his arm
squashed against my waist. As if he could read my
thoughts, he lifted it very casually, said, 'Do you mind?'
and before I could respond, he slipped it round my waist.

My heart gave an almighty thump, and for a dizzying
moment, I considered turning without another word and
kissing him.

No! You mustn't read too much into it, snapped the
voice of reason, as the rockets scattered crackling gold
and green stars over our heads like Space Dust. This poor
man found out this afternoon that his wife's going ahead
with the divorce. He's hurt! Just like you were after
Orlando, only a million times worse!

Jonathan moved his hand slightly on my hip and under
my thick coat a thousand shivers ran up my back, just
like the fireworks exploding in the sky above our heads.

Oh God, I despaired. I was so out of my depth here.
I knew I should say something Honey-ish – just to prove
I was the smart and sexy girl he thought he was with –
but my mind was a complete and total blank.

I savoured the feeling of standing so close to Jonathan
for as long as the fireworks lasted, praying we'd moved
on from that difficult question, but then during a brief
lull in proceedings, he lifted the flap on my hat and
shouted in my ear, 'So? You never told me – is your work
phone on or what?'

My confidence drained away and I bottled it completely. 'Jonathan, it doesn't feel like work!' I yelled back, hoping that would cover both eventualities.

His face froze a little, as the music dimmed slightly. 'But it *is*, right?'

'Well, yes,' I faltered, scanning his face for clues. Did that mean *he* thought it was? 'As you were saying just then, business and pleasure . . . well, you have to be careful, don't you?'

It was no use. Honey's chat had completely deserted me. I wanted him to say, 'But tonight is pleasure, not business!' but he didn't. And I just couldn't risk it. I couldn't carry off gestures like that.

'OK,' he said, removing his arm. 'OK, I see. That's cool. I apologise.'

'No, Jonathan, listen,' I gabbled. 'Don't get the wrong end of the stick, I don't mind you putting your arm around me. I mean, it's fine!'

But a huge barrage of shells, rockets, and God knows what exploded at that point, and I don't think he heard me. It was like the Somme up there and yet I have never enjoyed a firework display less.

I grabbed his arm to get his attention, and he yelled something back to me, with quite a stern expression on his face, but I couldn't hear a word he said, and my lip-reading is useless.

'What?' I yelled desperately. 'What? I can't hear you!'

You know that feeling just after you've dropped your car keys – when you can see them slipping out of your fingers, and you know you've struck the one in a hundred chance of them falling right down the drain, but there's absolutely no way of stopping them, and all you can do is watch as they slip down and splash into the slime?

Well, that's how I felt.

Abruptly, as if the council had unexpectedly run out of money, the fireworks ceased, there was a round of applause and suddenly relative quiet descended around us as the crowd began to disperse via the hot-dog stands and smelly burger vans.

How did that situation go so wrong, I wondered miserably.

With perfect timing, my phone started ringing in my bag.

I knew from the ringtone that it was my own phone, not my work one – which I'd only brought so Jonathan could get hold of me – but whatever I said now would look like a fib.

'Your cell phone is ringing,' observed Jonathan.

'I know. It's my own line. I'm going to ignore it.' I tried a big smile.

'Don't do that on my account,' said Jonathan, and his voice sounded polite, but distinctly distant, as though I were a client he was showing round a house.

I looked at him, hoping to see a twinkle in his eyes, but there wasn't one. Not even a twinkly reflection from the bonfire.

I unzipped my bag and extracted my phone.

It was Nelson.

'Where are you?' he demanded loudly. So loudly I was sure Jonathan could hear.

'Near the main gate,' I said, even though we were some way away from it.

'Good. If you can get to the car in the next fifteen minutes we're going to Nando's for chicken. Stuff that hat up your jumper and tell people you're pregnant – they should let you through faster.'

I looked at Jonathan as I slipped the phone back into my bag. He looked older, more grown-up than me, as though he should be there with two excited children clinging to his hands, and I was suddenly crushed by my own misreading of the situation. Without the euphoria of the fireworks and the music whipping me up into a frenzy of fantasy, it hit me like a ton of bricks. All that stuff about Carolyn and Hughy, then checking with me that I knew it was work: he was being kind, trying to put me straight. He was being a gentleman, which only made me feel more of a silly little girl. An inexperienced silly little girl.

My insides felt as if they'd been removed with an ice-cream scoop: I was completely hollow and numb.

'I, er, I have to go,' I said, suddenly desperate to be anywhere else but stuck next to Jonathan in a stationary crush.

Appropriate as that might be.

'Your room-mate?' he asked.

I nodded. 'Yes.'

'I *see*.'

I wanted to yell, 'No, you don't!' but what was the point? Even the word 'room-mate' sounded so juvenile; he'd be going back to that beautiful family home in Barnes, and here I was going back to a shared house in a run-down street in Pimlico.

I could virtually hear my father chuckling at my gaucheness.

'Honey, I've had a great evening,' he said, adjusting his scarf. 'Thanks for taking time out of your own Bonfire Night to organise it for me. Apologise to your friends for my taking you away, will you?'

'That's no problem,' I said faintly. 'Thank you for the whisky.'

He gave me a brief smile, and for a second I thought he was going to lean forward and kiss my cheek. He made a tiny movement, then checked himself, lifted a hand and, turning, marched off, in completely the wrong direction.

'Jonathan!' I yelled.

He turned back.

'You're going the wrong way!' I yelled, conscious of everyone looking at me. 'You need that exit over there if you want to get a taxi home.'

He shrugged, and carried on walking the way he'd been going.

I stared after him until his cashmere overcoat disappeared into the crowd, then I let myself be carried along like a zombie on the wave to the gate.

19

I woke up the next morning with a dull headache. Gabi and Nelson had wanted to make a night of it after our chicken dinner, but I hadn't been in the mood for drinking. However, in place of a hangover, a heavy sense of foolish anticlimax covered me like a smelly old blanket.

I was conscious that there was something sitting on my bed, and it smelled strongly of Jo Malone's Red Roses, which rather ruled out Nelson.

'Mel,' said a wheedling voice. 'Are you awake?'

I hadn't yet opened my eyes, so I tried to pretend I wasn't.

'Mel?' Gabi repeated, more insistently. 'I've brought you a cup of tea!'

That was when I knew she wanted something, and when Gabi wanted something it was best to capitulate as early as possible.

Without opening my gummy eyes, I flung back the eiderdown so she could get underneath. It was cold in my bedroom. Nelson liked to switch on the central heating at the last possible minute, to save on fuel bills, or, as he put it, 'to cut down on environmental pollutants'.

'Ooh, it's as warm as toast in here,' she said.

'Flannelette pyjamas,' I mumbled. 'You can't beat them.'

'Did you have a nice evening with Jonathan?' asked Gabi, wriggling herself into the warm bedding.

'Yes, and no.'

'I had a nice evening with Nelson,' she said smugly. 'A lovely evening.'

'Did you?' My heart sank. Now I was more awake, all I could see in my mind was the distant, adult look that had come over Jonathan's face when I'd failed his mobile-phone test. If it had been a test. Whatever.

Oh Lord. What a mess.

I shut my eyes again but the face was still there. I buried my nose in my pillow and tried to think about Emery's wedding dress, and the new designs she'd sent me in the post. It didn't help.

'Yes, we had a great old chat before you turned up,' Gabi went on. 'He was asking me about work and stuff, and told me all about this sailing trip to Ireland he's got planned with that plank Roger Trumpet.' She went quiet when I didn't respond, then said, 'Me-e-e-el . . . ?'

'What?'

'You know, I've been thinking really hard about what you said. About sorting out my feelings for Nelson before I work out what to do about Aaron.'

'I don't know that's exactly what I did say,' I began, but Gabi wasn't listening.

'Will you talk to him? To Nelson?' she pleaded.

It was just getting worse and worse.

'What do you want me to *say*?' I groaned.

'Just . . . just get a sense of how he feels about me. So I'll know.' Gabi twisted the duvet round her legs again. 'Then there can be no what ifs.'

I was fairly sure I could tell her right there and then about how Nelson felt, but my conscience cut in. Maybe

I didn't know. If she was asking me, I had to do it for her, as her best friend. And I'd have to explain Nelson's feelings to her, as Nelson's best friend. Anyway, just because I was feeling low, there was no excuse for taking it out on Gabi, and, if I did talk to Nelson, it might knock things on the head once and for all.

Besides, he might surprise me by declaring his hidden passion for her.

I surprised myself with a wave of new depression at that thought.

'Do you want me to say anything about . . . um, about how you feel about him?' I asked. 'I mean, what are your feelings?'

'You don't need to go into *my* feelings,' she said hastily. 'Not unless he admits he's been in love with me for years. Then you can say I'm quite fond of him.'

'OK,' I said. 'But you have to promise not to shoot the messenger if the news is bad. Bear in mind that I haven't had to do this since I was in the fifth form. And I wasn't very good at it then.'

'No problem,' said Gabi cheerfully, and wound her feet into the warm cotton sheets that were now cocooning her like a fat larva.

I made a lame attempt to get some of my eiderdown back, but Gabi had it firmly trapped. No wonder Aaron never slept over at hers. I gave up, got up and went for a shower.

Even after a shower with every single one of my 'saved for best' bath-time treats, a dismal sense of gloom hung over me. I couldn't face my usual Saturday morning tidy-up and I certainly didn't want to hang around to watch Gabi drool over Nelson, so I went to the one place where I didn't feel like a complete idiot: my office.

I didn't often go into the office on a Saturday, but recent events had left me somewhat behind on my paper-work. I'd been putting off my monthly financial review for ages, and if there was one thing growing up with my father had taught me it was to keep on the right side of the tax people. And if I got sick of that, there was always Emery's dress to tackle.

Just being in the office was reassuring: I was in control here. The open diary on the desk, the next few weeks filled with appointments in different coloured inks, gave me a boost, and I was grateful for it.

There were two messages on my answerphone: the first from Jonathan, who must have called just after I left to meet him in Battersea.

'Hey there,' he began with a clunk where he'd picked his phone up off speed-dial, 'really looking forward to this evening . . .'

I fast-forwarded it, unable to hear the rise and fall of his voice, so grown-up and assured, without cringing.

The next message was from Bryan Birkett, the man so wet he was unable to call off his own engagement. 'Hello, Honey,' he said. 'Um, you haven't returned my call from yesterday, so I'm leaving another, in case you, er, didn't get it. I was wondering if you were around for a drink sometime this week? I mean, I'm, er, I'm having trouble with my, um, mother's birthday present and I'd appreciate some advice. I'm free all week. I think you have my number – I put it on the remittance slip for your invoice, but in case you've misplaced that, let me give it to you again, it's—'

I fast-forwarded that too, before Bryan could reel off

his numbers. This was actually the third pointless message he'd left for me now; though I felt rather sorry for him, I was beginning to wonder if he was developing an unhealthy dependence. Some clients were like that: so relieved to find someone to make decisions for them that they quickly wanted to dump every single life decision in my lap. I tried to be kind but firm. Sometimes firm wasn't enough, but actively rude wasn't in my natural repertoire.

I made a note to put Bryan in touch with a tough-talking counsellor chap I'd met at a party in Islington with Jonathan. He'd have no compunction about telling him to get a life, and Bryan definitely wouldn't be tempted to ask him out for drinks.

I spent a few hours filing loose papers, making a list of invoices to chase up, and then cross-referenced my client file cards with the diary, checking for mothers with birthdays, or anniversaries requiring flowers, or godchildren who might expect attendance at confirmations. It was soothing, satisfying work, and time flew past, until the street lights flickered on as dusk fell outside.

Then my mobile phone rang, and I was shocked at how quickly I grabbed it, just in case it was Jonathan.

'Hello?' I said.

There was a long silence, then a familiar, absent-minded woman's voice ventured, 'Hello? Who's that?'

'Emery.' I leaned back in my chair and drew the curtains. 'How are you?'

'Oh, you know . . . Um, I was just phoning to check you got the parcel?'

I drew a deep, patient breath. 'No, I didn't. Which parcel was that?'

'The favours, dummy!'

Emery and I had spent an interminable afternoon trying to decide on new table favours since the wedding planner had absconded with Emery's 'final four choices'. I had no idea whole favour catalogues existed, filled with mind-boggling variations on the 'bag of sugared almonds' theme, but they did.

'I ordered them, like you told me to,' she said, sounding very pleased with herself.

'Did you?'

'Don't sound so surprised,' said Emery, in a hurt voice. 'I got a very good deal for them too. They were at least half what you thought they were going to cost.'

'Well done you,' I said, mentally scouring my brain for any stray parcels that had arrived. 'Did you, er, did you have them sent to Nelson's?'

'Dur!' honked Emery. 'Of course I did! Where else would I have them sent to, you idiot?'

'Um, good point,' I agreed quickly, then a fresh thought occurred to me. 'Emery, why *did* you have them sent to me? You're the one getting married, aren't you?'

The line went vague. 'Mmm. Got to go, Mel,' said Emery. 'Daddy's just come in with William. They've been out clay-pigeon shooting.'

I could hear the distant sound of an argument. Daddy liked to give his potential sons-in-law a rigorous preparation for their married life.

'Emery? Emery? Listen, we need to talk about your invitations. If we don't get them ordered soon, there won't be time to . . .'

As was her annoying habit, she hung up without saying goodbye, which left me gabbling away pointlessly to myself for a good two minutes.

With a big sigh, I closed my desk diary. No parcels

had arrived for me at home and I was sure I'd have noticed a box like that, but then recently Nelson had dropped one or two things off for me at the office, if I'd been working late and needed cheering up. There was nothing in my little foyer, so I went into the cupboard-like spare room, where I kept Emery's wedding bits and bobs, well out of Gabi's sensitive sight.

Lo and behold, under a bag with fabric in it, was a large box addressed to me from grace&favour.com.

I stared at it. It was a timely reminder of how I needed to get a better grip on what was going on in my life. How had I failed to notice that there? And how long had those clothes I'd sorted out for the charity shop been lingering?

I carried the box back into the office, wondering why it was so heavy. God alone knew what Emery had considered appropriate favours for her wedding tables – the last time we'd talked about it, she'd murmured something about lumps of pink clay at each setting, so guests could mould love-hearts for a massive sculpture for their new garden.

As soon as I got the box open, I understood why she'd managed to get such a good deal – and also why she'd had the box sent to me: it contained about three thousand circles of tulle, several hundred miniature rosebuds, half a hundredweight of multicoloured sugared almonds and enough ribbon to gift-wrap St Paul's Cathedral. Emery hadn't stinted on the optional decorations; she seemed to have ticked every box to be on the safe side.

And every bit was bloody self-assembly.

The instructions featured mother, daughter and sisters sitting round the family table, looking warmly at each other – a sort of hen night, but with paper rosebuds and home-spun advice.

Still, I thought miserably, helping myself to a couple of sugared almonds, at least it would take my mind off the accounts.

Which I still hadn't tackled.

I put Ella Fitzgerald on my stereo and had done about forty bonbonnières – enough for one table, the way the guest list seemed to be going – when my phone rang again: it was Nelson and I was astonished to realise it was half six already.

'Hello,' he said. 'Where are you? Don't tell me, I can hear soothing, spending music. Are you shopping?'

'I'm in the office. And I'm *working*,' I said. It gave me a warm glow of saintliness. I understood why Nelson liked to say it so much.

'Really? Are you going to come home for supper?' he asked. 'I've just bought some lamb so free-range it still has walking boots on.'

I looked queasily at the pile of sugared almonds in front of me. Pink ones, it seemed, did not have a different flavour to the lilac, green or blue ones. I was sure my tongue now matched my office decor. 'You know, I think I might have to stay here for a bit longer. But you go ahead and make supper for yourself if you want to.'

Nelson tutted down the phone. 'Come home, Miss Martyr,' he said. 'You've made your point. So you're now so busy and successful that you have to work weekends. Please come back. The house is too eerie and peaceful without you here.'

'Well, OK then,' I said. 'Are you, um, alone?'

'Quite alone, thank you,' he said. 'Gabi made a big point of telling me she was going home to her mother's, so we could have the place to ourselves. Do you know why she might have done that?'

'No idea,' I said, with a grim sense of obligation. 'OK, I'm coming back, but I should warn you that there are about two hundred and thirty-seven bonbonnières still to make.'

'What?'

'It's French for "waste of money".'

'Do you want to bring your accounts back too?' asked Nelson. 'I imagine you've been putting them off for a while and I'd hate to see you organise Emery's wedding from a prison cell.'

A tidal wave of relief and gratitude flooded my entire body, counteracting the sugar rush. 'That would be most kind.'

'No problem. See you in about an hour then,' said Nelson. 'Go and get a bottle of wine. None of your cheap rubbish either, please. My lamb has high standards.'

After supper, I cleared away the plates, and dumped my box of favour ingredients on the table, along with a second bottle of wine.

'Help yourself to sugared almonds,' I said. 'And ignore the illustration on the instruction leaflet. As you can see, a rose-tinted mother and sister are not provided. By rights, the instructions should feature a bitter, spinster sister.'

'You're sure you're not making the cake?' he teased. 'Emery hasn't signed you up to drive her to church?'

'Don't,' I groaned, gathering up four circles of net. 'I think this is Emery's way of getting herself banned from any more organising.'

'Not as dumb as she looks then,' said Nelson. He picked up some tulle circles with surprising enthusiasm. 'Right then. Let the bridal favours commence.'

We sat there fiddling with bits of sequinned tulle,

326 *Hester Browne*

listening to Frank Sinatra and arguing about who exactly he'd been married to and in what order. All the while, I racked my brains for a clever way to bring the conversation round to Gabi and how Nelson might feel about her.

Eventually, when Nelson went to get a third bottle of wine, in the absence of any inspiration dawning, I decided to jump straight in and hope for the best.

'I've been meaning to say for ages – you were so sweet to Gabi when she and Aaron split up,' I began. 'I don't know many men who could have passed paper hankies with that sort of sensitivity.'

Nelson shot me an arch look. 'Let's just say I'm an old hand. Anyway, she seems more cheerful these days. Whatever it is you're telling her, it seems to have worked.'

'Oh, it's all just women's magazine stuff. I don't know that I'm much help,' I said. 'I only told her to be honest with herself.' I looked over at him, but he was intent on his knots, his blond eyebrows knitted in concentration. 'Don't you think that's important, to be honest with yourself?'

'Indeed,' he agreed. 'But within reason.'

My attention was caught by the quick, deft way Nelson's fingers twisted the ribbon into perfect loops, then dispatched them into tight little knots. His paper doves looked as though they were billing and cooing, whereas mine looked as if they'd been recently winged by a cack-handed shot.

'Pass me another handful of net?' he asked, looking up and seeing me staring at him. 'What?'

'Oh, I was just admiring your, er, handiwork,' I said, sipping at my wine.

Hadn't it been Gabi who had said how strong and capable Nelson's hands were? It was funny how I'd never noticed things like that about him until she started banging on about it all the time. But he did have rather nice hands. Outdoor hands. Manly hands. Even when he was fiddling about with camp things like net and miniature turtle doves.

In Nelson's hands, they didn't look camp at all, come to think of it. Quite the reverse.

Nelson dropped a finished bonbonnière on the pile. His pile was about three times bigger than mine and three times more elaborate.

'So have they officially split up then? Gabi and Aaron?' he asked, as if he were enquiring about the rent.

Gabi. Yes. Back to the matter in hand, I reminded myself.

I took a deep breath. 'I think so,' I said. 'I think she's in love with someone else.'

'Oh,' said Nelson. 'Aaron's boss?'

'No!' I looked at him, trying to assess how serious he was being. Not easy, since my attention was being impaired by the wine and the fact that Nelson was wearing a new shirt that made his eyes look very blue.

Once you started noticing things like that, it was hard to go back.

I pulled myself together. 'No, um, someone very different.'

'Different from Aaron?' Nelson raised his eyebrows. 'Why? I think Aaron's the perfect man for her. Whether she wants to recognise that, of course, I don't know,' he added loftily. 'Why is it you girls always want to pretend you're something you're not, then try and find a boyfriend to prove it?'

'Meaning?' I demanded. Nelson could be unbearably smug sometimes.

'Well, Gabi obviously doesn't want to accept she's a dyed-in-the-wool material girl . . . Don't tell me. This other bloke – is he some kind of *Guardian*-reading, muesli-eating, save-the-whale kind of open-toed-sandal bore?'

'Yes, you could say that,' I snapped.

He shrugged. 'I rest my case. She's just having a last-minute panic with the absolute opposite of what she wants, just to be sure she wants Aaron.'

'You think so?'

'All girls do that,' he said confidently.

'What absolute nonsense. And you would know that *how*, exactly?' I demanded. 'In your vast experience of women?'

'Mel,' said Nelson, in his patience-of-a-saint voice, 'just because I don't have a girlfriend *right now* doesn't mean I'm some kind of eunuch. I'm not *entirely* without experience of the opposite sex.'

There was no obvious comeback to this, not without being actively rude.

'Well, no, I'm not suggesting you are,' I retorted, distracted by the sudden rush of blood to my imagination. I knew Nelson better than anyone, but there were still gaps when he'd been abroad travelling or I'd been living away at art college. What kind of experience *had* he had? What sort of girls *had* he been with?

Nelson finished off his wine. Over the course of a long evening, we'd drunk a fair bit, but it didn't seem to be affecting his knotting whereas mine was getting somewhat erratic. 'Still, I suppose it gets rid of the what ifs.'

'That's what Gabi said.'

What ifs. I looked at the almonds in my hands. My life was *full* of what ifs.

What if the fiasco last night with Jonathan was meant to bring me to my senses?

What if what I wanted was actually right here in front of me?

What if Nelson had brought up the topic of 'what if' to exorcise his *own* 'what if' . . . with me?

I fervently wished Gabi had never planted that idea in my head.

I peeked over at Nelson. His head was bent in concentration while he laid almonds delicately onto the lace circles balanced on his palm: a vision of graceful strength. His hair, which I'd always thought of as toffee-coloured, now seemed the exact shade and texture of a teddy bear.

Gabi was right: he was the perfect boyfriend. He was *lovely*.

'So are you going to tell me who it is that Gabi's secretly in love with?' he asked without looking up, breaking into my thoughts.

I nearly knocked over my glass. 'Um, do you want to know?' I stammered. 'Would you be jealous?'

Nelson roared with laughter. 'Of course I would! Surely if anyone's entitled to Gabi it's me, the amount of time she spends round here, flirting outrageously!'

I was surprised to feel a twinge of resentment in my stomach.

I was even more surprised to hear my own voice saying, in a rather childish tone, 'Well, it is you. And it's not a joke.'

That seemed to sober us both up, quick smart.

We sat there, not looking at each other and twisting silver ribbon round our fingers. The Frank Sinatra CD finished, and an awkward silence filled the space.

'Oh,' said Nelson eventually, all the teasing gone from his face. 'Right.'

'Are you in love with her? Could you be?' I asked in a small voice.

'Gabi is a *sweet* girl,' said Nelson. 'She's fun, and very pretty, and . . . you know. Lovable. But she's not really in love with me. She's just working her way round to getting married to Aaron, isn't she?'

'You're so sensible,' I moaned, wondering how I was meant to convey all that to Gabi without her going berserk.

'I mean, I can't *blame* her . . .' added Nelson, then paused.

I was about to berate him for being big-headed, when he went on, 'It's so much easier to have a crush on someone who you know isn't going to respond – it makes it nice and safe and you never have to humiliate yourself by getting knocked back.'

Did I mention that wine makes me weepy? And that I'd spent the past few weeks poring over white weddings I'd never have and ordering engraved stationery for someone else? And falling in love with an older man who thought I was sexy and metropolitan, when in fact I was pear-shaped, on the shelf and more parochial than the lady president of Ambridge WI?

Suddenly big fat tears were rolling down my nose and splashing onto the almonds in front of me.

'Hey! What's the matter, Mel?' asked Nelson in a tender voice that only amplified my misery.

'Come on . . .' I heard a handkerchief being whisked out of his pocket and flapped open. Then I felt it pressed up against my nose.

I took it gratefully and buried my face in it. It smelled of Nelson: warm, clean, and fabric-conditioned.

'Is it Emery's wedding?' he asked. 'Is it all a bit . . .

close to home? I mean, you're not crying because I don't fancy Gabi . . .' There was a sensitive pause, then he added, '*Are* you?'

'No!' I wailed. 'Of course not! I'm crying because I'm just fed up of being me!'

'What?' Nelson put his big strong hands on my shoulders and held me at arm's length so he could see my face, and so I could see the look of amusement on his. 'How is this suddenly all about you? I thought we were talking about Gabi, or me, at the very least.'

I got up and stumbled away from the table in the direction of my bedroom, but bumped into the sofa. I sank down on it instead, as if I'd meant to all along and put my head in my hands and sobbed.

Nelson came and sat next to me, wrapping his arms around me, and tipping my head into his shoulder. I melted into him like a half-set jelly.

'Hey,' he said. 'Come on, Mel. Tell me what's upsetting you. It must be tough, dealing with everyone else's problems and not getting any help with your own.'

'I've been so *stupid*,' I hiccuped. 'I've made a complete fool of myself, just like you said!'

'Are we talking about Remington Steele here?'

I nodded, miserably.

'You've started to feel, ah, more than professional towards him?'

I nodded again. 'He's so charming . . . and nice to me, but only because I was being flirtatious with him. And I was being flirtatious because he was *paying* me to be flirtatious!'

'Sounds all right so far,' said Nelson. 'Why can't you just agree that all bets are off and now you can be his real girlfriend? He obviously needs one.'

I lifted my tear-stained, blotchy face. 'Because he'd want *Honey* for his girlfriend, not me!'

'Don't be bloody stupid,' said Nelson.

But my misery engine was running at full steam now, and there was no way of jamming on the brakes. 'Anyway, even if he did fancy me, he's totally on the rebound from his ex-wife.' I wiped my running nose with the back of my hand. 'He's only being nice to me to make himself feel better. Then as soon as his heart's mended, he'll find someone new. Someone . . . proper!'

'Mel, there's no woman in London more proper than you,' said Nelson stoutly.

I ignored him and wiped my eyes hard with his hanky. 'Why does no one nice want me, Nelson? Am I going to spend the rest of my life organising other people's weddings, and sprucing up men for other girls to get off with? Am I really such a career spinster?'

Nelson squeezed me. 'Now you're just being ridiculous. That's just the wine talking. You're a wonderful, gorgeous woman! Everyone adores you.'

'Everyone adored Mary Poppins and she never had a boyfriend,' I wailed, fresh tears springing into my eyes. 'Just a huge . . . *bag!*'

'Oh, Mel,' said Nelson, hugging me to his chest. He probably thought I couldn't tell he was laughing because I couldn't see his face, but I could feel the vibrations in his chest.

Now this is the weird thing. I don't remember the order in which this happened, and bear in mind that we'd polished off a fair amount of wine, but not brainwashing amounts, but next thing I know, Nelson's nose is brushing mine, and I'm moving my head so we don't bump noses, and suddenly we're kissing.

Kissing! Me and Nelson!

At first it was quite soft and tentative, in case, I suppose, the other person backed off with a shriek, but when it became clear that neither of us was going to, I felt Nelson's arm pull me round so I was almost lying next to him, and I felt my own hand tangle up into his thick hair, and slide down his neck, which was surprisingly soft and, well, manly.

It came as something of a shock to discover that Nelson was a really good kisser. I'd never even wondered about it before. Well, not much. His lips were soft and moved just forcefully enough against mine to make me wonder if he'd be as masterful as Gabi reckoned in bed; meanwhile his hands cautiously stroked and explored over my back and waist, finding all the right spots without groping or grabbing or making me conscious of any rolls of flab.

It was so long since anyone had kissed me, and I'd been carrying so much pent-up desire around that it all seemed to flow out of me like champagne out of a bottle. Messily but enthusiastically. I could feel my whole body shaking, and Nelson kept wiping tears from my face with his fingers as he kissed me, and I was hiccuping into his mouth, which doesn't sound as sexy as it actually was.

All at once, everything made sense. That whole humiliating scene with Jonathan had been for a reason: to bring me and Nelson together at last! We had the best friendship in the world, and now it was going to move on to another level. It was Fate. It was right.

I pulled him even closer to me, and kissed him with renewed gratitude. Thank God he'd put up with my ridiculous behaviour for so long. That had to prove it, if nothing else.

Suddenly, Nelson caught my face between his hands

and pulled away to look at me. His expression was heart-breakingly serious.

'We can't do this,' he said.

I looked into his eyes. They were very blue, the colour of mussel shells, with tiny flecks of gold around the iris. Very beautiful. I'd never noticed that before.

Of course we couldn't do it. It would be treacherous to Gabi, it would ruin our friendship, it would mean a horrendous conversation in the morning. None of that explained the weird mixture of relief and disappointment that swilled around my chest.

'I know,' I mumbled. 'Don't . . .'

Tears started to slide down my face. I'd made a mess of everything. Again.

'Let me put you to bed,' said Nelson, picking me up as if I were a large sail bag.

I was so tired and weary that I fell asleep before he could haul my jeans off.

20

I woke up the next morning with the disorientating sensation of something being not quite right.

I peeled open one eye cautiously: I was in my own room. Fine. I was on my own. Good. I had a shocking red-wine hangover that meant every thought and movement was taking place in slow motion.

Not so good.

In my experience, in hangover situations my brain usually withheld key memories until it adjudged that I was in a fit state to deal with them: the worse the hangover, the more blank my short-term memory remained.

I lay there, concentrating on breathing quietly and, eventually, my brain ticked round to the fact that it was something on my body that didn't feel right. Slowly, I lifted up the duvet, and peered underneath, not sure what would meet my eyes.

I was wearing an enormous T-shirt with 'I survived the Dun Cow Pub Crawl' on it. Not that I could read that upside down. I just knew from having seen it on Nelson at times of low laundry levels. Underneath that, my knickers were firmly in place, but now riding up in a very uncomfortable manner.

I lay back on the flat pillows, staring at the ceiling with unseeing eyes while my mind struggled to piece together the small but vivid fragments now feeding back to me. I

honestly hadn't felt that drunk at the time but we must
have knocked back three bottles between us.

What had I done?

My overall memory of the previous night was a bit of
a blur, but the occasional bright tableau leaped out in
glorious Technicolor.

Like Nelson's face when I'd kissed him.

And the weird look in his eyes when he'd stopped it.

I groaned aloud. How could I have done that? How
could I have let Gabi down so badly? How could I have
made such an idiot of myself?

Rather than lie there tormenting myself, I decided to
have a shower and brace myself to deal with the conse-
quences in a mature, adult fashion.

I felt significantly better with clean hair and fresh clothes,
and set about removing all evidence of the previous night
from the living room and kitchen. Albeit in slow motion.
When everything was looking even tidier than normal, I
made myself some breakfast and distracted myself with
a wedding magazine feature about table decorations, post-
poning the moment when I'd have to deal with what I'd
done.

Then Nelson walked in, his hair still damp from the
shower. 'Morning,' he said. Too brightly?

'Nelson,' I began, gazing furiously at my plate. 'I, um,
listen, we have to . . .'

'No, we don't,' said Nelson. He slipped into the chair
opposite and grabbed my hand. 'Come on, Mel. Let's not
make this into a drama. It's just one of those things that
sometimes happens with old friends when they've had a bit
too much drink and they're feeling sorry for themselves.'

I felt a deep sting in my chest at that.

'Is it?' I said, still not looking up.

'Yeah. One day you might be saying the same thing to Roger.'

'I don't think so!' My head ricocheted up in outrage, and I realised Nelson was teasing me. His eyes were crinkled up with a tentative smile.

He might at least *pretend* to be devastated. 'Are you saying it meant nothing to you?' I demanded hotly, ignoring my churning hangover.

Nelson raised his eyebrows and poured the tea. 'Of course not! It was . . . very . . . very . . .'

'OK,' I said. 'Don't finish that sentence. I can't take much more rejection.' I sank my head into my hands. Faced with Nelson's matter-of-fact cheerfulness, my resolution to be adult about it was suddenly crumbling away.

'Oh, Mel.' A teacup was pushed in front of me and I took it automatically, letting it burn my fingers. I heard him put bread in the toaster. How could he be so *normal*?

'I'm not *rejecting* you, stupid,' said Nelson. 'We were both a bit tipsy, that's all. You really have to stop being so down on yourself. Or at least stay sober enough to remember what you've got up to.'

I pulled my shoulders back: I hadn't been *that* drunk!

But Nelson held up his hand to stop me before I could start. 'Listen, don't,' he said in an unbearably kind voice. 'You were upset, I was a little bit drunk, maybe we were both curious . . .' He stopped, coughed self-consciously, then began again. 'Mel, I'm extremely flattered that you could have even a passing drunken interest in me. But let's be realistic: you don't really love me, and you'd get very bored listening to me talk about rigging and tax relief all the time.'

'No, I wouldn't,' I protested. Irritatingly, Nelson had

chosen that morning to get the tousled bed-head look exactly right, after three years of looking like Father Jack Hackett until ten o'clock.

He lifted an eyebrow at me, and something in me cracked. Now he was telling me he wasn't interested, all my doubts about Nelson as a potential boyfriend abruptly vanished and I felt absolutely certain I'd just screwed up my once-in-a-lifetime, fairy-tale 'But your handsome prince is right here!' opportunity.

'But, Nelson . . .' I began, tearfully. 'I love you!'

Was that all I did these days? Stumble from one screw-up to the next?

Nelson burped into his hand, which brought me back down to earth somewhat. 'Scuse me,' he said. 'Look, Mel, I love you too – you're the sister I thankfully don't have. Of course we love each other.' The toast popped up behind him; Nelson buttered both slices, and handed one to me. 'But, much as it pains me to talk like one of your dreadful magazines, you're *in love* with Jonathan Riley, international man of mortgages, and I think you'd be making a big mistake if you ignored that. He's more the sort of man you need – high-powered, suit-wearing, you know . . . Anyway, it sounds like you'd be good for him. From the way Gabi talks about the work it sounds like he could do with someone to lighten him up a bit.' He bit into his thickly buttered toast, then added, 'And that's the only time I'm ever going to offer you advice like that, so you'd better take it.'

I wondered if Nelson had missed a great chunk of last night's conversation. Had he been listening to me *at all*?

'But I told you, he's not interested in me,' I protested. 'He just enjoys being with Honey.'

'Oh, for the love of God . . . When are you going to

get it into your thick skull that you *are* Honey?' demanded Nelson. 'Is someone hypnotising you before you go out?'

'Well, no.'

'Do you go into a trance state and start channelling Ava Gardner?'

'No.'

'So why on earth do you imagine that it isn't *you* entertaining this legendary humour-free man?'

'How do you know he's humour-free?' I asked, momentarily diverted.

'Gabi told me. Apparently his latest nickname is Simon Cowell because no one's ever seen him crack a smile.'

'Oh.' I couldn't even be bothered to put him straight about Jonathan's sense of humour. Jonathan didn't want me. Nelson didn't want me. I might as well just give up, buy a house, fill it with cats and spend the rest of my life writing complaining letters to the local paper about speed-humps.

'Mel, you only get one chance at life,' said Nelson, though his voice was gentler than his words. 'You can't go on hiding behind your persecution complex. I know your father is a shit and your mother has . . . her own problems, but you're going to miss out on so much if you don't start grasping the nettle a bit more. OK, so we could end up together, but you'd only be settling for me because I was safe and familiar. That's not enough.'

'Isn't it?' I said, my eyes filling up.

'No. Not at our age. Maybe when we're sixty and divorced and in need of a home for the Labradors. Oh no, please don't start crying again. I've seen more iron self-control at the Oscars.'

'I'm not sad,' I said, trying to smile. I wasn't sad

actually. I was starting to feel quite purged. 'But Jonathan's honestly not interested. He more or less told me so at the fireworks. He said mixing business with pleasure was a terrible idea.'

Nelson looked more sympathetic. 'Did he? Sorry, I didn't realise. Maybe you should just give it time. Or tell him you can't see him as much, and see if he still tries to book you for pointless trips around Tate Modern.'

'That wasn't pointless. He wanted a fresh eye on modern art.'

'I suppose your guilelessness is one of the things he finds most attractive about you,' Nelson observed, putting more toast in the toaster. 'You've got to make him divide business from pleasure, and if he won't, you've got your answer, haven't you?'

I pushed my chair away from the table. 'Well, speaking of guilelessness, I've got to go home to sort out the invitations for Emery. Apart from anything else, I want a word with her about those bloody bonbonnières.'

'Are you going to take the rest home for her to do?'

We both looked at the box by the coffee table, over-flowing with circles of net and ribbon. I tried to imagine my mother snipping and knotting, and failed.

'No,' I said. 'I'll just keep them here. Do a few every night while I'm watching television.'

'*Right,*' said Nelson.

'No, really.' I sighed. 'It'll be easier in the long run. Honestly.'

He wagged a finger. 'Responsibility never killed anyone.'

'I know. But choking drunkenly on sugared almonds might. Besides you're so good at them.' My mind skimmed to the thought of Nelson's fingers, quick and neat and dextrous . . .

A crimson blush spread all up my neck and swamped my face.

'Comes from tying fishing flies,' said Nelson calmly. 'Amongst other things. Don't worry, I'll hide it all if Gabi comes back. And don't worry about that either,' he added, as my mouth opened to speak, 'I'll have a word with her. And I won't mention last night.'

'Thank you,' I said, full of sudden, heartfelt gratitude. I was so lucky to have a friend like Nelson. I told myself that I should take better care of our friendship.

I grabbed my bag and Emery's wedding folder from my room, and headed for the door.

'See you later then,' I said, trying to sound as normal as possible. 'I'll bring a takeaway back if I'm home in time for supper.'

'Um, Mel.' Nelson caught my arm as I passed by.

'What?'

He looked up at me and I realised he might not be quite as unfazed by it all as he made out. 'Look, it happened, but let's not regret it. I don't.' He smiled his most disarming smile, and scratched his stubble wistfully. 'It was rather . . . nice.'

A funny little shiver rippled through my stomach, as if I'd swallowed a bee.

'Thank you,' I said.

His face turned serious. 'But we won't ever speak of this again until we're sixty and divorced and in need, OK?'

'OK,' I promised, and dropped a kiss on his damp hair.

Then I left the house and set off for my parents', feeling almost like Honey.

*   *   *

In a new spirit of positivity, I called Emery and made her come and pick me up from the station, instead of spending money on a taxi.

I deliberately told her the train would be arriving thirty minutes before it did, and she still managed to drift into the car park a good ten minutes late.

'How does William cope with you being so appallingly vague?' I demanded, shoving aside a pile of papers and parking tickets on the passenger seat.

'He doesn't notice,' she replied, narrowly missing the car-park sign as she swung left onto the main road. 'He says he's used to repeating everything nineteen times. He's a lawyer.'

'Well, he gets paid by the hour, doesn't he, Em? I don't,' I said, trying to be firm. 'I *cannot* leave today without having the final, *final* details for the invitations, or else they won't be ready in time. Then no one will be able to come to your wedding. Emery? Are you listening to me?'

'I love this song!' exclaimed Emery, turning up the radio. 'Don't you? It makes me think of oranges!'

I decided to leave it until we were home.

When Daddy wasn't in residence, my mother was more like the mother I remembered from the happier bits of my childhood. She didn't smoke, mutter or wander around in a state of vague panic as she did when he lurked around the house, popping up sporadically to bark instructions at her. Neither was she the immaculately dressed, perma-smiling MP's wife who accompanied him in public. Instead, the woman who greeted us at the door seemed pretty compos mentis, and pleased to see us.

'Hello, darling,' she said, giving me a one-armed hug. I didn't squeeze: this was the hug she adopted after she'd undergone some kind of light physical cosmetic improvement.

'No Daddy?' I asked, hopefully.

'No, darling, he's on a trip somewhere,' she said happily. 'Taking some constituents on his annual trip to London, I think.'

To be fair to him too, Daddy was a popular local MP. He was extraordinarily charming to everyone outside his immediate family, brilliant at talking to all manner of people, and ever ready to offer tickets to view the Houses of Parliament. His views pretty much mirrored those of everyone in the area – yes to the pound, cricket pitches and local businesses, no to huge supermarkets, vegetarians and anything 'Un-British' – and he was happy to hold forth for hours at any local meeting going. I had to admire the courage of his convictions, even if I didn't always agree with everything he said.

Of course, it didn't always do to enquire *which* constituents he was showing round the Houses of Parliament, so for the sake of Mummy's nerves, I didn't.

I wandered into the kitchen, and was surprised to see that the table was covered with pots of jam and a couple of Victoria sponge cakes.

'Have you been baking?' I asked in some surprise.

'What? That? Oh no, village bring and buy,' she replied. 'I lost my head a little. Still, all in a good cause.'

'I lost my head a little' was my-mother-speak for 'I went berserk and bought everything in sight.' Bond Street, the Boden catalogue, the village fete – she shopped as some women did yoga. For inner calm.

'Cake, darling?' she said, searching for some plates. 'We'd better eat the evidence before your father gets home.'

'Mel says she's going to get tough with us,' Emery announced, appearing at the door with one of the dogs in her arms. 'Brace yourself, Mummy.'

I put my file on the table. 'Sorry, but I am. How am I meant to organise invitations when you won't tell me who's invited?'

'It's so hard, darling.' My mother sighed. 'Your father keeps inviting people, then uninviting people in a fit of pique, and William can't make up his mind whether it would be infra dig to invite his children, so we thought we'd just wait until the last minute and take it from there.'

'You weren't so casual about Allegra's wedding,' I reminded her. 'That was like a military operation.'

'Yes,' she agreed. 'But Emery is a much more . . . relaxed person altogether than Allegra. And I did nearly have a breakdown after that, if you remember.'

I did remember. The report in the *Daily Mail* had certainly brightened up everyone's day in the office I was working in at the time.

'Anyway, listen, Mel, I sent out "save the day" cards,' protested Emery proudly, carving herself a transparent sliver of sponge cake. 'Aaaages ago.'

'Did you?' I perked up. Maybe disaster could be averted after all. I started going through the file. 'Well done, Em! So is the list in here?'

Silence. I looked up and met their guilt-ridden gazes. 'Please don't tell me you've lost the list.'

Emery gazed intently into the middle distance, and Mummy's calm expression started to slip a bit.

'Emery!' I snapped. 'Who have you invited?'

Mummy's hand twitched on the table, searching for a phantom packet of cigarettes. 'Mummy, you must be able to remember,' I said, turning to her.

'Oh God, Melissa, you sound just like your father,' she murmured.

A fresh horror struck me. What with William's busy schedule, Daddy's commitments, and Emery's inability to decide anything, the date of the wedding had moved several times in the last month alone. The vicar was barely taking my calls any more.

I fixed Emery with a basilisk stare. 'Tell me you told them to save the date you're actually getting married on now?'

More silence. I got up from the table, walked round, then sat down again. I didn't know why I was getting so wound up; it wasn't even my wedding.

'OK,' I said, very firmly. 'OK. So several hundred people may or may not have marked your wedding day in their diary. We'll just have to hope that the ones who don't now get invitations won't take it too personally. Go and get your address books. Now!'

Mummy and Emery exchanged fearful glances then scuttled out. I cut myself a large piece of cake.

After a couple of agonising hours, we finally had a list compiled. All we had to do was to whittle it down from five hundred and forty-three to something nearer two hundred and fifty. I phoned Nelson to let him know I'd be staying overnight.

Armed with my wedding file – the pictures of people actually getting married were necessary to convince Emery of the need for things like placement cards and table cameras – I began to make some progress on the arrangements, and by teatime, definite black ink had started to appear in my notes. My brain began to release comforting, planning chemicals into my bloodstream.

'I can't believe it's really happening,' said Emery, her face uncharacteristically animated with delight as she studied pictures of bouquets. 'It's just so exciting!'

The mind boggled. 'You haven't felt that before now?' I asked. 'Like, when William proposed?'

She put *Wedding and Home* down. 'No, not really. I mean, you know what he's like . . .'

'No, not really.'

'Well, he doesn't go in for big gestures.' Emery sighed. 'He was quite brisk about it, so, you know . . . One doesn't like to get too excited about things, you know, in case . . .' She looked at me, her eyes glassy with emotion. 'You know how things go wrong with this family.'

I suddenly felt a little bit sorry for Emery. She'd developed chronic avoidance issues for a reason, after all.

'Still . . .' she said and picked up the magazine again, beaming fondly at a photograph of a bride leaping gaily off a tractor in full meringue and wellington boots.

Although I didn't think William and Emery were exactly a match made in heaven, I didn't feel the burning need to intervene as I had done with Gabi and Aaron. For one thing, beneath that cloudy exterior, I knew Emery was far from daft. She knew precisely what she was getting into, and I had a feeling that, once installed in some big house with William, far, far away from my father's sniping, the veils of vagueness might lift and reveal a more decisive woman altogether.

William, though I still hadn't met him, sounded reasonable enough. There were many valid explanations, after all, as to how a man could accrue three wives by the age of forty. And that really wasn't my business, anyway. Daddy might be a selfish brute sometimes, but he wouldn't let his daughter marry a serial killer.

Not unless his business contacts were *really* impeccable.

'Where's Mummy?' I asked suddenly.

Emery looked up. 'Oooh. Don't know.'

'I need her to write some cheques.'

'Oh.' Emery's face fell. 'I wouldn't bother. Daddy's in charge of the money side of things.'

'Daddy,' I said, 'is not here, is he?'

'No,' said Emery.

I gave her a stern look. She could be very slow. 'But, Emery, this is urgent. No invitations, no corporate hospitality, no social debts written off. So let's find a cheque-book.'

'Oh! Oh, well, quite,' murmured Emery, letting a small smile play around her rosebud lips.

I pushed back my chair and went to look for my mother.

My granny often insisted to me that the secret of a long and happy marriage was a large house. Big enough to spend significant portions of your day pretending you were in fact still single, she reckoned. Two houses, if it could be arranged, was the ideal, as Allegra and Lars had demonstrated.

If size of house was directly proportional to happiness of marriage, my parents should have been pretty blissful: while my father had his oak-lined study to skulk around in, my mother had her own Wedgwood-blue sitting room, which looked out over the apple trees in the orchard.

Mummy was sitting in the window seat now, her small stockinged feet curled up under her. In her hand was a framed black and white photograph of her and my father, getting into his Aston Martin on their wedding day: it was my favourite picture of them. In it, she looked very young and radiant, he looked handsome and exceptionally pleased with himself. They'd barely changed in thirty-odd years.

'Hello, Melissa,' she said when she saw me. 'Just remembering how lovely it was.' She let out a big sigh. 'Of course, it was before the breathalyser.'

'What?'

'The breathalyser. He shouldn't have driven us away from the reception, you know. It was a wonderful car.' She sighed again and touched the glass with her finger. 'I still miss it.'

Really, my family were incorrigible.

I sat down beside her. 'Was Daddy terribly romantic when you first met? I mean, did he woo you with flowers? How did you know he was the one?'

She threw a couple of pine cones into the fire, and squinted hard, as if I'd asked her for the square root of three million. Then she said, 'You know, your father has the most wonderful gift for making one feel *special*. When I met him at my coming-out dance, he behaved as if I was the only girl in the whole room. He was even nice about my dress, which I know was completely ghastly, really. I should have known then what a compulsive fibber he was.' Mummy sighed, but not in an entirely disapproving way. 'When I was with him, I felt clever and beautiful and . . . and desirable. Because, you know, *he* desired me. And he was such a catch.'

Much as I disliked him, it was nice to hear evidence of my father being romantic, just to balance things up. 'But you were a catch too,' I reminded her. 'You were gorgeous! I mean, you still are. Daddy was just as lucky as you, don't forget.'

'Mmm.' Her brow creased. 'The trouble is, darling, when one has a gift like that, it's a bit like being a violin virtuoso. One feels compelled to share it with as many people as possible.'

I thought about Jonathan. When I was with him, I felt clever and beautiful. Maybe all his clients felt like that too. Was that a gift he could switch on and off?

'So why is he so vile to you now?' I asked, turning my attention back to my father.

Mummy looked surprised. 'Oh, he's not always vile to me, darling. No! He can be utterly delightful when he wants to be.'

I must have looked shocked because she laughed at the expression freezing my face.

'He can!' she insisted. 'You just see the worst in him.'

'It tends to stick in the mind.' Mummy was, I noted, saying all this with the luxury of having my father at a few hundred miles' distance.

'You know, it's much better to have a marriage with ups and downs than for it to be monotonous,' she went on, happily. 'More reason to stick together if you don't know what tomorrow will bring.'

For a moment, I couldn't hide my disbelief. I had spent my entire childhood convinced that my parents were constantly on the brink of acrimonious divorce. So had Emery. We had even discussed whether we should plead to be re-homed with Granny rather than split between our parents.

'And, of course, what you girls don't know is that your father is terribly good at—' Her eyes were twinkling.

I held up my hand in horror. 'Please! No! There are things I don't need to hear.'

'I'm not saying he can't be a total bastard,' she said

seriously. 'He can be perfectly filthy, for no good reason at all. I'm just saying that you don't see everything, darling. Marriage is complicated.'

'I wish he'd turn a bit of that charm on to me,' I blurted out.

She put her hand on mine. 'Oh, Melissa, I know Daddy can be a pig, but he *adores* you.'

'Don't make me laugh!' I objected. 'He takes enormous pleasure in making me feel stupid. He always has done. I seem to spend my whole life trying to make him happy, then he just cuts me down – for the fun of it.'

I bit my lip. I so rarely talked about my father, especially not to my mother. I was scared that once I started, I might not be able to stop.

'I know he's not very demonstrative,' she went on, 'but, darling, he was awfully proud of you at school.'

'Was he?' I squinted at her.

'Oh yes.' Mummy nodded. 'The way you always settled in straight away, and made new friends. He was so proud that you never made a fuss, like Allegra did. You just got right on with the task in hand. He used to call you his little soldier.'

'Did he?' Not to my face, at any rate. 'I wish he'd be a bit nicer to me now,' I said woefully.

She squeezed my hand. 'Darling, you're really terribly alike, you two.'

'I most certainly hope not!' I protested.

'Oh, you are. You get things done, just like him. And he trusts you. *You* are the only one with his keys to the London flat, don't forget. *I*'ve never had a set.'

I sighed. Emery and Allegra got Mummy's long legs and sexy cheekbones; I got Daddy's networking abilities. 'Big deal. He never argues with Emery and Allegra.'

'Oh, he *does*, darling,' said Mummy. 'He has shocking fights with Allegra over the phone and Emery just vanishes whenever she hears raised voices. You're the only one who sits there and takes it. Don't, is my advice. He likes it when you fight back. Makes him all warm inside. You should do it more often.'

'Why can't he just give me presents, like any normal father?' I demanded. 'I *hate* arguing with him! He's a professional arguer! And he's my father! I shouldn't be arguing with him at all!'

'Darling, just stick to your guns,' she said. 'When you're married, you'll learn to work out which issues are worth fighting for and which you have to sacrifice on the altar of expedition. Women's lib and all that.'

I gave her a hard look. This from the woman with multiple split personalities developed to cope with her selfish husband's private and public lives; the woman who shopped herself happy; the woman who thought learning tactics to counter her husband was better than getting him to stop being a bastard. Marriage as domestic guerrilla warfare, punctuated by emotionally loaded sex.

I shuddered at the thought and pushed it away.

'I don't think I *want* to get married,' I said. 'Not if that's all I've got to look forward to. Now, can you write me a cheque for Emery's invitation cards, please?'

21

Much as it pained me to take Nelson's advice, there was really no need for Jonathan to be seeing me quite so often now that any budding match-makers in his immediate social circle knew he had a significant other. If he wanted to make dates for sight-seeing, or just general company, I decided that I'd tactfully suggest that that was a whole different ball game. I just wasn't sure how I could suggest that it was a job for a real girlfriend without actually ruling myself out of the running.

As it turned out, Jonathan solved the small matter of post-Bonfire Night embarrassment for me with his usual mixture of gallantry and office efficiency. He phoned me, full of apologies, to explain that he wouldn't be around for a few weeks: he had to fly back to New York to deal with some Kyrle & Pope business, and to tie up 'some personal matters'.

From the tone of his voice, I could guess what those personal matters would be.

I thought about Jonathan a lot while he was away, and I missed his company. In comparison, the lads I had to escort to parties and office dinners seemed so gauche and dull. I went on a Murder Mystery weekend in Kent with a lecherous Welsh merchant banker who ended up being 'murdered' a little too enthusiastically; I spent another interminable evening at a St Paul's School reunion where every other girlfriend seemed to be hired too.

But I did my best, thinking all the while of my growing professional reputation, and by the time Jonathan phoned me on his return, it was getting on for the end of November, and I could say, quite honestly, that my time was at a premium.

'It's the pre-Christmas rush,' I explained to him when he expressed surprise that I had no free appointments that week. 'I've got Christmas shopping to do for various clients, not to mention some sprucing up, as well as all those Christmas parties.'

I also had to finish a wedding dress, arrange a wedding, and make another six thousand pounds to hand over to Daddy so I could walk into the church with my head held high. But in the new spirit of emotional distance, I didn't tell Jonathan that.

'Can you make some time for me?' he asked. 'I need your advice about gifts for the girls in the office.'

'How thoughtful of you!' I said warmly. Clever and generous gifts would be a great way of shattering his miserable office image. Quentin had never given us presents at Christmas: just a catering-size tin of Quality Street from Woolworths, which Carolyn purchased with petty cash, and went through first, removing all the praline triangles and the big purple ones with the nuts.

'A good manager keeps his staff happy, Honey,' he said.

I strained my ears to detect any new note of formality or detachment but it was hard to tell, when Jonathan's normal tone was so dry. I decided I couldn't really tell over the phone. I'd need to see him.

'Mmm,' I replied, ambiguously. I seemed to be developing my own version of Emery's 'still . . .' If I'd realised how useful it would be, I'd have done so years ago.

'Are you available for a lunch meeting or not?' asked Jonathan.

'No, I'm not,' I said truthfully, looking at my diary. 'Not this week.'

'I see,' said Jonathan, again, inscrutably.

'But how about next week?' I added. I *did* want to see him. It was no good pretending I didn't, but, I reasoned, as long as we met in a controlled and professional lunchtime environment, where I wouldn't be able to kid myself about his twinkly eyes, there would be less chance of me making a complete fool of myself.

'Next week looks good to me,' said Jonathan, in the same measured tone. 'When?'

I scanned the diary for a good long lunch space. 'Wednesday?'

'Wednesday looks good for me too,' he said, almost too quickly to have looked at his diary. 'Do I have to rush you back for another client afterwards?'

'Not really,' I said. 'You can have me for as long as you want.'

Jonathan laughed – his short, quick, dark laugh – and a little ache bloomed in my stomach. I hadn't realised how much I'd missed hearing it.

'Well, there's a tempting invitation,' he said. 'It might be an extended lunch. And then there's all that shopping to do.'

'Lunch, then shopping – what more could a girl ask for?' I joked, without thinking. 'Are you going to rub my feet afterwards too?'

There was an abrupt silence on the other end of the phone.

Horrified at myself, I sank my forehead soundlessly onto the desk.

'OK,' said Jonathan, sounding more brisk, 'I'll look forward to next Wednesday then.'

'So will I,' I said and put the phone down before I could ruin anything else.

There! All completely above board and professional. Now I could look forward to it without a shred of guilt.

I sharpened my pencil to block out Wednesday for Jonathan, when the buzzer went.

'Hello?' I said into the entryphone.

'It's me!' crackled Gabi's voice. 'Can I come up?'

I buzzed her in, and got out the tin of special biscuits from my desk drawer while her feet thundered up the stairs.

'Hello!' said Gabi, bursting into the office with a broad smile on her face.

'Hello, you!' I said, standing up to take in the full effect.

Gabi had had her hair cut short and flippy, with deep chestnut highlights that made her dark eyes flash. She was wearing a neat red skirt suit that showed off her legs, resplendent in a fabulous pair of black stiletto heels. For a woman who claimed skirts made her brain seize up, it was quite a transformation.

'You like it?' she asked, giving me a quick twirl, nearly knocking over a lamp as she failed to regain her balance on the new heels.

I clapped my hands together with pleasure.

'I've gone for the Honey Blennerhesket look, as you can see,' she added, tugging at her hem.

'I'm flattered! What's it in aid of?' I asked. Not Nelson,

I hoped fervently. I was curious to know how their 'little chat' had gone; Nelson had cooked Gabi supper one night while I was sticking pins in Emery over at her flat, and now he'd taken some time off work and gone sailing with Roger, with only a brief, disapproving 'Mind your own business' before he went.

'My new life,' she said, pulling up a chair and helping herself to coffee and biscuits. 'I had a really, really good talk with Nelson last week.'

'Did you?' I asked innocently.

'I did.' Gabi nodded. 'He's such a wise owl, you know. I can see why you've leaned on him so much over the years. He has this way of listening that doesn't make you feel stupid – you know what I mean?'

'Yes,' I said slowly. 'I am very familiar with that skill of his.'

Gabi beamed at me. 'I felt so much better afterwards – and he cooked me the most delicious grilled trout! Eyes still in it and everything. Anyway,' she went on, in semi-reverential tones, 'Nelson suggested, quite rightly, that I should start by working out what I need to make *myself* happy, not rely on Aaron to do it for me. So I've decided to make some changes. I've got myself a pay-rise at work, I've eliminated toxins from my diet, and I'm going to move out of my mum's place and find a flat of my own!'

'Wow!' I said. I'd almost forgotten that Gabi still lived with her mum: most days it felt like she'd actually moved into our house. Still, it was great to see her bouncy again. 'That's brilliant. Do you, er, would you prefer a cup of peppermint tea?'

Gabi looked down at the milky coffee she was dunking her chocolate biscuit in. 'Oh, never mind. I'm allowed the occasional one. It's more about the *decision* to give up toxins, isn't it?'

I nodded. 'So did Nelson have any advice about Aaron?'

Gabi licked dark Belgian chocolate off her fingers. 'Well, after I had supper with Nelson, Aaron and I had a good long talk, and we decided that he should do the first term on his pathology course, and I should focus on my career, then see how we felt at the end of six months. He was really impressed with my pay-rise. It's so nice having my own money to spend!'

I put aside my nagging suspicions about Gabi's sudden 'pay-rise' and her 'career'. I hoped it didn't have anything to do with what Jonathan had told me she'd seen in the conference room: blackmail was not a pretty word. 'But are you seeing him? For dates?'

'Who? Aaron?'

'Yes, Aaron!' I retorted. 'Who did you think I meant? Nelson?'

'You *might* have meant Nelson.' Gabi looked a little shifty for the first time and her mouth clamped shut.

I was so ashamed of my own mean-spirited crossness at the thought of her dating Nelson that I shut right up too.

'So . . . shouldn't you be at work?' I asked.

She shook her head. 'I've got the day off. I'm going to look at a few flats.'

'Did Carolyn print off a list of rental properties for you?'

'Noo!' spluttered Gabi. 'Do I *look* like I've got more money than sense? Of *course* I'm not going through Dean & Daniels.'

It dawned on me that Gabi might have come round to my office in search of something more than chocolate biscuits. 'Do you want me to come with you to ask the hard questions?'

'You? Ask hard questions?' Gabi looked frankly incredulous. 'Do me a favour. No, I've got a much better plan than that.'

The entryphone buzzer buzzed. 'Hang on,' I said. 'Let me just get this.'

'It's me,' said Nelson's voice. 'Can I come up?'

'Speak of the devil – it's Saint Nelson,' I said to Gabi with a shrug, as I rang him in. 'I hope he's brought me lunch.'

Gabi and I both surreptitiously adjusted our hair and clothes as Nelson's footsteps jogged up the stairs. This was the first time Nelson, Gabi and I had been in the same room since, well, since our moment of madness, and though I'd managed to shove it right to the back of my mind with lots of other things I didn't want to think about, I still felt rather awkward and guilty.

'Hello,' said Nelson, not bothering to knock.

'Hello!' beamed Gabi.

If Gabi had transformed herself, Nelson was also looking more stylish than usual too, in what looked like a new suit.

Still, I reminded myself, as Nelson said, these things sometimes happen. I simply *had* to learn to be a bit more worldly.

I drew up my spine, which in turn yanked my thick black stockings up my legs, which in turn reminded me that in this office, I was in charge.

'This is an unexpected pleasure, Nelson,' I said, bracing myself for the lecture about stupid women leaving their own house keys on the kitchen table. 'What did I forget at home then?'

'Nothing.' He looked blank, then looked at Gabi. 'Are you ready?'

'Ready for what?' I demanded before she could speak.

'Gabi's viewing some flats and I'm going with her, to knock on the walls and make a fuss about combination boilers.' He peered at me. 'Sort of the same thing you do, only I'm not charging her for it.'

'Oh,' I said, faintly.

Gabi was looking much less shifty and significantly more radiant. 'Shall we go?' she said, abandoning an open packet of Balhsen chocolate biscuits for the first time in our entire friendship.

'But, Nelson, you don't know the first thing about combination boilers,' I protested.

'I know enough,' he said, with a sideways smile at Gabi. 'And we might have tea afterwards, so don't make a big supper, will you?'

It occurred to me, with a loud internal clang of horror, that I might not have been the only one worrying about what Gabi would make of Nelson's and my little secret.

To take my mind off the troubling mental picture of Gabi and Nelson touring flats like a married couple, I spent the rest of the morning making phone calls. I'd realised that I could combine significant portions of Emery's wedding planning with my own business, and by lunchtime, I'd struck a most advantageous deal with a florist who was going to do the flowers for Emery at a bargain basement price, as a sweetener for being the sole supplier of my special 'Year of Flowers' package.

My seasonal specials were proving very popular amongst men who didn't like to think too hard about gift-giving. For the specially guilt-ridden, I was planning to offer outrageously expensive last-minute panic-buying outings, in which I'd whisk them and their credit cards round Selfridges in ninety minutes flat, the week before. For everyone else, I'd devised year-long packages of treats for neglected female relatives – manicures, blow-dries, flowers, chocolates and so on. All the client had to do was work out how much he wanted to spend, and then enjoy reaping the monthly rewards for the rest of the year.

Roger Trumpet was the first on my list.

'So you see, Roger, you don't have to worry about a thing. Your mum gets a huge bunch of the most gorgeous roses every month, and they take care of the delivery and message and everything,' I told him. 'All you have to do is listen to her sobbing with gratitude over the phone.'

'Done. Sold. Put me down for two,' he said. 'One for my mother, and another for my godmother.'

'Excellent,' I said, putting two ticks by his name.

'How's the lovely Gabi?' he asked in his new man-of-the-world voice.

'She's fine,' I said, thrown by his interest. 'Why? Have you changed your mind about having a girlfriend?'

'Good God, no, *I* haven't, but I think Nelson might have.'

'I don't think so!' I retorted automatically.

'Don't you?' he said. I reminded myself that Roger was a terrible old woman for gossip, accurate or otherwise. 'Oh, maybe I've got it wrong,' he went on airily. 'But that's Nelson all over, isn't it? He's got a bit of a Sir Galahad fixation when it comes to helpless women, hasn't he?'

I stared at the receiver. There was no polite answer to that. Especially coming from a man who now prided himself on offering women advice about their highlights.

'I hear you're escorting Miles Glover to a party tonight?' he went on, oblivious to my shocked silence. 'Be nice to him, he's not very good at these social dos. See if you can have a word with him about his BO too, will you?'

Really, I had created a monster, and no mistake.

Miles Glover, old friend of Roger Trumpet, was waiting for me in the coffee shop opposite the bar in which his office party was taking place. I would have known him for a friend of Roger's, if only from the prematurely middle-aged haircut and the nervous way he was shredding a paper napkin, as if he was waiting to be stoned to death, rather than drink a few glasses of warm white wine in a private room.

I wasn't really in the mood for someone else's office party, but a job was a job, and since I was scaling down Jonathan's appointments, I really needed to do more of these. So I pulled all my confidence and positive thoughts up into my chest, straining the buttons of my new Loden-green wool suit, and went over to Miles's table.

'Hello,' I said, slipping into the chair opposite. 'Is it Miles? I'm Honey. How do you do?'

'Hello.' He gave me a quick look, then cast his eyes back down to the table where there were four empty espresso cups lined up in front of him.

'Not looking forward to tonight?' I asked sympathetically.

Miles shook his head.

'Never mind, it'll soon be over,' I said. 'If it gets very bad, I can pretend I have a terrible headache, and insist that you have to take me home. Then you'll look like a perfect gentleman, I'll look like the prima donna and you won't have to stay for the speeches.'

That cracked a tiny smile out of him.

'Is there anything I need to know before we go in?' I asked. We'd covered the basics in our phone conversation earlier: it was an old-fashioned law firm, they were always on at him to bring a partner along, Miles hated Christmas parties and had always feigned last-minute ski trips but this year he was going for a promotion and had to be there.

'That they're a nosey bunch of bastards?' he suggested, bitterly. 'And don't drink the wine, it'll be poisonous.'

'OK,' I said brightly. This was going to be a long three hours. 'That sounds like most office parties I've been to.'

Miles made an enigmatic snorting noise, knocked back the dregs of his last espresso and off we went.

As Christmas bashes went, I actually didn't think it was a bad one but Miles clearly wasn't the sort of chap to wander round a party on his own, scattering chit-chat and jollity in his wake. He spent most of the first hour glued to my side, while I made increasingly desperate conversation about Roger and Roger's cousins. But I did notice that heads were turning our way, and every so often someone would pop up and linger next to us, until I said hello, and he grudgingly introduced them to me.

Then they went away again, rejoined their circle of mates and began gossiping furiously.

Most of my dates were just shy, but there was something else about Miles. He was shy and cross and seriously hard work. He was also knocking back the free wine like nobody's business.

My feet were hurting and my back was aching and I was dying to look at my watch, but I knew I couldn't. I hadn't had a date this tough since that horrible lunch for Mrs McKinnon in the Lanesborough. Being with

Jonathan had obviously ruined me for normal men – even with his unpredictable silences, I hadn't realised until tonight how very easy it had been. And if I ended our arrangement, it would all be like this from now on . . .

I shook myself.

'So, Miles!' I said cheerfully. 'Who's that big chap who keeps staring over at us? Should I go and say hello?'

Miles, who had no compunction whatsoever about checking his watch, snapped to attention at that point. 'Don't look at him. Don't!'

'Why?'

Miles let out a gusty sigh. 'He's . . . just someone I know from school. Called Ben. He joined the firm a few months back and all he's done ever since is spread . . . nasty rumours about me.' He downed the rest of his wine and took another glass from the passing tray.

'Oh dear,' I said, casting a brilliant smile at this Ben bloke, who blinked rapidly, then winked at me. 'What sort of rumours?'

'Don't want to talk about them.'

'Really? That bad? Surely not,' I said, soothingly. 'Oh look, he's coming over.'

'Shit,' said Miles.

'Would you like to put your arm around me?' I suggested.

Miles looked at me, and his face was frankly scared. So I put my arm around him.

'Hello, Miles, my old mucker,' bellowed Ben, and I knew at once what sort of man he was: head boy, captain of the first fifteen, everyone's mate apart from the ones whose lives he made a misery. 'And hello there to you, darling. Who are you?'

'I'm Honey,' I said, extending my hand politely. I didn't

flinch under Ben's firm grip and I withdrew my hand the second he held it too long.

He cocked his eyebrow. 'Didn't know Miles had a sister?'

'I'm Miles's . . . friend,' I said. 'Not his sister.'

'Well, well, well!' Ben laughed. 'Wonders will never cease. Never had you down as a ladies' man, Miles!'

I could feel Miles flinch. 'Why ever not?' I asked.

'Well, you know . . .' Ben did a rugby-club guffaw and now I flinched on Miles's behalf.

'No,' I said coldly, 'I don't know.'

'Between you and me, Honey . . .' said Ben, leaning so close I could smell the wine and cigarettes on his breath. Not nice. 'Between you and me, we had old Miles down as a shirtlifter. Didn't we?' he added, giving Miles a hefty slap on the back. 'Bit of an uphill gardener!'

I looked at Miles in horror: misery was written all over his face and his slumping shoulders told me everything I needed to know.

'How rude.' I pulled my shoulders back and tried hard to keep the anger out of my voice, while flashing Ben a look of pure disgust. 'Do you have a girlfriend yourself?'

'Abso-bloody-lutely.' Ben preened himself. 'Fighting them off with a shitty stick.'

'*Really?*' I said, sympathetically. 'Well, if you say so. Maybe there really is someone for everyone. Would you excuse us? Miles wants me to say hello to his secretary. I wish I could say it was lovely to meet you, er, Bill. But I can't.'

I gave Miles a gentle shove and made it look as if he were leading me away instead of the other way round. As we passed a door, I pushed him through it into the deserted buffet area, and he wilted onto a nearby chair.

'What was all that about?' I demanded. 'You know

bullying in the workplace is illegal these days? You can take him to a tribunal for behaving like that! What a revolting piece of pondlife!'

Terrible shoes too, I noticed, but didn't add this, as it didn't really seem to sit well with my moral outrage.

Miles shrugged hopelessly and looked round for a drink. He was distinctly the worse for wear, and we'd been there only fifty minutes. For a solicitor, he was very weedy. I wondered what he was like in meetings. Not exactly value for money. 'They're all the same,' he moaned. 'What's the point?'

'There's a big point!' I snorted. 'If you're not gay, it's a disgusting way of bullying you, and if you are gay, then . . . then it's sexual harassment!'

I paused, unsure whether I might have overstepped the mark. No mention had been made about Miles's sexuality, and I hadn't asked. But bigots like Ben made me so angry, and there was something about Miles that needed a good shake. 'Miles?' I said, nudging him. 'You're at work for a long time. If that creep's ruining your life, then you need to deal with it.'

Miles looked up at me with weariness in his eyes. 'And what if I don't know? What then?'

I knew he wasn't talking about Ben the bully then. I sat down on the chair beside him, tucking my skirt around my knees. 'Life's very short,' I said. 'You can't spend it pretending to be someone you're not.'

Given my own dilemma, I realised the irony of this as soon as I said it and was thankful that Nelson wasn't there to ram it home.

'Roger said you were perfectly happy to cover for him at his party,' Miles whined on defensively. 'You didn't give *him* a lecture.'

'Roger's different.' I helped myself to a lone sausage roll. It tasted of lard. 'I've known Roger for years and he's very comfortable with his sexuality.' I was about to add, 'What there is of it,' but didn't. 'Roger isn't particularly interested in girls or boys – he just wanted to get his mum off his case,' I went on. 'That's the only reason I was happy to do it. I don't think you're so sure, and, you know, it's not really very healthy to sweep it under the carpet.'

'You're saying you wouldn't act as an escort to a gay man?' he countered crossly. 'Isn't that discrimination?'

'I *have* acted as an escort to a gay man,' I said, thinking about a rather enjoyable evening of Scottish dancing a few months back. 'But the man I was escorting was completely relaxed about being gay, had a charming boyfriend, but he just didn't want to bring him to a cricket club event with a bunch of men he didn't know that well yet. I didn't say I was his girlfriend, just a friend.' I gave Miles a pointed stare. 'I think it's always easier to let other people draw their own conclusions than to start off with a lie.'

He let out a long sigh. 'I could leave.'

'You could. Or you could deal with the problem. It's your life, Miles. Do what you want with it. Just don't end up doing what other people want. You can only mask things for so long.'

What was I masking, I wondered. Why was I so determined to run away from Jonathan, from confronting my father, from saying no to people? Why was it so much easier, so much more rewarding to be Honey, and not Melissa?

We sat there in silence, listening to the party rumble on behind the closed door.

22

'Jeremy, put that down,' I said, looking up from the shopping list. 'You can't afford it. Step away from the display.'

Jeremy Wilde, reformed surf dude, obediently replaced the jar of Crème de la Mer he'd been fiddling with. We were in the beauty and make-up hall of Liberty, on the finishing straight of our Christmas shopping speed slalom. He was carrying the bags containing the gifts I would giftwrap overnight, then annotate with Post-it notes, all ready for his personal touch. I, meanwhile, was sipping calmly from a bottle of water, and beginning to understand why my mother treated her Peter Jones card like some women treated Valium.

Shopping for other people, with other people's money, was a surprisingly fulfilling career sideline, especially in the season of free mulled-wine snifters, mini-mince pies and the all-pervasive atmosphere of impulse buying. Thanks to the Little Lady, secretaries all over London would now be unwrapping something more exciting than three Roger et Gallet soaps on their last day in the office. And thanks to Honey's own personal research efforts in the field of boned and laced undergarments, some wives would be discovering some saucy undies they'd actually want to wear.

'Who's next, Jeremy?' I asked.

'Dad's girlfriend,' he mumbled, then squinted up

naughtily from under his shaggy fringe. 'Katinka. She's hot. Hyuk, hyuk. Mum hates her. Used to be our au pair – till she ran off with Dad.'

'Hmm. Nothing too sexy, then,' I said warningly, noticing Jeremy's eyes glazing. 'How about . . . cellulite cream?'

With three weeks to go before Christmas (and by the same reckoning, two weeks before Emery's wedding), I was inhaling more 'festive ambience' than one of Santa's little helpers. Sadly, my own spirits were less than festive.

Yesterday Daddy had left two messages on my mobile and one on our home answering machine, wanting 'to see you and your chequebook'. After those came a couple of messages from Emery, about her self-penned wedding vows and the possibility of hiring a small boy to carry her rings, since William's ex-wife was oddly reluctant to let her borrow their four-year-old Valentino, then a call from Gabi, looking for Nelson to help her view another flat, with only a passing hello to me.

None of these prospective conversations filled me with much joy and I was waiting for something positive to happen, in order to work up the necessary oomph to deal with the return calls.

'Hyuk, cellulite cream, excellent. Should I offer to apply it for her?' asked Jeremy, sneakily. 'She didn't have any last time I looked.'

'Scrap that. Pedicure socks,' I said. 'Girls love them. Big treat.'

My work phone rang in my bag and despite all the lecturing I'd given myself, my heart thudded in case it was Jonathan.

The number was withheld.

He could be calling from a foreign switchboard . . .

'Hello!' I said cheerfully, imagining a Starbucks Eggnog Latte, all steaming and festive and spicy. And American. 'This is Honey!'

'Oh, Honey,' whined a familiar voice. 'It's Bryan. I need some help with my Christmas shopping. What can I get my mother? She likes Lilliput Lane houses and baking.'

I suppose I should have been flattered that Bryan refused to give up, but it was getting quite wearing and I wasn't very good at being mean to men who clearly needed more help than I could offer. Since threats and crossness had only inflamed him – and I didn't have time to deal with him here – I decided to try another tack. I just couldn't be *mean*. I wanted to, but there was some kind of valve in my head that stopped me.

'All right, Bryan, but this will be very expensive since you've left it to the last minute,' I warned. 'Fax over a list of all the people you need to give presents to, with their ages and rough price guides and I'll get my assistant to look at it.' Half an hour on the phone to Gabi should sort him out. 'Now I have to go – there's another call waiting.'

I did have another call waiting, as it happened: also, enticingly, from a number-withheld switchboard.

'Hello?' I said breathily.

'Hello, Honey, this is your accountant speaking.'

'Nelson,' I said, letting the breath rush out of me, 'why are you calling me on my work phone?'

'Because you're at work? And because I've done your accounts. We need to go through them. Would you like to take me out for a sandwich? You may hear something to your advantage.'

My attention was drawn back to the display. Jeremy was slowly poking his fingers in and out of a large open

pot of home waxing gunk while the assistant glowered at
him.

'Stop it!' I hissed. 'Yes, Nelson, that would be fine.'

'OK, meet me at that nice café opposite my office at
about one.'

I looked over at Jeremy. He had abandoned the wax
and was inspecting a heated eyelash curler with curiosity
and fear in his eyes.

'Put it down,' I mouthed, and he did.

'Do you want the good news or the bad news?' asked
Nelson, tearing into an almond croissant.

The café was warm, cinnamon-scented and playing
Christmas songs, but I still felt unseasonably tetchy.

'The good news,' I said. 'Unless the bad news is so
bad you think I'll need a lot of good news to recover
from it.'

Nelson did a pretend double take. 'What has got into
you?' he said. 'You've been like an old biddy all week!
Get with the seasonal programme!'

'Sorry.' I pulled a face. 'It must be this wedding. It's
turning me spinster-ish.'

Nelson snorted something unintelligible. But it was
true: I was turning into a right old trout. Jeremy's dad's
girlfriend's pedicure socks floated accusingly into my
mind's eye. That had been mean of me.

'Well, the good news is that you are running a remark-
ably profitable little business,' he said, pushing a page of
accounts over the table.

I stared at the columns in front of me with a mixture
of delight and astonishment. Then I looked up at Nelson.
'Seriously? This is my profit?'

He rolled his eyes. 'No, you plank. Not unless you're

selling drugs on the side. That's turnover. *This* is your profit.'

He pointed to another column. It was still a surprising amount of money, more than I'd expected, even with my manic saving.

'Really?' I said, my face breaking into a smile. 'Wow!'

'Yup,' he said. 'You can stop cutting those "How to Pinch Pennies in Your Office" features out of the Sunday papers.'

I blushed and ran my eyes over the columns again. Wow.

Nelson raised his cappuccino cup to me and winked.

'Well done,' he said. 'I want to be the first to admit that I was wrong. You are a shrewd businesswoman after all, and I demand my share of the profits for giving you the idea in the first place.'

'Thank you,' I said, beaming so broadly I thought my face was going to split in two.

'So does this mean we get a much better Christmas?' he asked.

'Definitely!' I enthused, my mind returning immediately to Liberty, this time with my own shopping list, instead of Jeremy Wilde's. 'Santa might just bring you those slippers you've been hinting about, after all! And I'm going to treat myself to a really fabuloso pedicure somewhere, and get some new undies, and replace that knife of yours I broke, and . . .'

I tailed off as a much less cheery thought dawned on me.

Daddy.

I should pay that money back. I could write off nearly two-thirds of my debt in one fell swoop.

'What?' demanded Nelson, seeing my face fall. 'You

are going to treat yourself, aren't you? You've earned that money!'

A solemn sense of obligation and responsibility settled on my shoulders like a very heavy leather coat. 'No,' I said slowly, trying to wring every possible ounce of moral satisfaction out of the moment, in order to compensate for the loss of frilly Agent Provocateur knickers, 'I am going to pay back the money I owe my father and free myself from the shackles of obligation.'

'Do you want to tell me what you mean by that?' Nelson put his cup down.

It had to come out sooner or later, I suppose. I took a sip of coffee, and braced myself for the inevitable lecture. 'I owe my father ten thousand pounds. He lent it to me to invest in Perry Hamilton's ski business and of course Perry just vanished with it. It's been hanging over me all this time, and he's been using it as a stick to beat me with, but now he wants it back to pay for part of Emery's wedding.'

I looked up at Nelson. He looked furious. 'Are you mad at me?' I faltered.

'Yes, I am!' spluttered Nelson. 'Why the hell didn't you say something? We could have worked something out!'

'I didn't want to *work something out*,' I protested. 'That was the whole point – I wanted to pay it back myself! And now I can.'

Nelson looked impressed, despite himself. 'Well. I still say you should have told me.'

I looked him in the eye. 'I didn't want to. You'd have made me feel about four years old.'

'Only because I care about you, you stupid woman,' he said, in the caring way I had come to know and love and often mistake for curmudgeonliness.

'So you think I should pay him the money back, then?' I said hopefully. 'Get him off my case once and for all. Fund my sister's ridiculous wedding dream.' I paused, as a furious battle began in my heart between Honey and Melissa. 'Even if it means scaling down Christmas?'

Yet something still didn't add up, even to my innocent way of thinking. What did Daddy need my money for, when most of the wedding was donated, and he always seemed to have more than enough cash? Was he just trying to wind me up, or did he actually need the money for something else?

Nelson tipped his head to one side, in the manner of a TV relationship counsellor. 'What do *you* want to do?'

I pulled a face that I hoped reflected the titanic struggle between self and family.

'How much are you charging them for the dress, by the way?' he asked, waving at the waitress for another two cappuccinos.

'I'm not,' I replied, surprised. 'I mean, Emery's paid for the material and everything. I'm just making it.'

Nelson jotted a figure down on a napkin. 'OK, then, are you charging them anything for planning the wedding? Phone calls, faxes, emails . . . that sort of thing?'

'Er, no. I'm just doing it from the office. The office they're not meant to know about, before you say anything,' I added.

'And the planning – you billing them for your time?'

'No, but, Nelson, don't go down that road – it isn't worth it, honestly.'

He looked up. 'You know, if I were you, I'd inform your father that since you've saved him at least three thousand pounds, you should amend your debt accordingly.'

'I can't do that!' I protested, trying to imagine the look on Daddy's face.

'Melissa,' said Nelson, his voice very serious. 'Think about it. You've negotiated some cracking deals for this wedding. You've been tougher with those printers than I'd dare be with anyone at work. You're organising the lives of men much scarier than your father. What's stopping you taking that attitude home?'

I didn't want to say, 'It's Honey, not Mel,' because I knew he'd dismiss it out of hand. It was starting to sound like a lame excuse even to me. But that was the bottom line. I couldn't pretend to be someone I wasn't with people who actually knew me of old.

'He knows the right buttons to press,' I said wearily. 'It's just easier to pay the money and draw a line under the whole sorry mess.'

Nelson sighed. 'Fine. Be like that. But as your accountant, I strongly advise you to invest in your business.' He gave me a meaningful look. 'In whatever way you think best. If you get another wig, you could double your bookings. You could be Honey *and* Ginger.'

Oooh. My mind wandered happily down that road. Ginger could be a more feisty version of Honey. I could save her for the difficult jobs: the dumping of girlfriends, or the firing of cleaners. She'd have the same sexy undies as Honey, but in frothy sea-green lace, and deep midnight-blue satin . . .

'So. You want to hear the bad news?' interrupted Nelson.

The visions of deep suspender-belts vanished as I spluttered on a mouthful of milk foam. I knew it was too good to be true.

'OK,' I said bravely. 'What is it?'

'You'll have to pay tax,' he said. 'And you're paying for lunch.'

He leaned forward and wiped some chocolate off my lip. 'And you still can't drink cappuccino without covering yourself in froth.'

'Is that it?' I said, relieved. I peered more closely at Nelson's sudden shifty expression. 'Nelson? Why are you looking so guilty?'

He drummed his spoon on the table nervously. 'Oh and I, er, told Gabi she could stay with us for a few days until she finds another new flat.'

'You did what?' I demanded. 'I thought she'd found one!'

Nelson adopted his 'appalled saint' expression. 'Mel, don't be so mean. Gabi told her mum she was moving out, her mum went spare, crying, wailing, everything, then Gabi discovered there was some major problem with her new place. She couldn't face going through all that again, so she asked me if she could crash at ours while she found somewhere else. And I said yes.'

'I notice she didn't ask *me*,' I observed meaningfully.

'Yes, well, it's not your house.' Nelson looked guilty even before I had time to take offence. 'Sorry, you made me say that.'

'Fair enough.' I lifted my chin.

'Oh come on, Mel,' he said. 'I let you stay when you needed somewhere, didn't I?'

'Yes, but I wasn't trying to . . .' Our eyes met, and there was a slight moment of awkwardness. Was it really fair for me to stop Gabi and Nelson maybe getting together, just because he didn't want to get together with me?

The meanness of it shocked me. What kind of a cow was I turning into?

I swallowed, then said, in a bright tone, 'No, you're absolutely right! Of course she should stay!'

'Listen, I can sleep over at the office if you want,' he suggested.

'No need for that!' I trilled.

I wanted that bed kept in reserve for myself.

We parted on good-ish terms, and bearing Nelson's instructions about investing in my business uppermost in my mind, I decided to treat myself to a new suspender-belt anyway. I reckoned that Honey deserved a bonus, after earning all that money.

I knew my way to Agent Provocateur well enough: apart from my own shopping needs, I'd popped in several times recently on buying missions for shy clients. By now I knew better than to ask whether the measurements provided were for wives or girlfriends; after innocently putting my foot in it, I'd come to realise it was best not to enquire.

I was browsing through the various tiny hangers, enjoying the faint sense of naughtiness in the air and getting all tingly with excitement at the lovely fabrics and unexpected holes, when I heard a male voice sleazing away at one of the assistants.

'What size would you say you were, my dear? About a thirty-six D? Really? Fancy that! Yes, well, I am a pretty good judge!'

It sounded horribly like my father.

I froze for a second, hoping it would turn out to be no one of the sort. But then I heard him say, 'Do you get a discount if you buy the matching set?' and all doubt was removed.

My immediate thought, I regret to say, was one of

adolescent panic. There's surely only one thing worse than catching your parents having sex, and that's catching your father buying raunchy underwear for your mother. From a shop you buy your own seduction pants from.

I edged my way to one side, still clutching two forties-style balcony bras and matching tap pants with keyhole backs, to see if there was a way out.

There wasn't.

And now one of the assistants – Nicole, who had personally kneed me in the small of the back in order to lace me into the most dramatic corset ever – was approaching me with a handful of wispy undies.

'Hey, Melissa!' she said. She didn't have to raise her voice – it was a very small shop. 'Have you seen the new teddies?' she asked. 'They'd look fabulous on you. You need a bit of something up top to make them work, and a teeny waist like yours, of course.'

That, of course, was a red rag to a bull to my father – how could he help but turn round? The look on his face when he saw who the Melissa was, however, was almost as horrified as mine.

But Daddy had had many years' experience in recovering from embarrassing situations, and immediately transformed his expression from horror into paternal delight.

'Melissa,' he said, smoothly. 'What a surprise!'

'Um, yes,' I said, trying not to look at the large turquoise bra in his hands. My mother was nowhere near a thirty-six D. Nor did I imagine she'd suit the 1970s porn actress look that I understood could be very sexy on the right sort of woman.

'I've been trying to get hold of you,' he said, wagging

his finger. 'You're very elusive these days.' He peered at me beadily. 'That *temp* agency must be keeping you very busy.'

'It is,' I said, fighting the flush of blood to my cheeks. 'You know how it is, Christmas rush and all that.'

'Indeed.' He took a step back, gestured to get Nicole's attention, and waved the bra at her. I stared in fascination at the way the cups swung gently back and forth. You could have caught tiddlers in them. 'Nicole, could you put this on my pile, darling?'

Pile? He'd bought a *pile* of underwear? He wanted my mother to run through entire costume changes? I felt mildly faint.

'Um, which pile, Mr Romney-Jones?' asked Nicole discreetly.

He gave her the most lascivious wink I'd ever seen outside a *Carry On* film. 'Pile C, I think.'

Oh God, it got worse and worse.

'Now, Melissa, we need to talk,' he said, looking pointedly at the underwear in my hand. 'Because I think you have more pressing financial commitments than buying yourself frilly knickers, haven't you? Not what you'd call a necessity, in your case, eh?' He gave me a lechy look. 'Unless you're planning on reeling in a titled bloke to pay off your debts?'

If I'd had any reservations about paying that debt off and freeing myself from the lingering sense of obligation to this dreadful man, I had no doubts now.

'Actually, I want to talk to you about that,' I said, hoisting my chin high. 'I can give you a cheque.'

'For how much?' replied my father, quick as a flash.

'For five thousand pounds,' I said, bravely.

'Five thousand, eh?' Another beady inspection. 'What

sort of temping have you been doing, Melissa? Hmm? Quite lucrative, is it?'

How did he do that? How did he know where the vulnerable spots were?

'I've been saving up,' I said, going to put the pants back on the nearest rail. It didn't feel right, holding sexy knickers in front of my father. Then I heard Nelson's voice telling me to stand up to him. So I didn't put them back, I clung to them.

'And when can you give me the rest?' he demanded.

Oh God, this was it. The big test.

I could think of places I'd rather have faced it than surrounded by voluptuous models in thongs and nipple tassels. There were two barely covered crotches either side of Daddy's head. I didn't know where to look.

'Well, I've taken some money off for the wedding dress,' I began, determined to stand my ground, no matter what he threw at me. 'I've spent hours and hours on it, and I've saved Emery thousands of pounds by making it for her. And then there's all the wedding planning – according to Emery's magazines, it would have cost you at least three thousand . . .'

'Hold it right there, little lady,' said my father, raising a hand to stop me.

I stopped. Stupidly. But he had that magic effect on me.

Daddy picked up a transparent apricot chiffon chemise, inspected it, held it out for Nicole to collect. 'Pile B, I think, Nicole,' he murmured, then turned back to me. 'Really, Melissa. Talk about sharper than a serpent's tooth! You're going to charge your *father* to make your *sister*'s wedding dress? And you're going to bill your *family* for the time you've spent organising what should be a happy family moment? I can barely believe I'm hearing this. I lent you that money in all good faith, did I not?'

I nodded sulkily, though this wasn't exactly true – he'd spotted a business opportunity, whereas I'd wanted to help out a boyfriend. It was unfortunate that his business acumen had, on this occasion, been as lousy as my taste in men.

'Did I ask you to repay your school fees when you failed to get a decent job?' he demanded. 'Did I ask you to repay that money I spent sending you to that ridiculous finishing place your mother insisted you attend?'

A tiny angry voice inside me wanted to tell him exactly why he should be very proud of me indeed, but it was swamped by a tidal wave of guilt and misery. When you looked at it like that, I *had* let them down – what had I achieved, after all, but a series of dead-end jobs, and now a stupid pretend career, in which I'd met the man of my dreams, screwed it up, and exposed myself and my family to all manner of danger and scandal?

I fought back the hot tears that prickled at my eyes.

No, I thought fiercely, I am not going to let him make me cry in Agent Provocateur!

My father leaned in closer, and dropped his voice.

'And while you're here in person, Melissa, there's something I've been meaning to mention to you,' he murmured in his most dangerously silky tone. 'I'm happy that you're able to repay your debt, but I would warn you to be very careful about this . . . temping of yours.'

I gazed at him wide-eyed, like a rabbit caught in a tractor beam.

Without breaking eye contact, he reached into his pocket and withdrew something that he pressed into my hand. 'I have a reputation to uphold, even if you do not.

And if I find out you've been using my flat as a knocking shop ever again, I will come down on you like a ton of bricks. You will not know what's hit you!' he hissed.

I looked down at the fabric he'd pressed into my hand. It was a white cotton hanky, still crispy with something. I'd never seen it before in my life. I furrowed my brow, trying to think what it could be when it came to me in a flash: it was Jonathan's – the hanky he'd used to mop up his spilled tea the one and only time I'd held a meeting in Dolphin Square.

I looked up, about to explain, but Daddy cut me off.

'Don't even try to lie your way out of it,' he said with a self-righteousness that he carried off astonishingly well for an accomplished liar. 'I was in there myself this week. Jim the porter enquired as to how my interior decorations were going. I was taken aback. Until he explained that you had been there . . . meeting an interior decorator. Who just happened to be an attractive American man.'

I stared at him. If I didn't know better, I'd swear he had a crystal ball.

'Don't deny it,' snapped my father. 'You were seen. Dressed like some kind of upmarket hooker too, by all accounts.'

Given the stash of upmarket hookerwear he was buying, this seemed a little rich, but I was in no state to begin fencing now.

'I always had such high hopes for you, Melissa, but you've always let me down,' he said, with a final blast of menace. 'And I am running short of patience.'

I bit my lip until it went numb.

'Anyway,' he said, straightening up and adopting a warm, gentleman's club tone, 'you can let me have that cheque as soon as you like. I would hate Emery to get married in some sort of agricultural tent. Just think,' he added, patting me in what must have looked to the shop assistants like an affectionate gesture, 'it'll be your industry putting the roof over everyone's heads at her wedding. How proud you'll feel. Surely that's worth more than mere money?'

Mustering up every ounce of dignity I had, I said, 'I am doing this for Emery, because I love her. Unlike you, I can't put a price on that.'

Then I spun on my heel, ditched the bras and pants, and walked out, making myself walk calmly, even though my legs were burning with the desire to sprint away.

I couldn't bear to go back to the office after that. I just started walking in a sort of misery trance and before I knew it, I was outside my own front door, with my own straggly plant pots and my own gold doorbell.

I let myself in, walked through the empty house and threw myself face down on my bed, feeling like a lumpy, friendless, last-to-be-picked-at-games twelve-year-old again. I was too shattered even to cry.

I don't know how long I lay there. I couldn't move my arms and legs anyway. It was as though Daddy had drained my whole body of energy, leaving me an inert lump. Eventually, I heard Nelson come in.

'Mel?' he yelled, dropping his keys and his briefcase on the table.

Nelson didn't want me either. He had a new lame duck to help out. A new lame duck he'd probably end up falling in love with. It would all be like a Richard Curtis movie, but with me in the Kristen Scott Thomas brittle posh-bird role.

Brittle posh *abandoned* bird.

'Mel? Are you in the bath again?'

No one would ever want me. I might as well spend the rest of my life organising weddings for more attractive, more desirable women.

'Mel?' Nelson knocked briefly and then barged straight into my room. I couldn't summon up the will to lift my head.

'Oh, no. Melissa,' he said, crouching by my bedside. 'What happened?'

I still couldn't move, but I managed to croak, 'Daddy.' And then, 'Money.'

Nelson let out a long, cross sigh. 'Right. Get up.'

'Can't.'

I'll draw a discreet veil over the way Nelson manhandled me back to life, but he marched me into the kitchen, sat me down at the table, and cut me a large slice of carrot cake, which I toyed with unhappily.

'Eat it,' he ordered. 'Where's your chequebook?'

'In my bag.'

Nelson slammed the chequebook in front of me. 'Write that cheque to your bloody father,' he said. 'Give him the bloody money. You can make it again.'

'I don't know if I want to,' I said. Then the tears started falling. 'I don't want to . . .' My voice trailed off, but the voice in my head finished the sentence for me, '. . . fall in love with one of my clients again.'

'Oh, for heaven's sake, Mel, you're like one of those perpetual tear miracle statues. You never used to be like this.' Nelson searched his pockets for a hanky. 'I don't have a hanky.' He looked in my bag again and took out Jonathan's cotton square. 'Here, you look like a miserable panda.'

'Thank you.' I buried my nose in the hanky, breathed in a very faint trace of Jonathan's Creed, which set me off again.

'Here,' said Nelson. 'You dropped this.'

He handed me a hairclip: a large gold one with a red vinyl Chanel flower. I sniffed, and looked at it in surprise. 'What the hell is that?'

'It fell out of your hanky,' he explained. 'Not really you, if you don't mind me saying.'

'But this isn't *mine*,' I protested, turning it over. 'I can't afford stuff like this!'

Nelson gave me a dark look. 'Did you shoplift it?' he asked sternly. 'You're not turning into one of those deranged spinsters who start by nicking bridal magazines and end up stealing babies in prams from outside Boots?'

'No.' I turned it round and round in my hands. It must have come from Daddy's flat.

Had he thought it was *mine*?

And why did it look so familiar?

Then I remembered where I'd seen it before.

Stuck in Bobsy Parkin's stupid Horse of the Year Show mane.

23

Between juggling the final details of Emery's wedding and wrapping literally hundreds of tiny boxes for clients, early December rushed past in a blur – which was no bad thing, as it left me precious little time to dwell on Jonathan, Daddy's carrying-on or Gabi and Nelson's increasingly 'dinner for two' lifestyle. If it wasn't for my chocolate Advent calendar I wouldn't have had any idea what day it was.

I was in the office on 7 December (chocolate star), fiddling with silver rosettes when the entryphone buzzed. I panicked slightly as I wasn't in my full Honey regalia. I had no appointments – as far as I knew – so my skirt was unzipped for comfort and my stilettos were kicked off and lying under my desk.

I was still wearing the wig and a pair of seamed opaque stockings, however, just for fun.

I grabbed the receiver. 'Hello,' I said, sticking the rosette on my hand while my feet hunted for my shoes. 'The Little Lady Agency?'

'Hello,' said a distracted female voice. 'This is Miss Emery Romney-Jones. I am looking for Miss Melissa Romney-Jones.'

I stared at the receiver in shock.

'Hello?' said Emery again. She seemed very confused by the button and kept pushing it on and off. 'Is . . . Romney . . . am . . . for Melissa . . . Jones.'

What the hell was Emery doing *here*?

I shoved my feet into my shoes and pressed the entry button. 'Emery, it's me, come on up.'

While she was coming up the stairs, I scrabbled around in my mind to find an explanation as to why I had offices and what they were for. It didn't have to be that credible – it was only Emery – but she was bound to repeat it to someone who might ask more questions. Like my father. I'd managed to keep my new career from my family, and with their customary self-absorption, no one had been interested enough to ask.

Temping. I would have to be *running* a temping agency, not just working for one. It wasn't quite a fib, after all, was it? I was temping . . . sort of.

While my mouth dried with panic, I looked round the office for any incriminating evidence: I whisked a dry-cleaning bag of Jeremy Wilde's new suits into a filing cabinet and stuffed the bags of presents into the spare room. Then I rushed out to the top of the stairs to welcome Emery in, remembered at the last moment that I still had my blonde wig on, and was rearranging my hair as Emery floated up into sight.

'All ready for me?' she asked with unusual enthusiasm. 'You know, Mel, I never really enjoyed this whole wedding malarkey until you got involved. Oooh, nice shoes!'

I followed her into my office and closed the door behind us. 'Um, Emery, it's not that I'm not happy to see you, or anything,' I said, 'but . . . what are you doing here?'

She stared triumphantly at me, thrilled to have caught me out for a change. 'My fitting, you idiot. Had you forgotten?'

'Tomorrow, Emery! We said Thursday.'

'Did we?' Her face fell. 'I'm sure we said Wednesday.'

'No, we didn't.'

Emery looked totally crestfallen. 'Oh nuts. I thought I'd been so *organised* for once. I've come up to town specially. I've even got matching underwear on.'

I glanced over at my desk diary. There was nothing in it for the rest of the day, since I'd planned to pop out for some cakes and then crack on with my wrapping.

'Well, never mind,' I said, giving her an encouraging smile. 'You're here now. We might as well do it anyway.'

'It's really, you know, *nice* in here,' said Emery, looking around. 'Is this where you're living these days?'

That was a good point. 'Emery, who told you to come round here?' I asked.

She looked blank. 'Oh, I called by your house, and Nelson told me to try round here.'

'Nelson?' What was Nelson doing still in our house at ten in the morning? And more to the point, what was he doing telling Emery my secrets! 'He told you to come round here, did he?' I demanded.

'Well, to be fair,' she said quickly, 'it was actually Gabi who told me to come round. Nelson was umming and erring a bit.'

'Gabi!' *No!* 'What was *she* doing round there?'

'Oh, they were going house-hunting,' she said. 'Taken the day off specially. She reckoned Wednesdays are good for viewings.'

Nelson hadn't mentioned *that* when I left for work this morning. In fact, he'd gone very quiet on the whole subject of Gabi; when I'd tried to raise it tactfully, he'd just given me his Grade One Latter-Day Saint look, and told me I should be more supportive of her, and did I know she had given a whole load of her old clothes to a charity shop? They always seemed to be deep in private conversation, and clammed up suspiciously whenever I tried to join in. I tried to be Christian about it, but to be honest, I felt like both my best friends had been poached – by each other.

My face must have been a picture, because Emery added, 'Are they seeing each other these days? They seemed quite chummy to me. They had their heads together over _Time Out_ when I arrived.'

'No,' I said weakly. 'Well, I don't really know what's going on there.'

'Oh, yes.' Emery smiled. 'So is that why you're living here? Have you split up, you and Nelson?'

'Emery, for the millionth time, Nelson and I are not going out,' I said heavily. 'We've _never_ been going out.' There was nothing for it. I would have to make a clean breast of things. Well, clean-ish.

Emery looked at me, an expectant look on her face.

'Look, this is my office,' I said. 'I've started my own temping agency. I haven't been doing it long, and I didn't want to tell Daddy until it's all up and running, because he's bound to stick his nose in and ruin everything.'

Emery nodded sympathetically at that point. 'He'd want to vet your staff, I expect.'

'Quite. So keep it to yourself, OK?' I pleaded.

'Your secret's safe with me,' said Emery vaguely, her attention distracted by a new lipgloss I'd left on my desk. Luckily, curiosity wasn't one of her failings.

'Would you like to get yourself a cup of coffee while I get your dress?' I asked, edging backwards out of the room to check she didn't start poking about in my absence.

Emery's dress was on my dress-making dummy in the spare room and I was struggling through with it when the phone rang.

To my horror, Emery picked it up – probably the first time in her life she had failed to ignore a ringing telephone.

'Hello?' I heard her say, then, 'Oooh, no. I don't think so. Who? *Who?* No, not here. Are you sure you have the right number?'

I gestured furiously to her, as best I could with an armful of cathedral-length train.

'Can you hold for a second?' asked Emery politely, while looping a finger around her temple and rolling her eyes towards the phone.

'Hello?' I said breathlessly, wrestling the receiver out of her hands. I'd been hoping Jonathan would call for ages: typical that he'd ring now, when there was no chance of a proper conversation.

'Honey, it's me. Bryan.'

My heart sank. It was bloody Bryan Birkett again. I shifted the dummy under my arm.

'I need to make an appointment to see you,' he whined, self-importantly.

'Well, what's the problem?' I said, briskly. 'This is a very busy time.'

'I think I'm having closure issues about Camilla,' he sighed. 'I think I need to see you again, just to talk them through. Perhaps if I could take you out for dinner, I could use that as a way of moving on from her . . .'

'Bryan, I don't think you need me to move on,' I said. 'But you may need to discuss this with a trained counsellor. Have you considering going to Relate?'

'No, I think you're much better,' he said, obviously

enjoying the nannying tone. 'You drive all thoughts of Camilla from my mind. I think . . . I think . . .'

'Bryan, you're obviously thinking too much,' I said. 'It's not always helpful to think too much about relationships.'

'I feel my love life would run more smoothly if I had nicer clothes,' he insisted. 'Can I make an appointment for a wardrobe consultation?'

'Call me in the New Year,' I said, casting anxious looks in Emery's direction. Lipglosses could occupy her for only so long, so I nudged a wedding magazine in her direction. 'We can talk about the sales.'

I put the phone down on Bryan's protestations.

'Ooh, Mel,' said Emery without looking up. 'You are tough on the phone. I wish I could be so strict. Where did you learn it?'

'I didn't learn it anywhere,' I said. 'It's just normal.'

'No, it's not,' she said, finally looking up. 'You sound just like Daddy. And who's Bryan?'

'A client,' I said, switching on the answering machine and turning the volume right down so she wouldn't hear any messages.

'He must be a very good client if he calls you honey,' she observed.

'Something like that,' I said, taking refuge in bossiness. 'Now, put that coffee well out of the way, yes, right up there on the bookshelf, and try this dress on.'

It started drizzling, then raining, and as the rain lashed down outside, Emery and I passed a quiet hour or two fiddling with her frock, listening to Christmassy music and grazing on sugared almonds. She wasn't a fidgeter, so I was able to get some useful adjustments made while she stared into space and occasionally made some

comment about her wedding list, or William's latest anni-
hilation of the company squash ladder.

'You've made a super job of my dress, Mel,' she said,
looking at the dummy after a protracted pause. 'You're
really good at sewing, aren't you?'

I looked up at her, my mouth full of pins. I couldn't
remember anyone from my immediate family saying
anything complimentary about my dress-making before,
despite the fact that I rarely went home without being
cornered to sew on a button or tack some hem. A warm
glow of sisterly love filled my heart – although it could
have been the coffee.

'Thank you,' I mumbled, pinnily.

'I wish I had sexy dark hair like yours,' she mused.
'It's so gorgeous. Like molten Nutella. Or treacle.'

I ran a self-conscious hand through my thick mane.
Really, Emery said the oddest things. 'It needs a wash,
Em. But thanks.'

'Should I dye my hair black for the wedding?' she
mused. 'To match you and Allegra?'

'No!' I reined in my alarm. 'No, I mean, you have such
lovely hair, Emery. Don't do anything to spoil it.'

Emery cocked her head towards the door. 'Is that
someone on your stairs?' she asked.

'Can't be,' I said, shaking my head confidently. 'They
have to buzz to get in.'

As if in answer, there was a knock on my front door.

Visions of Bryan Birkett, armed with a knife and an
emergency wedding licence crowded my mind. I struggled to my feet and jabbed the pins into the pincushion
on my wrist. 'Must be the postman,' I gabbled. 'Or one
of the girls from downstairs wanting a button stitched on
or something. I'll get it. Don't move.'

I looked at Emery. The skirt of the dress was hitched up round her waist while I adjusted her underskirts, and she'd loosened the buttons 'for comfort' so her milky shoulders and what cleavage she had were on display.

'Do you want to . . .' I gestured around my own shoulders. 'In case they have to come in?'

Emery looked blank, then giggled at me. 'Melissa! You're such an old prude! Don't be silly!'

Prude, eh, I thought, walking towards the door and feeling my Honey suspenders slide against the inside of my thighs. Like she knows the underwear I have on right now. And it's not even a dressing-up day!

'Good morning,' I said, opening the door.

I wasn't expecting to see Jonathan there, holding a large bunch of orange roses and gleaming red berries. Too much exposure to wedding magazines meant I identified them immediately as Naranga roses and his dripping black umbrella as a perfect thank-you gift for ushers at winter weddings.

'Ah, so Fiona the receptionist exists, after all!' he said, with a courteous nod.

I froze.

Too late.

Jonathan took a closer look at me. 'Honey?' he said.

'No, Fiona,' I insisted with a brave smile. 'Honey's just popped out for . . .'

'Melissa!' barked Emery. 'Stuck! I'm stuck!'

'Melissa?' Jonathan's mouth twitched and he craned his neck round the door.

'Melissa,' I said, grasping at straws. 'Yes, I'm Melissa, the new receptionist who . . .'

'Now, hold it right there,' said Jonathan sternly. The twitch turned into a most ambiguous expression, and I couldn't tell whether he was amused or angry or disappointed or what. 'You can't pull this stunt on me. I'd recognise those brown eyes, with or without the blonde fringe.' He clicked and pointed at me. 'Hey . . . So Honey's real name is Melissa! Well, well, well. I thought I'd never find out the truth.'

I lifted my eyes from the floor and met Jonathan's grey-eyed gaze: his eyes were flashing with extreme amusement, and I felt my insides go warm and gooey, even though my skin was crawling with embarrassment at being caught out with manky hair and my fourth-best skirt on.

I was too stunned even to tell him off for pointing and clicking. I'd imagined this moment often in daydreams, but I'd always been freshly coiffed and definitely not so gormless.

'Score one to me, finally!' he cackled. 'I've caught you out! Melissa! You, Honey and I have an appointment for lunch and shopping? Or had that slipped your mind too?'

I thought fast. Damn. We did have that appointment – how could I have forgotten to put it in my diary? What was going on with me – first Emery, now Jonathan! That's what came of being too busy for your own good. I tried to rally as best I could while still in near-shock.

At least he didn't seem too horrified at my brunette appearance, I reasoned, but that was as much of my mask as I could let slip. I certainly couldn't let him meet Emery.

'OK,' I said, wedging myself in the door so he couldn't see round, even though he was trying. 'So now you know I'm not a natural blonde.'

'But I like it a lot!' he interrupted, then confided charmingly, 'I did guess it might not be your own hair. Not with big brown eyes like that.'

I filed that compliment away for later, while I struggled

to reset my brain into Honey gear. I wasn't sure I could deal with the situation otherwise. 'Um, it's rather embarrassing,' I said, with a winning smile, 'but would you mind awfully walking to the end of the street and coming back again? I'm afraid I'm right in the middle of . . .'

I felt the door being tugged and swung round to find Emery standing right behind me, half in and half out of her wedding dress. Twelve years at boarding school had left me chronically body-conscious, but it seemed to have had the opposite effect on her. Then again Emery had a lot less body than me.

'So sorry to interrupt . . . Melissa, can you undo me?' she said, offering her back to me, then her head swung round in a classic double take. 'Well, I never!'

'Hello, Emery,' said Jonathan. 'What a surprise!' He covered his eyes politely.

This was getting worse and worse.

I slammed the door, undid her buttons, then hissed, 'Right. Tell me how you know him. And no flannel, Emery.'

'Jonathan's our estate agent,' she said, surprised. 'Turns out William's best friend from law school – Darrell – was at high school somewhere out in the sticks with Jonathan.' Her smooth brow creased. 'Near Boston? I think that's right. It's quite complicated. Anyway, I've invited Jonathan to the wedding so they can have a bit of a reunion.'

'When?' I demanded, mentally scanning the guest list. How could I have missed Jonathan's name?

'Oh, this morning,' she said, airily. 'I don't think it was very nice to slam the door in his face, Mel. He's a real sweetie – once you get to know him.' She held out her arms so I could pull the dress over her head.

My mind was whirring furiously, but not getting any purchase. It was like trying to drive a Land-Rover out of a quagmire.

I sat down and forced myself to think. How long would it have been before Honey and Jonathan were invited round to dinner with Emery and William? At least I'd found out *before* I had to face my own sister over the smoked salmon.

'Get dressed,' I said. 'Has he met Daddy?'

'Don't be ridiculous!' snorted Emery. 'You think I make a habit of buying houses with Daddy in tow?'

'OK, fair enough. But I meant, does he know who Daddy is?'

Emery looked at me very seriously while she readorned herself in her swathes of velvet drapery. 'Melissa, Daddy may be rather embarrassing, but I hardly think Jonathan's going to cancel any temps you're supplying, just on Daddy's account. And believe me, dropping his name doesn't get you discounts with estate agents.'

There was a knock at the door. 'Melissa? Honey?'

'He seems rather fond of you too,' observed Emery. 'Do all your clients call you honey?'

'Stay there,' I said to Emery. 'Have a cup of coffee. Do *not* answer the phone or touch a *thing*. I mean it, Em.'

I grabbed my bag, took a step towards the door, then was paralysed by a tortuous thought. Which was more important right now? To keep Jonathan from knowing who I was, or to keep my agency a secret from the family?

Aargh.

As Gabi had made clear to me, Jonathan was an unattainable fantasy: a client who would soon want to find a real girlfriend of his own. *He*'d made it clear he didn't want to mix business with pleasure, and our relationship could end tomorrow. I could end it tomorrow if necessary. Indeed, I probably *should*.

Whereas my family were going to be around for a long, long time. And though I knew Daddy would have to find out eventually, I wanted to be able to tell him in my own way, and not because Emery let something slip at the wedding rehearsal about my client base.

And Jonathan understood about professional confidentiality, something that Emery couldn't even spell.

I took a deep breath. I would have to throw myself on Jonathan's mercy, even if it meant him having a good laugh at my expense.

'Actually, Em,' I said, spinning on my heel, 'would you mind popping down the road to get some fresh milk?' I pulled a 'silly me!' face. 'We've just finished the last of it and I'm sure Jonathan will want a cup of tea.'

'All right,' she said amiably. 'Which way do I go?'

'Out of the door, turn right, then left,' I said. There were at least three shops selling trinkety things between the office and the nearest supermarket in that direction, which, I reckoned, would give me enough time to concoct a suitable story.

Emery arranged another velvet shawl around her neck, which made her look as if she'd fallen head first into a dressing-up box, and pulled open the door. I heard her exchange a quick hello with Jonathan, then there was another gentle knock as Emery's feet clattered down the stairs.

'OK for me to come in now?' Jonathan asked, putting his head round.

'Please do.' I fiddled with the last few buttons on Emery's dress and put the dummy in the corner. I was vibrating with nerves. This was the moment I'd been dreading ever since I realised that it had started to matter what Jonathan thought of me – me, *Melissa*, as opposed to Honey. And if I'd got out of bed when my alarm went off, instead of dozing off again, I could have had clean hair.

'A-ha! The famous wedding dress!' He pointed to it with raised eyebrows. 'And that was the famous sister!'

'Now, listen, Jonathan, let me explain . . .' I began, wanting to get it all out of the way.

'No, me first,' he said, proffering the bouquet. 'Here, I brought you some flowers.'

'How thoughtful, thank you!' I said, rather more stiffly than I meant to. 'There's no need, really . . .'

Why did that come out of my mouth when I was secretly thrilled to get them?

'No, they're apology flowers.' Jonathan's expression turned serious; he did look quite stern when he was being serious. 'The last few weeks have been pretty hellish, to be honest with you. I've been working twenty-four-seven, and I haven't kept you up to speed with my movements, which was rude of me. You must have been wondering if something was wrong.'

'That's quite all right,' I said, faintly. I *had* been wondering but that was my problem, not his, surely? 'I mean, we did say it would make sense to scale the appointments down . . .'

'But you still need to know what's going on in my life,' he insisted. 'Otherwise it doesn't work. And it is working, you know – when people invite me out for dinner these days they only ask if you're around. And that never used to happen with Cindy, believe me.'

'Really?' I couldn't help being flattered by that.

'Really,' he said, looking round for somewhere to sit.

'I've never had a calmer or more amusing social life. You're doing a great job.'

A job. I sighed inside, but told myself it was just as well to know exactly where one stood.

'Thank you,' I said. 'Well, you're my favourite client, bar none.'

Jonathan settled into a leather armchair and flashed me a quick, warm smile that remelted my insides so fast that I had to turn away to put the flowers in water before I said anything I might regret.

It made it even harder to confess the stuff I now had to confess. Honey was just so much cooler than Melissa.

I took a deep breath. 'Jonathan, to be honest, I didn't want you to see me like this, but I'm in a bit of a pickle. As you saw, my sister's turned up and she doesn't know anything about the agency and . . .'

I trailed off as Jonathan raised an eyebrow.

God, without my Honey armour on, I just went to pieces.

'How do you know her?' I blurted out.

'The adorable Emery?' He gave me a teasing look. 'That her real name? Honestly, now?'

'Yes,' I said stoutly. 'It's just me with the alter ego.'

Jonathan dropped the quizzical expression. 'It's quite simple – she and William, who it turns out happens to be an old college friend of my best friend Darrell, approached Kyrle & Pope's office in Chicago about finding a house for them. Chicago suggested they speak to me since I was in London, and we put it together from there. Small world, isn't it?'

'Chicago?' I blurted.

'Yes.' Jonathan's eyebrow shot up. 'Didn't you know?'

'No,' I said. Emery? Looking for a house in Chicago?

'Um, I meant, I didn't know Kyrle & Pope had offices in Chicago.'

'They're looking at some of our London properties too,' he went on, 'in case the move doesn't come off, which is how I met Emery. She's pretty keen on Chicago, though.'

'I see,' I said. Emery hadn't mentioned moving to America. Or buying a house anywhere, for that matter.

Jonathan must have seen the confusion written all over my face. 'You English families,' he tutted. 'So stiff upper lip you don't even know where your own relatives live.'

I assumed by that that either Emery hadn't filled him in on our embarrassing family, or that he was so discreet he wasn't going to mention it.

'Hey!' he exclaimed. 'We'd have bumped into each other at the wedding anyway, then!'

Oh God. This was all falling to pieces faster than an IKEA table.

'Jonathan,' I said, sinking down into the armchair opposite his. 'Can I ask a favour of you? A, um, personal favour?'

'Of course,' he said, looking inordinately pleased with himself. 'Go right ahead. *Melissa.*'

My head jerked up at that: it felt weird to hear my real name coming out of his mouth.

I swallowed and composed myself. I had to get this right. 'It's rather awkward . . . and not very professional.' I looked at my hands and twisted my signet ring. What should I tell him? That Emery thought I was a primary-school teacher? That I was really an MI5 agent, posing as a dress-maker?

'Jonathan,' I began again, trying not to sound like a

nervous schoolgirl. 'My father's very old-fashioned, and, ah, somewhat in the public eye . . .'

Jonathan's expression had turned serious again, and he was nodding sympathetically, his face a picture of trustworthy understanding. I felt the truth suddenly rush out of me.

'My father is a politician who's constantly in and out of the papers because of one scandal or another, and he would go berserk if he knew I was running this agency. I wanted to keep it completely separate, hence my adopting a different name.'

'And a different head,' he added helpfully.

'Yes.' I coloured up. 'And the blonde thing. Anyway, I had no idea Emery was going to turn up here today – she thinks I'm running a temp agency. It would make my life much simpler if you didn't mention the, er, girlfriend element of our arrangement, and just stuck to the, um, personal assistant side of things.'

'I see,' mused Jonathan. 'But it sounds to me as if your father's more likely to ruin your reputation than the other way round?'

'Oh no, not at all. Quite the reverse! No, no, it would be a stain on the family name and all that. Of course, I'm terribly *proud* of my business,' I added quickly. 'But I do rely on keeping certain boundaries and limits.'

'Is this why you've been so careful not to tell me anything about yourself?' he asked shrewdly. 'You were guarding against anything getting around?'

'Partly,' I said. 'And also I think I need an out-of-the-office life as much as anyone else, don't you? Especially when I can't just switch off at five thirty like everyone else.'

He shrugged and a strange look crossed his face. I

realised too late that he might have taken that the wrong way, and I regretted it immediately.

'I can understand that,' he said drily, before I could rush out an amendment. 'Naturally it wouldn't do for it to get out that I was hiring my love interest.'

'Well, no.' I didn't add that nor would it do his reputation much good if he was dating Martin Romney-Jones's daughter, on either a professional or an amateur basis. If he didn't know that already, I certainly wasn't going to enlighten him. Well, not right now.

'OK, I think we understand one another,' he said. 'Temps it is.'

I smiled gratefully. 'Thank you, Jonathan,' I said. 'I'm sorry it's complicated. And,' I faltered, 'I'm sorry you had to run into my chaotic real life. Honey is much more organised. As you know.'

'No problem.' Jonathan winked. 'I kind of like Melissa. She reminds me of Snow White.'

I smiled dozily at him. I had to start taping him secretly to show Gabi just how endearing he could be. Meanwhile a sharp little voice in my head marvelled at how I'd started out this morning determined to keep Jonathan at a safe distance and yet had somehow ended up not only showing him my real self, but owing him a favour of discretion.

This wasn't how I was meant to be doing this.

'Sorry,' I said, again, then bit my lip.

Jonathan lifted his hands. 'Listen, don't apologise – I know what it's like having family embarrassments,' he said. '*Don't* I know about it! I was married to a woman who refused to go out for dinner without interrogating the hostess about the menu first.' He sighed. 'You have no idea what a novelty it is to see your dinner partner eat bread instead of making the sign of the cross against it.'

I knew he was only trying to make me feel better, but I was grateful, nonetheless.

'Anyway.' Jonathan slapped his thighs and made to get up. 'I can see you're tied up with Emery here. You want to rearrange that lunch and the Christmas shopping?' he asked.

'Oh, er, yes, of course.' I grabbed my desk diary. 'When's good for you?'

We'd just agreed on a time and place when Emery burst back in with several bags and, amazingly enough, a pint of milk.

'Jonathan!' she said. 'Cup of tea? Can we talk about houses? Do stay!'

Jonathan pulled a regretful face. 'I'm so sorry, Emery,' he said, sounding suddenly more formal. 'I'd love to, but I have to make a move. I just called in to check something out with . . . your sister.'

We exchanged a brief nervous glance. Well, I was nervous. He looked discreetly amused.

'About his temp,' I elaborated. 'He was just . . .'

'Checking availability,' Jonathan finished for me.

'Oh, what a shame!' sighed Emery. 'I got custard creams and everything.'

'Can we speak later in the week?' he said to her as he left, shaking her hand courteously. 'I've heard something on the grapevine about a fantastic property you might just love. But it's still top secret, OK? Husband doesn't know the wife wants to sell! Regards to William.'

'Bye, Jonathan,' said Emery, girlishly. She turned to me as Jonathan shut the door behind him, and mouthed, 'He is so gorgeous!'

'Isn't he just,' I said.

'You know his wife left him for his brother?' She pulled

a sad face. 'Poor Jonathan. I think he moved here to get over it. She wasn't very nice, by all accounts.'

'So I hear. And is he? Over her, I mean?' I asked carefully.

'Well,' said Emery, a gossipy expression stealing over her face. 'I have heard, from various *impeccable* sources, that he has a particularly foxy new girlfriend on the go. Cindy's livid, according to this friend of a friend of William's, but whose fault is that?' She raised her eyebrows. 'I'm glad. William says Darrell says Cindy was a real ball-breaker. Or was it pussy-whipper? Can't remember, but something like that. Some madly violent American expression. Anyway, they're divorced now, so what right has she got to be peeved if Jonathan's met someone new?'

'None at all.' Jonathan didn't look pussy-whipped to me, but it went some way to explaining his impassiveness. Maybe he'd just got used to stonewalling.

'I do hope he'll bring this new girlfriend to the wedding,' said Emery. 'She's got some fabulously racy hooker name – Foxy or Baby or something. Can't remember exactly. I think she sounds rather amusing, actually.'

'Oh, I don't think he will bring her,' I mumbled.

'Still . . .' said Emery, going thoughtful and dreamy. 'I'd love to meet her. I might ask him if she can come too.'

'I don't think she will,' I repeated, a little too insistently.

24

As Emery's wedding hove closer and closer into view, I found myself sinking into a tediously self-pitying frame of mind. I don't like being a moaning Minnie, but I've always been a little bit prone to imagining stressful moments as they'd be depicted in a film of my own life, and now I was being played by Audrey Hepburn at her most eyes-to-heaven (with obligatory Oscar-winning weight gain, naturally).

Maybe it was the mind-numbing effect of spending most evenings twisting hundreds of net circles together while listening to Nelson lecture Gabi with touching patience about tenancy agreements, while she did cruel impressions of Jonathan trying to grasp the concept of Secret Santa, and reduced him to helpless laughter.

Maybe it was the realisation that even my mother had a man who bought her saucy underwear, albeit as part of a bulk-buying deal.

Maybe it was the fact that I was about to be a brides-maid for the third time and Emery hadn't even checked whether I minded being consigned to superstitious spin-sterdom.

And so, as I threw the final bonbonnière in the box, I resolved that my Christmas shopping trip with Jonathan would be our last appointment. While he was still dating Honey there was no way he could date Mel. And if he didn't want to date Mel, I wouldn't see him again, not for a million pounds an hour.

Meanwhile, snuggled up on the sofa where I used to get my feet rubbed, Gabi and Nelson carried on talking about buy-to-let mortgages.

To prepare me for his shopping assignment, Jonathan had thoughtfully emailed me a list of people he needed to buy gifts for; his estimated costs were generous, and the list wasn't too long.

Our original plan was that we'd have lunch, discuss the list, then I would go off and do the purchasing for him, sending the presents round to his office in a taxi. However, when he walked into J Sheekeys, he was dressed not in his usual sober charcoal work suit, but a pair of jeans and a moss-green cashmere jumper that made his red hair gleam. He was also wearing a smart pair of horn-rimmed glasses instead of his contact lenses, all of which gave him the appearance of a trendy young web designer, not an estate agent. The effect was startling, to say the least.

It was the first time I'd seen Jonathan dressed so casually; he'd always worn a suit, even for our educational weekend visits.

'I took the day off,' he explained as I hastily fiddled with my napkin to stop myself staring too noticeably. 'I thought I might as well come along with you and learn something! Is that OK?' he added, peering at me. 'Do you need a hand there? Have you dropped something?'

'No, no! No. That's absolutely fine,' I spluttered. Suddenly my tailored skirt suit and knee-high boots seemed terribly overdressed. After revealing my real Melissa self, in all her greasy-haired glory, I'd rather gone to the other extreme when getting dressed that morning. My blonde wig had never been so neatly styled. 'Fine, no problem at all.'

'Great. You look stunning, as ever.' He pushed the glasses up the bridge of his nose and sat down. 'Wow! Fish!'

I wondered when I should tell him this would be our last appointment. Not just yet, I decided. Later.

Jonathan blinked rapidly and scanned the menu in front of him. 'So, hey. Hmm. What do you recommend?' he asked, looking up.

'Oh, er, fish cakes?' I wasn't letting myself even look at the menu. The truth was that I'd more or less abandoned all interesting food in order to fit into the bridesmaid's dress Emery had chosen for me to wear. There was no time to make something of my own, so she had gone out and bought me a column dress in pale green beads and silk from Monsoon: I was so touched by this act of thoughtfulness that I hadn't made a big fuss about the fact that she'd bought the size that had fitted her, not me.

After all, I had two weeks and a large selection of Pants of Steel. Columns didn't do much for me, not with my hips and bosom, but whose wedding was it, after all?

'Fish cakes,' mused Jonathan. 'Mmm. Interesting. What are you having?'

'Ooh, I don't know,' I said, in surprise. Jonathan never bothered to ask what I was having until the waiter came; he wasn't that sort of man. 'Grilled sole, probably.'

'Ah, yes. The Marilyn Monroe diet plan,' said Jonathan, knowledgeably.

'How did you know that?' I asked, curiously.

Jonathan pretended to look aggrieved. Well, I think he

was pretending. 'I'm not *just* an estate agent,' he said. 'I do have interests.' He flapped his napkin self-consciously onto his lap. 'And one of them happens to be Hollywood. Proper Hollywood, not all this computer-animated, McDonalds tie-in nonsense.'

I tried to keep my voice Honey-ish and dry, despite the quickening of my pulse. I had no idea we shared an interest. 'Now he tells me. Please don't say you like dressing up as Hollywood film stars,' I said.

'Ah, you guessed. Actually, it was my five-room collection of Judy Garland memorabilia that Cindy left me over,' he said, deadpan.

'Really?' I said, less certainly.

'Joking!' Jonathan rolled his eyes. 'No, I collect original film posters. Great investments, you know. I have a guy in New York who finds them for me and crates them out.' He leaned in and whispered, 'Actually, I'm having a bit of a *Vertigo* moment right here in this very restaurant.'

'Why?' I asked. I couldn't remember exactly what happened in *Vertigo*. Did it have something to do with mad birds? My stomach lurched unpleasantly and not because it was very empty.

'Because you're still blonde,' he said, staring at my ladylike up-do. 'And in that neat little suit. I kind of liked you in your natural state. Dark and mysterious and, ah, somewhat unbuttoned.'

I pushed my fringe out of my eyes awkwardly. Running alongside my impulse that morning to appear as smart as possible had been a totally contradictory feeling: since Jonathan had seen me as Melissa, the whole act of donning my Honey uniform suddenly seemed a bit silly, and fake. But I wanted him to choose between us, to know that Melissa and Honey were two different people.

'I came along off duty today,' he added, helpfully, gesturing to his glasses and jumper. 'I thought you might too.'

That off-duty thing again. What did he want me to say? Self-doubt swamped me. At least when I was concentrating on being Honey I could make conversation. When it came to making moves on Melissa's behalf, I bottled it every time.

'Jonathan, you're paying me for my shopping expertise,' I reminded him. 'And I shop better in my suit.'

'And a very glamorous suit it is. What red-blooded man could complain?' he replied gallantly and then the waiter appeared and I knew I'd missed another chance.

After lunch, I whisked up and down escalators all over London with Jonathan in tow, ticking off the gifts on his list while he patiently carried the multiplying bags and hailed taxis. As the darkness began to creep across the inky sky and the Christmas lights started to glow out of the dusk, I don't think I'd ever felt so happy or so festive.

I've always prided myself on giving just the right present, so I had to ask a few personal questions, but Jonathan seemed happy to fill me in. We bought old-fashioned shaving kit from Jermyn Street for his father, the Anglophile; bone-china coffee cups and Fortnum's goodies for his mother, the bridge queen; pink and glittery fripperies for his little nieces; and a gorgeous red-leather overnight bag for his Frequent Flyer sister. By the time we'd finished gliding through the tinsel-wrapped halls of Harvey Nichols I felt as though I knew his immediate family pretty well.

With two glaring exceptions.

Eamon and Cindy, needless to say, did not feature on

the list. Knowing how tense and horrible family Christmases could be, I skated around the topic sympathetically, but at the same time, tried to let him know I understood.

'I can't believe that's the lot. You've done a fabulous job,' Jonathan sighed, as we stood in the queue at Jo Malone, basket piled high with bath oil for the office girls. 'It never used to be so simple with . . .' His voice trailed off and an awkward expression clouded his face.

'With Cindy?' I asked.

Jonathan nodded. 'She wasn't exactly the spirit of Christmas, put it like that.'

'Well, not everyone is.'

'Not every wife buys workout DVDs for their husband's office staff,' he replied tersely. 'And not everyone fakes a cinnamon allergy and invents special religious restrictions to avoid seeing their in-laws over the holiday season.'

'Well. She's got an even better reason to avoid them now,' I observed. 'Clearly she'll stop at nothing to avoid that turkey dinner.'

Jonathan's sternness melted into a reluctant smile. 'Eamon. That poor bastard. Jeez.'

'Is it all finalised?' I asked. It wasn't really the place to ask, but I found Jonathan felt easiest with apparently casual discussions about anything delicate.

'It is,' he said, dumping the basket onto the counter. 'Tied up like a gift-wrapped Christmas basket full of shit. Pardon my language.'

The shutters had gone down on his eyes, but I sensed a sadness behind them, and didn't probe any further.

The sales assistant started ringing the boxes of bath oil through the till: one each for the various PAs, and a special large bath oil and body lotion set for Gabi, whose supplies of Red Roses had dried up now Aaron was no longer buying it for her. It gave me a pleasant warm feeling inside to know that the girls would at least be able to soak away the stress of the office this year; if nothing else, the combined floral fragrance emanating from them would mask any lingering evidence of Hughy's post-Christmas digestive problems.

'Make sure you tell the girls you picked their present out personally for them,' I reminded him. 'They'll be overwhelmed. Especially Gabi. Tell her you noticed she wore Red Roses and got this specially.'

'He-e-e-e-ey,' he said, suddenly clicking his fingers at me. 'Am I dumb or what? Why did I never make that connection before? *Melissa*, of course!'

'What connection?' I said innocently.

'You. You and the office. No wonder you know what to get people! You're Saint Melissa of the Photocopier. The one Dean & Daniels let get away!'

I put a finger to my lips and looked round mock-nervously. 'Shh! Don't reveal my secret identity!'

He gave me a playful push on the shoulder. 'Oh my God, you have no idea how jealous Carolyn is of you! She still gets all pissy when your name comes up.'

It occurred to me suddenly: forget Honey – the Melissa who used to work for Hughy and Charles was nothing like the Melissa standing there now. I really had changed. If Hughy met me now, he might not even make the connection, with or without my wig.

'Jealous of me or of Honey?' I looked straight at him. 'And why would they guess? Honey is a million miles away from the Melissa they knew.'

Jonathan handed his credit card to the assistant with

a friendly grin. 'Who couldn't be jealous of a bombshell like Honey?'

Wrong answer, I thought sadly.

Then he hesitated with the pen in his hand, and added, 'But if she met the Melissa who's running her own agency with such aplomb, I guess she'd be pretty jealous of her too.'

My heart turned a full somersault in my chest.

I wanted to ask him which one he liked best, which one he'd prefer to stick with, but somehow I couldn't make the words come out of my mouth. I just stood there like a lemon while sales girls squirted honeysuckle and jasmine cologne around us.

'Shall we go?' said Jonathan, balancing yet another set of bags.

'OK,' I said brightly.

We wandered down the street a little after that, picking up trinkety things for stocking fillers. I didn't expect Jonathan to be so into browsing, but he fell upon Smythson's with enthusiasm, and I couldn't drag him out of L'Artisan du Chocolat.

'So, that's the lot,' I said at last, as he hailed a taxi in Sloane Square and we scrambled into it with relief.

I had noticed, with just a smidgen of pique, that my name wasn't on the list of gifts to buy. I told myself I shouldn't really expect it to be, but then again, he'd bought things for the girls in the office, so why not me?

'Unless there's anyone you've missed off the list?' I added.

Jonathan furrowed his brow. 'No, I don't think . . . Oh damn, yes, I have forgotten someone.'

'Really?' I held my breath.

'My god-daughter, Hebe.' He clicked his fingers. 'Yet another one. Penalty for not having kids of your own. What do you think? Cash? One of those rattly things?'

'Do you want me to get her a silver charm-bracelet from Boodle and Dunthorne?' I said, trying to keep the disappointment out of my voice. 'Then you can just phone up and get them to send a charm to her every birthday.'

'Great idea!' said Jonathan. He was already checking his phone for messages.

'I'll do it from the office tomorrow,' I said and looked at my watch. It was nearly half past five. Time to go home – only I didn't want to go home. And I still hadn't told him that this would be our last appointment.

'No one loves me,' said Jonathan. 'No messages for me.' He sighed theatrically. 'So much for single life, hey? How about you? You heading out onto the town tonight?'

'Nope.' I shook my head. 'Just staying in, probably, playing solitaire with myself.'

'Ah. That's the terrible thing about single life, all that playing with yourself,' said Jonathan, soberly.

'Absolutely.' I nodded. I used to play Scrabble with Nelson, but he was rarely in these days, since he was usually with Gabi somewhere, and I wasn't about to ask *them* if they minded my tagging along.

I realised Jonathan was staring at me with a twinkle in his eye, and I wondered if I'd missed something.

Then it struck me. Dur. *Honey* should be out at a glitzy Christmas party, or at a fabulous book launch, not stuck in on her own, like *Melissa*.

'Listen,' he said, 'I was thinking about maybe taking in a film at the National Film Theatre – you want to come with me?' He pulled a wry grimace. '*It's A Wonderful*

Life – I know, I know, cheesy, but kind of festive. Could you bear it?'

My stomach flipped at the thought of two hours in the dark with him, then I reminded myself that it couldn't be easy, spending his first Christmas alone. It was my Christian duty to cheer it up as best I could.

'I'd love it,' I said. 'Thank you.'

Jonathan leaned forward to redirect the driver, then settled back into his seat with a contented smile.

It transpired that Jonathan had joined the NFT soon after he arrived in London, and regularly went to see old films on his own. I found this revelation rather sweet.

'It gets me out of the house,' he explained, as he bought me some nice chocolate to take in. 'But I try to avoid the other film buffs. They're kind of dorky,' he added in a stage whisper.

The cinema was packed with people and we had to sit quite close together, surrounded by our shopping. When the lights went down, I suddenly felt very tired but comfortable, and gently eased off my shoes once the auditorium lights were dimmed. It was pretty warm in there, what with all the people and my woollen suit, and my scalp started to feel rather irritated by my wig.

I wish my Christmases could be like Jimmy Stewart's – without the dying bit, obviously. I quite forgot where I was. As the film lulled me into cosy relaxation, my jacket came off, and the tight button on my skirt was loosened, and before long I was snuggled into my seat as if I was at home, letting tears run down my face during the sad bits and smiling like a simpleton when he came running back to his family, and everyone gathered around the piano.

It was a bit of a shock when the lights came up at the end, and I realised that not only was I living in full-colour twenty-first-century London, but I was also sitting with my left foot resting, shoeless, on Jonathan's knee, my blouse unbuttoned and my skirt about to fall down. I had to scramble to make myself decent, much to his amusement.

'I'd hate to see what you'd look like by the end of *From Here to Eternity*,' he said.

'Passion doesn't make me loosen my clothes, just central heating,' I replied. 'I'm English.'

'Then let's get tickets for *Lady and the Tramp*,' he said deadpan. 'I'll bring an electric blanket.'

I blushed and thrilled all at the same time, but didn't let him see.

We wandered out onto the South Bank, which was festooned with white Christmas lights and busy with late-night shoppers, laden down with bags, making urgent calls on mobile phones.

I knew it was time to go home, but didn't want to be the one to suggest it. I also knew that I hadn't yet got round to the sore topic of ending our business relationship, and that had to be done.

'Want a hot chocolate or something?' asked Jonathan, pausing by a café with outdoor heaters.

'Yes!' I said. 'Yes, that would be lovely.'

You've got to do it, I told myself. Just tell him. Get it over with.

I sat there, trying to make my brain come up with a sophisticated, confident Honey-tastic argument, but it was stuck. It had been such a lovely day. I absolutely didn't want to spoil it.

Then Jonathan returned with two large cups. 'This is pretty cool,' he said, nodding at the festive scene around us. 'I won't say this often, but you know, it's almost as good as at home.'

'Really?'

'Really.' He took a sip of his hot chocolate. 'It's really magical.'

'Good,' I said. 'Good. I'm glad.' I paused, and summoned up all my courage. 'Um, I don't know how to say this,' I said, biting my lip. I looked up and saw Jonathan looking straight at me, his eyes very serious.

'Go ahead,' he said.

'I think . . .' My eyes dropped to the messy table as my nerve faltered.

Come on! You're Honey Blennerhesket, bombshell extraordinaire. Get a grip!

I rallied myself, and went on, 'Jonathan, I think this should be our last appointment. I mean, you're more than settled in London, you're making new friends of your own, the divorce is finalised and I can't keep taking your money for . . .' I was going to say 'for dates I enjoy going on myself', but I changed it to, 'I don't want Honey to stand in the way of you finding a new girlfriend. You need someone to look after you for love, not money. You deserve it.'

I met his gaze as I said that, and hoped he could read between the lines. If anyone was going to come between me and the chance to be with Jonathan, I couldn't let it be *Honey*, for heaven's sake.

'I see,' said Jonathan, retreating behind his unreadable office expression.

'I mean, I'd quite happily carry on doing this for ever,' I added. 'But I think it's time you had a real girlfriend, don't you?'

He smiled but there was something detached about it, and I felt a little chill blow through me.

'Well, I guess so,' he said. 'Although Honey will be a hard act to follow.'

'Really?' For an ecstatic moment, I wondered if he was about to tell me he didn't want anyone to follow her.

'Oh, yes,' said Jonathan gravely. 'I don't know where I'll find a girl quite so popular, or gorgeous.'

Our eyes met and a shiver of pure happiness ran through me.

'No wonder she doesn't exist,' he said quietly.

Then my phone rang. My own phone, not my work one.

I froze. 'Ignore it.'

It stopped, and I breathed a sigh of relief.

Then it started again, at once.

'What if it's Emery?' asked Jonathan.

'Oh God, you're right,' I said, cursing mentally. 'She's probably phoning to see if I can get the Pope and Charlotte Church to do the service at short notice.'

I scrabbled in my bag. The number was withheld and the usual disturbing mental images of hospitals or police stations or my father sprang into the forefront of my mind.

'Hello?'

'Honey,' droned a familiar, whiny voice. 'Sorry to phone on your personal line, but . . .'

'Bryan!' I screeched. My skin crawled. 'How the hell did you get this number?'

'That doesn't matter. I need to see you . . .'

'No, you do *not*!' My teeth were chattering – with suppressed hysteria, not the cold. 'This is beyond a joke, Bryan. I've asked you politely to stop calling me, and now I'm telling you that if you don't . . .'

'We're meant to *be* together!' he yelled.

'No, we aren't!'

Jonathan clicked his fingers and gestured to the phone. When I didn't move, he reached over and prised the phone out of my trembling hands.

'Hi,' he said briskly. 'This is Jonathan Riley. I'm Honey's boyfriend. Now, she's a very charming and considerate lady, and she's too polite to tell you to back off and leave her alone. I am not too polite, however, and if you don't leave her alone, I'll come round and spell it out for you in sign language. Then I'll break your fingers. You got that? Yes? Good. Goodbye, Bryan.'

Then he hung up and passed the phone back.

'These imaginary partners come in handy, huh?' he said drily.

I swallowed. Jonathan Riley, Honey's boyfriend . . . That had sounded so easy.

'Thank you. He's not a real boyfriend or anything, just a nightmare client,' I explained. 'Won't leave me alone. I think he's got the wrong idea – you know, about how the client relationship works.'

Jonathan's mouth twisted. 'The lines got blurred, hey?'

'Something like that.' I was so thankful for Jonathan's intervention that my mouth just ran away with me. 'Some of my clients are a bit lonely, I think – not used to women being nice to them. It's easy to end up misinterpreting the situation so I try to be gentle about letting them down.' I pulled a face. 'Maybe too gentle sometimes.'

'Can't blame us lonely old men, though,' said Jonathan. 'Honey's the ideal girlfriend, even if she does only come by the hour.'

As he said that, I suddenly realised how utterly *wrongly*

my words could have been interpreted and I could feel
my face heat up with panic.

'I didn't mean . . . I mean, I wasn't . . .' I stammered.

'No need for apologies,' said Jonathan, a half-smile
twisting his mouth, but not quite reaching his grey eyes.
'I quite understand.'

Oh God. I looked at him, sitting there with faint traces
of stubble glinting sexily on his square jaw, the
programme from the NFT rolled up in his pocket, his
hair messed up in rough little waves, and I wanted him
so badly it hurt.

Just tell him how you feel! What have you got to lose?

'So how's the wedding planning coming on?' he asked,
changing the subject smoothly.

'Oh, you know, the usual nightmare,' I said. *Clang.*
Another stupid thing to say, in light of his divorce. 'It's
all last-minute panic,' I went on hurriedly, hoping he
hadn't noticed that either. 'Emery's losing weight in some
places and not in others, so I have to keep adjusting her
dress, then my mother seems to be getting more nervous
than her, and my . . .' I was about to start telling him
about Daddy's demands, but stopped just in time.

This, I reminded myself, is precisely why you can't see
him any more.

'I'll be glad when it's over,' I said flatly.

'Well, I have to say I'm kind of looking forward to it,'
said Jonathan, signalling for more hot chocolate. 'But
there's one problem that I'm . . .' He tailed off and looked
at me almost sheepishly.

'What it is?' I asked.

'No, I can't,' he said, fiddling with his empty cup.

'Go on!' I smiled encouragingly. 'Ask me anything. I
am here at your command.'

He met my gaze and his face seemed vulnerable, tentative even. 'It's a big favour to ask, but . . . Jesus, I haven't asked anyone this for years, but . . . do you have a date for the wedding?'

'No,' I said. Was Jonathan asking me to be Honey at my own sister's wedding? Surely not. 'I'm a bridesmaid. Emery told me I wouldn't need one. Why do you ask?' I asked, trying to ignore the crossness building inside me. 'Don't tell me you want to take Honey to the wedding?'

The hot chocolates arrived and I missed seeing the reaction on Jonathan's face. By the time the waiter had removed himself, Jonathan was concentrating on not burning his tongue on the drink, and I had wound my indignation back to manageable levels.

So much for thinking I really knew him! Obviously I didn't know him at all! I told myself he was taking liberties but, deep down, I felt about three feet tall and thirteen years old. My pride was utterly scalded.

'Well, I'm going to be there anyway,' I said, hoping he would hear the martyrdom in my voice. 'Why not?'

'Would you?' Jonathan looked relieved. 'You know the whole shebang about my going to school with Darrell, and Darrell being the best man? Well, he's invited a bunch of guys who it turns out I know from business school too, including some people who know Cindy, and . . .' He shrugged and let me fill in the blanks. 'They're great guys,' he said. 'You'd like them. They certainly like the sound of this amazing girl I've been seeing. And I know you'll be rushed off your feet, so I'd only need to borrow you for a little while.'

I stared at him, speechless. I had never had such an enjoyable and romantic day out, and Jonathan had never been sweeter or more relaxed with me, but all I could feel now was crashing, stomach-numbing disappointment. In him and in me. Because for the first time, it really brought home to me what I'd been doing. I'd managed to convince myself that our meetings were starting to mean something more, but at heart, I'd been renting myself out to him. And I still was.

And yet, why not, I thought fiercely, as my pride staged a late resurgence. Why not? I'll show him Honey bloody Blennerhesket. I'll show him exactly how glamorous and sexy I can be. I'll make him wish he'd put his cards on the table when he had a chance, then I'll never, ever see him again! The rat.

'It'll be a night to remember,' I said, exerting superhuman control over my cracking heart.

Jonathan's face creased into a smile. 'Hey, thanks. You're a star.'

My heart thumped in my chest, and I tried to ignore how boyish he looked when he smiled.

How could he look so cheerful? He wasn't even upset that he wouldn't be seeing me again! Thank God I hadn't made some girlish declaration of my own – how embarrassingly misplaced would that have been?

'Don't mention it,' I said, through tight lips.

I directed my gaze out towards the shoppers and buskers on the South Bank, and tried to quell the mixed feelings jumbling up inside. There was no point wishing Jonathan was asking me to the wedding as Melissa, when it was my own fault for inventing Honey in the first place. I had to get a grip on myself. And I had to do it quickly.

Before I could say anything else, he bent down and clicked open the catches on his briefcase.

'I've got something for you,' he said.

'Have you?'

He stopped rummaging and looked up seriously. 'Now, come on. You don't think I'd miss you off my Christmas shopping list, do you, um . . . ?'

There was a faint pause, where before he would have said 'Honey'; we both felt a little awkward, now we both knew that that wasn't my name.

'Should I close my eyes and hold out my hands?' I asked, gamely.

'You can do,' he said, playing along.

I shut my eyes, not to build up the suspense, but so I wouldn't have to look at him, relaxed in his baby-soft cashmere sweater, or see any expectation on his face. I didn't want to see what I was going to be missing.

Jonathan's voice broke through my concentration. 'You can open your eyes now.'

I opened them. He'd cleared the table of old cups and saucers and screwed-up sugar bags to give proper prominence to a tell-tale pale blue bag which now sat regally between us.

'Tiffany!' I breathed. 'Should I open it now?'

Quite a big pale blue bag. Too big for jewellery, though.

'Go ahead.' Jonathan leaned back in his chair. 'I know fancy English girls prefer Garrard's but this is a present from your favourite American client, OK?'

'OK,' I said, fumbling with the ribbon. Inside was a tissue-wrapped box, and inside that was a tissue-wrapped . . . silver photo frame.

I tried not to feel disappointed. He was a man, after all, and photograph frames seem to be programmed into all men's internal gift lists.

'Oh, thank you!' I said, trying to undo the tissue without tearing it. 'It's lovely.'

'You haven't seen the picture!' protested Jonathan.

A picture?

'I'm being careful,' I protested. How much did he want to rub it in, I wondered.

Crossly, I pulled away the last layer of tissue to reveal a photograph of me and Jonathan standing by a table at the Dorchester ball – him, dark and wry in his black tie, me, surprisingly luminous, wreathed in smiles.

I had no recollection of the photo being taken, but there were cameras all over the place that night, and I had been a bit squiffy. We made a really gorgeous couple, I thought, suddenly unable to be angry. Just like something from the smarter party photos at the back of *Tatler*. I really suited blondeness. Or was it just being with Jonathan that lit me up like that?

'You like it?'

'Do I like it?' I looked up, blinking back tears bravely. 'It's beautiful!'

'And the picture?'

'I meant the picture, stupid!' I said, without thinking. 'Where did you get it?'

Jonathan looked pleased. 'That would be telling,' he said. 'But, ah, you can change it if you want.'

'I don't think I will change it,' I said quietly. 'It'll remind me of a wonderful evening.'

Our eyes met, and the full impact of what I'd done hit me like a bucket of cold water. After the wedding, there would be no more balls, no more shopping, no more lunches. This was a going-away gift. And he meant it that way.

Jonathan lifted his cup. 'I know it should be champagne, but . . . Here's to Honey,' he said. 'A great girl, and an even better dancer. Thanks for the memories.'

I lifted my cup in silence, wrapping myself in a

haughtiness I'd seen my grandmother adopt to chilling effect. I refused to make an exhibition of myself now.

'Goodbye, Honey,' said Jonathan. The bastard looked almost cheerful.

'Goodbye, Jonathan,' I replied icily.

Jonathan put me in a taxi on the Strand and kissed my cheek tenderly. Twenty-four hours ago, I'd have called it romantic. Now it felt faintly mocking. 'I'll see you at the wedding,' he said.

I could only nod in reply. Then he turned and I watched his broad back disappear into the frenetic shopping crowds.

I just about held it together until I got home.

Then I put the photo frame on my dressing table, ripped off my stupid stockings and suspenders, and cried and cried until I had no mascara left on my eyelashes whatsoever.

25

With Emery's beaded, non-stretch size 12 frock hanging on the back of my wardrobe door as a constant reminder, and the dawn-till-dusk wrapping challenge at work you'd have thought the pounds would have dropped off in the last few days.

They didn't. Knowing my fondness for Belgian chocolate, quite a few grateful clients had sent me massive great Christmas boxes, and it was so easy to work my way through a layer at a time while I stuck labels on presents with one side of my brain and finalised seating arrangements for Emery with the other.

I was happy to be busy, though, because unless it was occupied with trivia, my brain automatically ran excruciating loops of my last meeting with Jonathan, allowing me to experience a whole new spectrum of emotions, from anger to bewilderment.

I wouldn't have been quite so stressed if Mummy and Emery hadn't booked themselves into a remote Irish seaweed spa for five days before the wedding, leaving me with all the final logistical nightmares of co-ordinating caterers and florists and so on. To give them their due, they did ask me if I wanted to go with them, but I couldn't take the time off work, and besides, if Emery was going to have the pre-wedding wobbles that all the magazines warned were inevitable, then frankly Mummy could deal with them in the comfort of their seaweed baths. I was having enough trouble getting the gold chairs to arrive at the same time as the marquee.

My London home wasn't exactly a haven of tranquillity either, and more unsettling was the vague sensation that I'd somehow created the problem myself. Gabi was still no nearer to finding somewhere to live, and she and Nelson and the property sections of most local London newspapers had become a regular fixture on our sofas. Even when I came in exhausted at ten at night, they'd be there, heads together, delicious little snacks balanced on their knees on Nelson's pensioner-special bean-bag TV dinner trays, imperiously crossing out houses with insufficient gardenage, or underwhelming amenities.

'How long is this going to go on for, Nelson?' I demanded, *sotto voce*, one evening while helping him with cheese on toast for three. 'She was only meant to be staying a few nights!'

'It'll go on until she finds somewhere to *live*,' he replied, sounding surprised and faintly reproachful.

'You don't think that the property she actually wants to rent might be *this* one?' I hissed and immediately felt terrible.

'Mel!' Nelson looked askance at me. 'Gabi's trying so hard to turn her life round. I think you could be more supportive.'

'Well . . .' I picked at the cheese. 'Just be careful. She and Aaron are meant to be on a break.'

'I know. I'm perfectly capable of being careful,' said Nelson huffily. 'And to be frank, Gabi's great company. I hadn't realised how funny she was, to be honest. We have a good laugh together.'

Between organising someone else's wedding and

sticking to my principles about Jonathan there wasn't much laughing going on for me. No wonder saints always looked so miserable on stained glass. No wonder Nelson had found a new best friend.

Emery's wedding was the week before Christmas, and on the Friday lunchtime before, I switched on the answering machine, gave my remaining chocolates to the girls in the salon downstairs and caught a train home.

I made it to the church just in time for the wedding rehearsal, and even then I arrived before Mummy, Daddy and Emery.

William was standing at the altar on his own with his best man and the vicar. It was, I thought, a good rehearsal in that he'd probably spend the rest of his married life wondering where the hell Emery had got to.

I ditched my bags at the back of the church and walked down the aisle. It was lucky for us that the village church was about as picturesque as one could wish for: thick stone pillars, richly multicoloured stained glass, and a gloriously ivy-covered graveyard for photos.

'Hello, William,' I said, giving the groom a polite kiss on the cheek. William was looking rather shell-shocked, as was his best man. I guessed that they'd made friends on the football pitch, since Darrell was about six feet five and built like a barn door. Next to Darrell, even William, the sports jock of the year, seemed slight.

'Darrell,' said William, with a courteous gesture. 'Darrell, this is Melissa, Emery's sister.'

'Hello, Darrell,' I said. 'You two look a bit stressed. Did you have a long journey?'

'Not really. We've been playing golf with your father all afternoon,' said William, almost succeeding in making it sound like a pleasurable activity. 'Don't worry, I let him win.'

'Oh. I see. And where is he now?' I asked, looking round the church. Daddy usually won anyway, one way or another.

'Don't know. We left him at the golf club,' boomed Darrell. 'Said he had some business to attend to.'

'Right.' I looked at the vicar, who was examining his watch.

'Are we in any danger of getting started?' he asked, wearily. 'I have a parishioner on her deathbed in Little Rugley . . .'

'Not unless you want to marry me and the lovely bridesmaid here.' Darrell nudged me playfully, nearly knocking me over. 'How about it, Melinda?'

William and I both shot him a dark look, and as I turned my head back, I caught sight of a dodgy-looking chap hanging about the lady chapel, fiddling with what looked like a mobile phone.

'Who's that lingering around the font?' I whispered to William.

'The photographer,' said the vicar.

'But I booked a *woman*!' I said, panicking. 'Dorothy Daniels, Wedding Photography.'

'The photographer from the *magazine*,' the vicar elaborated heavily.

'What?' I demanded, turning to William. '*Which* magazine?'

'Not *Which?* magazine, no,' he said. 'Some other one. Hi? Hey? Hiya? You'd need to speak to your father about that.'

'Would I?' I said grimly. 'You surprise me.'

Before I could put poor American William straight about *Hello!* Emery and Mummy waltzed in looking like

Zen yoga specialists, making me freshly aware of how much I looked like a limp rag. Emery was glowing and Mummy looked about twenty years younger than she should. If anything, I was the one who looked like she'd been steeped in seaweed for five days.

'So sorry, darlings! Bride's prerogative!' trilled Emery, landing kisses on William and Darrell, then me.

'Is your father here?' asked Mummy.

'Not yet.'

Her brows wrinkled. 'He's been most elusive of late,' she said. 'Anyone would think he didn't want to be found.'

I thought of the three piles of underwear and bit my tongue.

'Never mind,' she went on, more cheerily. 'Doesn't the church look super?'

I suggested we make a start, since the vicar was visibly flagging, and we got through nearly everything smoothly when the church door banged.

'You look terrible!' Daddy bellowed at me as he came striding down the aisle, an hour late and smelling of cigars. 'Belinda, I hope the make-up artist you've booked is good at tarting up corpses for open caskets. Melissa's going to need a whole hour on her own.'

I stared at him in shock.

'He doesn't mean it, darling.' Mummy was breathing serenely through her nose, one hand on her diaphragm, the other on a pew. 'He's been filthy all week. Just having a bad reaction to spending money.'

'Indeed.' Daddy eyed me beadily. 'Remind me to have a chat with you later, Melissa.'

'Well, that more or less covers it,' said the vicar, snapping his prayer book shut. 'Unless you have any questions?'

'Have you got your pre-nup signed yet, William?' asked my father unchivalrously.

The vicar looked as if Daddy had just exposed himself to the choir and asked if there were any takers.

'Not yet,' said William with admirable aplomb. 'I haven't had it yet.'

'You haven't? Well, don't forget,' said Daddy, laughingly wagging a finger at him.

'I won't,' said William, laughingly back.

I was not laughing. Neither was the vicar, nor Emery, nor, indeed, my mother.

As we trailed out of the church, I hung back to speak to Daddy, who was making a furtive call on his mobile. As soon as he saw me, he hung up.

'I've got that cheque for you,' I said bravely. 'I can give it to you now, on the condition that there is no mention whatsoever of this again. Especially not tomorrow.'

Daddy stopped by a large gravestone. 'Cheque? I thought we said cash.'

I stared at him. 'You think I carry five grand in used tenners around with me?'

'I need that money now, Melissa,' he said, and checked his watch. 'Plenty of time to pop into town. You bank with the same people as me, don't you?'

I nodded disbelievingly. As if I didn't have enough to do! There were still two hundred unwritten place cards sitting on the dining room table.

'Just mention my name, and they'll give you the cash,' he said breezily. 'Chop, chop!'

And he strode off, leaving me open-mouthed with frustration.

★   ★   ★

The wedding magazines, on which I could now have written a PhD, recommended that the bride spend the night before having calming baths, pedicures and heart-warming conversations with her nearest and dearest.

We didn't, of course. We had a row instead, just to get Emery revved up for married life.

Mummy and Daddy celebrated Emery's final hours as Miss Romney-Jones by having a spectacularly pointless argument about what had happened to the family tiara, last seen on Allegra's head at her wedding. By the time Em and I slunk away upstairs to watch television, it had degenerated into a pointed row about the guest list and why there were so many of Daddy's work-experience girls on it. We could still hear the ebbs and troughs of their yelling when we turned in for bed.

My room had been commandeered by Granny, and all the guest rooms were full of aunts and second cousins. I was bunking up with Emery, sleeping on a Z-bed last used in about 1987. It wasn't ideal, but I tried to concentrate on the fun 'midnight feast' aspect of it, instead of the less fun osteopathy aspect. I painted my own toenails Fireball Red, and let Emery witter on about how ruthless William had been on the paintballing stag weekend. We were so relaxed for once that I couldn't bring myself to ruin everything by asking about Chicago.

At about midnight, Mummy popped her head round the door before she went to bed. She looked distinctly flushed and her hair was dishevelled. 'Who wants a Mogadon?' she cooed, as if dispensing cocoa. 'Help you get a lovely night's sleep before the big day!'

It wasn't as if I needed sleeping pills, being on my last legs with total exhaustion, but knowing what I now knew about the contents of her lingerie drawer, I was more than happy to be rendered insensible until the morning.

'Night then,' I said to Emery, as we knocked back our pills. 'See you in the morning. You want me to wake you up?'

'Um, yeah.' Emery inspected her alarm clock as if unfamiliar with its mode of operation. 'Does this thing work?'

'I hope so,' I said. 'I need to be up early to make sure the marquee's still OK.'

She peered down at me from the heights of her four-poster bed. 'Are you comfy on that thing?'

'Not really.'

'Do you want to bunk up with me?'

'Do you mind?'

'Not really,' she said, then spoiled it by adding, 'I don't want the wedding pictures ruined by you cricking your neck and looking like Quasimodo.'

Gratefully, I climbed off the Z-bed, trying not to trigger its temperamental spring reaction, and slipped under the duvet. Emery had very cold feet. Literally, I mean, not metaphorically.

We lay there, staring at the tapestry and waiting for Mummy's Mogadons to kick in.

'Is it normal for mothers to drug their daughters before a wedding?' asked Emery.

'Only in Victorian melodramas.'

My mind wandered to Jonathan, and how it would feel to see him in the church. I'd hidden my bag of Honey clothes in our old toy cupboard in the music room: to be honest, I was sort of looking forward to being Honey. She'd at least have more fun than Mel would at this wedding, even if it was just for half an hour or so.

I was going to miss my Honey dates with Jonathan. I really was.

'You will talk to Jonathan, won't you?' said Emery sleepily. 'I don't think he knows anyone except you, and William and Darrell.'

'Darrell the best man?'

'Mmm. Awfully sweet but quite hard work. Not all that good socially. Bit like Jonathan.' She yawned.

'Really?'

'Oh God, yes. He's OK when he's showing me round houses – he's got all the chat for that – but outside work . . . God almighty. He's either desperately shy or just socially maladjusted. You have to *drag* conversation out of him sometimes. Poor Jonathan,' sighed Emery. 'Some men *need* a woman there, just to remind them they're in company. Still, his divorce has come through now, so maybe he'll cheer up a bit. Cindy's got most of it. But I think he's over all that.'

'Really.'

Emery rolled over onto her elbow. 'I've put him on the same table as Bobsy. Do you think they'd get on?'

I sat bolt upright and turned on the bedside light. 'Bobsy? Bobsy Parkin?'

'Yes.' Emery blinked hard. 'Can you turn that off? What's the matter?'

'Why have you invited Bobsy Parkin to your wedding?' I demanded. This was all I needed! 'I didn't know you even *knew* her!'

'Oh, come on,' said Emery. 'Practically everyone we've ever met is coming to this wedding. My estate agent's coming. Your flatmate's coming. Anyway, she's a friend of mine from school.'

If anything she was a friend of *mine*, surely? 'I didn't

know you were still in touch with her,' I said, trying not to sound hurt. 'When did you invite her? I don't remember sending her an invitation.'

Emery wrinkled her nose. 'Oh, you know . . . I saw her for lunch the other day – I bumped into Daddy in town, then we sort of bumped into her too, and we got talking about the wedding and . . .' She trailed off. 'Come to think of it, I think it was Daddy who invited her.' Emery squinted at me. 'They did seem awfully familiar. Do you think that's what Mummy and Daddy were arguing about at dinner? You don't think he's knocking off Bobsy on the side? Oh my goodness! And he's invited her to my wedding?'

I turned off the light and rolled onto my back. If I mentioned my suspicions it would ruin Emery's day. Besides, they were only suspicions. 'I don't think even Daddy would do that,' I said, without much conviction. 'It would be an appallingly selfish, arrogant thing to do.'

The Chanel hairclip floated into my mind. I pushed it away.

Emery, naturally, didn't notice the fact that my face was telling a different story. 'Oh, good,' she said. 'I'm glad you think that. I was a teeny bit worried. Still . . .'

Another nasty thought crowded in while I was contemplating Bobsy and my father. She wouldn't say anything about Mrs McKinnon at the wedding . . . would she?

Would she?

'Can you hear that?' murmured Emery.

'Hear what?'

'That . . . banging noise.'

'No,' I said firmly. 'I can't hear anything.'

What if Daddy . . . and Bobsy . . . and Mrs McKinnon . . . and . . .

The sleeping pill began to soften the corners of my

brain as I fought to stay awake long enough to organise my defences.

'Gosh, these pills are good,' murmured Emery. 'Must ask Mummy where she gets them from . . .'

Within minutes she was snoring while I struggled with jumbled images of Jonathan dancing with Bobsy Parkin, and Daddy demanding his money, and stacks and stacks of gold chairs all marching themselves into the marquee while I backed helplessly into a corner, flinging wads of cash around.

Then I fell into a deep, immobile sleep.

The alarm went off at seven thirty. Emery, naturally, didn't stir. I lurched to consciousness with a very thick head, and an already simmering feeling of panic. Nevertheless, I hauled myself out of bed, into the shower, then got dressed to bring Emery breakfast in bed, as per the bridal magazine guidelines.

'Wake up, Emery,' I said, dumping the tray on the bedside table and shaking her. I helped myself to a croissant and bit into it, trying not to get crumbs over the file with the wedding timetables in.

Emery rolled back over. She was always a bit of a slug in the mornings.

'Come on,' I shouted, 'you've only got an hour before the photographer arrives to do the breakfast photographs.'

Emery groaned. 'The what?'

'Don't blame me,' I said, counting out five timetables. 'I gave you and Mummy that checklist and you definitely ticked breakfast photographs.' I poured the coffee. 'So you've got an hour to get your face on.'

'Thought you booked a make-up artist?'

'I did. But she doesn't come till eleven.' I swigged some

coffee and felt better. 'But you don't want to look like a hound in your pre-make-up wedding shots, do you?'

Emery didn't move, so I whipped off the duvet and dropped it on the floor so she'd have to get up to retrieve it.

The marquee was standing in the paddock and, although I say it myself, it was pretty splendid. We'd left it too late to get a white frilly one, so in the end I found a gorgeous red and gold Indian wedding tent, with jewel-coloured flags outside, sumptuous embroidery on the inside and gold poles to hold the whole shebang up.

Everything else was themed around it: I knew it would be cold, so we picked spicy Indian food to warm everyone through – kedgeree, and delicate curries, and Indian sweets, and fresh mangos. Daddy was delirious with joy when he found out Emery was having a Last Days of the Raj wedding. Well, as near as he could be, given how much it was costing.

I took my files with me and sat on one of the gold chairs, making last-minute phone calls to the photographer, to the caterers, to the band who'd be playing at the evening reception, ticking and double-ticking against my timetable.

When I was happy that everything was in order, I put my phone down and looked around me.

If I ever get married, I thought, I want one of these. If.

'This way for the hotplates, love?' yelled a man in a white coat.

I nodded and showed them where to set up.

Back in the house, Mummy, Granny and Emery were sitting around the kitchen table, pretending to have a girlie chat over tea and croissants while the photographer – the lady I'd booked, I was pleased to see – shot them from flattering angles. Mummy was in full make-up, Granny was wearing a scarlet silk turban that gave her a discreet face-lift and Emery was wearing a pair of dark glasses.

'Love the shades!' gushed the photographer. 'Very cute!'

'Didn't rinse her contact lenses,' Granny informed me. 'Looks like she's got myxomatosis. Silly girl.'

'Where's Daddy?' I poured a cup of tea and attempted to stay out of shot.

'Nowhere. To. Be. Seen,' said Mummy through her mother-of-the-bride smile.

'Can you move out of the way, please?' asked the photographer.

The doorbell rang and I went through to get it.

'Hello! Congratulations! Are you all ready for your big day?' cooed another woman with large hair.

'Not exactly.' I opened the door for her to wheel her beauty trolley in. It was so substantial it nearly took out a mahogany Victorian umbrella stand. 'Through here.'

I led her into the kitchen where Mummy was now pretending to be overwhelmed by a large bunch of flowers from Emery. They were, in fact, the flowers I'd arranged for William to present Mummy with later at the reception.

'Right,' I said, handing out timetables. 'Can I give you each one of these? It's a timetable of events so you know where we are.'

'Gracious. Will there be a test later, darling?' asked Granny.

'Look, I don't mean to be bossy, but it's the only way of organising all this,' I explained, feeling self-conscious in front of the photographer.

'Melissa!' roared my father from somewhere upstairs. 'Melissa?'

'Humour me,' I said, pleadingly, and went up to see what he wanted.

Daddy was in his study, in his brocade dressing gown, eating a plate of croissants and slugging back coffee. He looked grim. Any thoughts that he might have wanted to offer a few quiet words of grateful thanks for my hard work evaporated.

'Melissa,' he said and rubbed his thumb and fingers together. 'I believe you have something for me.'

I gave him a wedding timetable.

'Very amusing,' he said, looking distinctly unamused. 'I was thinking of something more . . . cash-like.'

'It's in my room,' I said dully. Even now I was clinging to the vain hope that it might all have been an elaborate test: get me the money and I will rip off this mask of villainy and reveal I've invested the cash for you. But no. Apparently not.

'You do realise the marquee people don't need paying in cash?' I tried. 'I spoke to them on the phone yesterday, when they were setting up. The remainder of the invoice can be settled within three weeks. They were awfully sweet about it, actually.'

Daddy looked blank for a moment, then went back to looking grim. 'It's not for the marquee.'

'I thought you said it was.'

'Melissa, hospitality is an expensive business,' he said evasively. 'The father of the bride needs a certain amount of largesse at his disposal.'

I stared at him. What *did* he need cash for? The reception was in our paddock. Visions of Daddy peeling off twenties and tucking them in the vicar's surplice floated into my mind.

'Be a good girl and pop off and get it for me . . .' he said, absent-mindedly running his gaze over the front page of the *Telegraph*.

I trudged along to my room, got the envelope out of my bag, reminded myself that this freed me from my debt (nearly) and that it was a liberating achievement.

I thought hard about these things as I handed it over.

'Good girl,' said Daddy, scarcely bothering to look up as he tucked the envelope into his desk drawer and locked it.

'Is that it?' I demanded.

He raised his gaze from the paper. 'I think so.'

I locked eyes with him, willing him to thank me.

'Run along, poppet.' He flapped his hands dismissively. 'You don't want to miss your Polyfilla.'

Hating myself for being such a pushover, I stormed back to the kitchen.

Emery was sitting at the table being worked on by the make-up artist. She looked like a Botticelli vision of serenity and for a terrible moment, I felt rather jealous of her. How come everyone else got help except me?

Then the phone rang and I had to deal with the nice WI ladies who were finishing off the church flowers in return for a sizeable donation to the roof fund. Daddy didn't know yet just how generous he'd been.

Up to twelve thirty, everything was going exactly according to my timetable: the caterers were in, the band had set up and were having a spot of lunch and Nelson had called to say he and Gabi had set off. I had wedged myself into my severest Honey underwear in order to squeeze my curves into my bridesmaid's dress, and Mummy and Granny were even exchanging happy memories of their own wedding days while the make-up artist and hairdresser worked soothingly around their heads in the sitting room.

Then Daddy stormed in with a face like thunder.

'He's not going to get here in time!' he roared. 'Bloody, bloody hell! It's a total cock-up! Where's Melissa?'

I sprang off the window seat in panic. 'William? What's the problem? Oh God, don't tell Emery.' I'd already told her the wedding would start a whole hour before it actually did in an effort to get her there on time.

'Not William,' snapped my father. 'The solicitor! He's meant to have got those pre-nups here to me by courier last night!'

'For God's sake, Martin,' breathed my grandmother.

'Emery's not marrying him without signatures on the dotted line!' insisted Daddy. 'Melissa, you'll have to go and pick them up.'

'What?'

'It'll take you ten minutes. Nip into town, pick them up, fetch them back here.'

I stared at him in sheer disbelief.

'Well, come on,' he urged. 'There's ages yet. It doesn't start for another two hours. Chop, chop. The longer you stay here arguing, the more you're holding us all up.'

To my own astonishment, I found myself getting into Granny's car, driving into town in my bridesmaid's dress, collecting an envelope from an openly sniggering receptionist and haring back against the flow of Saturday traffic. As I turned off the main road into our drive, I nearly crashed into a Renault Scenic on its way out.

'There,' I gasped, slamming the envelope down on the

kitchen table. I had thirty minutes before the electric cars arrived. Deep breaths. Deep, deep breaths. I looked around and realised I was on my own.

'Emery?' I yelled. 'Granny?'

The sight of Emery in her wedding dress at the top of the stairs brought me to an abrupt halt. She looked beautiful: the long lines of the satin dress and the embroidered girdle around her slim hips gave her the air of an Arthurian queen. Sleek curtains of nutmeg hair fell around her serene face and as she raised her hand to touch the crown of flowers on her head, the trumpet sleeves of her dress fell back, revealing her soft white arms and diamond bracelet.

'Emery,' I whispered, forgetting all my bubbling annoyance, 'you look *wonderful*.'

She smiled and even her habitual vagueness now looked quite regal.

'Where's the make-up woman?' I asked. 'I need to get a move on.'

Mummy clapped a hand to her perfectly lip-lined mouth. 'Oh bugger. Sorry, darling.'

'She's gone, hasn't she?' I said flatly.

'She was in a rush,' Mummy explained. 'She had another wedding to go to.'

I put my palms over my eyes. Making a scene now would ruin everything. 'Fine,' I said. 'It's fine. I'll do it myself.'

'No, darling,' said Granny, taking me by the elbow. 'I'll do it.'

Someone with even greater authority than my father clearly intervened at this point, because the next thing I knew, the Romney-Joneses were assembled outside the church and it wasn't even raining. The horse and carriage supplied by the Green Energy people was delightful, the villagers had come out to throw confetti and only one or two guests were still lurking outside having a last-minute cigarette.

'Wait here,' said Daddy, helping Emery down from her carriage. He looked distinguished and very handsome in his morning dress, and his perfectly groomed hair made me wonder if he'd availed himself of my make-up-artist time.

He strode off towards the church door and gave something to one of the ushers.

'Oh, Emery, don't you look wonderful in that cape!' exclaimed Granny to distract her attention from the mutterings. She adjusted the snowy fur framing Emery's face, and arranged the folds so it fell down to the ground luxuriantly. 'It really does suit you far better than it ever suited me.'

'A gift?' asked Mummy archly. 'From an admirer?'

'Naturally,' replied Granny without even turning her head.

I looked around to see if I could see Jonathan, but presumably he'd gone in already. I tugged at the neckline of my dress and consoled myself with the thought that at least he'd see me in something more attractive later on. Granny had done a pretty impressive job on me, although my resting expression was now one of mild surprise.

'Right,' said Daddy, hurrying back. 'You can sign later, Emery. No need to spoil the moment, is there?' He smiled benevolently at the four of us, disarming any protests in an instant. 'What a lucky man I am, surrounded by four such gorgeous ladies!'

It was true, we did look pretty gorgeous, especially Mummy. She was very much in her public mode, champagne-blonde and poised, and almost as serene as Emery, although I did wonder how chemically assisted that serenity was. Her hat was spectacular but didn't detract from the smoothness of her skin or the high, cat-like cheekbones that made her real age an unguessable quantity.

One of the ushers appeared and held out his arm to her. She accepted with a graceful nod and walked into the church. The rest of us watched in sheer admiration as her ladylike wiggle, demurely contained in a mint-green suit, vanished through the Norman arch of the church door.

I held my breath for Daddy to say something to ruin it, but he didn't. He just smiled to himself, then fingered something in his inner pocket nervously.

'Good luck, darling!' Granny held the drooping feathers on her hat back and kissed Emery's cheek. 'Now and for ever.' Then she too vanished, on the arm of the best-looking usher, into the church.

'Ready?' said Daddy.

I took a deep breath. 'Yes,' I replied.

'I wasn't talking to you, Melissa,' he snapped. 'Emery?'

'What? Oh, er, yes,' murmured Emery, plucking at her bouquet of lilies and red berries as both photographers snapped away.

I lifted the fur hood up over her head, picked up the trailing lengths of her train, and the three of us walked slowly into the incense-scented darkness of the porch.

26

The ceremony itself went off without a hitch. I was pleased to see that the vicar had put his foot right down about 'Angels' by Robbie Williams not being an acceptable hymnal choice, even if played on a harp by someone we were both at school with.

The church itself looked glorious, with candles around the pillars and curling ivy and bright orange Chinese lanterns on the end of each pew. I sat with my back very straight all through the wedding ceremony, knowing that somewhere behind me, in the sparsely populated groom's side, Jonathan would be watching.

Seemingly moments later we were standing around outside again as dusk fell and the photographers – now joined by a grumpy-looking teenager from the local paper – scrabbled to get pictures before the light went completely.

Tears of emotion and beads of perspiration had wreaked havoc on my make-up, so I slunk away to a flying buttress to repair the damage as best I could with my powder compact.

'Wasn't that lovely?' I heard Gabi's voice say, somewhere behind me.

I hesitated, puff on nose. I didn't want to eavesdrop . . . but the temptation to listen in on what they were really up to was irresistible.

'Yup. Lovely,' agreed Nelson, not sounding quite so enthusiastic.

Good, I thought. If they were romantically involved he'd at least have warned her he wasn't prepared to splash out on such a lavish do.

Gabi sighed. 'So? Have you told Mel yet?'

I held my breath. Told me *what*?

'No,' said Nelson. 'Not yet.'

I heard Gabi's familiar huff of impatience. 'When? When are you going to tell her? When can we show her the . . . thing?'

The *thing*? What on earth were they talking about? Details of a flat? A ring? A *scan*?

'When the moment's right, Gabi.' Nelson now sounded more excited. 'She's rushed off her feet. I don't want to spring it on her in front of her family, or that great stiff, Jonathan. I need to get her alone.'

I stared at my stupefied reflection in my compact. Was Gabi moving in? Were they now going out? What was so awful that Nelson needed to talk to me on my own? Why did no one tell me anything any more?

How much worse could today *get*?

I hurried out from my hiding place to catch them, but they were already disappearing towards the cars, Nelson with one arm slung around Gabi's shoulders, the way he used to sling his arm around me. My heart gave a great thud of misery as I spotted another couple also heading that way, also deep in animated conversation: Daddy, and Bobsy Parkin, her racehorse legs very much on show in a silk dress and baby-pink tweed jacket.

Clearly something was going on. And I was going to find out what. Bobsy had no right to ruin my sister's big day. Being as how she could easily ruin *my* whole life with the wrong word in my father's ear . . .

'Let's have one of me and my sisters!' announced Emery, gliding up behind me and putting her arm through mine.

'Yes, let's,' deadpanned Allegra. 'I've never been photographed with a life-size globe artichoke before.'

'Hello, Allegra,' I said. She and Lars had flown in that morning and gone straight to their hotel, then to the church. She knew from long experience that minimal exposure time was the key to preserving family harmony.

Married life hadn't diminished Allegra's Gothic looks at all: she had Granny's long nose and piercing blue eyes, intensified by her long straight jet-black hair, and she was wearing a black, scarlet-lined cape that Dracula would have rejected as a tad flamboyant.

'She doesn't look like an artichoke!' protested Emery, as the photographers jostled for position.

'Thank you,' I said, gratefully.

'More like . . . a leek,' sniggered Emery.

I scowled, and wished I'd accepted Mummy's kind offer of a Valium with my pre-wedding Buck's fizz.

I'd like to draw a veil over the wedding speeches. The best thing one can say about them is that they lasted only forty minutes. Unfortunately, thirty-eight of those minutes were taken up with my father's speech, leaving William and Darrell with two minutes between them before the band started.

It isn't really in anyone's interests to rehash my father's show-business monologue, in which he managed to remind everyone of Emery's brief eating disorder, revealed Mummy's teenage drink-driving conviction, made some off-colour jokes about nurses, cast aspersions on the marriage habits of American lawyers, and slandered at least two other local MPs. In fact, the only people he remembered to thank were the various organisations who had provided free stuff for the wedding.

I honestly tried to keep my face rigid with disapproval, but I couldn't. My father is an utter snake, but a very funny one.

Not that I was really *expecting* any thanks, even though the food was utterly delicious and the marquee looked like something out of the *Arabian Nights*. But as Darrell garbled something about William being a great guy, and Emery being a peach, then sat down with a thump, I couldn't help feeling rather as I did most Speech Days at school, when the headmistress finally reached the 'Neatest Dorm' prize, and I was still the only one sitting there without a book token.

But it was Emery's big day, I reminded myself. Any thanks I needed were right there in her glowing face.

I was consoling myself with a second chocolate marquise from the huge table of extra puddings, when a warm hand fell on my shoulder.

'I've been looking for you all evening!' said a familiar brisk voice. 'Where've you been?'

Jonathan.

Clouds of butterflies rose in my stomach, fluttering up into my chest and all through my body. I had been avoiding him, it was true; the more I wanted to see him, the less I felt able to behave in an appropriately distant fashion.

Plus, my leek dress wasn't exactly flattering.

'Hello, there,' he said, kissing my cheek in urbane

greeting. 'At last I get to say hello. You've been very elusive. Or do I mean busy? Where was your bunch of flowers for organising this whole bunfight?'

I was temporarily lost for words. Jonathan looked ridiculously handsome in a dark suit and tie, his hair tousled slightly and a bright pink rose in his buttonhole.

I held up a warning hand. 'Don't say anything,' I said, stickily. 'Please.'

'Ah,' he murmured, looking sympathetic, 'bad time?'

I'm at my sister's wedding, dressed as a transvestite Nell Gwyn and I didn't even get thanked in the speeches, I wanted to yell. And the alternative is dressing up as Honey to meet your friends! At what point do I ever get to be Melissa?

'No, it's not a bad time,' I said, battening down my rage. 'But, like you, these puddings deserve my undivided attention. Let me finish one so I can concentrate on the other.'

'Flatterer,' he said, with a hint of a wink. 'The food has been amazing. I suppose we've got you to thank for that? You've done a fantastic job.' He topped up his glass from an open bottle on the table and poured one for me. 'As one would expect from the woman who makes Wonder Woman look like a flaky amateur. Do you want to come over and meet my very oldest school friend now? The American contingent is dying to meet you.'

'And I'm dying to meet them,' I said, taking a restorative sip of champagne. I hadn't yet planned exactly how I was going to avenge my wounded pride. I was hoping the spirit of Honey would rise to the surface and take over. But now the moment was approaching, and Jonathan was right here in front of me, a small voice in my head was starting to doubt whether I had the bottle to be anything but compliant Melissa.

'Great! Um . . .' Jonathan dropped his voice, cast his eyes from side to side theatrically, looked significantly in the direction of my head, and murmured, 'Listen, Wonder Woman, do you . . . um, need to . . . freshen up first?'

I gazed back, slightly dazed by the conspiratorial look in Jonathan's eyes, until it clicked that he was meaning 'get changed'. I was Melissa. And he wanted Honey.

Ouch. I'd spent the past few days riling myself up so that snub wouldn't hurt, just make me crosser, but it still stung. I noted that the arrogant, thoughtless bastard was already casting glances over towards his friends, probably not wanting them to see him with frumpy Melissa the bridesmaid.

'Yes, of course,' I said, mentally calculating how long it would take me to transform, given my underwear head-start. He was going to get the transformation of the century. 'Give me . . . five minutes?'

'OK.' Jonathan smiled and gestured with his eyebrows towards the dance floor. 'But don't be too long. I need to give you a spin around the dance floor before that grandmother of yours claims it for herself. I'll be by the chocolate fountain. Which I *love*, by the way.'

'I'll be quick as I can,' I said with a stagey wink, and slipped off, seething.

I wasn't sorry to get out of the heavy bridesmaid's frock; by now it reminded me all too itchily of how little my family actually thought about me and my feelings. Simply zipping up the fitted satin sheath, in palest ballet-slipper pink, and pulling on a long pair of evening gloves, made me feel lighter, quicker, and more 'me' at once, even though it was part of Honey's wardrobe.

I pulled back my hair into a bun in readiness for my

wig, while I focused all my thoughts on being Grace Kelly: ice cool and distant. My fingers slipped and pushed, now well-practised, and suddenly there I was, Honey in the mirror, golden and assured.

Sounds of distant partying floated back through the house as I slicked black eyeliner over the top of the pastel shadow I'd worn so as not to upstage Emery, and lined and filled my lips with sexy scarlet gloss. A quick dust of blusher over my cheekbones was like painting water over a magic picture book: my face seemed to come to life. I smacked my lips together and smiled to check there was no trace on my teeth.

Should this be the final time I'd see Honey too, I wondered. Should I retire her wig for ever after tonight? I wasn't sure I could go through this again.

I pushed away the nagging thought that I'd hidden most of my angst about the wedding from Jonathan out of pride, and that it was *me* who had called an end to the Honey dates. All I could see looking back from the mirror was a woman – a beautiful, confident woman – who could be taken advantage of: for free by my family, and for cash by everyone else. And I'd let them.

It was like seeing myself for the first time.

What on earth had I been playing at?

All the irritation that had been building up in me all month suddenly rose to the surface, galvanised into action by the wig, the satin gloves, a few glasses of champagne, and the high heels. Honey's dynamic approach to other people's lives had finally turned on my own. My selfish family, Nelson and Gabi, the constant demands of work – every frustration began to fizz into my bloodstream like Alka-Seltzer until my skin tingled.

'Right, you bugger,' I said, glaring at my smouldering

reflection and secretly liking the flare in my nostrils, 'I'll
give you Honey Blenner-bloody-hesket.'

I stalked through the house, nearly bumping into
Darrell, who was stumbling around, a ladies' handbag in
one hand and an empty champagne bottle in the other.
'Hey,' he slurred, then did a double take and added, 'hey,
've we met?'

'Do not use the lavatories in the house!' I snapped as
I brushed past him, sending him reeling. 'The Portaloos
for guests are outside!'

The band had come back from their break and had
swung jazzily into a selection of Rat Pack show tunes, as
requested by me.

The whole wedding was requested by me, I thought,
striding past the beautiful tables, now strewn with empty
glasses and wilted buttonholes. Chosen by Emery, but
bloody requested by me. This was the best wedding I was
ever going to have, and I wasn't even the bride.

Jonathan was, as he had said, by the chocolate fountain, chatting to a couple of men, and a tall woman with
her back to me. As I approached, I saw him raise his
hand, begin to smile and then suddenly the smile froze
and a look of confusion replaced it.

Too late, I thought, stonily, enjoying the swing of my
hips in my high heels as I crossed the remaining space
in a few quick strides. The conversation stopped instantly
as their heads turned and took me in as I slid a long,
gloved arm round Jonathan's waist.

'Hello, there!' I said, flashing a wide smile to the assembled company. 'I'm Honey!'

'Melissa?' said Jonathan.

'No, Honey,' I said through gritted teeth. 'That's who
you invited, isn't it?'

Jonathan pulled himself free to stare at me fiercely, but I refused to drop my gaze.

'What the hell are you playing at?' he hissed.

He had a nerve! *I* was the affronted one here!

'I could ask you the same thing!' I hissed back.

Jonathan grabbed me by the elbow. 'Pardon me, folks, I just need to have a quick word with my guest,' he explained suavely. 'She's having one of her blonde moments.'

He propelled me across the dance floor with a strength I would have found rather attractive had I not been so outraged.

'What the hell are you doing?' I demanded, furiously, shaking myself free once we were outside. 'Get your hands off me!'

'I could ask you the same thing.' Jonathan's grey eyes were blazing.

I'd intended to play it icy and cool, but now I found I simply couldn't; I was morphing from Grace Kelly into, oh dear, Maureen O'Hara.

'It's one thing to hire me to be your date, at my own sister's wedding, but that does not give you the right to manhandle me!' I yelled. 'There are limits to what you can ride roughshod over, you know! You can't treat me like you treat your minions in the office!'

'What?' Jonathan ran his hand through his hair in a quick, exasperated gesture. 'What are you *talking* about?'

'What am I talking about?' I glared at him. 'Isn't it obvious?'

'No,' snapped Jonathan. 'It's not.'

'It's *not obvious* that I might be offended by having to dress up as someone else, to be your date for my own sister's wedding?' I roared. 'It's *not obvious*? Have you any idea how that makes me feel? Today, of all days!'

'Melissa, did I ask you to dress up as Honey?' demanded Jonathan. 'Well? Did I?'

'Yes!'

'No, I didn't.' Jonathan dropped his voice as a couple walked past, casting inquisitive glances in our direction. 'Quite the reverse, in fact.'

I stared at him dumbly. 'You *did*. This is not something I would do for fun,' I hissed back. 'Believe me.'

Jonathan raked his hands through his hair so it stood up in choppy peaks, and the light from the torches outside the main marquee reflected copper and gold like licks of flame around his head. 'Melissa, did we, or did we not, say goodbye to Honey while we were sitting drinking hot chocolate on the South Bank? I thought we drew a line under all that. How much clearer do you want me to be? Do I have to get down on my knees or something?'

'But . . .' My mind boggled as I tried to separate all the strands of confusion into something I dared take at face value. 'But just now! You told me to get changed just now!'

'I meant you should go and wipe the chocolate off your face!' Jonathan spluttered. 'Not go and dress up in your damn wig like you didn't want to be seen with me yourself!'

I flushed scarlet. 'But I thought you were asking for an extra favour – I thought we'd agreed to end our arrangement.'

'We did! And if I wanted to see you, it would be as you!' Jonathan huffed impatiently. '*I thought* that's what you were saying to me with all that "you need a new girl-friend!" business. *I* thought you were basically telling me to date you as Melissa!'

'But that would have been *incredibly* forward,' I exclaimed.

Jonathan's glare softened into a grin. 'Well, yes, now you mention it, I did think it was a tiny bit presumptuous, but that's one of the things I like about you. You know what you want.'

'Oh, no,' I said. 'No, that's not me, that's the sort of thing Honey . . .'

'Oh, for Pete's sake . . . Honey is in your head!' said Jonathan, grabbing me by the arms and shaking me. 'Not in *my* head. You know back there? I've been telling everyone about this fabulous girl I'm dating. Yes, I call her Honey – it's our joke – but her real name's Melissa. She makes me laugh, she's smart, she knows the best places to buy cheese in London . . . What more do you want me to say?'

I looked up at him miserably. 'That's *not* me, though. That's the whole point. You don't know what I'm really like. I just let people trample all over me like a herd of rampaging elephants.' I bit my lip and opened up my worst fears. 'I don't want Melissa to be an anticlimax. I don't want you to be disappointed.'

'Oh, give me a break,' snapped Jonathan. 'You organised this wedding, you organised *me*, you organised *yourself* – OK, so you sometimes wear a wig to do it in.' He boggled his eyes at me. 'So what? It's still you. Do you think I'm completely stupid or something? Or have you got some kind of mental illness you should tell me about?'

I met his gaze, and it was fierce, as if he were trying to bore a hole in my mind to let the truth in. I'd heard Nelson say the same things, but I hadn't believed it coming from him, my best friend. Yet now, hearing it from Jonathan, I felt the first, faint inklings that it might really be right.

Jonathan took my hands and shook them as you'd shake a small child's. 'I didn't fall for you as *Honey*,' he said softly. 'I fell for you that day we went on the London Eye, the day you were so cool, taking my side with Bonnie and Kurt, even though you didn't need to. And afterwards, when you let me open up to you, and you opened up right back, so I wouldn't feel so dumb. That wasn't an act, that was you. And I never thought of you as Honey after that, even though I didn't know your real name. You're just not a good enough liar.'

I dug my nails into my palms and held my breath, unable to speak.

'I really thought we'd cleared all this up the other day. So when I saw you there just now, in your wig,' he went on, 'can you imagine how disappointed I was? That you wanted to disguise yourself in front of my friends?'

I shook my head, unable to take it all in.

'Hey,' said Jonathan, suddenly. 'Am I making a fool of myself here? Was this your polite way of telling me to back off? Shit.'

I snorted. 'By dressing up in a wig at Emery's wedding? By risking making a complete exhibition of myself in front of everyone I know?' I couldn't stop a giggle breaking through. 'Getting changed in an upstairs lavatory like Wonder Woman?'

'Did you?'

'No, actually,' I confessed, 'it was the music room. There wasn't enough space in the loo.'

We looked at each other, and I felt as if I were teetering on the edge of a very high diving-board. My stomach fluttered with butterflies as Jonathan inclined his head a tiny, tell-tale angle, and fixed his grey eyes on mine.

'I think we can get rid of this now, can't we?' he murmured, and reached forward, gently easing the blonde wig off my head.

He pulled a few hairs out, along with the Kirby grips, but I didn't squeak.

Jonathan carefully placed the wig on a round box tree, and with his strong hands, unpinned my hair so it fell around my face in dark, chestnut hanks. True to pernickety form, he put each hair grip neatly along his top pocket. Then he ran his fingers through my hair, stroking my scalp, outlining my ears with his fingers as if he were sculpting them, then my eyelids, then my lips, until finally his warm hands came to rest on either side of my face.

'Melissa,' he whispered, gazing into my widening eyes.

And I knew, this time, he was definitely about to kiss me.

'No!' A familiar female voice scythed through the night air, followed by a ringing slap. Was that . . . Bobsy?

'You little hussy!' That was definitely my father's voice.

'Excuse me,' I said, fearing the worst. There were still a couple of photographers lurking around. 'I really should . . .'

'No, excuse me,' said Jonathan and swiftly pulled me close to him, sliding one arm around my waist and reaching up to cradle my jaw with his other hand. Then he leaned forward and kissed me so hard I thought I was going to faint with the sudden flood of pleasure surging through me: the smell of his suit, his shampoo, his musky Creed cologne in my nose, the warmth of his lips on mine, the sweetness of the champagne and chocolate in his mouth. He kissed me so hard and so sexily that it took me a couple of seconds to regain enough control over my motor functions to kiss him back.

'Jonathan,' I began.

'Melissa,' he said, deadpan, just like Rhett Butler, and pulled me close again, nuzzling his lips against the hollow behind my ear, while one hand buried into my hair and the other stroked my back. His warm breath and surprisingly confident manner melted my insides like the chocolate fountain.

'Martin!' screeched Bobsy, now sounding nearer than before.

With a massive triumph of will over desire, I pulled away from Jonathan. My father really was the ultimate passion-killer. 'Jonathan, I'm so sorry . . .' I bit my lip and strode off towards the sound.

Enough was enough.

It didn't take me long to stumble over the unpleasant scene unfolding by the rose garden. Daddy and Bobsy were circling each other like cats around a large lavender planter: Daddy with a livid red slap mark on one cheek, waving a mobile phone, and Bobsy clutching a brown envelope.

'What's going on?' I demanded.

They both spun round in surprise.

'Ah, Melissa,' said Daddy, as if we were all having cocktails inside. 'You remember Eleanor, don't you? She's a hooker these days. And a blackmailer in her spare time. What little there is left of it, given her devotion to her job,' he added with a spiteful glare in her direction.

'Blackmail?' I stared at her with a prickle of self-interested panic but she was too busy grabbing for the phone in my father's hands.

'Yes.' Daddy moved effortlessly out of range. 'Eleanor seems to think that the national press would be interested in the sordid details of our meetings and—'

'Not the *meetings*, Martin,' Bobsy interrupted in her new breathy voice. 'In the awful things you made me—'

'Enough!' I roared, holding my hands up. 'I do not need to know.'

'I'm just phoning Eleanor's parents now, in fact, to break the dreadful news to them,' he explained, very reasonably.

'You are not,' hissed Bobsy.

'Then give me the money back!'

'No!'

My father studied the phone. 'Melissa, do show me whether I've pressed the right button . . . Oh yes, it's ringing.' He looked up at Bobsy with a charming smile. 'Your mother still a practising QC, Eleanor, or is she a judge these days?'

'Give me the phone!' she howled.

'If there's one thing I've learned in politics it's that everything has a price,' my father hissed at her.

'And the price of your embarrassing proclivities is ten thousand pounds,' she hissed back.

'Ten thousand pounds?' I shrieked.

In other words, I'd been slaving my arse off to pay Bobsy to eat whipped cream off my father's riding boots or whatever he'd had her doing.

'Give me that!' I snarled, catching them both unprepared, and grabbed the envelope out of her hands. Then for good measure, I grabbed the phone too.

They both glared at me.

'Don't bother,' I snapped, holding up a warning finger. 'Either of you. I feel I should warn you both that I have *finally* reached the end of my tether.'

'Well, in that case,' Bobsy retorted, dropping the breathy tones and glowering at me in a very unladylike manner, 'there's something *else* you ought to know, Martin.'

'What's that, Eleanor?' asked my father silkily, but he was looking at me too. And I knew that he knew already.

'Your goody-two-shoes daughter—' she began, but Daddy's mind was working faster than hers ever could.

In one swift motion, he moved to my side and put his arm round me.

To be on the safe side, I tucked the envelope of cash down my bra where he couldn't get at it.

'Eleanor, I do hope you're not attempting to add slander to your tacky repertoire,' he chided. 'We have no secrets in this family. So if you're about to tell me that Melissa was involved in your seedy operation, let me disabuse you, my dear. Melissa's involvement was purely to investigate how best she could help her father extricate himself from your sordid grasp, wasn't it, sweetheart?'

'Er, yes,' I stuttered.

Bobsy looked as though she'd been kicked in the stomach by a particularly sneaky horse.

'Really, there's nothing you can tell me that Melissa hasn't confided in me already. Please don't degrade yourself any further, my dear. So, now we've got all that cleared up, shall we return to the party?' He paused. 'I think it's time you went home, though, Eleanor. Shall I ring for your father to come and collect you?'

With a snorting sob, Bobsy spun on her heel to storm off. Unfortunately, the gravel was rather sparse and her heels were rather flimsy, and she stumbled over a miniature rose bush, revealing a sturdy rear end and a string of horsey expletives.

Daddy steered me away from the scene, but instead of returning to the marquee, he headed for the house.

'Where are we going?' I asked.

'Out of earshot,' he snarled through the wide smile he was flashing at passing guests.

I realised with a burst of dread that I wasn't out of the woods yet.

He marched me up the drive and into the hall where a large flower arrangement filled the fireplace once used to roast oxen. I had a feeling it was now my turn to be similarly roasted. Once we were alone, he turned to me with a look of absolute fury on his face.

'Give me that money,' he demanded.

'No!' I said, clasping a protective hand to my bosom.

'Give me the money!' he repeated.

'No,' I said stubbornly. 'It's mine! And besides, I've just saved you from blackmail, haven't I?'

'Christ Almighty, Melissa!' he roared. 'You could have destroyed me! What the hell did you think you were playing at? I knew you were a bit thick, but I had no idea you were living in some kind of moronic fantasy world!'

My lip trembled. 'How did you find out?'

'Oh, for . . . How did you imagine I *wouldn't*?'

We glared at each other. I was practically nauseous with fear, but there was no way I was handing that money back. I'd earned it. A large vein was throbbing on my father's forehead and he looked on the verge of apoplexy.

'I must say, for a hooker, you dress very badly,' he added. 'Did no one tell you that you don't have the legs for that dress? Eleanor at least has a decent pair of pins on her.'

'And you'd be the best judge of that, wouldn't you?' I retorted. 'That flat of Granny's must be like the Royal

Enclosure at Ascot, the number of fillies you parade around it.'

It wasn't as coherent as I'd have liked, but it was the first time I'd ever dared talk back to my father and I don't mind admitting I was pretty scared. Not so scared I wasn't raging, though.

'How dare you be so disrespectful?' bellowed my father. 'How dare you? After all I've done for you! After all the sacrifices I've made for my family, you dare to bring *my* name into disrepute with your filthy gutter behaviour!'

The sheer hypocrisy of this took my breath away, but even though I knew it was utter tosh, part of me was still quailing beneath the onslaught.

He hadn't finished, merely dropping into the oily nastiness he used to such deadening effect in the House. 'What have you done with your life, Melissa? Hmm? With your myriad advantages? Absolutely nothing. So much for all your talk about having a career and being independent.' Daddy laughed offensively. 'Come to think of it, considering your track record with men, you couldn't have picked a less auspicious career to follow.'

I felt sick to the stomach. My knees were starting to buckle and I wobbled on my high heels, when I heard a discreet cough behind me.

My father spun round. I didn't even want to look to see who it was.

'What the hell do you want?' Daddy demanded. 'Can't you see we're having a private conversation?'

'Forgive me, sir,' he said in a mild tone, 'but I couldn't help overhearing. And I'll have to ask you to take that back.'

Oh hell. It was Jonathan. If he'd thought I was Honey

deep down before, this was going to crush the illusion for him for good.

'And you are?' enquired Daddy unpleasantly.

'My name is Jonathan Riley, and I am one of Melissa's clients,' he said, with more courtesy than I thought possible under the circumstances. 'A client of her agency.'

'I should have guessed. I can see she takes her customer service responsibilities very seriously,' said Daddy. 'Even makes sure they're invited to her sister's wedding. The hooker with a social conscience. Well *done*, Melissa.'

Jonathan bridled. 'I'm also a friend of the groom. And I must take great exception to your calling Melissa a hooker. She is nothing of the sort.'

I looked nervously from one to the other. I wasn't sure if Jonathan talking like something out of *Gone with the Wind* was going to make things worse.

'Really?' Daddy's face softened into a reasonable expression that I knew of old was not a signal to relax. 'Do enlighten me,' he oozed dangerously. 'I should so love to be proved wrong. It isn't every day one discovers one's daughter is selling the pleasure of her company.'

Jonathan, to my relief, wasn't taken in by the change of tack. 'You couldn't be further from the truth if you tried. Melissa runs a life management agency, with more charm and efficiency than I've ever encountered in an office, either here or in the States,' he said. 'It's not an escort agency in any way *you* may have encountered. It's more like a nanny agency for grown men. I can see how cynical people might make insinuations, but Melissa is a talented and ingenious young businesswoman. You should be proud of her.'

I could tell Daddy was a bit taken aback by this

unexpected back chat, and Jonathan pressed home his advantage by taking a step forward. Daddy, trapped by the extravagant flower arrangement behind him, was forced to meet his eye.

'More than that, don't you owe Melissa a debt of gratitude for all she's done today?' said Jonathan mildly. 'I gather that she undertook most of the arrangements for Emery's wedding, and yet she wasn't mentioned once in the speeches. Not once.'

'We're not all brash about our achievements,' snarled Daddy. 'Modesty is still a virtue amongst Englishwomen. And I hardly think it was appropriate to start advertising the availability of my unmarried daughter on Emery's special day, do you? Particularly when I imagine her services are probably being gossiped about on most tables already.'

I cringed.

'Do you realise how talked-about Melissa's agency is?' demanded Jonathan, not entirely truthfully, I suspected. 'She even has her own magazine column!'

'I hardly think Melissa's advice is worth the paper it's written on,' sneered my father. 'She has the business acumen of a hamster. Has she told you about that? Or should I say, have you invested in any ski resorts recently, Mr Riley?'

'Well, actually . . .' said Nelson, who had appeared behind Daddy's shoulder, summoned, presumably, by the bat-sonar distress calls I'd been emitting. 'Mel's made a bit of a profit.'

Daddy wheeled round at the magic word, profit. 'What? Nelson, this is a private discussion, if you don't mind. Really, can a man not get any privacy in his own home?'

Since we were standing in a marble-floored hall, with wood panelling and echoing stairwell, I thought this was a bit rich. Still, it served him right for being unable to contain his need to get his mitts on the cash long enough to drag me to the lockable confines of his study.

But even I didn't want to be bawled out in public, nor did I want Nelson fighting my battles for me. 'Can't it wait, Nelson?' I appealed. 'We're, er, just sorting something out.'

'Sorry,' said Nelson, apologetically, 'but no. I've been trying to catch up with you for days. I was going to take you out for lunch and surprise you, but you've been so busy. You haven't even been picking up Gabi's calls. Anyway, look, I drafted a letter of investment based on the notes and emails you had from Perry and got him to ratify your share in his business.'

'He still has a business?' I gasped. Honestly, I thought I had seen the last of that money when Perry stopped returning my emails. I assumed *Watchdog* had been onto him. 'Really? How did you find him?'

'Well, Gabi and I had a job finding him. You weren't really looking in the right places,' explained Nelson, kindly.

'I wasn't?' I said faintly. Was that what they'd been up to? Was this 'the thing'?

'It took us weeks,' said Nelson. 'Gabi even had to pretend to be you at one point. Her idea, not mine,' he added.

'Is that what you've been doing?' I asked, my heart lightening.

Nelson nodded. 'Well, yes. That and finding Gabi somewhere to live.'

'Go away!' said my father, flapping his hands at Nelson.

'Go away! I am having a private discussion with my daughter!'

'Fine,' said Nelson, raising his hands. 'By the way, are you going to give Mel a bouquet or something for organising all—'

'For the last time, piss off, Nelson!' roared my father.

Nelson raised his hands again, and backed off. He didn't leave, though. I could see him still lingering by the door, making vague 'I'm here if you need me' gestures.

'Now then, Melissa,' began Daddy in his low-level hectoring tone. 'I think you should be a good girl and hand over that money, don't you?'

'No,' I said, grabbing my courage and my dignity in both hands and straightening my back inside the corset. 'No, Jonathan is right. I think you do owe me a thank you. I worked bloody hard to make this a lovely day for Emery, and I did it because I love her and wanted her day to be special, and not ruined by you making a scene. And you have made a scene, but I absolutely refuse to join in.'

I took a deep breath. Daddy's face was going beetroot and his vein looked set to pop.

'I do own the Little Lady Agency, yes,' I admitted, my voice rising in the manner of a WI president. 'Its aim is to make life easier for men who don't have girlfriends or wives to smooth things out for them. And I set it up because I didn't ever want to be taken advantage of by a man like you, a man who expects his wife to be his secretary, his mother, his child and his whore, and yet who still cheats and lies! Everything I do for my clients is appreciated and done with good grace.'

'And an invoice!' he shouted.

'And what's the difference between that and you

footing Mummy's detox bills when she's driven mad with your horrible parties?' I demanded. 'Or giving your tart tarty underwear?'

'I have no idea what you mean by such . . .' faltered Daddy, trying to throw his voice backwards towards Jonathan and Nelson and anyone else who might be listening.

'But at least I'm not confusing it with *love*,' I said, giving him a tentative shove with my finger. Daddy looked horrified, so I did it again. 'I'd do all that for *nothing*, if I thought I was getting *love* in return. I don't have any love right now, so I'm doing it honourably for money. And I'm doing nothing you could possibly be ashamed about. If you must know, Granny lent me the money to start it up, and she thinks it's a great idea.'

Daddy laughed. 'Yes, well, darling, she would, the raddled old tart.'

'Who's she, Martin? The cat's mother?' Granny appeared at the top of the staircase. 'Or, in your case, the alley cat's mother-in-law?'

'How long have you been there, you old witch?' demanded Daddy.

Granny descended the staircase with consummate elegance, taking her time with each step. 'What a way with words you have, Martin,' she observed acidly. 'It astonishes me each day that your toxic genes have managed to produce offspring who don't communicate entirely in grunts and snarls.'

'Well, it's obvious where Melissa gets her whorish leanings from,' he sneered. 'I wonder if she can make as successful a career of it as you did, Dilys.'

'I *beg* your pardon?' Granny paused on the penultimate step, giving herself a height advantage over Daddy's sneer. 'Melissa is not a *whore*, and neither was I. The only person who takes cash for favours in this house is you. You and your grubby little EU cheese producers.'

'That is a lie!' he flashed back, with a shifty look in all directions.

I wasn't listening, though. I was stumped by his previous revelation. Elegant, cosmopolitan Granny – my absolute model of womanhood – couldn't have been . . . one of those upmarket hookers . . . could she?

'Granny?' I said, my heart beating hard. 'What on earth does he mean?'

Granny looked me up and down, and her proud gaze never faltered. She looked magnificent in the half-light, her skin porcelain pale and powdery, her eyebrows arching in graceful query. If I could look half that lovely at eighty, I thought, I'd be more than happy.

'Go on, Dilys,' needled my father. 'Tell her, why don't you?'

Then she smiled, as if she was amused, rather than angry, though the twitch in her mouth betrayed annoyance. 'Why not? I've nothing to be ashamed of. What your father is referring to, Melissa, is the fact that for many years, before your mother was born, I lived in a rather lovely flat in Mayfair as the companion of a well-known gentleman.' She held up a long white hand. 'I don't wish to say whom. But we had an arrangement, not dissimilar to yours – I had no desire at the time to marry and become a household matron, and he preferred the company of a charming woman who would be entertaining, and not demanding. I had a wonderful time. So did he.'

'And so did many other people,' sniped my father.

'Oh, do be quiet, Martin.' Granny didn't even bother

to look at him, holding my gaze instead. 'It wasn't love, and we both knew that. When I did meet love, it all changed. But he and I remained friends until he died, and I have hundreds of wonderful memories. And I don't feel a moment's shame. That's what your father's trying to insinuate – in his tacky, small-minded little way.'

'Oh,' I said, faintly. Certain things were falling into place now. Half-comments, old photos, all those amazing clothes . . .

'I'm *terribly* proud of you, Melissa,' said Granny, seeing my distress and taking my hands in hers. 'We all are. You're a charming, practical young woman, far more resourceful than your sisters, and a much nicer person than the rest of us put together. You don't think badly of anyone, and that's something we could all learn from. But you must stop being such a wilty wallflower!'

'Oh, you know how I hate blowing my own trumpet . . .' I began, embarrassed.

Granny shook my hands until her bracelets rattled. 'No, none of that. It's about time you *did*. You've always been so kind and thoughtful and clever – it's just taken you until now to find the right outlet for your talents!'

'How extraordinarily remiss of us not to have considered courtesan as a career option,' said Daddy. 'I knew there had to be *something* she was good at. Remind me to get on to the careers department at Melissa's old school, first thing Monday.'

'Oh, for pity's sake, Martin, bloody well shut up!' snapped Granny. 'Just because you've never had an original idea in your life! I will *not* have you putting her down any more! Melissa,' she said, turning back to me, 'if you give up this wonderful agency idea, I will personally haunt

you for the rest of your days. Just get on with it. It's a
gift.'

I looked from her, to Jonathan, to Daddy.

Granny's face shone with an encouraging smile.

Jonathan looked amused, and rather impressed.

Daddy looked as if he was about to spontaneously
combust.

And suddenly I felt a real warmth spread through me.
A sort of strength. I don't think I'd ever heard anyone be
so *believing* in me before, and it was, well, rather nice.
What was stopping me, after all? I had bookings for
months.

'Very nice, round of applause everyone,' said Daddy,
coming back to life. 'Now, give me that cash before I put
you over my knee and wallop you like the little tart—'

I didn't let him finish. I flashed him one of his own
imperious looks and said, 'You can have what I owe you
and not a penny more. I'll pay back your loan, I've paid
back Granny's loan, and I'm damned if you're going to
make me feel bad about doing something I'm actually
rather good at. So let's draw a line under this conversation and . . . try not to spoil Emery's day any more than
we already have.'

I wanted to finish with something rather more dramatic,
but adrenalin was slowly tightening up my throat.

Jonathan nudged me in the back. 'Where's that thanks?'
he muttered.

'Forget it,' I muttered back.

'No, I won't. Mr Romney-Jones,' he said, in the brisk,
arsey tone I recognised from the office, and never thought
I'd be glad to hear, 'isn't there something you want to say
to Melissa?'

My father looked as if he'd been forced to swallow a

pint of fish guts, but being a consummate politician – with a captive audience behind him – he knew when to stop. 'Erm, thank you, Melissa.'

'How touching,' said Granny. 'But I think this deserves a wider audience, don't you?'

And with her diamond rings digging into my hand, she dragged me down the drive, into the paddock, past the flower displays into the marquee, through the crowd of assembled guests, who parted like the Red Sea to let us through, and up onto the raised platform where the toastmaster had been stationed.

Daddy scuttled along behind, trying feverishly to rearrange his features into an expression which suggested that it was his idea all along, while Jonathan and Nelson followed on, to make sure he didn't scuttle off in a different direction altogether.

Granny silenced the band with a dismissive gesture – midway through 'Fly Me to the Moon' – and waved for attention.

'Ladies and gentlemen,' she said, raising her voice. She didn't need a microphone. 'Could I have your attention for a moment? There's one more person we need to thank today, someone without whom none of this would have happened.'

I felt my face turn crimson.

She put her arm around me, enveloping me in a cloud of Shalimar. 'Melissa arranged everything, in her own time, and with the sort of brilliant attention to detail that she's famous for. So I think her father would like to say a few words on behalf of her terribly grateful family.'

There was a round of applause and I saw my father mount the stage, assisted by a small shove in the back from Jonathan.

Daddy coughed, then switched on the sort of charm that could blind small animals. He wrapped one arm paternally around my shoulders and used the other to make statesman-like sweeping hand gestures around the marquee as he spoke.

'Melissa, as you all know, is my middle daughter.' Pause for uncertain laughter. 'And as *some* of you may know, Melissa is a very busy *working girl* these days, so it was particularly good of her to make time in her heaving schedule to help us out.'

Did he deliberately say working girl there?

'Fortunately for us, she's generously devoted nearly all of her spare time, when she could have been out trying to find a rich husband of her own, to making her little sister's wedding a day to remember. I think we all agree she's certainly done that.'

Pause for applause. I cut a sidelong look at Daddy. I was sure he was taking the mickey. I just wasn't sure quite how.

'So thank you, Melissa, for all your hard work,' said Daddy. 'And as a little token of our appreciation, your mother and I have arranged a special surprise holiday for you!'

Round of loud applause and whistles.

'Have you?' I gasped, as my father embraced me for the cameras that were suddenly flashing all around.

'No,' he hissed back. 'Well, not yet.'

He disentangled himself. 'Anyway, ladies and gentlemen – especially gentlemen! – I should stress once more that Melissa is unattached at the moment, and it's my duty as a father to announce that she's available for weddings and parties, and at very reasonable rates!' he trumpeted.

Now that was uncalled for. I hesitated, sensing from long experience that his temper was cracking under the strain of appearing jovial.

'Don't say a word,' he hissed through a wide smile.

Fortunately for me, a press photographer appeared right in front of us before he could say anything else, and Daddy's politician's instinct took over, as he embraced me warmly and smiled into the lens, clicking his fingers out of shot for Emery to come up and join us for an even better 'family values' picture.

I astonished myself by thinking immediately of the business, and the attendant publicity, and I embraced the old bastard right back.

Then without warning, Granny was back on the podium with us, this time equipped with a microphone to override any attempts from my father to shout her down.

'Will you join us for the next dance, please?' she announced. '"You'd Be So Nice to Come Home To!"'

I looked out into the mass of tipsy guests and saw Jonathan stretching out his hand to me with a smile that lit up his face and crinkled up his eyes. My heart flipped over in my chest.

And as the band struck up the opening bars, and Granny began singing in her husky but still clear alto, I stepped down from the platform and took Jonathan's warm hand in mine. He slipped his arm around my waist, and pulled me so tight that my nose was buried happily in the woollen shoulder of his jacket, and I let him guide me around the crowded dance floor, which suddenly felt like the soundstage of an MGM studio.

Over Jonathan's shoulder I could see Mummy and Daddy swirling round the floor like an exhibition couple, toes practically touching as they locked eyes fiercely; I could see William hauling Emery around in small circles, her feet trailing off the ground; I even spotted Lars and Allegra stalking up and down to a completely different rhythm altogether. I caught sight of Gabi leaping up and pulling Nelson onto the floor, where they began to move so well one barely registered the height difference.

But no one was dancing as well as me.

I was dancing on air. I was dancing like Ginger Rogers. And that was largely because I was dancing with Gene Kelly.

'Thank you,' I whispered.

'No, thank you,' Jonathan said. 'Please don't change ever again.'

'I won't,' I said happily.

I leaned my forehead into Jonathan's shoulder as he manoeuvred me expertly around the floor, and sighed in absolute bliss.

'Melissa?' Jonathan muttered into my hair.

'What?'

'Stop leading, honey.'

'Sorry,' I said, happily, and closed my eyes.

Hester Browne's Polite Thank You Notes.

I simply must acknowledge the wise and gentle guiding hand of Lizzy Kremer. Also her big stick, which gets results when the wise and gentle guiding hand is not enough. I am most grateful for both. Without her, the Little Lady would still be merely the interfering voice in my head, telling me not to waste money on fashion shoes.

Thank you also to Sara Kinsella, and Sheena Craig, for great patience and good humour; and to all the charming Nelsons, Rogers, Hughies and Jonathan Rileys I know. May your repartee sparkle, your trousers hang perfectly, and your engagement diaries always be bursting at the seams.